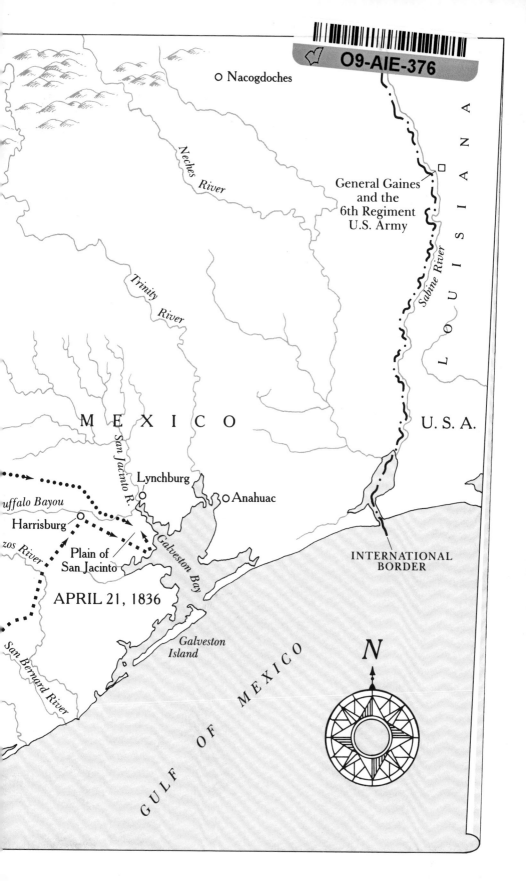

O Nacogdoches

Neches River

Trinity River

General Gaines
and the
6th Regiment
U.S. Army

Sabine River

L O U I S I A N A

M E X I C O

U.S.A.

San Jacinto R.

Lynchburg
O

O Anahuac

uffalo Bayou

Harrisburg

INTERNATIONAL
BORDER

zos River

Plain of
San Jacinto

APRIL 21, 1836

Galveston Bay

*Galveston
Island*

G U L F

O F

M E X I C O

San Bernard River

N

EMPIRE OF BONES

Also by Jeff Long

The Ascent
Duel of Eagles: The Mexican and U.S. Fight for the Alamo
Outlaw: The Story of Claude Dallas
Angels of Light

EMPIRE OF BONES

A Novel of Sam Houston and the Texas Revolution

Jeff Long

WILLIAM MORROW AND COMPANY, INC.
NEW YORK

It is the policy of William Morrow and Company, Inc., and its imprints and affiliates, recognizing the importance of preserving what has been written, to print the books we publish on acid-free paper, and we exert our best efforts to that end.

Library of Congress Cataloging-in-Publication Data

Long, Jeff.
    Empire of bones : a novel of Sam Houston and the Texas Revolution
/ by Jeff Long.
        p. cm.
    ISBN 0-688-12252-3
    1. Houston, Sam, 1793–1863—Fiction. 2. Texas—History—
Revolution, 1835–1836—Fiction. I. Title.
PS3562.04943E47   1993
813'.54—dc20   92-38397
                                                                CIP

Printed in the United States of America

First Edition

1 2 3 4 5 6 7 8 9 10

BOOK DESIGN BY M. C. DE MAIO

For John, Wesley, and Blake

ACKNOWLEDGMENTS

BECAUSE THIS BOOK emerged from my research for *Duel of Eagles*, I wish to repeat my thanks to all who helped with that project. One person in particular helped bridge the gap between that history and this fiction—Elizabeth Crook. Among the many documents she shared with me was a Texas Highway Department publication bearing the unpromising title *Sidelights on the Battle of San Jacinto*. Wary of a state travel brochure, I found instead a virtual Nuremberg trial of participants in the massacre at San Jacinto. *Sidelights* was in fact a two-volume compilation of depositions taken in 1859 from participants in the 1836 battle.

At issue was the cold-blooded killing of a Mexican woman a quarter century earlier. Eyewitness accounts identified one officer, John Forbes, as the killer. Ironically, this was not a war-crimes trial but rather a libel case run by Forbes against a historian and fellow soldier, Dr. Nicholas Labadie, who dared to resurrect the sordid tale. Testimony was taken from two dozen ex-soldiers, including Sam Houston, on the eve of the Civil War. Judgment waited until 1866, when a weary Dr. Labadie issued an apology and Forbes dropped his suit. If not for Dr. Labadie, the incident would have been covered over long ago. Many thanks to Elizabeth for introducing me to forgotten realities.

I wish to thank my editors at William Morrow: Elisa Petrini, Lisa Drew, and Katherine Boyle, and my agent, Doe Coover. Without their efforts, this book would still be galloping wild.

Above all, I thank my wife, Barbara, whose long patience even a Texan can brag about.

PROLOGUE

March 6, 1836

ONE FINAL BLIND shot through the loophole—touch the trigger, weather the hangfire, take the kick—then he drew the long rifle back into the room and did not load again. It was not because of the pitch darkness nor for lack of powder or patching or balls or any poverty of targets. But because the shooting had lost all profit, it only made him feel worse.

He pressed one eye against the hole. His hair dangled in long greasy strings. "Oh Lord," he softly groaned.

Part of him wished he'd stayed out in the open to do this down to the ground. From the start it had rankled him, getting penned up in this Alamo. Now he'd gone and penned himself tighter in an outright crypt.

Behind him the darkness spoke. "Colonel Crockett?" it said. "Tell us what's to see."

Crockett couldn't place the voice. Survivors coiled in the blackness, wracked and anonymous, one man panting in rapid bursts like a woman in labor. The sprawled barracks were honeycombed with these small cavelike rooms. Because it was so dark, Crockett had no idea how many men had taken refuge in this particular cell nor who they were. But someone knew him. Now they all did. Even here he was still accountable to his legend. They would not release him.

"Well, boys," he rasped to them with artificial cheer. How could he begin to describe what was out there? "We have made the dawn." That was something anyway, wasn't it, to reach one more tomorrow?

9

"No more?" a voice pleaded with him. They wanted salvation. Crockett kept his eye to the loophole and thought how it should have been ugly and loathsome out there. In truth the view was so opposite, he couldn't pull away from it.

The plaza cupped a million twinkling stars it seemed, hung them in a fog of pale blue and white and dirty rose gunsmoke. Animals surfaced in the cold mist, some slow—eels sliding through a sulfur sea—some quick—hummingbirds, hurried, quizzical. Here and there they came together and grappled as if rutting, not stopping until one or the other put his head back to howl or shriek. They were soldiers, of course. But trapped between night and day, flight and crawling, they had become something else, enchanted creatures in a purgatory of noise.

Underneath the cracking gunfire a steady patter of hailstones slapped against the limestone and adobe, raking their wood and bullhide door, the plaza, the sky, the earth, the soldiers—the whole world. Crockett pulled away from the loophole and turned around and sat against the wall. He cradled his Betsy across his lap. He couldn't see the smoke bleeding from the pan and barrel, but the smell of his own powder was familiar.

Something slippery snaked up Crockett's bare lower leg. It reached into his lap, fumbling, and found his hand with a desperate grip. Crockett squeezed the hand in return, wondering whose it was. It was a thin hand hard with callouses and he went on holding it.

A rattle of bullets gusted against the barracks wall.

"What's that?" a weary boy's voice asked.

Crockett rested his skull back against the chill stone and closed his eyes. *Pretend,* he wanted to tell the child. *Pretend the spring rain has come early.* He managed to conjure a quick image of cornstalks shooting green from the black dirt, of calves and foals and lambs dropping in wet bundles onto yesterday's loam. Boys would be hunting first flowers for their sweethearts soon. It was that season.

The hand had gone dead in his. Crockett let go.

A vast noise shook the walls, the very air, evoking goddamns and a cry of sheer terror from the men jammed into the darkness. Knees snapping, Crockett got to his feet again. He spied through the loophole.

A twelve-pounder cannon—one of their own—stood

smoking not fifteen feet away, aimed point-blank at the neighboring door. That meant the Mexicans had swept the walls and overwhelmed the Alamo's interior, all in a matter of an hour or less. Crockett was stunned by the speed of the Americans' defeat. It made a charade of their two-week "defense." All too obviously the Mexicans had allowed them to squat in this godforsaken place and at their convenience were evicting them.

The Americans' artillery had been wheeled down from the ramparts to flush the last resistance out with grapeshot. Even as a dozen soldiers with bayonets swarmed through the shattered opening next door, an officer was directing his team to haul the cannon around, pointing at Crockett's little den with his sword.

"Boys," Crockett pronounced to his invisible cellmates, "they'll be coming for us now."

"Our Father . . ." someone prayed.

"Someone of you come help me hold the door," a man commanded them.

"You'd best get down," Crockett told him. "We're whipped."

"You're whipped yourself. Not me."

Through the loophole Crockett watched the Mexicans swab and load the cannon. They were using for shot what the Americans had used on them, chopped bits of horseshoe and iron scrap, a mutilating round. Another officer was rounding up soldiers to storm the room once the door blew in. With their bayonets fixed the muskets towered taller than the men toting them. On the far side of the plaza the mission walls had grown luminous, the color of ripe peaches.

Crockett dropped to his hands and knees. He patted around in the blackness searching for a possible excavation. His hand landed on a dead man's face and he felt the liquid eyes staring before he could lift his fingers away: bad luck. He felt arms and legs moving, a hot rifle barrel, a cold knife blade. There was no trench dug into the floor in this room. Returning to the wall, Crockett lay down and socketed his face and chest and legs hard against the limestone.

"Help me hold this goddamn door," the man bellowed at them.

The door lifted inward with a rush of clean blue light. The explosion deafened Crockett for a minute, then he heard a hog squealing. It was the wreckage of a man. Through the smoke

and dust, he saw how tiny the room was. Along the base of the
back wall the earth moved, the dead stubbornly climbing back
to life.

The death squeal pealed on, finally tightening into a rattle.
After the shock of daylight and thunder subsided, Crockett
shook himself and cast around for a weapon, anybody's, anything. But the ceiling wands had torn loose and everything lay
heaped in old dirt.

Crockett pulled away from the gaping door on his elbows.
He twisted onto his rump, jammed his back into the corner,
and fixed his stare on the glowing entranceway, for it was the
gate of hell.

But no legion of dark angels issued in. Eyes wide, Crockett
waited. Minutes passed. No enemy materialized. No shadow
assaulted the bright doorway. Smoke and dust braided the air
in slow eddies.

"How come don't they come?" An apparition had risen to
Crockett's left. His face and hair and red beard were powdered
white with thick limestone dust and he lay propped on one
elbow.

Around the room the debris rustled and slowly produced
several more figures. Crockett didn't recognize a single one by
name, and the politician in him felt a little irresponsible about
that. One man had a bead of blood running from an empty eye
socket. Yet another began to howl and flail, throwing blood
everywhere.

"Hush, goddamn you," the man with one eye whispered,
"they have forgot us and gone by."

"Yes, that's so," hoped the boy Crockett had heard in the
darkness. Crockett looked closely and tears streaked the child's
grimy face. His fingernails were chewed to the quick. It had
been a very long two weeks.

And still the doorway remained empty.

At last their wait ended. "In the name of God," an operatic
voice boomed from the light, "if there is anyone in there, surrender and I will spare your lives."

The words—in an English too refined for most Americans—knifed through the gunsmoke. Crockett drew a breath.
He opened his hands and saw they were filled with dirt, not
much of a weapon. Until that instant he had not realized the

depths to which his faith had fallen. The possibility of escape beckoned brightly.

"Surrender?" the one-eyed man said. He sounded awestruck.

"But what would Colonel Travis say?" the boy remonstrated. "Fight, he'd say, I reckon. I reckon we should fight."

Travis! That name again, that uncertain consideration. Crockett wanted to spit the bad taste out. But Travis was of their own doing. They had let the half-baked zealot seduce them into this madness. Crockett blamed himself more than the others for letting the monster go on. For one thing, at forty-nine years old, Crockett was older than almost anyone else in the Alamo. And for another, few knew demagoguery the way he did. He had seen the crazed glint in a president's eye, he had heard famous men rave wildly and be applauded and get elected.

From the start this sprawled, crumbling fortress had felt to Crockett like a jailhouse. All too quickly it had come to remind him of an asylum, and yet he'd kept his mouth shut. Each time Travis emerged from his dark cave he'd seemed more disoriented than before, as if the sun were turning circles in the sky and he'd lost his north. When he spoke it had been to deliver their own hopes back to them, and that was where Crockett had failed them, for hope is never reality and he should have said so loud and clear, him or Bowie, except Bowie had drunk himself into foolishness and a deathbed. So it had been Crockett's place to be wise. He should have told them Texas wouldn't drop into their open palms like a ready fruit. He should have chided them for believing so fiercely in the whiskey patriotism they had grown up hearing their grandfathers concoct on cold evenings around the fire. They should have smelled the stink of their own recklessness and bolted for safety. They should have tied Travis up or turned him loose to wander in the Mexican desert or cut his throat. *I should have split his tongue so his words fell among us like a beast grunting.*

"Travis?" another voice registered. The corpse that had squealed its life away shifted, then raised up and flopped over. A man surfaced from underneath, shoving the masquerade away with his feet. Layered in gore, he was badly hurt himself.

"Travis," the man repeated. "I seen Travis before I run to here. He was first down, by God, down along the north wall."

"Them goddamn Meskins!" the one-eyed soldier swore, and pawed at the dirt ferociously.

"Wasn't Meskins kilt him."

"Who then?" Crockett asked.

"Travis kilt Travis. Took one look at the odds and put a ball between his own eyes."

"That ain't so," Crockett's neighbor objected. "That was George Mitchell, he's the one shot himself in the head."

"Maybe George Mitchell done it, too. Maybe a lot of boys. But I seen Travis. He took the dark leap on us."

The fact—even the possibility of it—sobered the one-eyed man. The child was looking from one man to the other. All that showed in his mask of dirt and smoke were eyes as green as a Kentucky summertime.

Crockett couldn't remember if this was a Sunday. But the Alamo was a church and so, somehow, resurrection didn't seem all that farfetched. After all wasn't it the chance for a second life that had drawn him to this primal land in the first place, to this giant sky and these far spaces? A second chance to be a congressman. A second chance to settle paradise, to restore his name, to have it all. Well here it was. His second chance.

Then and there, Crockett resolved not to squander the opportunity this time around. He would walk through that door and get a horse and ride back to Tennessee. He would kiss his stern lonely Betsy and watch the seasons mount and fly from a chair upon his porch. He would let himself get old and tell his tales to grandchildren and the children of them, too. All it took was to quit.

Crockett crawled into the word headfirst. *Quit.* Well it wouldn't be the first time, just the most public. And the alternative? Unthinkable.

He got to his feet. Bits of warm grapeshot fell from his torn clothing and hit the floor like music falling apart. His belly clenched with dysentery and the backs of his legs were foul with liquid. Ears ringing, Crockett nearly fainted. He had to lean back against the wall. But he was on his feet, that was the important thing, up and ready to cast his vote for the promise. If it meant walking into the light alone, that's what he'd do.

One by one the others threw in with Crockett. The one-eyed man staggered right, blinking, and staggered some more, not quite aware he'd lost half his vision. The boy migrated to

Crockett's side. His shirt was missing: not a hair on his chest nor chin. Crockett absentmindedly brushed the dust from the boy's wheaten head. One of the other lads couldn't seem to find his balance and kept falling down, but Crockett didn't have any strength to lend. All told there were six of them, nine counting the dead and last gasping.

"How should we do this?" someone asked.

"Hell, I ain't never quit before."

Outside, the squall of gunfire had ebbed. The rampant shouting and screams of agony were getting displaced by more businesslike commands in Spanish. Crockett took a peek through the loophole. Low angled sunlight was stabbing in through the smoke. The supernatural contest, animal to animal, had evaporated. Where before he'd witnessed shapes shifting, the plaza now displayed relatively calm drabness. The only figures still standing were Mexican soldiers in blue jackets. They steamed like horses in the cold March air.

"What say, Colonel?"

"The battle's done," Crockett said.

"Then let's get this goddamn over," the man with red hair declared.

"I'd let them season a bit," Crockett recommended.

"Hell," the red hair said. "A promise is a promise."

"At least hallo 'em. Say you're coming. Ask for safe passage."

"I'll quit, by gum, not beg." Red pushed away from his wall. He bulled through the open doorway with his own best version of a contemptuous stride.

No sooner did he leave than he returned, mincing slowly backward on tiptoe. His teeth showed in a mighty white grimace. A musket barrel appeared to be attached to his stomach. Now Crockett saw the tip of a bayonet standing through his back. Red stayed high on his toes, dancing away from the pain, absolutely silent except for his grinding teeth. After a minute he gently tiptoed forward, drawn away like a speared fish.

Terror bounded into the room. Crockett had thought he had no more fear left, but his bladder released warmth down his thighs and the one-eyed man started howling. The boy slid to his haunches.

A loud burst of Spanish erupted in the plaza. Someone with big lungs and a deep bass was losing his temper out there.

The unmistakable cadence of orders being given and passed along followed. Five minutes passed.

"Look it," someone shouted. A miserable-looking face had poked through the doorway, a Mexican soldier's face. Almost before Crockett saw it, the dark face was gone.

"Now we're kilt, now we're kilt," the one-eyed man despaired.

The Mexican's head appeared and disappeared again. He tossed a quick glance around the room. At last he dared to enter, in a fighter's crouch but with his hands empty.

"Quick, kill the bastard," the one-eyed man urged. But right behind the soldier came a tall, patrician officer with silver hair and a uniform still smoldering from powder flash. He shoved the soldier to the ground with despite.

"Here is a hand and a heart to protect you," he said to the huddled survivors and touched his big chest. "This reptile has shamed the Mexican army of operations with his disobedience. I offered you protection. I repeat my offer, gentlemen. Surrender to me and I will save you."

These Mexicans were a tricky breed, Crockett ruminated. But at least the man was of the white persuasion, or seemed so with his sunburned nose and blue eyes and silver hair. Crockett unfastened the boy's embrace from his leg. While the offer was still warm he stepped to the middle of the room.

"I do. We will," he said with a touch more enthusiasm than he intended. There was a code of manliness among these people and it was especially pronounced in the creoles. It wouldn't do to show too much relief. He started over.

"If you're an officer, and that's your word, so be it," Crockett said. "We will place ourselves at your discretion."

The Mexican general was momentarily thrown off guard as Crockett threw his pumping hand out for a shake. When Crockett's meaning dawned on him, he took the hand in his own. "I am General Manuel Fernandez Castrillón," he said.

Crockett's heart leapt. A general? Their luck was improving. "Crockett," he said. "I am David Crockett." He considered appending a credential or two, just to establish some pedigree. As it turned out, General Castrillón was quicker.

Castrillón's eyes brightened. "David Crockett, the great naturalist?" he asked. "The frontier clown?"

Crockett had never heard it put quite that way and wasn't

sure he liked it. "The former congressman from Tennessee," he answered with a slight bow picked up in the corridors of the House. "At your disposal."

"Yes, yes," Castrillón said. "I have heard of you, you see. How small our great continent is."

Crockett straightened his ragged nor'easter jacket and squared his billed cap and regretted the loss of his collar and tie. At one point on the long journey to Texas he'd nearly traded away his city clothes for a hunting shirt and a buffalo robe. He was glad now that he hadn't.

"I present to you my companions," Crockett graciously remembered. He felt downright drunk with hope. Only a moment ago he'd been scratching the earth for his very existence. And now look, he was swapping chatter with a grand general of the enemy. New possibilities crowded in on him. The Mexicans would parole the prisoners—what else, Mexico was a civilized republic—then put them on a boat. By the time they reached New Orleans, Crockett could maneuver his role among the men, become their leader, and land a hero. Written up properly, it might even fuel another run for Congress. The sky was the limit, especially with King Andy decrepit in the White House and the Whigs clamoring for a man of the people. If only he'd been wounded!

"Come." Castrillón motioned toward the door. "I will take you before the commander in chief. It will be safe there."

Crockett fixed his sights on the radiant doorway. Stooped with stomach cramps, he stepped across the torn remains of the doorman at their feet. A new wave of cramps doubled him up. There was a touch at his elbow, a helping hand. It was Castrillón. "Allow me," the general said.

"*Gracias,*" Crockett said, exhausting half the Spanish he knew.

"Life is a circle, I think. Perhaps one day your people will do a kindness to me."

My people, Crockett thought. Unless Castrillón meant by that his stay-at-home Tennesseeans, Crockett had no people. Certainly not these poor limping remnants of Travis's calling. Crockett understood the Anglo-Saxon need for elbow room. "Be sure you're right, then Go Ahead" had served him well for a campaign slogan. He'd even come here to sample this wholesale takeover of foreign territory. But over the past fortnight he'd realized that understanding these invaders and their illusion of what was right was beyond him. Taking land from Creeks and Cherokees by inches and miles was one thing. Conquering a space larger than the thirteen colonies put together was another. There was so much empty land here that only a fool would want more. And yet they did. Well before this morning Crockett had felt defeated. Coming here had been a mistake, and not just the coming to the Alamo. Texas—a mistake. He didn't belong here. It was for a people different from him.

Despite the early hour, the light outside was blinding. Crockett slit his eyes and licked the gunpowder out of his teeth. When his vision finally pieced together again he stopped, stunned. Behind him the other survivors disbelieved the sight, too.

"It can't be," a Georgia man protested.

The plaza was no longer a place of misty beauty. There was still an hour left to the sinking moon, but the sun was up and the smoke had dissipated, exposing a stage of hideous ruin. Between the front of the chapel and the far north wall, the acres of enclosure were littered with weapons, expended cannonballs, torn uniforms, musket balls, and severed limbs. Hundreds of dead and wounded men lay where fate had tossed them. The cries and groans were like cattle lowing.

Mexican soldiers circulated through the mass of bodies. Some were washing the faces of the dead with gourds of water, and Crockett wondered if it were some sort of Papist habit. Others went about sticking and resticking the pale bulky American bodies with bayonets and lances and bending to swiftly strip away clothes or artifacts. He hoped whoever found his Old Betsy would treat her well. On second thought, he hoped it would blow up on them. That's how he would tell the story anyway, *she snapped like a turtle and rearranged that dusky old hook's thieving face right there upon the bone.* The prospect of aggrandizing on events put some vinegar back into his bloodstream.

Guided by the general with the silver mane, Crockett and his huddle of survivors passed among their former friends and comrades. In the heat of battle men's hair and clothing had ignited from sparks and gunpowder, burning away their scalps and beards, denuding them of their vanities. It was horrible to see their teeth bared in grins that had no jokes, to see their skinny legs or barreled bellies, the inside of their rib cages. It was immodest. Crockett had seen much death in his day. It always made him blush.

Side by side the two old men, one helping the other by his arm, threaded their way to the front of the hospital quarters. Blood had guttered into wheel ruts and depressions in the broad muddy plaza. Men had been dragged from their sickbeds and mutilated.

"A sad day," Castrillón said.

"Just put us with the others." Crockett could scarcely think.

"The others?"

"Let us have the comfort of our fellow prisoners."

They would be gathered inside the hospital, hurt and scared, in need of a leader to soothe and assure them and negotiate fair treatment and a speedy parole. Suddenly it struck Crockett that this might be the very reason he'd been drawn to Texas and the Alamo, to lead these poor sheep away from destruction. He would bring them from this place back to their rightful homes. It would be biblical, their return.

Castrillón broke in on his thoughts. "But you are the last ones," the general said. "The only ones."

Crockett's lower lip worked nervously, contradicting his careless bachelor's beard. It hadn't crossed his mind that there would be a tax to his survival. No one else was left who could bear witness to the final days of some two hundred men. All those strands of life lay in his hands now. Just remembering their faces could take a whole lifetime.

"I wish I'd never come to this place," he murmured.

"But you are here," Castrillón shrugged.

"It was an accident." Crockett was struggling to retrieve his composure, to make sense of his presence in a scene beyond his imagination.

"Of course," Castrillón said.

"That's the actual truth," Crockett lied, and in the lying remembered himself. It was one thing to have a true rifle and a sharp eye in this dark, tangled forest called life. But long ago he'd learned that the most dependable weapon, the finest warmth, the best banquet, was generally fashioned from the words that came out of one's own mouth. Folks never tired of a tall tale. Now Crockett tailored one of his tallest.

"I came as a traveler to your country," he said. His head ached and he felt starved for the wildman language that was his trademark. His tongue seemed swollen and it was hard to think. But he forged on.

"Amazing." Castrillón was nodding, and not unsympathetically, Crockett decided.

"Yes." He warmed to it. "It was the hunting that drew me deeper. Things are so plentiful out here in this country. The game is twice as fat and the days are twice as long. And the Indians, every tribe I met, they were talking about a giant buffalo." His mind felt clarified with each new syllable. He was finding his stride again, the old Crockett.

"Yes, sir, pure white," he went on. "Far to the far west, they said, always further on. It was that buffalo I was after, General, somewhere out upon the Staked Plains, as it's called. That's when I chanced upon this town, looking for a pinch of powder and a peck of human society and maybe a horn or two of the creature. By coincidence your army was just entering. Not knowing the local situation, I naturally took refuge in this sanctuary and have been trapped here ever since." Crockett stopped with his overall delivery. Had he been stumping, about now would be the time to refresh the voter with jug and twist. Get them to crack a smile and they would be *for* you.

"Ah," said Castrillón, but now he seemed disappointed. "Another captive of fate."

Crockett frowned. Had someone else used up the same lie then? The thing of it was, fundamentally he wasn't lying. He had come to Texas to hunt and drink and talk and chew, not to provide cannon fodder for a real estate grab led by Jackson men and the land companies. His presence here this morning was altogether an accident.

They turned the corner of the barracks building. Castrillón brought the little group of exhausted prisoners to where a quiet, remarkably still Mexican soldier was viewing the washing of corpses' faces. He looked serene in the midst of all the activity. The officers surrounding him were mostly larger men in elaborate military costume, but for some reason Crockett's eye fastened on this quiet man. Dressed unpretentiously in a plain blue field uniform, he could have been a chaplain overseeing the belated baptism of these dead souls. He was Crockett's height, perhaps five foot eight, but much thinner in the waist, much younger, and handsome.

At Castrillón's approach, the man turned and Crockett had

second thoughts. The soldier was eating a chicken leg as they cleaned the faces and his eyes were black as a savage's. There was red nigger in his blood, Crockett estimated.

Castrillón stopped the prisoners. "Wait here," he told Crockett. "Perhaps His Excellency will want to speak with you."

"It's Santy Any," the boy whispered to Crockett. "Why if I just had my frog sticker . . ."

For an instant Crockett imagined himself springing upon the Mexican ruler like a tiger and snapping his neck and biting out his throat before the balls and blades chunked him to pieces. The absurd fantasy passed. "Hush, child," Crockett said, "he's about to grant us our lives."

Crockett marveled. Here was the great tyrant himself, the most powerful man in Mexico. He had no horns sprouting from his skull, no tail nor fangs. Self-consciously the frontiersman who had dreamed of becoming president scrutinized this president who dreamed of becoming an emperor. He hunted for any clue to Santa Anna's uniqueness. What was it about a man that drew people to him on such an epic scale? Crockett had spent a lifetime despising and mocking such men and at the same time struggling to learn their secret in order to become one of them. Maybe someday he'd figure it out.

Castrillón spoke with the commander for a minute. He went on for a long minute. Santa Anna glanced over at Crockett from the center of his ring of officers. Apprehending that he and his fellow prisoners probably looked like so much livestock bunched together, Crockett folded his arms and drew his chest up. *I'm a ringtailed roarer,* he wanted to bellow. *Half horse, half alligator. I wash my hair in the hurricanes and clean my teeth with lightning.* But his bowels spasmed again and he was left hoping the introductions wouldn't take too long. He had a powerful need to lie down and rest. Some water would help, too, say a gallon or two to wash out the taste of the war. Meanwhile he had to stand here with his belly sucked flat.

Crockett tried to prepare a suitable greeting for Santa Anna, something bold but not insulting. You wanted to be first with the handshake, that was one thing. He'd known tyrants all his life, from shuffling brutes in buckskin to serpents like Daniel Webster and Calhoun and Biddle and Adams and the demon himself, Andy Jackson. It was a mistake to wait for their pleasure because they would stomp you flat. No, an aggressive strategy was always best, nothing invasive, mind you, but forward moving, definitely. They respected that.

Santa Anna had the look of a family man, Crockett concluded. Family circumstances usually tempered a fellow, made him less wolfish about the head and ears. No doubt the Mexican would be suffering Crockett's same thousand-mile homesickness. Maybe they'd get around to discussing wives and children and how far away everything that really mattered was. First, no doubt, there would be some curiosity about what had brought a famous politician all this way to Texas, and Crockett would answer how that was like asking a man why he dreams his dreams, or where is the wind born, or how deep is the sea.

Castrillón's deep voice barked suddenly, startling Crockett from his reverie. The conversation fell to silence and Santa Anna turned his back to Castrillón. He began pointing at a row of torn-up bodies. Now Crockett comprehended. The faces had been washed to distinguish the Mexican dead from their enemy. In pairs soldiers dragged each American body by the heels toward a large pile of wood, leaving long blood streaks. The Mexican bodies were getting loaded into a big two-wheeled cart for transport elsewhere.

Castrillón's face darkened. Crockett tasted bile and his belly convulsed again.

"What's going on?" the boy asked Crockett. "They're arguing."

"Don't worry," Crockett said. "They are a tropical people. The sun gets in their blood and it makes them disputatious."

Castrillón was attempting to resume the discussion with Santa Anna. All too clearly the commander had developed other priorities, though. Castrillón tried talking over Santa Anna's shoulder, which provoked several officers to angrily chastise him. One stocky man with a moustache and a small gold earring and a clean uniform started arguing with Castrillón. Castrillón cupped a beseeching hand toward the prisoners.

Crockett looked away quickly.

The sun had pried loose of the eastern flats, striping the clouds from the inside out. Doves and mockingbirds, disturbed by the battle, were returning to the big pecan tree and the cottonwoods. Cocking his face to the warm rays, Crockett closed his eyes. He drew their song to him, pulled it right through the plaza's bedlam and stench.

Her brow would blow sharp with wrinkles, he knew. But she wasn't going to weep, not Betsy. He hoped she would feel more sorrow than disappointment, then changed it around and hoped she would go ahead and get mad, maybe cuss him with those severe lips, anything to keep her eyes dry. Even with all he'd put her through over the years, Betsy was a woman who liked to keep her chin high and back straight. It was a quality that had inspired him, though he'd never told her so. There were a lot of things he'd never told her. She deserved everything, and yet year after year he'd provided her with next to nothing except more work, more worry. *Forgive me.* The words jumped into his head.

Just then the long sound of steel sliding free brought his eyes open. Crockett looked over and now Castrillón was gesturing at the stone walls, railing to himself. Several others had faced away, too.

It was going to be the officers then, the lackeys who had missed their chance at combat. Swords in hand they were spreading out, circling the prisoners. Crockett felt his neighbors back against him. He would have preferred Castrillón were in on this. He'd felt a spark of companionship there.

"Dear Jesus no," the one-eyed man begged.

"Colonel?" the boy wondered.

But Crockett had no answers left, only the gift to give to Betsy. With all the grace that was in him, Crockett opened his arms wide and held them out. He reached as far as he could reach and then started walking due east, into the sun.

Someone screamed behind him. As high and deep as he could throw it Crockett released his soul toward the dawn, and suddenly all there was to hear was the birdsong, those doves in the cottonwoods and pecan. He took another step.

The sun split in two. Like a golden apple separating into even halves, one for each hand, the brightness fell open along a thread of steel. Crockett reached for each half of the light, certain at last that he was going to make it all the way to wherever he was going. Now there would be a tale worth telling.

CHAPTER ONE

March 6, 1836

NEAR DARK THE WIND took on a taste.

Alone, weary from a long week of spread-eagle revolution talk, Houston sat napping in the saddle, an old cut-down Mexican job on loan, his own having been taken for a monte debt. Rocking gently, the general covered a possible mile with that odd touch of smoke on his tongue. His skull wagged to the rhyme of creaking leather, and he verged on a dream of wine-dark seas and a crew of loyal sailors and monsters without end.

At last something, maybe lice, maybe old memories, startled him awake. His gray eyes shot wide and Houston reined his yellow pony to a halt in the piney barren, somewhere—nowhere he recognized—deep in Texas. For the third time today he'd lost the trail. With an empire waiting for his direction, it seemed he couldn't even lead a horse straight.

There he sat on a pathway choked with soapweed and buffalo grass, staring all around as if discovering a strange new land. Texas was like that, part dream, part faith, one minute a dark bayou roaring with gators, the next a prairie so flat and golden it hurt to see. One day you thirsted, the next you swam. Close your eyes on a field of white flowers and you could open up to a thousand white cranes springing into the moonlight. It took a quick imagination to keep up with this land, and Houston figured that included visions that weren't bound by time and place. Sometimes you had to get lost in order to find your way. At least that was the hypothesis Houston kept handy for such moments as this, when the bearings were unfamiliar. In a way, it didn't matter where he was. He'd been promised a scout was waiting at some point along the way and would lead him on to his destination.

Two days ago, in some rare bright sunshine in a shantytown grandly named Washington-on-the-Brazos, the revolutionary government had crowned him major general of the Army of the Republic of Texas, granting him sweeping control of all regulars, volunteers, and militias. With a hasty minimum of fanfare, the rebel convention had anointed him their military messiah and dispatched him to the western front at the head of a nonexistent army to save their nonexistent nation. It was said that a pride of several hundred Anglo-Saxon fighters stood in wait for him at Gonzales. Supposing that were true—and Houston knew his stock better than to suppose any such thing— it still wouldn't be good enough. A few hundred could never hope to stem, much less beat back, the dark tide of thousands of Mexican soldiers. On top of that, thanks to Bowie and the young maniac Travis, the Alamo needed rescuing before Houston could even begin his consolidation of Texas.

The town of Gonzales lay roughly one hundred miles to the southwest. That would take three days of this kind of riding and he was glad for it. In between here and there was much to do. For one thing he had his usual cogitations to sort through, and then there was the war plan to craft, and some corncob and jerky and his thumbworn copies of Caesar and *Gulliver's Travels* to digest, and sleep to recover. When it came time to hit the enemy, he wanted his strength up and his spirits high.

But that scent in the wind . . . it troubled him. He sampled the air. He worried it. It was so faint—just a touch of smoke— that it may as well have been nothing. Rain was coming, there was that in the air. And while it was too cold for flowers still, the oaks were budding, a woody musk for the tree frogs. Old horse dung festered in the trail. But it was none of those things. He let the air loose.

The pony shifted under Houston's weight, some 240 pounds last time he'd bothered with a feed scale. She was a sturdy mountain mustang, just as happy with grass as oats, which extended the range he could travel on her. But her legs were short and his were long and that left his boots dangling ridiculously close to the ground for the commander of an army and a founding father of a nation. He could have regretted her for humbling him so publicly. But the truth was he found it charming that she should burden him as much as he did her.

The pony cropped a mouthful from a patch of threadleaf sedge. The sedge was early. Most years, a short winter would be cause for celebration. Not this year. *Lord.* Houston prayed, working his chew. He spit. *Spare us your goddamn bounty.* His wasn't the only pony that could thrive on the local grass. The Mexican horses ate it, too, and so did Comanche stock, being stolen Mexican horses. Every sort of enemy would be mobile now. They would have to guard against the north as well as the south this season.

He searched the darkening sky for his totem eagle. It usually came to him in times of need. At Horseshoe Bend, as he lay dying of bullets and the arrow, the eagle had appeared and given him hope. On his first trip to Washington as a Tennessee senator it had come again, drafting on the river heat. And again, after the belle Eliza left him in ruins and he fled into the wilderness, the eagle had cut overhead and showed him the way. But with dusk dropping fast all that appeared was a wedge of honking geese.

He dismounted and started up the trace on foot, due west—upwind—toward the sinking sun. At a slight knoll he came to a halt and waited patiently for the next good current. When it came he drew a deep lungful and the black frock coat lifted with his rib cage. Slowly, delicately, he separated out the wind's parts.

Somewhere nearby a fawn was watching him. He could smell the doe's sweet milk and the fetal sac, not yet eaten by the owls and beetles nor dried out by the sun. That would make the fawn a day old, younger by just a few hours than the self-declared Republic of Texas. With a soft "howdy do," the commander in chief welcomed mother and child under his breath. It wasn't a birth he was smelling for, though, and he tried again. This time he caught it, or almost did. But there were too many echoes in the wind.

"Goddamn it," he muttered, and then the wind shifted slightly. This time he got met with a burst of smoke blown raw from someone's new-made campfire. Judging by the smell of rabbit grease, the fire wasn't far off.

Houston scanned the treetops. It was too dark to see the smoke but just dark enough to spy the glow, probably a mile off. He'd been figuring on a cold camp tonight. Now, with care, he might actually land some meat and a piece of company for the night.

On board his pony Houston made for the evening star, off which he'd marked the twinkling campfire. Fifteen minutes passed before he closed on it. The trees took on sharper, cleaner silhouettes as the glow magnified. Riding slow, he whistled a tune to advertise his presence.

It came as no surprise when he entered a well-lit clearing that was empty. He reined up and took stock of the camp. There was a good-sized rabbit—bullet creased across the spine—roasting over a one-man fire, conservative, built for the meal and little else. Houston could tell an early-to-bed man because his own fires were so opposite, constructed for good illumination and late reading.

It was a white man's camp. Indians—Cherokees and Creeks, anyway, the tribes Houston knew—fed a campfire with the tips of wood, edging the logs in as needed. White men burned everything, middle out, gorging on the light and heat. Some travelers declared that was because the Anglo-Saxon naturally had more appetite than the common heathen. Houston had come to believe his people just had more demons and night fears.

Something moved in the penumbra, back among the trees, a large shape, a small motion. Houston froze. Texas was filled with every breed of outcast—dimwits and lunatics and recluses and plain bad men. And he had just laid himself at a stranger's mercy. Part of him regretted his bold entrance. On the other hand, fate had her ways.

After a minute there was another motion and he saw that it was a horse in the shadows, shifting from one hobbled leg to another. She was a big black Spanish mare with white stockings peeking at him from the trees. That was the bait. Any horse thief foolish enough to grab for her would end up rotting in the needles.

Houston sat there and kept his hands still and clearly on the saddle horn and waited for the gun. It would surface on a side, he decided, that or from the back. He waited. It seemed like three minutes passed. Houston was starting to feel foolish sitting there with his rusting dress sword and the slouch hat which he'd shaped into an old-fashioned Revolutionary War–era tricorner, a leftover from some speech he'd made years ago dressed as George Washington. Finally four feet of glistening hexagonal barrel came sliding out from the brush on his right. Houston turned his head to face it, smiling, meaning to be smooth about this. What he saw made him start.

The figure looked for all the world like an orange-haired gargoyle, a man dressed as an animal or an animal disguised as a man. He was crouching on the brink of shadows with the barrel of a beautiful Pennsylvania long rifle trained on Houston's belly. The two studied each other.

"Evening," Houston greeted him.

The man stood up and stepped back, surprised, as if Houston's language itself were a weapon. His serape spread like broad wings. Underneath it he had on a forest green frieze coat. His sombrero, dangling back on a thong, formed a dark leather halo. A fresh scar ran across his forehead, purple and furrowed. The man didn't answer. Instead he held one finger to his lips in the manner of hushing Houston, that or listening to a faraway sound.

The man finally reached a decision. "You're Houston," he said, and let the cock down to half-cock and lifted the barrel. The voice was so high it piped like a young girl's.

"I am." Houston waited. When it became apparent the gargoyle wasn't going to volunteer a name in return, he ventured a question. "Are you my scout then?"

"Evidently you don't need one." He spoke with a slight Spanish cadence, less an accent than a melody. "I was told to find you. You found me."

"I was smelling the wind," Houston explained, "something in the wind. Then it turned all to meat. Your rabbit there ruined the wind."

The scout regarded his supper. He made another decision. "Light, General," he said. "Rest yourself."

Houston got down and unsaddled the pony. He laid the saddle blanket out by the fire, then sat close to the heat. However warm it got in the day, when night descended, winter was waiting. Houston envied the man his serape, a red and white beauty with a tight weave that would keep the rain out and the cold off.

"Supper?" the man offered.

"That's yours," Houston politely declined, then waited for a second invitation. There wasn't one.

"Well then," the scout said. Cradling the spit of rabbit in his lap, he started picking pieces off with his fingers.

Here was a blunt, literal man. It paid to select your words carefully around folks like this. Houston unbuckled his saddlebags and rustled around for a corncob. He shucked the leaves and propped it by the fire, a poor second to the rabbit.

"It seems there's a storm coming in," Houston offered. But the homely fellow didn't reply and Houston returned his attention to the bright flames and the snap of resin. On a thought, he shucked his boots. While his supper cooked he passed his boots back and forth over the fire, a Cherokee preventive against snakebites. Some said it worked against bullets just as well.

After maybe five minutes of silence the scout suddenly spoke out. "It is my opinion we have brought a tempest on our heads," he volunteered.

"Is that so?" Houston said.

"It is." The scout evicted a rabbit bone from his mouth.

"And who might you be, sir?"

"I am Erastus Smith."

The name meant nothing to Houston. There were a thousand Smiths flooding the territory. He leaned forward, twisted his roast. "This being a military affair, do you mind sharing with me your rank, Mr. Smith?"

"No rank, no title," the scout answered. "We are all good Christians in this grand war." The "grand" was mocking and that aroused Houston's curiosity.

"You sound almost sorry for the fight," he said.

"Not almost," Smith said, then shut up.

"There's men who came two thousand miles to put themselves in harm's way," Houston said. "Now here it is at last, the war."

"I would go all the way to the Indies to get away from what's coming." The scout's homely face was creased and sunbaked right up to his baby-white hatline, with not a trace of laughter in his whole life.

"And what's that what's coming, sir?" Houston asked, and caught his breath. There was a species of person who could see into the future, and he'd always figured scouts and trackers were born of it. If Smith really did have the sight, it might help to keep them all alive.

The scout's eyes shaded over, though. It was obvious he was simply despairing at the violence in general. Still it was comforting to know Texas held at least one sane man besides himself.

"I have to say you've got me confounded," Houston said. "Louisiana's not half so far as the Indies. For a man who doesn't like war, there's many another place to be than here."

Smith fixed him with a look through the camp smoke. "If I could find my family, that's where I'd surely be, another place."

That only deepened the mystery for Houston. It made no sense how a pacific man—a scout, no less—could misplace his family this close to a war, especially with every white woman and child who wasn't in Gonzales safely back in the settlements further east. And then it came to him who this particular Smith was.

This was the one they called El Sordo, the Deaf One. Or near deaf. Houston had heard of him. A buffalo hunter and surveyor and small-time *ranchero*, he'd been living in-country so long, married to a San Antonio Tejana of such beauty, that many questioned if Deaf Smith might not have gone completely native and become, in the jargon currently at large, a Tory. Houston had suffered similar misgivings himself from his years spent among the Cherokee with his own dark-eyed beauty, a wife of sorts, Tiana. Civilization had a way of drawing a very thick line around itself.

"Is your family trapped in Bear?" Houston asked, using the American slang for San Antonio de Béxar.

Smith cut him a hard glance full of suspicion. *I'm the first to ask after their welfare,* Houston realized. The man had no friends out here. He was an exile among exiles.

"Travis asked me to ride a message out from the Alamo, and ever since there's been no getting back in. Not into the town. Not now." Smith's worry showed in the way his boney hands went blank and lay motionless.

"The Mexican army will let them go," Houston said, then handed Smith's own words back. "We're all Christians in this one." In truth Houston didn't know the Mexicans at all. Like

most Americans in Texas he'd stuck to the eastern country
where Mexicans generally didn't stray unless they had horses
to sell or tobacco to buy. Tales of their barbarity had hatched
like mad hornets over the past few months. Suddenly every
Mexican was lazy and bloodthirsty and lusted for white women,
but that was all propaganda written for the American uprising.
Houston knew, because he'd written some of it himself and seen
it distributed on broadsides crying for more men with rifles to
come to Texas.

"Maybe so," Smith reckoned.

"They will have as much mercy in them as we do in us,"
Houston declared, and it seemed to relax the scout's knotted
face. "Now, Mr. Smith, what can you tell me about my army?"

"Which one would that be?" the scout gently scoffed. It
wasn't a malicious reply, just one stripped of all the niceties.
Texas was in chaos, and only partly because Santa Anna had
brought 6,000 soldiers up to defend Mexican territory from
what the Americans were calling a revolution.

In point of fact they were lucky to have the Mexicans to
call their enemy, otherwise there might have been bloodshed
among their own factions. There was an army of 500 men under
Colonel Fannin at Goliad, an army of 150 under Colonels Bowie
and Travis at the besieged Alamo, plus a few hundred men
theoretically awaiting Houston's command at Gonzales, and
who knew how many other bands of armed men roaming
around. Combined they would have amounted to a force ex-
ceeding one thousand. The problem was that, to this date, none
of the officers along the western front seemed willing to follow
a single instruction Houston had issued them, nor to pull back
from their forts and pool their numbers. And now, like hounds
that wouldn't heel, they had a mouthful of porcupine quills.

"The Gonzales bunch, let's start with them," Houston said.

"They're coming in by twos and threes. By the time we get
there we'll see three hundred maybe. On the other hand we
might see none. They're not the sort to wait for long. There
was talk of going on."

"Where to?"

Smith shrugged. "Deeper."

"The Alamo," Houston said. "Tell me about them, then.
How were the Bear men managing when you left them?"

Smith tsk'd. "Travis had their heads stuffed with nonsense.

And there were some shooting stars one night. They're sure of victory."

"How about you?"

The scout fiddled with his lapful of rabbit bones. "They said the place would hold. I said, t'won't."

"I warned them, too, both of them," Houston confided.

Smith stared at him skeptically.

"Bowie carried the order, my order," Houston said. "Back in January, before Santa Anna ever got close. I instructed him to destroy the Alamo, then fall back. And now . . ." He left it dangling to see what Smith had to contribute.

Smith's sorry-looking face stayed sorry. "It's a sin to kill yourself."

"It's a worse sin to kill your command," Houston said.

After a minute of thinking about it, Smith visibly arrived at a decision. "Well," he said, "we'll need leading." Not they. We.

Houston nodded, pleased. He had won the man. Here was his first soldier. He spit on his fingertips and lifted his dinner away from the fire and bit in.

The two men didn't talk anymore. There was no awkwardness to it. Smith watched the tiny flames for fifteen minutes, thinking his thoughts. Then he lay back and went to sleep.

Houston pulled out his Swift and added a few twigs to the fire. He turned to the passage about the warmongering Lilliputians. Usually that piece appealed, but tonight it unsettled him. After a few pages he tucked the book back into his saddlebag and lay his head down to sleep.

He dreamed, but it was more like walking through a memory. He was a young man in a blue uniform, leading a charge on foot against the Indian breastworks, fanning his sword, bellowing war cries, vaulting feetfirst into battle. By the time his men could join him, he was reeling and bloody, with a barbed arrow jutting from the side of his groin. The stone tip grated against the inside of his pelvic saddle and Houston ordered a friend at sword point to jerk the arrow free. The hole was big enough for a surgeon to insert four fingers. Then General Jackson came riding by on a great white horse and looked down at him.

He dreamed of a gaunt wand of a man papered with yellow skin and eyes so jaundiced they were nearly golden. The long skeletal face appeared above him with his white hair slashed upwards, a lion's mane, and the apparition smiled. He spoke. *Samuel.* It was the name of God.

"General." There was a whisper, a touch upon his shoulder.

Houston woke. Deaf Smith was squatting to one side, blocking the spray of stars with his head. It was the wolf's hour, not yet dawn. Beneath his head Houston felt his books and his two pistols inside the saddlebags. The fire was dead and he was curled in on himself, sweating and shivering at the same time.

"What is it?" Houston copied Smith's whisper, uncertain if they were in peril.

"You said you smelled something." The scout stood up, agitated in his own way. "Is this it?"

Houston unhugged his arms and took his hands out from inside his jacket. He got to his feet, his old injuries aching with the cold. He put his hat on.

"It woke me," Smith said, nosing the air.

Houston pulled the morning breeze in through his nose, eyes closed, part contemplation, part pain. He exhaled in a burst, shocked. The air was thick with the smell.

So it was true.

Here was how it had smelled a quarter-century earlier at Horseshoe Bend after Old Hickory gave the gee-haw and loosed them on a nation of Red Sticks tucked in the distant brakes. It was the smell of sulfur and woodsmoke and scorched limestone. Reluctantly, necessarily, Houston breathed the wind again. And there it was, his final proof of battle. The stink of meat.

Burnt.

Human.

Houston snorted to get the odor from his nostrils. He knew how far the scent had carried: two hundred miles, give or take. But that was logic, not sense. Two hundred miles was the distance from here to San Antonio.

The fall had come then.

The Alamo was gone.

CHAPTER TWO

HOUSTON DISPATCHED Deaf Smith in the direction of San Antonio. "There will be survivors," he told the scout. "There always are. Find them. Bring them to me at Gonzales."

Smith started off, then paused and twisted in the saddle and said, *"Vaya con Dios."* He said it shyly like a blessing.

"I will," Houston lied and plowed on alone.

It took four more days to reach Gonzales. He followed the old scout's careful directions—to jog left at the oak split in thirds by lightning strikes, to follow his morning shadow in a beeline, to ford the fourth stream two hundred yards below the blaze marks, and so on. He found his sudden urgency a good compass.

Each day the north horizon bruised bluer and bluer. The temperature sank like a pebble in a rainbarrel. *I was born for a storm,* Jackson once confided to him. *Calm does not suit me.* He'd known the old tyrant's meaning instantly, because no storm had ever failed to embrace him either. Riding into the wind Houston breathed battle smoke the whole way.

The town of Gonzales represented the farthest reach of Anglo-Saxon colonizing. For a scant decade it had grown up against the prairie's edge, a tenuous bridging of eastern Texas's American energies and the *ranchero* economy of the Latino west. In asserting their roots, the Americans of Gonzales had eschewed the Tejanos' adobe, preferring split oak to sheathe their frame-built houses.

Houston reached town at dawn in a cold blue drizzle. His

35

shocked first impression was of a massacre. Hundreds of men lay everywhere, in the dog runs, on the street, piled against the houses, curled around trees. For a bad moment he thought the Mexicans had swept through here, too, and left him a town full of dead. A bear dog with wet tan fur came up, the sort that could bite through a cow's spine, and it sniffed at Houston's stirrup.

He nudged the pony's ribs and moved among the bodies. It took no effort to smell their liquor and vomit and hear their breathing. A single fire hissed in the center of the lane, steaming gray under the fine spray. Beside it a sentinel slouched over his knees, dozing, toes bare. He had no blanket, and his hunting shirt—soaked by the rain—had more patches than cloth.

The firepit showed a mesh of charcoaled fence posts and a chair leg. A half-burnt page lay in one corner. The soldiers had been burning books. Houston bent forward and twisted his head. It was a title page. *The Black Dwarf*, by Sir Walter Scott.

Houston nudged the sentinel with his boot tip. "Wake," he said.

The slouch hat lifted. It was a child, not thirteen yet. His eyes peeled open sleepily.

"Give me the watchword, boy," Houston demanded.

"Watchword?" the boy answered.

"How about a drum? Is there a drum to beat reveille with?"

"No drum, by gawd."

"Goddamn it," Houston grumbled. Most of these warriors had never seen a war nor served a militia nor heard a command. It was going to take a sharp knife to cut Texas free from Mexico, and what he had instead was a blunt stone. "Is that yauger loaded?" he asked.

The boy nodded.

"Hand it up then."

"Me gun?"

Houston reached down and took the contraption from his reluctant grip. It was of old Harper's Ferry manufacture, stamped 1803, a rusty-looking thing with its lock strapped tight with a sewn, tacked buckskin patch and the barrel wired to the stock with buckskin lacing and loops of buckskin underneath to hold the ramrod. In ordinary times if Houston had spotted such a weapon lying in the road, he would have ridden right over it as a piece of scrap. It was hardly worth chopping into chunks to shoot as grape from their cannon.

Water beaded the long barrel, but the boy had managed to fall asleep with the flintlock mechanism protected in his lap. Houston pulled back the cock, aimed at the sky, off toward where the sun ought to be rising, and pulled the wobbly trigger.

Flint sparks jumped in the gray light, followed by a dull crack of slow smoky powder. A flock of starlings jumped into the air. Houston sniffed at the cloud of gunsmoke. This wasn't the Double Dupont he was toting in his horn, not close. The boy must have loaded up with some of that Mexican powder the Americans had captured at the Alamo during the fall campaign. The powder was worthless, close to shooting with ground charcoal. The charge he'd just fired wouldn't have thrown a ball fifty yards.

The gunshot's effect was almost as slow as the shot itself. All around him Houston's army emerged from the mud like maggots in a wound. "Rise up, rise up," Houston called through the camp. The dog followed him off to one side.

They surfaced from their blankets and draped coats and, the lucky ones, ponchos that were nearly waterproof. Some of the men wore striped hickory shirts, some linsey-woolsey cinched at the waist with bale rope or strips of animal hide, deer, cow, horse or snake. Buckskin clothed some, city cloth others. Houston passed a foxskin cap, ears alert on top, the red tail hanging to the man's liver.

There was not one stand of arms in the whole mass of them, no military order at all. It was every man for himself. Most carried butcher knives heavy enough to fell small trees; otherwise the array of weapons was more a menagerie than an armament. It even included tomahawks, axes, and a few Mexican lance tips mounted on long sticks.

All told there were a half dozen handmade long rifles in the bunch, as exquisitely crafted as they were expensive. But most of the firearms Houston could see came in the form of double-barreled shotguns, ancient muskets, pistols, and even a blunderbuss or two. If there was a standard in this pack of arms, it was the British-surplus Brown Betsys captured from the Mexicans after the first "fall" of the Alamo back in December when the Americans had overrun San Antonio.

They'd laid siege, they'd shed blood, they'd gained a town in the deep west of Texas. Commanded by the Alamo's huge eighteen-pounder cannon, San Antonio de Béxar had been theirs for a matter of only three months. All they had to show for it now were a few dozen surplus muskets and some kegs of inferior powder. Houston sighed. They had squandered their advantage for nothing. Now they were going to have to begin all over again.

"Who's in charge here?" Houston demanded of the sleepy men.

"Houston?" A man hailed him from a doorway with horsehide for hinges. He had cropped yellow hair and a blue jacket too tight across the shoulders. Houston was relieved that anyone among these flea-bitten strangers recognized him, though wary that it was Ned Burleson doing the recognizing.

"You've come from Washington-on-the-Brazos?" Burleson asked. He had a face like a dirt clod, common and forgettable, but he possessed a violent Scotch-Irish integrity that border men liked and trusted. His neck was bigger around than his head and his eyes were small and dangerous. If he said something was going to be done it generally got done, one way or another.

"I'm fresh from the convention."

"Did they do their job?"

"We have a declaration of independence," Houston confirmed.

"Independence," Burleson snorted to himself. It was a charade, of course, and anyone who'd lived in Texas for more than a month knew it. From their declaration of independence to their broadsides against taxation without representation and their committees of safety and even their antiquated weaponry, they were plagiarizing the theater of their grandfathers' glorious Revolution. They didn't want independence nor, with the Mexican army advancing, did they really want defense. What they wanted was to be left alone on the land, and that meant conquest, plain and simple.

"So they've done their clerking," Burleson said. "We got our piece of paper. We're official now. And what about you? Have you your star?"

For the last few days Houston had been hoping Burleson wasn't going to begrudge him the promotion. With enormous guile and stern gray eyes and his meaty handshake—talking cracker to the squatters and high finance to the eastern land agents and patriotism to all the rest—Houston had gained the leadership of an army that rightfully belonged, by some interpretations, to the man standing before him.

Last fall Burleson had tried his hand at leading the army against San Antonio and the Mexicans holed up in the Alamo. Houston had missed the excitement, but from all accounts Burleson had treated warring like a farm chore: plow, sow, and reap. That was fine in itself, except that Burleson had lost his entire army. He'd lost it, not to the enemy, but to the army itself. When bands of dashing mercenaries with names like the New Orleans Greys and Alabama Red Rovers had showed up from the States, Burleson's plowboy approach had offended them. The ugly fact was that the men had mutinied and the officers had usurped their clay-footed general. Humiliated, Burleson had sat out the conquest of San Antonio in a tent.

"I got the star," Houston acknowledged. "They voted me commander in chief." He waited to see the reaction. He wanted Burleson with him, or at least not against him. Houston had thought this through and decided Burleson's abysmal failure as a military leader was a crucial asset. The man had made serious mistakes during the fall campaign, but one way or another Houston meant to learn from them. This was a different season, and hopefully, with Burleson close by, he could make this a different army.

Burleson wrinkled his pug nose, digesting his fall from grace. Finally he said, "I don't want the goddamn army. All I want's my fight."

Houston relaxed. "If we must fight, we will," he said.

"We will," Burleson insisted. The man had much pride to recover.

"Has my scout Smith showed up yet?"

"Deef's not with you?" Burleson said. "Then he's gone back to his *casa* and chile. We figured him to jump the line."

"You figured wrong," Houston said. "I sent him spying." Then, to get it out of the way, he added, "Colonel." Not Ned, not General. Colonel.

Burleson's jaw bunched at the word, but he swallowed it. "No matter," he said, "we can find our way without a scout."

"How many men have we got here?" Houston asked.

"With guns or without?"

"Total."

"Last night, three hundred seventy-four. And their blood is up. Some of us have been waiting here for a week or more. We can leave inside the hour."

"Leave?"

"Go," Burleson growled peevishly. "To the Alamo."

That startled Houston. He studied Burleson's eyes to be sure he was in earnest, then checked through the soldiers' faces around him. Hadn't they smelled the death in the air? But there was too much bravado and listless optimism everywhere, not a hint of grimness. They didn't know about the Alamo, hadn't even guessed. And since they hadn't, Houston saw no reason to panic them.

Houston's musket shot and the ensuing commotion in the streets had woken the whole town. Right through the slat walls, he heard babies crying and mothers cooing hush. Dogs barked, igniting some Mexican donkey's bray. Children darted from houses, ganged together under a tree, started a game. Houston smelled coffee.

For some reason, the tan dog had taken a shine to him, or at least to his ancient sword. Feeling a tug at his belt, Houston looked down and the animal had the tip of his scabbard in its teeth and was yanking tentatively. "Get," Houston told the dog, and pushed it hard with his boot.

Up and down the brief street Houston's other officers began appearing at doorways with bits of straw in their hair, itching at bug bites, opening their flaps or untying their strings to piss into the muddy street. Wylie Martin, who belonged in a rocking chair not a saddle, began muttering vile curses at his reluctant bladder, for all the world a demented old monk. Most were faces Houston knew, a distinct advantage. Like officers in any war they had garrisoned themselves in the best accommodations, in this case anything with a roof over it.

Houston swept his gaze through them and was startled that they looked so mortal and more, downright vulgar. *Misfits.* The word jostled into his head. Maybe it was the hour or their shabby backdrop, maybe it was their week of waiting for a commander, but his officers looked flaccid and bored and irrelevant. They lacked a pattern, and not one had a hungry look to him. There was no telling the colonels from the majors or the majors from the men sleeping in the street. Except for Colonel Sherman and his bunch, brand new to Texas, there wasn't a uniform in the lot. One and all, they looked like they'd just tumbled from a New Orleans brothel. Judging by his wild hair, John Wharton had fallen asleep upside down. Three-Legged Willie Williamson could barely keep aloft on his wooden crutch, he was so hung over.

The officers became aware of Houston incrementally, eyeing him as he eyed them. Like a colony of prairie dogs, they peered at him from their doorways, measuring the authority about to rule over them. Only one seemed happy to see him, and that was the regrettable Colonel Forbes.

"Great God, the general's come!" he boomed out.

Houston hissed under his breath. Forbes was a stout Cork-born Scot, blessed with great leonine cheek whiskers the color of sea sand, but cursed with the manner of a motherless calf, sucking whatever tit came in reach. He'd first met Forbes in November, shortly after the man arrived in Texas and started granting all other newcomers like himself certificates of citizenship. Inventing his own jurisdiction, he had sworn in three quarters of the Americans now posing as Texans. The line between being a mercenary and a revolutionary was very narrow this year, and Forbes considered it a patriotic duty to boost every manjack he could into a facade of respectability.

"Do we march for the Alamo before or after breakfast?" Forbes cheerfully bayed.

The whole street seemed to grow quiet and Houston silently damned the colonel. Even if he had defined a strategy, a public street was not the place for revealing it. But all eyes were on him.

Just then a pair of men clutching books emerged from an empty shed like children heading off to school. Houston saw his escape and took it. "You soldier boys," he called to the two, and the attention of the street swung away from the general's battle strategy. "Take back those pages," he commanded.

The two soldiers stared at Houston as if through eye holes in old battle helmets, the fine rain draining down their whiskers and scar lines and crow's-feet. "Who are you?" one said.

"I'm Sam Houston, and I'm the general."

"Well I'm cold."

"Heat up, boys," Houston told them, "but not with those books."

After a moment one snorted indignantly and dropped his handful of books in the mud. His partner did the same and they slapped away on bare feet. Houston dismounted. He went across to pick up the books.

Every last one had come from the pen of Sir Walter, and Houston almost chucked them back in the mud. The sooner Americans quit pretending they were buckskin knights and highlander warriors and took on homegrown American heroes, the better. So far as he was concerned, Scott's windy romances and fool talk about the Great Heart were a plague upon the South, seducing young men with notions of aristocracy and confederacy and pretty militarism. But for every Ivanhoe or Waverly they burned in their campfires, a Virgil or Homer or Plato would go up in flames as well, and Houston was not about to help create a Texas barren of poets and scholars.

He stacked the books neatly on a plank—at the same time leaving them exposed to the drizzle—then turned and threw his voice hard so the entire street could hear him. "We've come here to build a nation, not loot it," he said. "The next man who burns a book or fires a fence or a stick of furniture, I'll have you court-martialed and horsewhipped."

But a woman's roupy voice reached across. "You didn't say, mister," she said. "When are you off to Bear?" In light leached gray by the rain, the rawboned woman looked a century old, though she couldn't have been out of her twenties. Her blouse was open to the belly and she had an infant at one nipple and a sticklike child of four or five leaning against her hip, sucking at the other.

Houston flinched. They wanted answers and weren't going to let go of him until something got said.

"Madam," Houston said, and gave her part of a French bow.

Stone cold she stared like he'd just asked her for a dollar. "Two weeks ago we sent our men off to the Alamo. My brother, my husband, her father, her two kin," she pointed at other women crowding doorways, "her uncle, her son. More than twenty of them. And when our men left they said, Don't you worry, more fellers will come on later. And now more fellers come, you fellers. But look at this. This ain't right, all these men in my street and our Gonzales men all off to the Alamo."

"I count every life as precious," Houston evaded her. It was the kind of thing a politician was expected to say.

"Whoever you are," the haggard mother said to Houston, "take this army and go on to Bear. Fetch back our men."

Houston took a deep breath. Texas had not been kind to this woman and it was about to be less kind still. But short of telling her the time had passed for saving the Alamo, what could he say? It seemed too soon for such tragedy, too soon for terror. Besides, except for the stink of dead souls on the wind, he had no evidence. Houston stood there in the center of the street, freighted with his own ignorance. He wanted to say something true and comforting to her, to all of them, the way great leaders did in storybooks. But the sky was falling and he felt helpless to spare them what was about to come.

"Get on to the Alamo," the mother railed at them, "or goddamn you all."

But then another woman's voice broke in. "Don't you goddamn them. They'll go when they go," it said from a house. Mosely Baker happened to be occupying that particular doorway, and the woman with the voice stood behind him in the shadows. Wearing his round hat with half the brim trained up and a long black raven feather in the band, Mosely was a handsome Black Irish, one of the best-looking men in Texas. He craned his head around and admonished her with a whisper. But it was too late.

At the sound of the voice the skinny mother went from sour to mad. "You," she yelped at her hidden neighbor and twisted so fast her nipple popped from the boy's mouth. Her long breast dangled naked like an eyeball out of its socket. "What do you care, Molly? You'd be happy if my brother never come home."

"Aye, you'd be happy, too," the shadow woman answered from behind Mosely. "Simon's a hard brute of a husband. I'm tired of his beatings. I didn't come to Texas for hard knuckles and no whip. I come to be a bride and be loved."

Mosely shifted uncomfortably. He detached his shoulder from the doorframe and grinned self-consciously. He had some sort of connection with the woman called Molly, and it wasn't hard to guess what sort. Colonel Baker was good friends with another eager lawyer turned to military opportunities, Buck Travis. Houston remembered the pair from last spring when they'd taken nine dollars from him in an all-night card game. With Travis's reputation for bedding whatever moved, it was no surprise that Mosely would have found some amusement here in Gonzales. Now he was paying the piper.

"You come because your husband said so," Simon's sister said.

"Well, I don't want for a husband no more. I don't care if he never comes back."

"See!" the mother cried. "She wants my brother dead. Her own husband. You heard the evil woman. She's cursed our kin."

Houston grimaced, feeling caught in the middle. He wanted to walk away, but intuited he was somehow part of this. And all he'd wanted was to ride into town and take possession of his radiant army and maybe hear the people cheer a little.

"That ain't so," the invisible Molly retorted.

" 'Tis," the hag wailed, "and if you kill Simon you kill them all, that's how the hex works."

Now the woman called Molly barged past Mosely into the light of day and Houston's jaded petulance melted away. She was a tall beauty with a dense bundle of red hair that blazed in the drizzle. Her beauty tugged at him like a promise of something larger or better than this muddy street. Right away Houston judged that on the eve of war his handsome colonel had found himself a sloe-eyed lass to fall in love with. It was a natural thing to do. In a way so was the fact that one soldier was cuckolding another. What was different was how extraordinarily fine the two of them looked together, and it lifted them above what might have been carnal or just plain common. Reading Homer could be like that, too.

Out in the open now Molly blinked at the size of the crowd and turned bashful, and Houston saw why. From chin to eye the girl's right side was streaked with a narrow crimson birthmark. It was a mark, and Houston understood about disfigurement, hidden and otherwise. Molly darted her green eyes around at the watching faces and licked her lips. She pawed at her mass of red hair, shielding herself, and swallowed hard. But for all her shrinking she stayed her ground and had her say. "I ain't evil," she murmured.

"Look at you, like a bitch mutt in front of the whole town." The older woman spat and glared right past Molly to her colonel in the doorway. "Where's your shame, sinner?"

"My sins ain't none of your business," Molly whispered.

"When Simon comes home from soldiering, we'll see whose business, sure."

"I won't have him back."

"You're in his house, witch."

"I'll leave."

"He'll hunt you."

At that the girl trembled. Houston had once known a sweet girl like this Molly. She'd had a lover, very possibly one as dashing as Mosely, certainly one who was younger than the man her family meant her to marry. The marriage had happened, only to end weeks later in disaster, in divorce and scandal and the end of Houston's governorship of Tennessee. His golden-haired bride had gone back to her family and, after a fashion, Houston had come to Texas. Eliza had broken his heart and he still couldn't forgive her. Even so he was grateful she'd been spared this kind of public scourging. At a certain level, unfaithfulness was almost the same as love. They were matters of the heart and Molly was right, such things were no one else's business.

Now the wags started in. "Come to the bower with me, Molly darling," someone called from the crowd.

"I got a silver peso," another offered. "I'll be your husband."

Molly's gauntlet had begun. It would get crueler, Houston knew. Catcalls were how a mob tiptoed into being.

In the background Mosely's jaw bunched, but he kept his distance. *Come on out here and save your poor gal,* Houston silently urged. He tried to recollect from their May card game what kind of man this Mosely might be, but all that came to him was the memory of a hot night with fireflies and a cow in the yard. The cow was trying to give birth and kept mooing, which progressively annoyed the players. Now he remembered that Travis had recommended shooting the beast to be rid of the sound, but Mosely had suggested reaching in and turning the calf or tying a rope to it and pulling. Nobody had done anything, of course, and the game had dragged on. The point was, Mosely had it in him to ease this Molly's suffering. But as miserable as he looked, the colonel couldn't seem to find his gallantry. That's how young men were, always too little or too much.

Molly had begun leaking tears. The catcalls were getting lewder. They were building a credibility of their own, making her into something she wasn't.

"Enough," Houston suddenly blurted out.

The harpy's eyes bulged and Mosely jerked as if getting kicked awake. No one was more surprised than Houston himself. There was nothing to gain by stepping between two town women in a squabble. But having opened his mouth he went ahead and physically placed himself between Molly and her fury, his shoulders and chest like a log wall.

"Sure, you say," the mother hectored him. "You lay your army on our town. You sleep your soldiers in our homes and foul our street. You eat up our corn and chickens and burn our property and steal our women. But you won't go fetch our men. And you say enough? Our men are alone out there. And you stand about and curse them with your cowardice."

There was a grousing through the crowd. She had stung them.

"Hush, woman," said Houston. He looked down into her face. The eyes were bloodshot from breakfast smoke and ringed with her children's same pinkeye. Her hair hung in dirty strings, what teeth she had left were too crooked to chew with or else rotting in the gum. Anger and worry and spite had twisted into a mask that was easy to loathe. There was precious little to love in that face with its sallow bones and hateful desperation. Houston tried to open his compassion to her anyway.

"Don't you hush me," she snarled, and her spit flew. "I'll put the whammy on you and yours."

"Quit that juju talk or you'll kill us all." He said it sternly, but without edge. "Now you cover up your nakedness. Take your children home." Houston wiped the rain from his eyes. He scraped through the ugliness and mean poverty standing before him and searched for the beauty that was going to be Texas. It would have been far easier to find in a pretty young belle like Molly, but that wasn't the crux of the matter.

The woman winced at his soft words. Her fury shifted, emptied like a sail dumping loose its wind. A teardrop welled in one eye and her cheek twitched, and now it was her turn for the tears to run. Houston didn't dare touch her head, afraid she might react strangely, with a rake of her fingernails, say. She had so much fury and malice in her. But this mother and wife and sister was about to suffer more than she'd ever suffered. If the Mexicans were truly on their way here, then the very earth was about to disappear—literally—from under her feet. She needed kindness and mercy and whatever inspiration Houston could offer.

"I know it seems our army has invaded your home." He cast his voice like a fisherman throwing his net. He wanted everyone to know what this was about, even though he wasn't quite sure himself.

"On to Bear," someone shouted. "Let us catch Santy Any and kill him."

"No, to Goliad," another cried. "We can join Colonel Fannin in his fort and draw the Mexicans south to us and hold forever."

As Houston had feared, they all had plans to promote.

"Go south. Matamoros lies open to us," yet another insisted. "We can lay their town to waste."

"Here's the place to stay," another voice hollered out. "Let them come into hell."

"North, by Jesus, cut them off on the Camino Real."

"Which goddamn way, General?"

Houston waited for the hubbub to dwindle and the eyes to come back onto him. In the excitement, Molly had been forgotten.

"Were I to consult the wishes of all," Houston said to them, "why I'd be like the ass between two stacks of hay. One says up, the other says down, one north, one south, one west. No, sir, they are many, and we are few. So we must find our place."

"One more time, Houston, what place will that be?"

"I will know it when I see it," Houston said.

"Ha," someone brayed. "Through the lens of a jug you'll see it."

Houston pretended not to hear. He made his face stone. What else could he do? If they ever did try to usurp him the way they had Burleson, it would be with a joke, not a bullet. As much as he feared their sloth and violence and illiteracy and, yes, their patriotism, he feared their wit even more. But their slander would have to come sharper than calling him Big Drunk and sniggering about his jug. For one thing he'd sworn off the ardor on his way from Washington-on-the-Brazos. This would be a cold water campaign, at least for him. Cold water and hot coffee, if they didn't run short of the black bean.

"What is important," Houston called to the jeering crowd, but they weren't really listening. Already his army was falling to pieces. He tried again. "What is important is to remember, Santa Anna is out there."

Houston swept his arm up. He pointed off to the dark western horizon. And at that something remarkable happened and it made the whole town fall silent.

Taking Houston's motion to be a command, the ugly tan mongrel with the fierce jaws laid the remains of his chewed ears back along his skull and suddenly dashed off toward the west. It was as if Houston had just fired a bullet at the enemy, that muscular singleminded sprint. The dog didn't look back once. A minute later it was almost out of sight, still tearing into the barren reaches. It was frightening and magical at the same time, like an ability to rule the animals and the elements. Houston was stunned, too, but he recovered fast enough to keep the moment his.

"You aren't a town," he spoke to them, making it up instant by instant, "and we aren't an army, not unless we are a people, all of us together. And we cannot be a people so long as we savage ourselves. It will be a long pull and a strong pull and a pull all together. That's the only way we'll get Texas. In the days ahead, we must reach inside us and find the best in ourselves. We must be better than our enemy. We must be worthy. That is what Texas will be made of."

It was a good enough speech, Houston could tell because every eye was on him and the catcalls had died. He could hear the children playing in the distance and a late rooster cracking the dawn. He started to step away, highly pleased with himself, thinking the people—his people—had listened with their very souls. But that spiteful woman caught him by the sleeve.

"What about my chickens?" she demanded.

CHAPTER THREE

HE HAD FLED the heartbreak of Eliza on a raft up the Mississippi, fled like a fugitive, leaving behind everything so that he could be free for a new beginning. That's how it felt now as Houston closed the door and shut the world out, as if he were casting himself upon a river. For the rest of the morning he took his time and let himself settle into the empty shack. He hadn't occupied a place of his own for years, not since leaving the governor's mansion. As a result Houston had developed the wanderer's trick of inhabiting wherever he was, for as long as he had it, as if it were home.

Someone had carved a primitive sunburst into the edge of the mantle. Because there was no furniture, the general sat crosslegged on the dirt floor, choosing to face the hearth and its sunburst. He dragged his saddlebags close and withdrew his two pistols, his Caesar and Swift, a long twist of tobacco, and a hawk wing, plus some smaller fetishes and good luck pieces. Last of all he found his packet of writing gear wrapped in a tube inside an oilcloth.

Setting out his paper, ink, and pen, he got his thoughts straight, then leaned over his knees and wrote two dispatches. One was a war report he'd promised to the convention members, the other an order to Colonel Fannin down at Goliad. He reread his words while the ink dried. Satisfied, he folded the letters and took them outside to the couriers who were taking turns with tongue twisters. He sent two of the three riders galloping off, one to the east, one to the south. Back inside, he

49

pegged the door shut again and did some reading and took a nap, resting, waiting.

Around noon Houston emerged from the shack to warm himself. The drizzle had ebbed. A pewter sun was swimming in the overcast. He caught a passing soldier by the sleeve.

"Do you know the man they call Deaf Smith?" Houston asked.

"I know who he is," the soldier answered.

"Has he come into town this morning?"

"You're the only one, General."

"If you see him, you tell him I'm here. This house here is headquarters."

"If I see him."

Houston found a stick the size of his forearm and took a seat on an anvil rusting by the wall. He unfolded his clasp knife and set to whittling. Cutting, chewing, he filled his lap with fragrant blond curlicues of wood and listened to the children. His knife went still and Houston circled back through his schoolmaster days when he'd held class with a fresh hickory stick in one hand, half white, half blue from the fire. His hair had been thick back then and he'd kept it bound in a Revolutionary War–style queue that dropped between his shoulderblades. They had called him Master Houston and loved him for his stories about life among the Cherokee and because he didn't whip them. He leaned out to see them down the street.

The children had cut some river cane for guns and made touch holes above the green joints with a cobbler's awl. Some amused soldiers had donated a few measures of gunpowder and the children tamped it down their cane barrels, using rocks for musket balls. With burning twigs, they fired away. Naturally, it didn't take long for the combat to draw blood and raise knots and bruises, at which point mothers and older sisters searched out their wounded and dragged them home to do chores.

Houston had long recognized that there was a warrior in every child. That was easy to trigger: Hand them a stick and a war cry and let them go. The real challenge was to somehow preserve the child in every warrior. That was how he preferred to see his soldiers at any rate, not as a necessary evil but as a loan against their fundamental innocence. His perception didn't change facts, of course. Their little revolution was still a bald land grab. But he kept hoping it could be something more, too, something different, maybe even democratic.

Houston enjoyed another fifteen minutes with his dwindling stick before the colonels approached. They came in a pack down the middle of the street, sidestepping tree stumps that the Gonzales men had never quite gotten around to pulling. Houston bent and spit in the shavings nested between his boots.

The colonels were spread out, breasting the still air with fierce, martial expressions. Houston leaned back against the wall and the nails squeaked in the clapboard under his weight. He'd known their breed all his life. From genesis, it seemed, America had abounded in the species, bright-eyed men from the dark side of the Appalachians, hungry to where you could see their ribs, dry to where a spark—one word, even—would detonate them. He watched them come on.

J. S. Neill was bringing up the left with his lank lope of a walk and his starved-looking beard. He was supposed to have been commanding the Alamo garrison, but just a few weeks before the Mexicans showed up he had taken a leave from duty. He was a man with natural good fortune.

Sidney Sherman carried the right side of the pack. By virtue of having shown up with his own militia—the Buck Eye Rangers or Kentucky Rifles or some such—the tall red-haired businessman had brought with him the rank he'd bestowed on himself back in Kentucky. Houston hadn't met him yet, but he envied Sherman's fancy uniform with its squared shoulders and buttonholes embroidered with silver thread. Besides giving real stature to what was otherwise ordinary-looking clay, the uniform showed a wife's loving touch. Houston wondered what Sherman would say if it were recommended that he ought to leave Texas and return to his wife before this thing became an outright war, and on his way out to hand over his uniform for a general to wear. Houston wanted that uniform, but he also wanted Sherman to clear out. He and his men had showed up scarcely a week ago bearing a silk flag and the bloodlust of crusaders first hitting the Holy Land. So far they'd been nothing but trouble.

"Houston," Wylie Martin announced. "Since you won't see fit to call your officers to a war council, we've done it for you." His manner suggested that there was a time when his voice had cracked like a bullwhip and men obeyed him. That would be back in the days when he'd been thick with Aaron Burr and his grand scheme to take Texas, back before the disgrace. After that Wylie had come to Texas and become a Mexican and snatched up much of the prime land and sat on it, waiting for the United States to come in and with it citizens eager for real estate. It had been a long wait. Wylie had gotten old. His voice was like fingernails scratching against the window.

"Is that so," Houston said mildly. He carved a long white slice from his stick, then another. If there had been a child at hand, he would have put his knife to work sculpting a frog's head or a dog's. For the little girls, and the big ones, too, he usually liked to cut a heart.

"The Alamo cries to us," J. S. Neill said.

"Cries to us," Houston drolly repeated. He stood up, dusted his pants of shavings, and walked inside the shack, leaving the door open for the colonels to follow him in. There was no sense sharing their rancor with the street, though these walls weren't likely to hold much in. The officers filled the tiny place.

"We must save her," Neill pleaded from the hearth with the sunburst. "Buttressed with our courage and arms, she can hold back the dark tide. I know those walls."

"Tell me," Houston asked him with an offhand curiosity, "when Bowie brought to you my order to destroy the Alamo, how come you didn't obey?"

Neill stiffened. "It wasn't mine to obey. My wife was sick. I had to leave. I gave my command over to Bowie."

"And what was Bowie's excuse?" Houston bore down. He wanted this beanpole of a colonel to know that his insubordination had not been forgotten in the sweep of events.

Neill narrowed his eyes, resenting the humble pie. Houston didn't mind Neill's bitterness one bit, especially if his example would serve to keep the others obedient in the future.

"We talked about your orders," Neill said. "We went walking around the outside of the Alamo and Bowie told me those walls were as sacred as liberty to him. He called it a chalice of holy freedom."

Houston doubted it, but didn't waste his breath saying so. Bowie was nothing but a con artist. His greed for land and money would have been extraordinary if not for all the other world-class opportunism going on in Texas. Bowie cared for one thing: Bowie. That was straight from the horse's mouth.

Houston could hear it still. Floating drunk upon the Mississippi, his head full of suicide and Eliza, Houston had come upon Bowie and two mountain men in a riverside den. That would be '28, maybe '29. The date was out of reach, but Houston couldn't forget that fleshy face with stones for eyes and a reptile's philosophy. *I'm the center,* Bowie had declared from a throne of pressed beaver pelts with his own vomit on his bare feet and a loaded pistol in the hand without a bottle. *I can stop the Mississippi. I can erase the sky. One bullet into my brainpan and I can stop the dream cold. And every one of you bastards dies with me.* He'd gone on like that all evening, waving the pistol, threatening to destroy the universe. After that Houston had never entertained suicide again. Nor believed Bowie's threats.

"Those walls are worthless," Houston said. "That's why I ordered the Alamo abandoned. The forts are beyond our capacity to supply them." He looked up and marched from eye to eye.

"Goddamn it, Houston," Wylie objected. His overgrown eyebrows looked like an explosion. "The presidios are our western front. Without Goliad and the Alamo there is no line."

"There never was a line," Houston quietly replied. "The Alamo was never a real presidio. And besides that, Goliad is gone." He let the notion of disappearance sink in.

"Gone?"

"In effect. My order went out to Colonel Fannin this morning. He is to spike his cannon and destroy the presidio and fall back to meet us. Immediately."

"Destroy Goliad?"

The very thought of it staggered them, all of them, passing like a bolt of lightning through a herd of cattle.

"No, sir," another man declared.

It was John Wharton, a dark-eyed firebrand who had practiced some law with, and against, Travis. It seemed that every lawyer in Texas had gunpowder for brains . . . and Travis for a friend. Houston was not surprised by his excitability. "Fannin will never give up the presidio," Wharton stated. "Not to Santa Anna. Not to you. Not the Fannin I know."

"Then Fannin will be court-martialed," Houston quietly delivered to them.

The colonels didn't care for that one bit.

"You can't mean to court-martial Travis and Bowie, too,"

Wharton challenged. "They are heroes. They've captured the imagination of the people."

If they had survived their battle at the Alamo and he could ever get his hands on them, Houston thought it might be most fitting to just shoot them out of hand. Goddamn them for not blowing up their pile of mud and falling back. Bowie and the young maniac Travis had deliberately disobeyed his orders. They had stayed in their forts showboating with their own command. As a direct consequence of their hubris they had sailed off the edge of the world with some hundred and eighty men in that worthless mission corral.

"Heroes? They're insubordinate and fools," Houston said. "Their recklessness borders on treason."

"So you say, Houston. But those brave men are holding the line." Wylie Martin returned to his theme. "They are occupying the forts."

"The forts are coffins."

"Goddamn you, Houston." They seemed stuck, unable to conceive this fight without those stone anchors.

"Goddamn the forts," Houston retorted.

"But what of Fannin?" Colonel Forbes asked with poorly disguised guile. "Where have you told him to rendezvous with us?" It was a backdoor question, not at all naïve. Forbes was trying to elicit Houston's direction for the army.

In a way, Houston didn't mind if Fannin never showed up, though he didn't say so out loud. The man's incompetence ran dead even with his plantation arrogance. So far as Houston knew—and he prayed it was true—Fannin was the sole instance of a West Point education in Texas. Personally Houston despised the very concept of a national military academy. It was tantamount to taking the eggs of a dunghill fowl and sneaking them into an eagle's nest. No, there was only one way to learn war and that was by surviving war, though at this rate, with men like Bowie and Travis and Fannin in command positions, there was going to be no one left to learn anything.

"Not here," Houston told them. "And not at the Alamo."

"Then where?" Wharton demanded.

Houston laid down his knife and stick and pulled a rolled map from his saddlebags. It was a copy of the same map of Texas that Stephen Austin had drawn and given to the Mexican government as a gift, the same one Santa Anna would now employ to hunt the Americans down. He threw it into the middle of the room. "Since you insist, my answer lies in there."

"So you refuse to help our beleaguered comrades and you think to destroy our forts." Wylie trembled. "What else do you propose, sir?"

"I don't propose a thing," Houston said.

Wylie fixed him with a withering glare. "You may sleep the day away, Houston. But I warn you, we are men of action."

Someone had peeked through the shack wall and seen him napping that morning, then. But Houston wasn't bothered that his officers were spying on him. It meant the colonels didn't yet know what to make of him. Just the same Wylie's threat was not an idle one. Several of these very officers had mutinied against Burleson last fall.

"Gentlemen." Houston sighed. "I don't mind your company. But you'll need to excuse my participation. Somewhere in here," and he held his whittling stick to the light, "there is an animal waiting to be released. I can feel it all ready to leap out. But it's going to take some concentration for me to find the proper contours." That said, he sat in the dirt against one wall and returned to his whittling and would not talk.

Wylie and Wharton and a few others stamped off to continue their plotting. Several stayed on, though. Whether to curry favor or satisfy their curiosity or just to show they weren't part of any conspiring, at least not yet, Forbes and Sherman and Williamson and Mosely Baker made themselves at home. Finally, with nothing else to do, they unrolled the map of Texas and pinned it flat with rocks. It showed a crescent of land curving along the Gulf with tiny towns bearing American names along the eastern rivers and tiny towns with Spanish names on the western rivers. Above the 31st parallel there wasn't much of anything to show, because the northern reaches were largely unexplored.

Before long, the colonels were boldly reconfiguring the map. Houston listened with bemused disbelief as the men proceeded to draw Texas with wilder and wilder strokes. Shucking his crutch and sprawling beside the map, Three-Legged Willie declared that Texas needed more elbow room than to stop at the Nueces River, the traditional border between Texas and its neighboring state Coahuila.

"Nueces, hell," he said. "I say the Rio Grande is more fitting for a region of Anglo-Saxon. We are a bigger, more vital people." In his day Burr had dreamed similar wild dreams, from snatching New Orleans to stealing Texas to conquering Mexico herself and crowning himself an emperor, Aaron I. His soldiers had called themselves colonists, no different from these colonels stabbing at Houston's map.

It was Forbes's turn next, then Burleson threw in. Before they were done the colonels had pushed the western border of Texas all the way to the Pacific Ocean and north most of the way through Canada. The only thing restraining their reach was water and the northern ice. They talked of invading deeper Mexico, driving all the way to Mexico City and her gold. As he listened to them, Houston thought he'd fallen into one of Swift's tales of human folly.

At last the colonels tired of Houston's taciturn company and drifted away. The afternoon stretched on. The rain returned. Houston lay on his horse blanket on the floor and stared up at the dripping ceiling, trying to decide what to tell the army and the townspeople. He wanted to give them hope and at the same time kill their hope. He wanted to put wings on their ferocity, but also to rope them tight and keep them safe. He wanted to tell them about the Alamo even though he didn't know anything to tell them.

All he had was this idea called Texas. And yet for all his faith in ideas, he didn't trust them, and if he didn't, why should anyone else? An idea didn't have the weight of a penny. It was something that traveled with you anywhere, like a star in the night sky or like notions of east or west or high or deep. It was forever out there, no matter what few inches of dirt you were standing on. You could wander all over the earth with an idea and still be nowhere. Sometimes Houston wondered why he was here at all.

At long last, at five o'clock that afternoon, Deaf Smith arrived, escorting two Tejanos who were on horseback. One was young and scared by the crowd of several hundred men who billowed up from the woods and street, massing to hear their story. The other was tall, probably a generation removed from living the cannibal life-style of his Karankawa ancestors.

"I found them hiding in the chaparral south of San Antonio," Smith explained to Houston at the entrance to the shack.

"What news?" a soldier shouted out. Houston saw several

of his officers approaching and some of the town women were
nosing their way through the crowd.

"Bring those two men inside," Houston said to the scout,
"and you two soldiers," he addressed a pair, "you make sure no
one gets in through this door. Understand?" Then he shut the
door and closed the army and town folk out. There was no fire
in the fireplace, but Smith and the two Tejanos gathered there
anyway.

"It's like you said," Smith said. "Santa Anna overran the
Alamo a week ago."

"With what casualties?" Houston asked. "Tell me the
wounded first." If the dead and wounded amounted to even 50
percent of the Alamo garrison it would be too many. What
little morale his army had left after a week of stasis would
disintegrate. He was praying the numbers were low and Travis
and the majority of his band had been captured.

"There weren't any wounded," Smith said.

Houston's spirit lifted, though the rational part of him
knew it was impossible to have a battle without wounded. There
were always injuries, if only from powder burns on a soldier's
hands.

"Every man died," Smith said.

"Every man?" Houston's throat clenched tight. There were
always survivors. He'd said so himself. "How can that be?"

"It just is."

The scope of Smith's news dazzled Houston. He couldn't
fathom such a battle. Even at Horseshoe Bend where the Red
Sticks had refused Jackson's offers to surrender, even there
where the killing had been so utterly compressed, there had
been survivors.

"Tell me what they say, Mr. Smith," Houston said, mostly
because he couldn't think of where to begin asking questions.
His fingers traced in and out of the carved sunburst. *What can
I tell them?* But it was up to him to transcend the shock. He had
to forge the information to his advantage. He was their general.
"Start at the beginning," he told the scout.

Deaf Smith asked something in Spanish, his voice high and
singsong.

"They are *vaqueros*, and they live around San Antonio. I
know this one," he said pointing at the tall man, "not this one.
They say they were hiding from the Mexican *sorteo*. The draft.

The battle took less than an hour and a half. It was finished before the sun came up. They say that Mexican soldiers who fought in the battle told them that Colonel Travis shot himself in the head, that Colonel Bowie died in bed, possibly by his own hand, and that seven prisoners were taken, then executed." The Alamo—mauled into American control only last December—was once again in President Santa Anna's hands.

"Ask them about the burying," he said. Deaf Smith put the question to the younger boy in fast Spanish. He got part of an answer.

"They took the Mexicans to Campo Santa. That's the cemetery." To be sure Houston understood, Smith reminded him. "The Catholic cemetery. Consecrated ground."

Houston didn't begrudge the old scout his religiosity. They all had their destinies to obey, and loving a Catholic wife was a destiny, too.

"And the American dead?" he asked.

The younger Tejano told Smith in a very quiet voice.

"They couldn't be put in holy ground."

"I know that," Houston said. "Where did they get put?"

"They got gathered," Smith translated. "One layer wood, one layer man. Up and up. Then it got fired. Anselmo here, he says the flame went five hundred feet high. He says it burned for three days and nights."

Houston took it all in. He was aware of cremation in other societies and among some of the tribes. But most Americans hearing this would go cold. Fire was for Inquisition purposes, not for burying human beings, not white ones anyhow. He couldn't have invented horror better than Santa Anna had just handed him. They were Go Ahead folk, these Anglo-Saxons. For fifteen years now they'd been struggling to shape this corner of Mexico in their own image. They stubbornly believed Texas had opened her prehistoric arms to them, that she had invited their powerful hand, their radical voice, their ax and gun, their seed . . . cotton and otherwise. Every one of them had arrived white hot with Texas fever. In a way, thought Houston, it was only natural they should end as ash.

"Does anyone else in Gonzales know what we've just heard?" Houston asked.

"Just us two and them two," Smith said.

"Then let us keep the secret." He needed time to absorb the tragedy, time to shape his words, his plans.

The secret held for less than an hour. At sunset a shriek pierced the town and shortly afterward the sound of women wailing told Houston that the wives now knew they were widows. Under the quarter moon more than a hundred men fled from town. Colonel Burleson came at two o'clock in the morning to tell him so.

"By morning you may have no army," Burleson warned him.

"Let them go," Houston said and turned over on his blanket. It wasn't hard guessing which direction the deserters had gone, back to their homes to collect their families, those who had them, or else straight for the Louisiana border.

At dawn Houston came out of his shack and what was left of his army stood waiting. He found a pitch keg to stand on, then got up and faced them.

"Citizens of Texas," he spoke. They fell silent, for his was a voice that could throw a half mile without shouting. He could reach all the way into the cold pebble of a congressman's heart and yet not wake a sleeping baby.

"Your country is desolate, your cities are burned with fire," he called out to them. He listened to his mother's faraway echo, the Scripture, the sound of neighbors digging a grave for his father. He carried it up and gave them his grief. "Your land, strangers devour it in your presence, and it is desolate."

"Desolate," some man in the crowd murmured.

"Yes," said Houston. "Overthrown by strangers."

The men bent to his words. They wanted to hear him. He saw the confusion and terror in their eyes. J. S. Neill's gaunt face was pale with turmoil, part grief, part ecstasy. He'd slipped death's talons by not being where he ought to have been. His look of horror and joy said he obviously hadn't decided what that meant. In the background, scarcely muffled by the clapboard, some of the widows were howling to Jesus.

Then Houston told them everything that was known about the Alamo battle, trying to dispel their wilder notions. He called them soldiers and defenders of the people.

"Is it true they split Bowie's jaw open and cut out his tongue and threw him alive on a fire?" someone yelled.

"Is it true they roasted our boys and ate bits of their flesh?"

"Just tell us when's our fight?" a sour man bellowed.

"We will fight, boys," Houston assured them.

"Where at?"

"We will fight," Houston repeated, "but it will be on our ground, not theirs."

"This y'ere's our ground," one shaggy fellow pronounced. He looked enormous in a shaggy buffalo robe. One eye was dead, part of a fleshy seam cutting from forehead to chin. The good eye glittered up at Houston, sly and brute, challenging. His hair hung in greasy braids ornamented with red and white beads. And then Houston saw the scalps. There were a half dozen of them sewed along the shoulders of the robe.

"It's not our ground," Houston pointed out for the record, "not yet."

" 'Tis," the buffalo man responded. "And I say, slay them bastards y'ere." He grinned with black stumps for teeth.

Houston realized he was afraid of this man. And suddenly it struck him that he feared all of these men, even the boys. The recognition startled him. But this was no time to untangle the emotions. He had chaos to overcome.

"No, sir," Houston said, "they are many, and we are few. So we must find our place."

"Stand here, lads. Here's the place," the shout rose up. A gun went off into the air, then another. Some of the voices belonged to his officers. Worse, they stood scattered through the crowd, so that he couldn't see and silence them. The army was falling into panic and chaos.

"We must go from here," Houston said.

"Not east, by gad, or else," someone swore. Houston looked quick and it was Mosely Baker. He had a peculiar darkness in his face, a desperation Houston hadn't seen yesterday. His frontier rose was nowhere to be seen in the crowd.

"Else what, Colonel Baker?" Houston gently asked him.

Baker swiped one hand across his nose. Houston had caught him flat in the open. He grew quieter, if not less passionate.

"Give us our fight," Mosely said. "You'll find the whole army with you. We'll follow you to the very devil."

"I thank you," Houston said. "But the devil is not our direction."

"What then is our direction?" some other dark voice challenged from the crowd.

Houston reached into himself and found some calm. He didn't answer right away. Instead he waited. His eyes strayed up from the turbulence spreading all around his little raft of a keg. Out beyond, the sun lay sparkling on the eastern skyline, a momentary jewel between the dark jaws of earth and storm clouds. Houston felt the warmth on his face like a whispering in his ear.

"Why, we will go into the light," he replied simply.

Baker frowned. It occurred to him to turn and look at whatever Houston was looking at. When Baker saw the sun, he erupted.

"Now see here, General," Mosely started in. "Gonzales must be defended."

The babble of voices climbed. Men on horseback were wheeling in the background and flintlocks banged away at the emptiness. The army was slipping from Houston's hands and they'd barely begun their war.

Houston stepped down from his keg. He shouldered a channel through the tight pack of humanity straight through to the largest of the mess fires burning in the street. As if he were all alone and there weren't some three hundred men watching on, Houston took his time selecting just the faggot. It was a good six inches thick and four feet long and half its wood was blazing. Houston grabbed the torch and returned through the crowd, not particularly careful where he waved the flame. This time the men were quicker to open a way for him.

They gawked and grew more attentive, uncertain what their general had in mind. Trailing sparks and frost, Houston strode back to the little shack he'd called headquarters. Without a word he pitched the torch through the open door.

He'd prepared. The house was safely empty except for a pile of straw in the back. His rig and possibles were stored in a stable down the way.

The straw lit in a puff of orange fire. In no time the clapboard caught. Men scrambled to back away from the heat. Suddenly the roof burst into flame and big pieces of burning debris lifted over the crowd, then hit the cold air and pelted down. The mob scattered. Across the path, another roof caught on fire.

"Put the women and children in wagons," Houston shouted
at them. He was risking everything. Only yesterday he'd cau-
tioned them against burning novels. Today he was burning an
entire town. There was no telling where this would end. "Pack
your gear. We march east. Gonzales is no more."

The peculiar part was that Houston felt hope.

CHAPTER FOUR

FOR A WEEK then more, Houston's army fled. It was like the Flood, a world of water, of rivers escaped, of the fields flooded, drowned cows dangling in the mangroves, of cottonmouths and other reptiles swimming loose and alligators with white mouths and a bold taste for man, and not just for slave children fishing and skipping rocks while they watered the beef, but for red-blooded Anglo-Saxon meat, too.

Squalls of hail and pea snow swept through in pitch darkness rattling in the branches like skeletons on the loose. The only good thing about the rain was that it washed the Alamo's death smoke from the air. Houston felt like he could breathe again. By day the mud trapped their feet and hooves and bogged their wheels. By night the cold plagued them and brought pneumonia and strep, killing two of the infants plus three soldiers already sick with lung diseases. One half of the McCavish twins woke to find the other half dead, his brother's face glazed with a mask of diamond ice.

With time the women and children went one way, north and east to catch the grandly named Camino Real, or King's Highway, which would take them to the Sabine River and Louisiana. The army went differently, straight east, just like in the Bible, east from Eden as if Houston had some definite destination in mind.

Day after day the cold rain lashed their backs, driving them on. They were being whipped from the Garden, Houston saw, all of them, punished for sins they had committed or were about

to. Like Adam they bent their collective head in despair and
trudged blindly into the wilderness. Like Cain they raged
against their exile and fought with one another even as they
fought the wilderness.

With the sun sunk deep in clouds their clockwork became
a spectrum of grays, lightest at noon. Their feet flowered with
green moss inside their brogans, the ones who had them. Otherwise it was bare feet, soft and puckered and turning pale am-
phibian. Houston had one of the only pair of boots in the army,
though a good deerskin moccasin would have been preferable
because with his pants tucked into his boot tops, he collected
more water than he shed. Every time he got off his yellow pony
to empty his boots Houston had to pick slick black leeches from
between each toe.

Back and forth, up and down, Houston rode his stout pony
through the red and black gravy, counting his soldiers with one
finger. The total was never the same, but that had nothing to
do with his arithmetic. They'd been marching for more than a
week and his army had grown, but now it was melting away.
At one point they'd numbered over eight hundred. But on
Houston's very next pass down the wagon trace the count had
dropped by a hundred. Today the sum barely hit four hundred.

Men came and went as they pleased. Scarcely a quarter of
his army had been in Texas for more than a few months or
weeks. They had come to Mexico alone or in packs, with long
teeth and flat bellies and an appetite for free land, between six
hundred and twelve hundred acres depending on when they'd
showed up and how long they'd signed on for. But until they
yanked it from Mexican hands these grand soldiers of fortune
wouldn't own one stick or inch of Texas. Soaked, frozen and
famished, many realized they stood to lose nothing by high-
tailing it back across the Louisiana border.

There was little to do about these hour-by-hour "migra-
tions," as Three-Legged Willie termed them. A few among the
colonels demanded a set of executions to cure the desertion
fever. "You got to make the troops fear you more than they
fear the enemy," Colonel Wharton explained. He'd been ill
lately and there was a cadaverous suck to his cheeks. "Then sir,
then you can call 'em an army."

Houston considered a killing for the sake of discipline.

That's how Jackson would have done it and Houston had seen it work: the soldiers assembled, a quick shooting, an open grave. Lord knew this rabble would only hear through its back, and Houston knew it would be a mistake to spare the whip. But he wasn't Jackson. *What am I capable of in the name of Texas?* he wondered and looked around. What were *they* capable of?

Houston couldn't bring himself to shoot or hang a single deserter. For one thing, he couldn't square killing a runaway when the fact was they were all runaways. The men themselves had taken to calling their backward march the Runaway Scrape.

More important the deserters were purifying his army with their absence. The men who remained were pulling together into a legion that was moved by something larger than any of them, though not one in fifty would have said so out loud. The most philosophical the troops got was to crow about the livers they meant to carve from Mexican soldiers and the fields they would irrigate with Mexican blood. But as coarse and stupid and violent and debased as so many were—or pretended to be—they were reinventing themselves step by step. Houston had faith in it. He believed as much as an adult could that they were marching backward into innocence, and in a way the desertions simply confirmed the bigness of their quest. The more men dropped away, the higher the mountain proved to be.

"When do we turn and fight?" Wylie Martin demanded. It had become a daily tax.

"Not here," Houston sighed.

"But we must draw a line. We must make a stand. We must fight." Very like a tombstone left too long in the elements, Wylie had a square, dour face bracketed with spiky curls. These days he seemed mostly held together with a whalebone corset and leather strings tied at each ankle and wrist to keep the leeches out or the life in. Except when he was hectoring Houston about their retreat Old Wylie kept his jaw locked tight, as if his surviving teeth might try and escape when he breathed.

"Not yet," Houston told him.

"We must."

"When Fannin joins us," Houston said, "maybe then." It was a sop he threw them. His colonels delighted in the possibilities. They knew that with Fannin's troops, the American army would swell to nearly a thousand. Strength would give them options, and options were opportunities, and opportunities were Texas. The problem was no one knew where Fannin had disappeared to. After a dispatch from Goliad stating his retreat from the presidio was about to commence, Fannin had fallen into silence.

Mile by mile, Houston kept his army moving away from the enemy. The farther east they marched, the deeper they penetrated their own American construct. The zigzagging wooden fences, the brick-lined wells, the square wooden houses, even the livestock spoke of a familiar order. No round-cornered adobes or twig *jacales* here, nor brindled range cattle with wide gutting horns, nor small Spanish ponies that could live like goats on the wild fescue, nor Mexican corn with its soft white kernels.

They came upon American houses and American towns and words printed in English on American printing presses and fields ripped neat with American plows and corn grinders nailed to trees and a cotton gin built along the river and black-smith anvils and cooper's rings and a surveyor's tripod and a hundred other things that spoke of who they were and where they'd come from. Ordinarily the sights would have buttressed their morale.

But there were no people.

Everywhere they went they found emptiness and lonely hounds and cats that ran up mewing. The houses were occupied all right, but by huge hogs that had broken open the doors to root and vandalize and by goats and dogs who slept on the corn-shuck mattresses. Houston was reminded of Circe's island where Odysseus had found the men magically changed into beasts.

Every settlement came out of the rain like cold blue burial grounds. Indeed, many seemed to have sprouted fresh graves with wooden crosses as if the cholera were making another sweep or the Mexicans had already come through. Even after Deaf Smith and Ned Burleson and other Texas veterans demonstrated that the new graves had been dug to fool the Mexican army and only contained settlers' buried possessions, not corpses, the soldiers remained skittish.

These were men schooled since childhood in backwoods taboos. It was a given that if they accidentally stepped across a grave, they would immediately jump back over it to reverse their trespass. In a sense the entire army was jumping back over the Anglo-Saxon grave.

On and on they retreated and the further they marched the more they pillaged, burning the worm fences and homemade furniture and books for their heat and shooting milk cows for meat and looting smokehouses for pork bellies and smoked venison and in general erasing the Anglo-Saxon presence as they fell eastward.

Since ordinary flint sparks couldn't combust their damp tinder, they started fires by pouring a shot of gunpowder down the muzzle, then stuffing in a piece of dry rag saturated with more gunpowder and tamping it with the ramrod. Aiming at their pile of kindling, they triggered the charge and the rag shot out flaming, and they stuck it among the twigs and blew it to a blaze.

How strange, thought Houston. Like many, he'd heard Jim Bowie's tale of the golden bullets, about how a party deep in the Staked Plains up north had discovered a cache of Spanish doubloons. But upon running out of food they had been forced to chop the coins into bullets to shoot jackrabbits on their long hungry march back to civilization, and so had shot away their fortune. In a sense Houston's army was the logical extension of Bowie's wanderers, penniless, reduced to shooting bits of their own clothing and burning their own homes just to heat a few cobs stolen from the corn cribs. At this rate they would exit Texas naked as infants.

The army crossed the Lavaca and the Navidad rivers, forcing the passages. They found ferry rafts hidden in the brakes or else made them out of trees and pieces of houses, and Houston ripped his jacket on a hinge nail. If it was shallow enough they simply breasted the current. They forded creeks named Ponton and Mixon and Big Becky and Cedar and creeks that had no names because in ordinary times they weren't creeks at all, just dips and wrinkles in the land.

They got to the Colorado and found it swollen wider and deeper than anyone could remember. On the opposite bank Jesse Burnham's ferryboat rocked up and down on the nut-brown waters, and higher up the shore was a stone blockhouse, the trading post. They located the ferry horn dangling by a rawhide string from a giant willow with names carved in it.

While one man blew the horn, a few of the soldiers shielded their guns from the rain and carefully loaded powder and fired blank rounds. But neither Burnham nor any of his thirteen children came to the signals.

The army stood in the pelting rain and looked forlornly across at the boat. Sitting on their horses with the water sluicing down the manes and saddles and creases in their clothing, Houston and his colonels tried to figure things out.

"Where's that Jesse at?" Wharton groused. "Don't he know there's a war on?" He had a dashing white hat with one swept-up side to the brim, in the same fashion affected by Mosely Baker and their dead friend Travis. It was a beautiful hat, but it channeled water straight down the colonel's collar. As a direct consequence his cough was getting worse, but the hat stayed.

"Could be the Karanks finally got him, them or Comanches," Burleson postulated. He didn't like Indians and was famed for his savagery when he went rangering after them.

"Maybe the goddamn Cherokees went wild," Three-Legged Willie tossed in. That was aimed straight at Houston. The Cherokee were Houston's second family—third if you counted Jackson's embrace—and he was considered soft on hostiles because of it. After Old Hickory banished the Cherokee from the United States, one branch of the exiles had settled in the Red River country of upper Texas where they had demonstrated nothing but peaceful ways. Nevertheless men like Burleson and Willie couldn't wait to go raid and despoil them. They knew their talk bothered Houston.

"Is there any other way across?" he asked at large.

"There's Montezuma way," Burleson answered, which was the same as saying no. Montezuma lay a full day south. If Santa Anna was hunting them, he'd go straight for Montezuma. And even if he wasn't, Houston could take his army down and find no ferry there either.

"Can we get a man over to fetch that boat?"

"Don't we have no Meskins?" Wharton asked. "They can swim slick as fat."

"Juan Seguín's got all the greasers with him," Old Wylie said. "No telling where that pack is off to."

"There's a fellow in Baker's company," Colonel Forbes volunteered. "They say he's half fish."

"Bring him up then," Houston said.

Somebody found Robbie King, a gentle young cooper from San Felipe de Austin. "I hear you can swim," Houston said to him. King had long fingers and Houston wondered if that might not be his trick.

"It's true," King said.

"I'll give you a dollar if you can swim over," Houston said. He hoped the man wouldn't want more. All he had was two dollars.

King didn't answer right away. He screwed up his eyes, then took a handful of grass and threw it on the water and calculated the river's force. "A dollar and a league," he told Houston.

Houston didn't blink. A league amounted to more than four thousand acres, and while it was all meaningless until they owned it and he admired capitalism as much as the next man, still Houston didn't like the appearance of getting bested in a deal.

"A dollar and a mile," Houston said, then added, "soldier," just to remind the cooper he had certain martial duties. A mile was only 640 acres. The cooper was happy with it.

"I'll go get my horse," he said, for he meant to swim with his horse's help.

Even as they waited for Robbie King the storm slackened and a rainbow sprang up, generating a discussion among the slogging soldiers.

"Look it there," one soldier pointed. Their gloom fell away. "She's touching down along the Colorado." All of them knew rainbows sprang up from the finest soil.

"I'll take a place along here," said another. "It will be black, the earth. It will be a place to build a home. And I'll paint 'er white so as to bring my house out from the northers and contrast the piney barrens."

"First I'll plant me some corn," a stark fellow with a bulging goiter voiced. "Cotton later, or sugar, I don't know. But the corn first, yeah. Throw it down among the stumps."

Houston watched the men bend and pinch up the dirt under their feet. All along they had been paying as much attention to the ground as to their looming enemy. They tasted the dirt for the presence of salts. They smelled it for its minerals. Few would actually be farming it, but all meant to take chunks of this land to pass on to others, and the price would rise if they could lay title to the sweetest soil available. Even in retreat these soldiers saw their fortune in the dirt.

Some men looked up, not down, to judge the ground, debating the tallness of trees or the density of fifteen-foot-high canebrakes. They were searching for hickory and sassafras and walnut, Houston knew, for those marked the best picking. They would know better than to believe in the Spanish oak which could grow in just about anything. The prairies were a complete loss, of course. Not one of them would trust a soil without trees.

With great animation and wisdom, they shared their alphabet of the earth. Black soil which cut like butter, which didn't stick or clump, which was short and light and broke into small clods, that was what they wanted, a soil as good as gold. But so far such a soil had eluded them. Either it was sandy-bottomed or slick with blond clay or mixed with iron, which would stunt the crops, or it had been "crayfish" soil, white and sterile. They'd crossed miles and miles of yellow sand, which had some life to it, it was true. But this was Texas and they'd come to seat King Cotton on the richest blackest throne they could find. They wanted only the best.

"Bless you poor bastards," Houston whispered to them. All the while the rain pocked the thick brown river with rapid dimples.

At last Robbie King was ready. He showed up buck naked on a bareback roan and seemed to know his business. Except for a hickory switch he had no equipment, not even reins or a bit for the horse.

The cooper directed his mount upriver a hundred yards, estimating the eddies and curls and Houston didn't know what else. Picking a place, he entered the water slowly. For maybe thirty feet the roan kept her footing on the riverbed, then the current took them and man and horse began to swim. While the horse moved her legs underwater, King paddled on top of it with cupped hands.

To Houston's surprise, the cooper and his roan actually gained distance through the thick muddy water. They were three-quarters across by the time the current brought them opposite the army. Another fifteen yards or so and the pair of swimmers would touch the far shore.

That was when the water parted in a twenty-foot-long riptide, green and slow. At first only the soldiers saw it.

"Robbie King," they yelled at him, "best hurry or that gator come bite your ass."

The army laughed and joked because King's eyes got big as lemons and he started moaning "Oh God, oh God, oh God," and lashing the water to a froth with his hickory switch. With only ten yards to go, the cooper's predicament struck Houston as comical, too, and lord knew they needed some humor. No possible harm could come to King, not from this slowly drifting animal, not with a whole army present with guns.

Several men stood on the riverbank chuckling and, just for the target practice, pinked away at the monster. But their lead balls only slapped against its stony scales like raindrops.

"I'll be goddamn," one sharpshooter said and reloaded quick to try again.

Then the jaws opened like a small cave. King quit his prayer. One minute he was above water, the next he was gone, taken under to another world.

"By God," a man murmured. The hilarity died.

"Robbie King?" one of his San Felipe neighbors called.

King's roan made it to shore and climbed bareback from the water. She took one look around, then bolted north, freed forever from human hands. She'd gained her liberty and Houston doubted any man would ever get within rifle distance of her again.

"A goddamn waste of a man," Ned Burleson said.

"Now what?" Wharton wanted to know. He was looking weak and flinched at the raindrops.

"Maybe Mr. Forbes has another swimmer for us," Three-Legged Willie suggested with a wicked glint.

At that moment the door to the stone hut slid open and the whole army quit its agitation. A man dressed in skins stepped outside and studied the sky. He started whistling to himself, Houston could hear it plainly, and headed over to his woodpile. It took him another full minute before he found time to look across his river and catch sight of the Army of the Republic of Texas stretched out along the banks. He stopped, less amazed than Houston would have thought possible. His head perked a spot higher, the way a squirrel's does.

"Who the hell are you?" he shouted over to them.

"We're the goddamn army of God," someone yelled back.

"What do you want?" Burnham wanted to know.

"What's it goddamn look like," Burleson bellowed back. "Get your goddamn ferry y'ere, Burnham."

By nightfall half the army had crossed to the east bank, with Houston taking the final boat over. He rode up the trace past Burnham's stone hut with a sweet twig sticking out between his teeth and found his soldiers occupying an abandoned set of shacks.

"Light, sir," someone invited him. "Stake out your hoss."

"I swear," someone joked, "the general's mount do grow shorter everyday." Just then, with the pony's hooves deep in mud and Houston's long legs dangling down, his feet nearly touched the ground.

"Who ordered the halt here?" Houston asked them. Deaf Smith had indicated a better campground lay another half mile on. Socketed in a low hollow, this particular clearing was as opposite to defensible as a man could pick. Besides that Houston had resolved to sleep his army of predators as far from settlers' dwellings as possible. But these men weren't budging for the night. Houston gave it up.

The soldiers set to rifling the little dogtrot house and dismantling the worm fence and chasing down the chickens and cutting the heifer's throat. Soon their mess fires were smoking away. Just to break the place in several men started fighting like trappers' dogs over some eggs hardboiling in a pot of coffee. The grappling turned to teeth and eye-gouging. One combatant parted with a tip of his ear. A butcher knife was pulled.

"Come let me tickle your gut with my Arkansas sticker."

"Why you," said the other and pulled a heavy faggot from the fire for a club.

Blood and sparks flew. Men cheered and bet. Someone uncovered a barrel of liquid corn hidden in the brush and they drank it dry. More fights broke out. Some put the excitement to good advantage and went off to claim the best, driest ground for sleeping. Most stayed to watch, grinning with cheeks packed with chew and a glee so primal it came up from their groins.

Houston looked about at these shouting men dressed in animal hides and patched-up rags smeared with red and brown and yellow and black mud, feeling their same muscular pull toward abandon. The soaked firewood smoked and the smoke hung in a dense green pall. It erased their names and faces and made them just a clot of primitives drunk on coffee and half-raw beef and cold rain and some shared notion of a direction. He watched them and felt like he was standing on the brink of a cliff, ready to fling himself into their violence and amnesia and anonymity.

It always ended like this for him, or started, however one looked at it. As a boy he'd escaped from school and his father's harrowing apparition and the stifling discipline of clerking in a general store by running off to join the Cherokee in their forest. As a governor in disgrace he'd run again, floating off on a raft to mate with black-haired Tiana and live in her wigwam, drunk and delirious with opium and malaria. And when Jackson had tried to civilize him and bring him back into the political fold, Houston had fled into the wilderness again, into this Texas of renegade men and boiling anarchy.

He loved chaos. He loved it more perhaps than any constitution or marriage vow or logic in the world. Chaos had soft breasts and wet fur upon its pubis, it lurked as shadows and cries in the woods and in the rivers, defying neatness and measurement and laws with its gigantic mountain ranges and tangling roots and swift current and its million constellations hanging unnamed behind the few stars that did bear names. Chaos had taken Robbie King off into the earth.

One shout, one lurch forward into the hurly-burly and Houston knew the ecstasy that would take him over. She was waiting for him deep inside the folds of wild roses, in the seep of pure ponds, atop the northern mountains. In these men's savage roar she was calling to him. And all he had to do was lift his voice in answer. Houston could be one with the tribe.

But he held himself back.

"Enough," he shouted to no one in particular and spurred his pony into the thick of the fighting, knocking men right and left. The net effect was merely to reconfigure the fighting, matching men with new opponents. At last Houston lifted one of his pistols, the one he'd carved with a dog's head, and pulled back the cock and fired a shot in the air. His little mare could have bucked or jerked but she held steady, something worth noting if the Mexicans ever did catch them and force a fight. He cocked his second pistol, the one with a carved rooster head, and fired it off, too.

The men paused in their pummeling and wrestling. "Save it for Santa Anna," Houston told them.

That was good enough for them. Bruised and muddy, the happy mob dispersed. Soldiers straggled off to their fires or into the dark woods fringing the hollow to settle for the night. They had raided the corn crib and Houston could smell ears propped upright by the flames, roasting, and johnnycakes frying, and pieces of meat getting seared on sharpened branches. Their cooking would continue far into the night, long after he beat tattoo for them to turn in. Once again he would have to drum them to consciousness in the morning.

Houston wandered toward the dogtrot to see about his chance of a dry floor for the night. But the area surrounding it reeked of urine and fresh human dung, and both cabins and the sheltered gallery between them were jammed with men. No one volunteered to move. He could have cleared a space for himself with a single command, of course, but he was weary of commanding for the day.

He meandered off, working up a nearby hill to find a place to lie down. Sleep would probably elude him tonight, no different from the last week of nights. An hour, three if he got lucky, and then for the rest of it he would just lie in the darkness and let the visions take him over.

He passed through the twilight camp like one of Homer's eavesdropping gods, undetected in the gloom, listening in on his mortals. Under trees, sharing blankets, clustered around campfires, or just muttering to themselves, the army spoke to Houston. There was the usual bellyaching about hunger and the rain and blisters, the usual bragging about how fast one could run or hard another could hit or far a rifle could shoot. But underneath that surface chatter Houston heard revelations. In snatches and murmurs his soldiers spoke of their heartache, their night dreams, their demons.

"I left a wife. . . ."

"I married two. . . ."

"I killed a man. . . ."

"I made another man's slave bury my children and he got their cholera and died. . . ."

"I sold land that wasn't mine. . . ."

"I stole my neighbor's hog. . . ."

He listened to them as if thinking to himself. He made their sins his own confessions. Maybe Robbie King's death had put them in a thoughtful mood, maybe Houston was just hearing them for the first time tonight. What impressed him was how they had quit talking about Texas. Not one spoke of what had brought them here. Rather they talked about what they had left behind. Their imagination was dying out, extinguished by their backward journey.

Not all was nostalgia, of course. Skirting one bright fire, he saw a father teaching his son how to slit a man's windpipe. By the light of another, he saw a man's bare buttocks and on the other side a man's bearded face. Houston drew closer. The buttocks belonged to Three-Legged Willie, the beard to Dr. Labadie, a walleyed healer with a black felt stovepipe on his head. He was lifting Willie's penis on the tip of a stick.

"That's pox, all right," the doctor affirmed.

"Goddamn her," the cripple swore. "Travis warned me she was afflicted. But a half dollar seemed a fair market price for such pretty eyes."

"That's the problem with pretty eyes," Dr. Labadie said. "They can lure strong men away from their chosen path." He threw the stick into the fire.

The colonel hitched his pants up. "Well, the heat in this thing's likely to carry me right into distraction. What's your relief?"

"I'm out of blue pills," Dr. Labadie said. "You'll have to take your mercury neat in liquid form. . . ."

Houston moved off, his curiosity satisfied. Willie's was a confession, too, a remembrance.

It was dark now and he still didn't have a place to lie down. With his saddlebags in hand Houston took care in placing his feet. In moccasins he would have felt it when the roots started to tangle his ankle. But the thick boots gave him no warning at all. The roots suddenly snared his foot and he tripped. He fell to his left and thrust out one arm, wrenching around for balance. Right away he felt the old arrow wound open in his groin.

The pain blinded Houston and ripped the breath right out of his lungs. It took a full minute to get enough air for even a single goddamn. He lay on the cold slimy hillside holding the wound and gritting his teeth. He reached inside his clothing and his fingers came away wet.

Even in the best of times, the hole seeped constantly, weeping a clear rancid fluid. Every now and then he'd twist wrong, and it would pull wide open again and bleed and stink for days or weeks. In the morning, when there was light to see, he would have to go search out Labadie, even though no doctor had yet figured out how to get the hole to seal shut for good. One had reckoned that this was Houston's stigmata and he'd just have to learn to live with it. Usually they gave him laudanum or plain unmixed opium and told him not to twist himself anymore.

"General Houston?" A man was leaning over beside him with a small torch in one hand. He had a pleasant face and green spectacles and city clothes, frayed at the ankle where weeds and stones had been nibbling at him. Clearly he'd traveled here on foot. "Let me help you from the mud, sir."

Houston accepted the hand. His jaw muscles bunched. He hunched over and rested on his knees. Whoever that Indian archer at Horseshoe Bend had been, he was surely smiling at this moment and the thought of it made Houston grimace right through his pain.

"Maybe you should sit."

Houston stayed on his feet, breathing carefully, finding his way around the pain.

"This mud's a wonder," the samaritan observed in a friendly manner. "When you don't need a grip, the stuff sucks your foot to the knee. And just when you could use some traction, it sends you skating."

The muscles around Houston's wound quit pinching. It felt almost as if the hole were healing shut again, temporarily anyway. He tried easing himself to straight, but the wound caught with a stab and Houston grabbed at his lower abdomen.

"Come to our fire, General," the samaritan said. Houston gave a swift nod and the smaller man took the general's left arm over his shoulder and they finished climbing the rest of the hill.

"I'm Mirabeau Buonaparte Lamar," he introduced himself. His voice had a tenor lilt to it and was pleasant to the ear. Houston wondered vaguely, instinctively, if the man had any political background. "If I do say so, it's a great huge name for a rather little private, especially one still so green to the country. I reached your army just in time for the *volte-face*."

"Well you reached us in time to catch a general," Houston

managed. He was feeling better now and took his arm off the helping shoulder.

"My pleasure," Lamar said.

Houston tried to pretend his limp was a cautious gait in the darkness. The soldier pretended to be a slow walker. They moved side by side.

"So you have come to fight for Texas," Houston said, just to say something.

"Actually I came to buy Texas," Lamar replied. "Or at least part of her. I'm an agent for a New York real estate syndicate, and I have a bit more than six thousand dollars in bank specie and gold on me. I was on my way to find my friend Colonel Fannin and offer him a partnership in the venture. But this war jumped up, so here I am."

Houston prized the man's candor. "You belonged at the convention," he said. "There's where Texas is getting bought and sold."

"Oh no, sir. Here's the future of Texas. Right here," and he didn't mean this place, but this man. His eyes twinkled behind his green spectacles.

It was a perfect remark, carefree and calculated, one that might have been flattery in another man's mouth. On the surface it sounded like a pledge of allegiance to the army or to Houston or to both, but it wasn't, not coming from this quick little bantam. If Houston had heard correctly, Lamar had just declared the future of Texas lay in Lamar himself. It was a long reach for a private with such short arms, but Houston had to admire the man's pluck. Certainly there were more Young Turks in Texas this season than fleas. Most had showed up with an esquire or doctor or colonel attached to their name, and that made this man with no title all the more entertaining.

They found Lamar's mess in a smear of smoke beneath a sprawling live oak. "Here we are then," the private said.

A half dozen soldiers were sitting around the fire carving leaves of seared beef with their butcher knives and passing a jug that came, no doubt, from the ferrymaster's stock.

"General Houston?" One man squinted through the smoke. "Well, I'll be."

"How are you boys tonight?" Houston asked. He edged his way among them, lowered onto a rock, and draped his saddlebags over one knee. It took remarkably little time for the men to get used to having their general share the same fire. They passed him the jug, but he passed it on.

"We were just recollecting about an old friend of yours, General," said one fellow with bear grease in his hair.

"Which friend?"

"The late Colonel Crockett, sir."

Crockett had been neither a friend nor a colonel, but Houston tipped his head in recognition. "What was it you were recollecting?"

Several of the men exchanged daring looks in the firelight and suddenly Houston realized he'd come to the wrong place. With a guide as clever as Private Lamar he should have known the talk would be political here.

"It's no secret Old Davy hated Andy Jackson," the man with bear grease said. "No secret, either, that if he'd showed up at the constitutional convention, he might just have got your job. Nor any secret that this army is more than just an army, it's a constituency. Crockett thought he'd make a pretty good general, you know, and a pretty good president, too."

Someone's spit snapped against the fire. It sizzled. They waited for Houston's reply. The accusation was clear. Houston had just been charged with getting Crockett out of his way by sending him to the Alamo. It was a cynical thing to say, as false as it was bizarre. Houston had been off negotiating peace terms with the Indians when Crockett arrived and he'd had nothing to do with posting the poor washed-out dupe to the Alamo.

Houston's first instinct was to attack the slander straight on, for here was the beginning of a mutiny. But how many other campfires were illuminating similar talk? He couldn't answer them all. Instead he kept his expression wry and glanced around through the smoke and saw their eyes fixed on him, all except for Lamar's. Houston's little samaritan was innocently studying the flames. He wasn't part of this, he wouldn't be, not yet. But he understood everything. Their discontent smelled of blood and musk, a pungent smell that gave away their waiting.

Houston had dueled once, a political matter disguised as a defense of honor. Bloodthirsty old Jackson had personally provided him with both pistols and instructions. *Bite down on one bullet while you shoot another. It will steady your aim.* In a Kentucky pasture draped with blue fog, Houston had bit, ending the affair by shooting down an old terrified man. He had emerged with no illusions about his marksmanship or his luck. This time, if he took on his accusers directly, it would be him lying in the grass, turning gray.

Finally Houston spoke. "The last time I ever saw David Crockett, he was bowing to himself in public," Houston said. "It was in a theater in Washington, in some play called *The Lion of the West*, as I recall, and there was some actor up on stage playing the part of Crockett. It was a sight, gentlemen, this buffoon all rigged out with a bobcat cap and animal skins and a mouthful of frontier nonsense: I'm part snapping turtle, I can whip my weight in panthers, that kind of thing. After a bit I saw that Congressman Crockett was in the audience watching his own image ape around on stage. And goddamn me if he didn't think that was himself up there. When it was all over, that actor stood in front of Crockett and Crockett stood in front of him, and the two of them bowed and applauded and complimented each other. It was a strange sight to see the creator meet his creation."

Houston polled the firelit faces. The majority were confused or simply carried away with the story. The man with greasy hair looked resentful at Houston's detour. Private Lamar alone seemed to have enjoyed or understood the tale.

"Wonderful," he said. His green spectacles glittered. "But would you indulge me, General. I fancy myself a poet of sorts, and yet I'm not sure I understand. Is your point that Crockett failed his illusions, or that his illusions failed him? Because if it's the first, then it makes the congressman a sad old fool who grabbed at empty air. And if it's the second, then he was wrong to come to Texas. And if he was wrong, then maybe we all are, because the illusions could fail us all, couldn't they, including the illusion of this army and even the illusion of Texas?"

Now the soldiers were truly bewildered. Not one of them understood what the private named for Napoleon could be driving at. "Take the jug and shut up, Lamar," one prescribed.

Houston spread his hands over the fire and took his time. He listened to the drizzle cut against the leaves like ants chewing. The night was growing chill against his back, reminding him that he still had to find a place to sleep. Some scamp had stolen his horse blanket, and so he needed a dry patch of ground or just a nest of needles under a pine.

"Crockett said it best," Houston finally responded. "Be sure you're right, then Go Ahead." He looked up from the fire and the conspirators seemed like figments of smoke and shadows, like momentary spirits.

"But Go Ahead where? You can't go where your imagination doesn't lead you. Texas isn't going to be won through a rifle barrel, gentlemen, but through this," he tapped his skull. "This. A blast of dreams. Here's the weapon."

He was about to stand up and leave, but on second thought pulled out his whittling knife and unfolded the blade from the handle. He leaned forward and sliced off a prime chunk of the beef, then rummaged through their fire and helped himself to a torch. Sparks blew and Houston's assassins blinked and snorted.

"Sleep well, boys," he said and got to his feet, stretched his big shoulders, and stepped into the darkness, away from their fire, out where the alligators were roaring in the night.

CHAPTER FIVE

IT WAS BEFORE DAWN in their third week of the fallback. They had fallen asleep alongside the twin ruts of the wagon path and fog was skimming their campsite in cobalt rags. They were exhausted. But at the sound of a hoof puncturing the paper-thin ice glassing over a puddle, Houston came awake instantly.

The horsemen materialized the way Homer's spirits did from Hades, amid a pool of cattle blood and smoke. Houston recognized Juan Seguín. The great *ranchero* was mounted on a huge, still, black stallion rigged with a Spanish saddle and oak and leather stirrups that must have weighed five pounds and a vicious-looking bridle that could have been mistaken for a steel trap. The hair of its chest had been eaten to the hide by alkali dust. The horse had seen much territory, much weather.

Seguín was equally still as he surveyed the camp of sprawled soldiers. He had easy, wide shoulders and his hooflike jaw was scraped clean. Leather chaps half-covered his skin pants that were unbuttoned down the outside of each shin. Strapped to each black boot he wore heavy spurs with rowels the size of dollars. He had thrown back one corner of his dun serape, exposing a short buckskin jacket and under that a woven shirt.

What startled Houston more than the early hour was Seguín's astonishing dignity. To his surprise Houston felt jealousy shoot through him. He wanted Seguín's horse, and his calm, his certainty. Seguín belonged, Houston could tell. Wherever the man went, he belonged.

Grouped around their boss, Seguín's *vaqueros* sat in their

horses so naturally they looked almost like a painting of centaurs Houston had once seen when he was a congressman in Washington. There were ten or eleven of them. Dressed in buckskin and old cloth with boots or thongs on their feet or just barefoot with spurs bound to their heels, none presented so magnificently as their leader. But under their wide hats and black Indian hair, their eyes glittered with Seguín's own self-possession.

The sleeping army became aware of the newcomers with comic suddenness. "Goddamn," wailed a soldier. "The goddamn Meskins got us." That would be one of Sherman's, Houston guessed, some newcomer who'd never seen a Mexican and couldn't tell the friendlies from the hostiles.

The men reared up and stumbled, panicked by Seguín upon his midnight horse. Their eyes burned white in faces blued by their mess fires and by every variety of filth. They had twigs and dung in their hair and beards and their teeth were frightful. Here and there bundles of rags lay quivering in the grass: malaria.

Houston only wished he'd woken an hour earlier and the Mexican could have found him sitting by a fire, reading or writing dispatches or just diligently whittling. As it was, Houston had to separate himself from the cold ground and stand up and limp through the mud with frozen joints. He seated his tricorner hat upon his head and had the distinct feeling it wasn't on straight.

"*Generalísimo*," Seguín greeted Houston. The frost poured from his mouth. Then his Spanish issued forth in a gush.

Houston caught less than three words in the whole address. "Mr. Smith," he called out.

"Deef's gone spying," someone said.

"Go find an interpreter," Houston ordered. "And be quick about it."

A slight young man in a hunting shirt stepped forward. "I've studied the language, sir," he offered.

"Mr. Bryan," Houston said, relieved. Moses Bryan was a blood relation to Stephen Austin and had his wizened uncle's big doelike eyes and thin shoulders and outsized forehead. "Please welcome Captain Seguín to the headquarters of the Army of the Republic of Texas," Houston said.

Moses Bryan and Seguín were no strangers. They carried

on in rapid Spanish for a minute or two. Finally Seguín threw a command over his shoulder and one of the *vaqueros* nudged forward on his mount. The man's right arm was crooked around a bundle of weapons which he now lowered to the ground and let drop in the mud.

Houston's soldiers clustered around the weapons and stared as if these were artifacts from China, say, or the Sandwich Islands. There were two broken-off Mexican lances in the bundle, plus four or five British Betsys with bayonets fixed. Houston also saw a pistol and two swords without sheaths.

"Captain Seguín wishes to present you with his latest harvesting of the Mexican army, General. These arms were captured from a forward patrol under General Ramírez y Sesma."

Houston's soldiers murmured contentedly like lions catching the scent of prey. At long last, here was proof of a war and an enemy. Houston sucked his teeth and looked around at his sorry bunch. This heap of weapons was the closest nine out of ten of them had ever gotten to a battle. At this moment he wouldn't have trusted them to face a herd of cows, much less an army drawn on the Napoleonic model. They suffered from the same diseases Travis and Bowie had, hubris and ignorance. They despised their enemy, and they didn't even know him.

"Look here," a man cried out. He pulled a rifle with a broken stock from the pile of weapons. "I know this gun. It's Colonel Crockett's, by God."

"Hold her up," another soldier demanded, "show us Old Davy's rifle." The crowd pressed closer.

"Pass her back, let us touch that gun."

"Blood!" someone declared. "See upon the stock." It looked more like common barrel rust leaching onto the cherry wood to Houston, but the soldiers accepted it as blood. That led to other conclusions.

"Mexican blood!"

"And a busted stock, by God. He clubbed his rifle, boys! Old Davy went down swinging!"

"They say he took ten of them with him."

"I heard sixteen."

Something was happening. Before Houston's eyes, a broken rifle was being transformed into a holy relic. Crockett was getting deified. Houston frowned. He stepped away, trying to concentrate on business.

"My congratulations to the captain and his men," Houston said to Bryan. "Has he come across Colonel Fannin, by any chance?"

Bryan had already asked. "No sir. Not a sign."

"Ask him, what can he tell us about our pursuers?" Ordinarily Houston would have taken the intelligence in privacy, but he wanted his men to hear the details themselves. Maybe it would curb their arrogance.

Bryan and Seguín exchanged words for a couple minutes.

"The captain estimates that twelve hundred troops under Sesma crossed the Colorado at Beason's Ford," Bryan said. "A second column of seven hundred under General Antonio Gaona is approaching Bastrop to our north. And General Urrea is far to our south with another fourteen hundred men, sealing off the coast."

Seguín added something more.

"Urrea is like a wolf among sheep," Bryan translated. "The people say he captured a small group of Americans going to Matamoros and that he executed his prisoners. They speak of more death at his hands."

That would be Johnson or Grant, Houston knew, the only two men in Texas who were bigger fools than Travis. He'd warned them not to take their bands of men deeper into Mexico, but they'd insisted there was gold and booty at the port city. Now they were dead.

"Goddamn me if I believe a word," some grizzly soldier huffed. "You believe a goddamn greaser?"

Whether or not Seguín comprehended the man's English, he understood the sentiment. Without so much as a look at his detractor, he handed back some words of his own. Bryan made the translation.

"Captain Seguín says that a month ago, he placed a scout along the Rio Grande. This scout sighted the Mexican army on their approach to San Antonio. He rode day and night to give an early warning to Bowie and Travis. But they were dancing at a fandango. He says Travis refused to listen. Travis wanted to dance."

Bryan paused, then resumed. "No one will accept the truth from a Tejano. Captain Seguín says it's sad that only the dead will listen to him."

Seguín shrugged and flicked at his thigh with the tip of

one rein. Houston envied the man's discipline. It showed in everything from his tamed stallion and straight spine to his *vaqueros'* silent obedience. With a hundred men like Seguín's, Houston knew he could defeat Santa Anna. Between the rivers that cut Texas into a hundred battle zones, such a force could strike and disappear and strike again. That was exactly how the Russians had exhausted Napoleon. But Houston had only this riot on feet.

"You say, you greaser, you say," a mud-caked soldier blustered up at Seguín. He was dressed in the uniform of Sherman's Buckeye Rangers. Then Houston saw that this buffoon *was* Sherman, his red side whiskers crusted with mud or dung on one side. The man had been into the jug already this morning or was barely out of it from last night.

"You tell that goddamn high and mighty greaser . . ." someone else pealed.

Seguín glanced down at Houston. In that instant Houston could see the Mexican was ashamed for him, and he blushed.

"General," Bryan lowered his voice. "The captain says they captured a courier of the Mexican army. The courier told them that Santa Anna wishes to compliment our fast legs. He said we run quicker than rabbits. He wishes to quit chasing us. Santa Anna invites us to meet him upon the prairie and engage him in combat."

Seguín's words set the army off.

"Goddamn Santyany," someone howled. "I'll kill that goddamn Santyany, I'll kill ever goddamn Meskin, I'll kill . . ."

"We should have held them at the Colorado," a man declared. Houston thought he recognized Wharton's hoarse voice.

"By God," someone yelled out. "Let us see the color of their blood. Let us smell it. It will smell like ditchwater, I say, mixed of every low race upon our continent."

"Fight, boys, we must fight, boys." It was Colonel Sherman.

I'm being tested, Houston realized. *Tested or baited. But why?* It was a hell of a time and place to make the test. The army resented Seguín's presence and Seguín was doing nothing to lessen their resentment. Not only did the Tejano have dark skin, not only did he speak the language and practice the religion of the enemy, but he had fought and they were running. He had the dignity of arms. They had none, none that could be demonstrated. He was very deliberately pricking their pride. Having lit the fuse, Seguín calmly watched Houston from atop his black stallion.

Unless something was said, and quickly, Houston could see the morning blowing up with violence. Someone might just decide to shoot one of Seguín's *vaqueros*. They might shoot Seguín himself. And as valuable as Seguín was for his ranger skills and the information he brought, he was more valuable because of his color. Scarcely a handful of Tejanos had allied with the Americans to fight for Texan "independence." Seguín and these few horsemen were all that clothed what was otherwise naked theft.

"Mr. Bryan," Houston said. He reached for his old stumpmaking vocabulary and darkened his voice so that it would throw the extra stretch. The din subsided. "I want you to convey to Captain Seguín my esteem for his manly vigor. He has met our enemy and defeated him on the field of battle. He has struck a blow for independence."

Bryan translated swiftly. Seguín watched Houston's face and was suitably unimpressed with the flattery. It wasn't for his consumption anyway. Houston was talking to his own men, trying to curb their stampede of emotions.

"We must keep our army organized and disciplined," Houston spoke. "That way, and that way only, can we meet and vanquish the despotic thousands. Never forget, we are battling for human liberty. Reason and firmness and wisdom must characterize our acts."

He went on in that manner for a few minutes more, plundering snatches of speeches he'd heard Old Hickory emit, speeches which Jackson, in his day, had plundered from Revolutionary War leaders. Over and over again he sang out the key words: liberty, blood, despotism, patriotism. The passions cooled beneath Houston's song. His herd calmed.

"Under the hand of you yeomen warriors," he said, "we shall convert this howling swamp to a gentle field, we shall tame these rivers and bring commerce forth from the field. We shall make land of this wilderness."

In the distance they could hear the wind mounting, another storm getting ready to blow.

"Hell, General," a man called out. "I ain't no farmer. I come to try my spunk, is what."

"Good man," Houston soothed him.

Seguín seemed amused. He spoke to Bryan.

"The captain's prisoner had one more thing of interest," Bryan relayed. "He said that Santa Anna has put a price of five thousand dollars on your head, General. He wants to take it back to Mexico City in an iron cage and hang it from the walls of the national theater."

For an instant Houston was fascinated by the image, his own head captured like an exotic bird, dangling in some exotic capital.

"I know the Mexicans," a voice called out. Wharton again? "They got black hearts and mean ways and they are Papists, all of them. They kill prisoners. They are mercenaries and pirates. They'll rape our women. We must fight."

"Why are these Meskins in our camp?" another cried. "They are spies, by gad. They'll tell."

Houston raced to get control again. "Where is Captain Seguín's prisoner?" he asked.

"The courier?" Bryan translated for Seguín.

"Yes, the courier. I want to talk to him myself."

Seguín solemnly ran one finger from ear to ear.

"You see?" an excited fellow shouted. "They kill their own people."

"Goddamn it," Houston swore to himself, then spoke loud. "Mr. Bryan, you tell the captain this army has a policy of not killing prisoners. I want that clear. We are different from our enemy." *We are better than them.* "There will be no more killing without my say-so."

Bryan told the *ranchero* and Seguín smiled coyly, almost as if he'd expected the chastising. "General, since that's your policy, the captain says he does have one prisoner. He says he'll gladly give this man to you."

"He captured another courier?" Houston said.

"No, sir. He says he caught this one yesterday."

"Well who is he?"

"He says there are men out there who are more like animals," Bryan said. "They come riding up to the rear of refugees in flight and spread the alarm that the Mexicans are coming. The poor women and children panic and drop their bundles and leave their wagons and run. Then these animals take their time picking through the goods. This is one such man. Captain Seguín's rangers caught him thieving the refugees," Bryan translated. "He was drunk. Also he was raping a refugee woman. A white woman."

The crowd went utterly blank for a moment.

Then men began screaming "Dirty Meskins" and "They've caught our women" and "Whip out the greaser."

"Here's my rope," a soldier offered. "We'll string him high."

"Captain Seguín asks what kind of justice you will show such a man," Bryan said.

"He will be held as a prisoner of war," Houston said.

Seguín shook his head no. "This man is not an enemy soldier," Bryan said.

It took Houston a moment to realize Seguín might be turning over one of his own people, possibly one of his own *vaqueros*. Houston was baffled. Seguín had either an extraordinary code of honor or else some other motive. It could be he was trying to curry favor with Houston or to prove himself to the Americans. But Seguín wasn't the sort to need favor or popularity. It was unlikely such a proud man cared what anyone except for his God thought of him.

"In that case," Houston muttered, "tell the captain that his soldier will receive justice like any other accused of a crime."

When Bryan told him that, Seguín grinned. Bryan edged closer to Houston, a confused look on his face. "Captain Seguín says, we will see."

Seguín motioned with his chin. One of the *vaqueros* spurred his mount and dashed into the woods to get the prisoner. While they waited, Houston drew Bryan to one side.

"What game is he playing, Mr. Bryan?" Houston demanded under his breath.

"I don't know, sir." Bryan kept his voice low, too. "We've talked many times before. All I can tell you is that the captain feels very strongly that this revolution does not belong to us. These Tejanos have seen people like us come and go with our filibusters. Twenty years ago an army of *norteamericanos* came to San Antonio with great promises of independence. But then the Spanish army arrived and defeated them. The Americans who didn't get killed fled back to the States. For many years afterward, it was the people of San Antonio who suffered for a foreign adventure. Their men were executed. Their women were raped. He has joined our fight to ensure that never happens again."

"But what is it about this prisoner? This feels like an ambush."

"My guess is that Captain Seguín wants some sign of good faith on our part. Maybe some kind of sacrifice. I don't know."

Just then Seguín's *vaquero* returned, leading the prisoner out from the woods on a rope, and Houston's mouth went dry. His boisterous army quit its yammering. The prisoner was a skinny man with a wispy beard and no hat. A rope bound him around the chest and his hands were cinched with rawhide. Now Houston understood. Captain Seguín had delivered to them an American. The prisoner was a white man.

"Morning all," the prisoner said.

No one replied. The entire army had lost its balance, its voice, its spirit, all in a heartbeat. *What now?* Houston asked himself.

"Somebody get this rope off me," the prisoner said.

A soldier started forward, but Houston stepped in first. He felt Seguín towering above him.

"You," Houston said to the prisoner, "give us your name."

"Johnny Jarvis, by God. But I am known as Popcorn." Except for the rope, he seemed perfectly at ease.

Houston paused. "How come 'popcorn'?" He had to know. Sometimes a man's etymology explained everything you needed to learn about him.

"I settled up the popcorn patch near Brazoria," the prisoner answered. "Then the Meskins come and said you got to be baptized to keep land, and I said well then baptize me Popcorn. Popcorn Jarvis." He displayed a mouthful of twisted teeth which Houston took to be a grin.

"If you will, Mr. Jarvis, explain how you got to be in your present circumstances?" Houston asked.

"Say what?"

"Why are you in a rope?"

"Meskins."

"What were you doing with the refugee column?"

"Looking for you," Popcorn said. He made a shrug, mostly to point out that, despite his request, the ropes still bound him. "I come to volunteer."

"Captain Seguín says you're a thief and a rapist."

Popcorn spit. He turned his whole body and faced the army. "And he's a goddamn Meskin."

The crowd shuffled. There were murmurs of retrospection. They were second-thinking the accusation now. But closer up, Houston could see the fingernail marks on the man's face and neck. In fairness they could as well have been scratches from thorns.

"The captain alleges you were stealing from the refugees," Houston said. His lawyer days were a thing of the past, and he felt stale trying to remember how to prosecute such a charge. At the same time, it wasn't his place to prosecute this at all. He was a general, and this was a war, not a courtroom.

"I was confiscatin', I'll admit," the man said. "I was hungry. And I was coming to volunteer."

"Captain Seguín also alleges you were raping."

"Hell," Popcorn said.

Houston turned to Bryan. "Ask Captain Seguín, did he bring the alleged victim along with him?" He wouldn't have, but there was a form to these inquiries.

Before Bryan could put the question, however, Popcorn reacted. "Victim?" he sputtered. "Why it was just some prairie gal. She's been married to every man in Gonzales anyhow."

Now Mosely Baker stepped in. "What gal?" he said.

Popcorn smiled fondly, a wrong thing to do as it turned out.

"Popcorn Jarvis," Mosely said with cold eyes. "Here on, you be Dogal Jarvis." One of Seguín's *vaqueros* lit up with a broad white grin.

"Doe-gal?" the prisoner said. His burst of good humor crashed against Mosely's sinister mood. "What's it, doe-gal?"

Mosely got up close to say it. "That's Mexican. It means noose." Then he looked away. Houston was inclined to pass the same judgment. Jarvis looked guilty, he acted guilty, and, with Juan Seguín looking on, a quick hanging of one of their own would confirm the equality of American vengeance. He was about to sentence the prisoner when several other colonels appeared in the front.

Colonel Forbes spoke first. "For my vote, gentlemen, there can only be one outcome, and it just got wisely pronounced.

Capital punishment, swiftly executed. So be it. What do you say?"

Houston scowled. That might be his own judgment, but this wasn't a court martial. The matter wasn't open to a vote of the colonels and he had no intention of sharing authority with subordinates. If he hadn't known Forbes better, Houston would have accused him of being clever.

"You can't kill me," Popcorn protested, apparently convinced Forbes had just solicited his opinion. "I come to volunteer."

Now Private Lamar squeezed out from the mass of onlookers. "Since Colonel Forbes has raised the issue of a voting up or down a man's life," he said, adjusting his green spectacles, "and since the man in question has had no benefit of counsel, I hope you'll allow me to introduce a rudimentary point of law."

It was something like this that Houston had been afraid would happen. If not Lamar, it would have been one of the officers, making what was simple complicated. Anymore these challenges were coming at him constantly, on a daily, sometimes hourly basis.

"Speak your piece," Houston said to the private.

"The accused . . ." Lamar began.

"The condemned," Mosely Baker amended.

"This fellow unfortunately named Popcorn," Lamar said, and that drew an appreciative guffaw, "he has had no proper trial nor credible witnesses. These are serious charges and our commander in chief has rightly promised Captain Seguín a display of American justice. But what's unfolding here is an aberration."

Colonel Wharton cut Lamar off. He was brusque. Of late the malcontents had taken to haggling among themselves and that sometimes provided Houston a respite. "All right, Mr. Lamar," he said, and Houston was surprised that the private was known by name to the colonels. "You've made your point."

Wharton turned to the prisoner. "Are you innocent?" he asked Popcorn. When that got no response, Wharton tried it the other way. "How about guilty, how do you plead?"

"I'm a white man," Popcorn told him.

"And a goddamn pity that you are," Wharton responded. "You've pillaged. But worse by far, sir, you've defiled a woman."

"Maybe he has, Colonel, maybe he hasn't," Lamar per-
sisted. "But my point here is that General Houston has instructed Captain Seguín there will be no killing of prisoners
without his approval. And I'd just like to get on record what
the highest authority in the land has to say about mob justice."
He faced Houston with a pleasant smile.

"I'm sure you didn't mean to call the Army of Texas a
mob," Houston parried. The ugly reality was that for weeks
now they'd been in the mood for blood.

"Of course not," Lamar demurred. "What I meant to refer
to was the effect, not the cause. And, forgive me, sir, my question still stands. Do you call this justice?"

"If we are not here to fight evil," Houston sidestepped him,
"then why fight?"

"A quaint notion," Lamar responded with enough courtesy
to cover the insult.

Houston knew that was how it might sound. His problem
lay in making these hundreds of men believe in their righteousness the way he believed in it. *But do you really?* a voice surfaced
in his mind. *Do you believe?* Houston's head snapped away from
the thought. He went on searching for high-minded words to
seduce his army back from Lamar. But that terrible instant of
doubt tangled him like a serpent. What if he didn't believe?

"We are near the edge of the world," Houston said, trying
to buy himself more time to think. "We are the law. We are
pathfinders in this wilderness. Without us, there is no justice."

"All I'm saying," Lamar appealed to the crowd, "is that we
should be sure that our justice is fair. With our enemy so close,
maybe we should just draft the accused and put a rifle in his
hands. Later let us sort out his guilt."

Houston felt dizzy and unclean. Lamar was right. They
should wait. Even if this gatemouthed Popcorn was guilty, waiting would lend gravity to what ought to be a state function, not
a mob action. Because otherwise, all he was doing was presiding
over a lynching. For the first time Houston felt the awful weight
of being more than just a man. As commander of an army, he
was also an instrument of the people. But what did that mean,
to be an instrument? Was it his role to be wielded by the people,
to carry out their passions, to lead where they were already
going? Or was he here to guide them into civilization, regardless
of where they wanted to go?

Houston considered some way to concede Lamar's point and postpone the killing and at the same time to impress upon Seguín that justice would be done, that his word was not in doubt. He could say he was taking the issue under advisement or call for a formal investigation of the charges. He could do anything he wanted because he was the general, the highest authority in a land at war.

"Popcorn Jarvis," he said, "until such time as a formal court of inquiry can be arranged, you are hereby inducted into the Army of the Republic of Texas."

"But General," Mosely Baker started to protest. Houston wondered if Mosely had decided it was Molly who'd been violated out there. Houston couldn't help that just now, nor could he help that Seguín was probably ruffled, too.

"Hurrah," someone shouted, for something about the moment suggested an element of heroic vindication. Popcorn had just glimpsed his own specter and yet survived.

Lamar cocked his head, lips pursed midway between a smile and a thought. The mysterious private was done playing for now, Houston could see. Lamar seemed to know he had won his point, and something more. He had exposed Houston to himself.

Houston looked around and Seguín was staring down at him from his midnight stallion. Abruptly the Tejano flashed his white teeth in a dangerous smile.

"Be with God," he said to Houston in English.

Seguín and his rangers could have thundered off into the forest for the outright drama of it. Instead they left slowly, without another word.

CHAPTER SIX

FOR FIFTEEN YEARS, ever since Mexico had opened eastern Texas to settlement, the little town of San Felipe de Austin had been the heart and soul of American propriety with its cluster of neat log cabins and its air of commerce about to happen. Here Stephen Austin had shaped his kingdom within Mexico, crafting deals with tyrants and ruling over his expatriates with a missionary's guile. Here American settlers had seen hope.

Reaching San Felipe, Houston's army found it nearly empty. The general took one look around, then ordered the town looted for supplies. The soldiers pitched in with relish. One thing led to another and soon one house, then others were on fire. Rather than try to save what the Mexicans would burn anyway, Houston pulled his army to the outskirts and they watched the entire town light up.

With the flames licking high, Houston was reminded of Washington when the British put it to the torch. He had arrived in the capital within weeks of the 1812 sacking and had felt shame and grief and outrage. This was different. He'd never much cared for Stephen Austin and his unending compromises with Mexico City. Firing San Felipe felt like a cleansing.

Houston kept his jubilation to himself, however, because some of his men had made homes there. Moses Bryan wept as if it were his uncle himself going up in flames. Bringing up the rear, Mosely Baker arrived to find his town sacked and burning and gave Houston a glare of such hatred that Houston almost reached for a gun. Ever since Gonzales, Mosely's happy-go-lucky élan had darkened and become unpredictable, sharpening into something that had two edges and no handle. Houston had thought it reduced to worry over his lover Molly, but Mosely wasn't heartsick. His sunny expression had turned to cold night. He seemed possessed, though by what Houston couldn't say.

"You mean to burn your way to Louisiana, is that it, General?" the colonel shouted over the roar of flames. He had more to say, but then caught sight of Three-Legged Willie. Colonel Williamson was doing a strange frenzied jig upon his pegleg-crutch, laughing at the destruction.

Houston had long admired Willie's almost supernatural capacity to not just get around but always be in the thick of it. Even with that crutch strapped to his crooked leg, the lawyer could ride, talk, and dream with the best—and worst—of them, and probably would have died with his friend Travis if not for his sharper instincts. But something had shifted in him over the past few weeks, too, though in a way far different from Mosely. Willie had always had a smaller man's daring. It had twisted into a recklessness without any purpose, a delight in sheer anarchy.

"You've lost your minds," Mosely said. He pointed his finger at Houston, then cut his reins at his horse's flanks and bolted off.

After torching San Felipe, the army marched on. Next morning they woke early to the eerie glow of San Felipe still afire in the gloom. Like a lantern in a bayou, the luminous ball lit the dark western horizon.

"Look," an old man with a billy-goat beard called out to the soldiers, sweeping his hand from west to east. "The sun sets, but it rises. Dusk and dawn, all in one. Gee, gad. Scripture said it, two suns, one day. I tell you, lads. The Beast."

"Quiet down, old man," someone said. "Scripture don't say no such thing."

"The Beast," the old man warned them. "He's walking the land, sure."

"Let him come on then," shouted a young bravo. He shook his long musket in the smoke of their mess fires. "I can put one ounce of lead through either eye, you pick which one. Then I'll skin what beast it is and wear it for my sweetheart."

"But what if?" wondered some gaunt boy trembling with

sickness. He could barely stand. "Maybe this time it's come. The apocalypse and second coming. What if?" Through the mud on the boy's face, Houston could see the angry crusted spots of chicken pox.

" 'Tis evil walking," the old fellow muttered. "The Beast afoot. Afoot and among us."

"Where at? Where among us?"

"Don't you see him? He's here," he trembled. The old fool looked around at them with madness gleaming out through his shadowed sockets.

"Easy does it," a man quieted them with a voice of authority. It was a new voice, new to the campaign anyway. Houston knew that voice and turned to it.

As if he'd been among them all along, Tom Rusk, their newly appointed secretary of war, was standing there in rotting buckskins, his brown hair plaited and clubbed on the back of his head the way Daniel Boone used to keep his. Rusk wasn't particularly imposing with his small shoulders and solid waist, but that in itself was something to trust, a young man with no vanity and a bushelful of high intent. Houston hadn't seen him since the convention and could only guess Rusk had arrived during the night. Rusk winked at Houston, then proceeded with his little exhortation.

"We ain't the Beast afoot, but Democracy on the shoot," he said to the men. "We are the flaming sword. Why, if we want, we can light the valley of darkness all the way to the halls of Montezuma."

"There," a soldier said. "you see there, old man."

"I see what I see," the old fool called back.

"Well then, goddamn you," and someone threw a rock at the wild prophet. They catcalled at him. But he had shaken them with his omen.

Houston shook Rusk's hand good and hard. "Mr. Secretary," he said with a smile, "I am glad to see you." Here was a friend, one of the few men Houston could turn his back to without fearing a knife. Like Houston, Rusk had lost his sweetheart and come to Texas. They had similar fits of melancholy, too, though Rusk's fits had no escape hatches to them. Alcohol didn't work for him, and laudanum only made his moods blacker. He'd tried to kill himself twice that Houston knew about, once that Houston had talked him out of. It was probably a matter of time before suicide took Rusk away.

"You may not be so glad once you read this." Rusk handed him a letter sealed with red wax that bore a plain square imprint. Houston had seen President Burnet's ring print before and it usually meant bad news.

"Are they taking the army away from me?"

"God no, Sam," Rusk said. "This here is more along the lines of inspiration."

Houston opened the letter. Even the president's handwriting looked pinched and lead-footed. "Sir," it read, "The enemy are laughing you to scorn. You must fight them. You must retreat no further. The country expects you to fight." It was signed. That was it.

Houston handed the letter back to Rusk. "So my retreat is not a popular thing," he said. He wondered if there was a single voice of support anywhere for what he was doing.

"The president almost put his fist through the table stamping this," Rusk told him.

"I suppose you want to take a reply?"

"Do you have one?"

"I'll have to think."

"Well don't think too long. Burnet and his government are running faster than anyone else. They were headed in the direction of New Orleans last I saw."

"When do you leave then?"

"Me?" Rusk said. "I'm not leaving. I figure you're the only one that knows what you're doing in this whole country, Sam."

"Do I?" Houston wondered.

"That's why I've come," Rusk said. "I figured you might need a friend."

Houston stopped. He looked around to be sure they had moved out of earshot. "Is there any news from General Gaines?" He asked it casually.

Rusk was surprised. "There are rumors that Gaines may be bringing up thirteen companies of the U.S. Army. They are near or upon the far side of the Sabine River," Rusk said. "But how could you know that, Sam? I only learned it an hour before departing for here."

"A lucky guess," Houston said. Houston hadn't known

which regiments would come, nor that it would be Gaines for sure, nor even that U.S. troops would actually get called up to the border. But Jackson had intimated it. The stratagem was loaded with risk, not the least of which was Jackson's presidency and an international war between the United States and Mexico.

"What do you know?" Rusk asked. As secretary of war, it was his right to ask. But as Jackson's confidant, Houston didn't have any right to answer.

"I'm sorry," Houston said. Rusk did what he could not to look hurt by the secret. Houston truly was sorry, too. Rusk was right, he did need a friend.

"Do you know which companies?" Houston asked.

Rusk withheld nothing, possibly to shame Houston, which it did. "The word is they're from the Sixth Regiment. Twelve hundred of them. Red hot from fighting Seminoles and Creeks in Florida."

"Excellent," Houston said. These would be combat troops and regulars, not a whimsical pack of mercenaries, squatters, and colonists playing soldier boy.

"We could take all of Texas if Gaines crossed the border," Rusk said, probing Houston's reserve.

Houston didn't budge. He knew too much, including the fact that Gaines's presence on the Sabine guaranteed nothing. For one thing, Edmund Gaines was a wily career officer and an old crony of Andy Jackson's, meaning he played games within games. And for another thing, if American troops crossed the international line it would constitute an act of war. Such technicalities had never slowed Gaines or Old Hickory in the past, of course. The two of them hadn't hesitated to invade the Spanish Floridas back in '18, even though it had risked pitting an infant United States against the Spanish empire. From private conversations Houston had shared with both, he knew the old soldiers feared Mexico even less than Spain. But they needed a catalyst to invade. And that was Houston's job. Just as Travis had baited Houston to bring his army to the Alamo, Houston now had to try and bait Gaines to bring American regulars into Mexico.

"I think the best thing for us is to count on ourselves," Houston said. After that Rusk didn't bring up the subject again.

The army followed the Brazos River searching for a sanctuary. They'd been on their feet for weeks and needed to rest. A day north, Houston selected a ravine for his exhausted army.

It was an old riverbed on the west side of the Brazos, close to Jared Groce's big white house and slave shacks. Old Man Groce let them use his land for free, a patriotic contribution that had mostly to do with keeping the voracious army away from his plantation.

The ravine was deep and wide and out of sight and it was protected from surprise attacks by swollen creeks in all directions. But Houston knew it wasn't impregnable. The Brazos had a way of turning red as arterial blood after each rainstorm, and he feared the river might jump its banks upstream and flood the ravine and drown them all.

All the same they occupied the ravine for a week, then two weeks. Houston had come here to restore them and restore himself, but the longer they stayed the more he despaired. He had headaches for one thing. And what was left of his fingernails were cracked to the quick. His bowels were a battleground for dysentery and worms. Every time he doffed his tricorner there was hair in the brim, and every time he passed a hand across his head he found hair between his fingers. At this rate he was going to end up as bald as a baby.

Some of this had to do with the opium, of course. From half a lifetime of quaffing and chewing the bitter yellow rose, he knew the effects, good and bad. The diarrhea, the queasy mornings after, the headaches: Usually they were worth the release from pain, even when the pain changed into matters of the heart and midnight sweats. But lately he'd begun to question if the opium Dr. Labadie had given him wasn't magnifying his despair. It had grown almost out of his control. When Houston walked through camp that was all he felt, black defeat.

It wasn't that his men were slipping away from him, but that they were slipping away from themselves. His soldiers had become plastered with red mud. Their beards and hair and clothing were caked with it. They were losing all outward aspect of their humanity except for the eyes peering from their earthen masks—and those showed human only when they managed to get sober or healthy, which was more and more seldom.

They lived in filth and drank from a common pool in the pit of the ravine. It was bad enough the water was stagnant, but they fouled it further by pissing and washing their clothes and watering their livestock in it. All manner of debris floated in the pool, even gaseous white and purple guts of butchered cattle and wild game. As a result, the whole camp quickly fell to overlapping plagues of whooping cough, mumps, measles, chicken pox, pinkeye, and diarrhea.

Not a day passed that someone else didn't die. Some mornings it was hard distinguishing between the dead and the living because so many men had worn out their clothing and had taken to wearing plantation shirts sold to them by Old Man Groce. Normally given out to slaves, these shirts were slit up the sides and made of cotton sacking, and in the present circumstances they looked exactly like shrouds for corpses. More than one man came awake when the daily burial detail went through camp and mistakenly grabbed him by the foot.

Memory was their sanctuary. They were an army of other lives, and with the presence of so much death they became an army of other deaths, safely distant, even wonderful. Houston listened to them through the walls of a tent sold to him by Old Man Groce.

"Remember Matthew Turpin?" Houston heard a man speak by a fire. "He was my cousin's grandpa and he got killed picking mulberries fifty years ago. Out along the Clinch River."

That prompted a second hungry man. "What about those Smith brothers at Palmyra, kilt when they went for strawberries."

"My great uncle Robert Ramsey," a third recalled, "he got an Indian hatchet whilst going for paw-paws and wild cherries and grapes along the Hartpeth near the Highland River."

They reached backward in time, thirsting for fresh milk from family cows or clear water from springs they hadn't seen for many years. "Before I die I dearly want for rosen yers," a soldier wished out loud, and Houston could practically taste the plump green corn his own mother used to fry up and serve with milk and butter.

What startled Houston most was how his grand army was being leveled by childhood diseases. Something about the notion gave an innocence to his primitive warriors. It lulled him. He felt almost fatherly, as if he were leading a children's crusade. It made his aging—the thinning hair, the broadening expanses of forehead, the rheumatism in the morning—more bearable. His soldiers did childish things, though every now and then he caught glimpses of something hard and mean and even evil, and it made him wonder if he could be wrong about them.

One afternoon in broad daylight a boy in nut-brown home-spun came running through camp shouting an alarm. He dashed pell-mell through the barnyard slop, planted himself in the middle of the camp, and screamed it loud.

"Meskins! The Meskins coming!"

Houston was sitting on a stump trimming his toenails with his clasp knife, idly contemplating whether his feet had always looked so flattened out and pawlike with toes gone nearly to claws. The latest norther had passed and its blue clouds had sunk off the Gulf horizon, leaving the afternoon bright and sultry with some tropical edge for a change. At this rate, he allowed, most of his clothes might actually dry out.

His first reaction to the alarm was flat annoyance. It seemed much too fine a day to waste on a fight. His second reaction was curiosity. For a camp about to get overrun by Santa Anna, the soldiers had all the calm of a plow horse on an August noon. Except for the highly animated harbinger, barefoot and shirtless and flapping his arms, hardly anyone was inclined to move at all.

Houston lowered his big foot to the cool mud. He scrutinized the camp. Over there beneath a tree stood a pocket of stationary officers swapping chew or gossip or land talk—or waiting for something about to happen—and none was about to relinquish the shade. Everywhere else men and boys went on lounging like they were deaf. Some were honing their butcher knives or counting, endlessly counting, their lead balls or trading for flints or reconfiguring muskets like good soldiers. There was a man carving himself a brand new rifle stock out of oak, shaping a cheek rest that was just right. Others catnapped under their slouch hats or were weaving palmetto into fanciful animals or jawboning while they whittled. But they were watching, those who bothered to wake up, all watching in a particular direction. Houston followed their eyes, just in time.

Abruptly Colonel Forbes burst from his tent. The man had obviously been deep asleep. His vest was open and his pants were falling and he looked nearly demented with panic.

It was impressive, the degree to which the colonel had memorized his escape route. As Houston and the entire camp watched on, Forbes didn't bother to stop and assess the emergency. He didn't measure his soldiers' movements, didn't even take the time to estimate which way the enemy might be pouring in. He just went into action.

Wild eyed, his sandy muttonchops furred out like a scared cat's tail, Forbes sprang upon his mule. Obviously he'd placed the mule close for this very eventuality. He heeled its ribs with all he had. "Gee gaw, Maud," he yelled and with a snap whipped the reins against his mule's neck. "Gee gaw."

At some point in this furious display, the mule came awake and leapt to the flight. But her wings were clipped. Someone had hobbled the colonel's beast fore and aft and all poor Maud could do was hop around and try to keep her balance.

Forbes slashed the animal with the reins and pummeled her ribs with his bare heels and bellowed his get go, but all he gained was more frantic hopping. The mule realized the predicament before her master did and finally decided a complete halt was in order. The mule's stasis drove Forbes to greater frenzy. He whipped and goddamned and hammered at her, but she wouldn't bulge.

Meanwhile, the entire army looked on. They had planned the prank, unmistakably, but succeeded beyond all reason. The soldiers were too flabbergasted by Forbes's antics to even begin their laughter.

"Stop yourself, Colonel," Deaf Smith commanded Forbes from a nearby mess fire. He was wearing a disgusted frown.

The wildness in Forbes's eyes slowly burned out. He lowered his elbows and quit kicking and the terrible realization drained his face. The colonel sat there high atop his mule, too stunned to blink much less dismount.

Houston sighed a purling curse. The Cherokees had done something similar to him once, painting one of their Negro slaves with whitewash and dressing him in Houston's favorite bobcat skin vest and seating him in Houston's place at the tribal council. They had humiliated Houston for his drunken, visionary excesses. With their black clown they'd effectively banished him back to his own people.

Now it began for the man on the mule. Someone cried out, "Who rode off on a hobbled old Maud?"

And like a Greek chorus, men throughout camp answered

with one voice. "Colonel Forbes," they shouted boisterously. Their laughter washed back and forth.

Houston pitied the devastated colonel. They had chosen their victim with care. Besides being pompous and high-handed with the troops Forbes had been Houston's choice to oversee the army's commissary. It was Forbes's misfortune to have inherited an empty larder and an army that was as unforgiving as it was hungry. The reins had slipped to the ground and Forbes was staring at his open palms. He was paralyzed up there. No one could rescue him.

Houston returned to his trimming. He carved off the tip of another horny nail, then investigated his other toes. *Goddamn them all.* They wouldn't drill properly, they wouldn't follow orders, they wouldn't even clean away their own filth. They shit in the very water they drank. The joke on Forbes had turned out more cruel than it should have, mostly because of Forbes himself. All the same their brutality appalled Houston.

Some part of him had hoped that by his garrisoning the men in one place they would become more civilized. Wasn't that how history worked? The nomad settled. Cities grew. Poetry and science blossomed. But his army had only gotten more insubordinate and bestial. At night when he paced through the camp unable to sleep, Houston had even heard some of the soldiers rutting with the livestock, something farmboys did, not grown men. They were slipping into pandemonium here and he was becoming less and less certain they could ever crawl out of their muddy red pit.

It became plain to him. Houston was no longer sure he wanted to be their general. He didn't dare to share the realization, not even with Tom Rusk. Early on, Houston had feared the army would consume him with its desires. But it was Texas herself that was eating him alive. His only salvation lay in fleeing from their descent. And yet, like Crockett who had never wanted to go to the Alamo but went anyway—and stayed— Houston knew he couldn't leave. He had nowhere else to go.

He had nothing to show for his forty-three years on this earth—no child, no money, no home, no legacy, no wife, no land, no country, even that. In order to gain his acres of free land, he'd renounced his American citizenship, given up his faith, and been baptized a Roman Catholic Mexican: Samuel

Pablo Houston. Like so many other men shipping from New
Orleans or swimming the Sabine River, he had signed away his
nation of birth in order to get a foothold in Texas. Unlike most,
the sacrifice bothered Houston. He worried they might have
given up too much of themselves, and that was before losing
what they'd thought to be getting.

Travis had once yipped something about their deceptions
being camouflage, that they were like chameleons who'd turned
brown so they could turn Texas white. But to Houston that
conjured an image of snakes shedding their very skins for the
chance to get within striking distance. Well, they had made their
strike and they had missed, and there was no hole left to slither
back to except the country they'd renounced. *We're poorer than
we know,* Houston thought. *We have damned ourselves to Texas.*

They could return to the States, but it would be to carry
on as twilight creatures living between the margins of night and
day. Years ago Houston had met Aaron Burr upon a porch.
Desiccated with age and bitterness and the failed chance, the
old traitor had clung to his wicker seat like a bat in a cage,
sipping mint juleps and staring out at the world with black beads
for eyes, the soul gone out of him. Houston had shuddered at
Burr's terrible fate, never imagining he might face it himself
one day.

Then something happened that returned Houston to himself and to his army. It started early one morning with the whole
camp waking in terror because the earth was quivering under
their heads. Desperate men screamed out that a trembler was
about to wreck them, and it did feel like the great 1811 earth-
quake of their youths which had toppled chimneys and knocked
cabins to pieces, when the waters of the Mississippi had risen
and fallen like an ocean's tide and lightning bolts had sprung
from the hot earth. Houston remembered how his little sister
had declared the angels were about to come and lift her up into
their dead father's arms. But it wasn't that. Even after a sentinel
in a pecan tree pointed out the north-moving phenomenon, the
army shivered in ignorance because all there was to see out
there was a vast mobile blackness, like ink spilling off the page.
The fact that it was a buffalo stampede eventually settled the
men down.

But Houston knew better. This was a premonition. He'd
been reading the western sky for days now, deciphering blood

in the patterns of black and green clouds. His dreams had been trying to tell him something, too.

A group of the officers, Houston included, mounted up to track the herd and bring in some buffalo. Hunting parties had been going out every now and then to supplement the beef Groce sold the army on credit. Today's excursion was partly meat-minded, but mostly just a frolic to escape from the squalor and tedium of camp life.

The pack of horsemen broke loose of the cedar and oak woods at about the time the sun cut a hole through the clouds, and all agreed the prairie was a beautiful sight. Poppies blazed red. Bluebonnets mixed with white sorghum. The grass was knee-high to a man in his saddle and the plains stretched lush and emerald under the sunbeams.

The buffalo path followed the line of least resistance along the earth's contours. Mile after mile the turf lay chopped and the grasses were pounded flat. As if following a roadway the hunters rode with a springtime abandon. A jug passed back and forth. The horsemen told stories and boasted and joked and made light of each other's guns or rig or horses. Houston kept to himself for the most part, unable to shake the feeling that something terrible had happened or was about to.

At last, just as Burleson wondered aloud if they'd accomplished the impossible by losing an entire buffalo herd, the hunters came upon their prey. The animals were grazing in a gigantic loop that stretched all the way around the hill. Men reined up to load or check their powder charges. Bets were placed on marksmanship. The jug made its final rounds. The group splintered into pairs and trios, fanning out to bracket the rear of the column.

Houston split left with Tom Rusk. Crossing behind a bluff, they lost sight of the herd. Five minutes later they came into the open upon a spit of high ground. Their vantage point hung within thirty yards of the closest buffalo.

"Close enough," Rusk murmured to Houston. The two men dismounted and Houston held their rifles upright while Rusk staked both horses to a rock. They crept up as far as possible, crouching in the tall grass. Then both stood up and, by whispered agreement, shot at the same animal.

Their buffalo was a black and tan female and she dropped onto her knees and slowly keeled over onto her side. The gunshots startled the herd around her, and maybe a hundred or two hundred animals rushed away. In no time their small stampede inspired a larger one. Houston saw Mosely Baker and Forbes and Sherman and others popping up from the grass to get off hasty shots. Three more buffalo fell, but one managed to get up and walk off before anyone could reload.

The grassy chute emptied of buffalo. Except for the earth trembling up through the long bones in his legs, Houston could have believed there'd never been a thousand buffalo spread before him just a minute earlier.

"Come on, Sam, let's claim our kill before one of those poor shots does," Rusk said. He was in a fine summery mood and Houston was glad to see him boyish for a change. Maybe Texas *was* good for forgetting.

They went back to their horses and rode down to the black and tan buffalo. Her black tongue was hanging in the dirt, but she was still breathing. Rusk took a pistol and shot her through the eye and her suffering was done.

Spread out over two hundred yards or so, the men grouped around their kills and drew knives. The butchering went on for a good part of the afternoon. It was bloody work, but the sunshine held and that put everyone in high spirits. They lay the cuts out on the pure green grass to let the meat cool before starting to load it on the pack animals. Houston forgot his earlier dread. The sun soaked in through his back, sweating him pleasantly.

When the sound came, no one paid any attention.

"Oh," it soughed.

Houston heard, but it wasn't much of a noise. It could have been a bird or a bit of stray breeze across the plains.

The second time it drifted through, their horses startled. Willie's strawberry mare took off across the prairie. This time men reached for their guns. Those who hadn't reloaded yanked butcher knives from the meat or dirt or their sheaths. In the confusion the sound came again.

"Oh," it shivered.

And there he was, standing in the grasses.

"Goddamn me," bellowed one of the frightened officers.

If not for the creature's standing upon two legs, Houston couldn't have told it was human, and even then his first thought was of the graveyard. Naked, every rib pronounced in the yellow sunbeams, his meat withered down to where each knee and elbow bulged like piney knots, the figure just stood there staring at the slaughtered meat lying on the grass.

"Oh," he said again. It was impossible to tell from his flesh that he was a white man, for he was painted with every color of mud and where skin showed through it had been seared by the sun or lacerated by thorns. His legs looked like a tailor's pincushion with hundreds of cactus needles bristling out. His hair was straight, however, and it was bleached white by the elements. It was a white man all right.

"Don't shoot him," Houston yelled. "He's one of our own."

Ned Burleson sheathed his big shovel of a knife, out of temper for having no one to use it on. "You took some wrong track, mister," he growled.

The man was lost, in every sense lost, that was plain to see. Edging closer, Houston discovered the man was just a boy. The hollowed face barely showed sideburns and his lip was still fuzz. He looked fifteen at the oldest.

Houston set his teeth. The child's condition unnerved him. It wasn't that he'd never witnessed starvation and disease on the front edge of Anglo-Saxon settlement. To the contrary, he'd seen men and women worse than this, but those had been fugitive Negroes newly caught and whipped and manacled or slaves fresh in from Africa or the Caribbean. And there'd been that white girl bought back from the Comanches with her nose burnt off and just a hole in the middle of her face, a hideous sight.

What he'd never seen, though, were eyes like these. They were enormous and owllike and they saw, but didn't see. That's what scared Houston. To this ghost the men on horses surrounding him were just ghosts themselves. They were simply illusions. That seemed unbearable to Houston. It made the world a trick of the mind.

"Come here, son," he said.

The boy peered at Houston but didn't move.

"Tell us what happened," Houston said, and opened his arms and began to approach him.

"Talk, boy," Sherman demanded.

Nothing worked. Like something born out of the wind the prairie child trembled with each breeze, bending with the grasses. He had forgotten everything, even language itself.

"Where'd he come from?" Colonel Forbes wondered.

"Maybe the Comanches. Maybe he slipped the Comanches," someone ventured. "Maybe he just run away from home and here he is." Strange things happened out here. You never could tell. One thing was certain, the boy had suffered. He had a deep laceration along one shoulder and most of his fingernails were torn loose, probably from digging for food.

When he shied at riding a horse, they tied the frail creature with a rope to transport him back to camp. Lifting the poor child onto his own saddle, Houston was surprised because he weighed hardly more than a bagful of butterfly wings. Houston circled his arms around the boy. Like that they returned to camp, and before three minutes were gone the child had fallen asleep.

Soldiers were flocked at the neck of the ravine and lining the gully walls, eager to see what kind of meat the hunting party was bringing in. Coated with mud they blended in with the red clay and it looked like the earth itself were coming to life. The men were rambunctious and playful after their day of rare sunlight. But when they caught sight of the bound naked animal asleep against Houston's chest, the soldiers quit their whistling and mud throwing and grew still.

"What's that you catch, General?"

"Don't know, boys," Houston answered.

"You sure that ain't Indian?"

"He's white."

"By God."

"Somebody fetch Dr. Labadie," Houston said.

Houston took the boy directly to his tent. He wouldn't let anyone else carry the child. Inside Houston laid him on his blanket and untied the ropes. The boy went on sleeping.

"Let me through," Dr. Labadie told the soldiers gathered at the door of the tent. "Get out of my way."

The surgeon ducked into the tent, stovepipe first. "Jesus, look at this," he muttered, tipping the boy onto one side to look at his back. "It makes you wonder about God's love sometimes. What happened to him?"

"He hasn't said one word."

"He'll need those thorns out and some sewing. And I better open a vein," Dr. Labadie said. "I'll have my supper here, General. This will take some time."

Around sunset Deaf Smith brought in a second wanderer. Houston was standing by his tent, eating some of the buffalo. Squatting around their big mess fires, soldiers looked up with sparks dancing around their heads. The scout rode through the center of camp.

This one was a man dressed in rags and a loincloth and Smith was keeping him warm with his serape. This second discovery spooked them more than Houston's child, because as Smith rode through camp his passenger hooted at the army.

"Hoo, hoo," he sang to them. Nobody damned him because he was already cursed. Rangy soldiers quickly turned away, afraid of the evil eye.

Houston watched the procession for a minute, then whistled through his fingers and gave the scout a call. Smith steered his discovery toward the tent and lowered him to Houston and another soldier.

"I found this one southwest, clear over to Cedar Crick," Smith said with his high voice.

Inside by the light of a smoking tallow candle and with the aid of a pair of pliers, Doctor Labadie was pulling barbed thorns from the legs of Houston's prairie child. The doctor's long polished forehead showed the strain in beads of clear sweat. With each tug, he got a festered tab of flesh. The boy had awakened but seemed oblivious to the pain, staring at a gecko on the canvas ceiling.

Doctor Labadie glanced up from his bloody chore. He saw the cactus thorns jutting from the new man's legs and groaned. "If these were coon dogs, I'd say just shoot 'em. I'll be up all night pulling barbs. And they're like to end infected anyhow."

"Well, it's got to be done," Houston said.

The doctor scowled and bent back to the leg.

"Does he talk, or just do the hoot owl?" Houston asked Smith.

"He did speak on the ride, General. He had a rough go, one thing and another."

"What in heaven is going on out there?" Dr. Labadie wanted to know. "Have the Indians entered into this thing?"

Smith's expression said he knew, but there were soldiers bunched all around. He said, "I believe he's shy, General."

Houston acted. "You soldiers," he said, "clear out from here." When they were gone Smith revealed the answer.

"We've been waiting for Fannin's army," he said. "Here they are."

Houston felt sick.

Smith patted his wanderer on the shoulder. "This fellow talks crazy, but here is what I gather. Fannin burned his fort. He started to retreat like you told him, only too late. That one named Urrea hunted him down. There was a fight."

"These are survivors of the battle?" Dr. Labadie asked.

The scout shook his head no. "Fannin's bunch ended up surrendering. They got marched back to Goliad. For a week they were held prisoner. Then the Mexicans took them out and shot and bayoneted them. This one, he run, then he swum a crick, then he run some more."

"Fannin's army is dead?" It was unthinkable. Houston needed those men.

Smith nodded his wild red head. "On Palm Sunday the Mexicans formed them into groups. They started each group off in different directions. The men figured they were getting paroled and getting marched off to home. So they sung the Yankee Doodle and 'Home Sweet Home,' that kind of thing. Then it started."

"But there were almost five hundred of them," Houston said.

"There were," Smith said.

The survivor sat in the dirt hooting gently. He lay back.

Houston stood over him. His head felt ready to split open. First the Alamo, now this. He tried to imagine what the news of disaster would do to his army. He wondered what it would do to him.

Since learning the details, Houston had not been particularly shocked that Bowie and Travis and Crockett and the others had died at the Alamo. Most of them had gone down in the heat of battle. But this violated the rules of warfare. What had happened to Fannin's men violated logic. Worst of all, it violated Houston's imagination. He simply could not fathom crafting a mass execution. That was the part that fascinated and repelled him the most. What sort of imagination could piece together such evil?

Above all the loss of Fannin's men gutted Houston's plans. In a coded letter to Jackson he had projected an army two thousand strong. Such an army, he'd promised, could savage the Mexicans guerrilla-style in the woods and bayous of eastern Texas. They wouldn't whip the Mexican army, but they would fight long and hard enough to convince the world—or Congress, at least—of their sovereignty. American intervention, in the form of U.S. regulars, would finish it. But now, with less than seven hundred ragamuffins, Houston had lost the ability even to create a fiction. They had been reduced to what they were, an ambition.

Over the next three days Deaf Smith and several of Seguín's *vaqueros* brought in five more survivors. Some bore saber wounds or bullet holes. All had starved on their solitary journeys. They entered camp shimmering with the strange translucence of desert monks. Their eyes were huge from starvation and too much sheer faith.

Each time, the army stilled and watched, every soldier looking for himself in these wracked transcendent survivors. Their bravado melted. Houston noticed that the soldiers had quit their horseplay and fistfights. Everyone who had faced Santa Anna's army this winter was now dead and burned. Only a handful of men had survived the Mexican army's great wrath.

Houston kept Fannin's men in his tent. He watched over them, making sure they were fed and given water and kept warm and dry. He provided them with blankets, including his own, and called Dr. Labadie back anytime one of the survivors seemed not to be getting better. They had terrible nightmares and Houston comforted them, telling stories or listening to their horrifying tales.

Their worst dreams tended to be about fields of tall undulating prairie grass. One way or another, these seven had flung themselves deep into the land. They had become the land, the land had become them, an agonizing mystical act of communion. Separated from one another after the massacre, each had thought himself the sole survivor, at least until they began coming across traces of one another: a signature scrawled in charcoal upon a plank of wood; footprints; once, a distant sighting of a running nude.

They had wandered, lost. They had tried to imagine the map of Texas, but couldn't. Some had walked in circles. Others had taken their bearings where they could think them up, off a patch of tree moss, from the sun, from a flock of geese heading north. *And now they have me,* thought Houston.

So far as the seven survivors were concerned, they had been delivered from the wilderness by the hand of Sam Houston. Their gratitude was simple. It came in bashful thank-ye's which Houston deflected with his own thanks for their sacrifices. Over and over it came in their eyes every time he entered his crowded tent.

Remarkably, as the survivors recovered, so did Houston. Hour by hour, ounce by ounce, his despair fell away. These skeletal survivors had been delivered to him from the desert. That's how he felt. They had come to lead him back to his army, to lead them all out of this filthy dead-end ravine.

The boy he'd found on the buffalo hunt began to recuperate, at least physically. He could sit up and drink broth and down johnnycakes and chew meat and his eyes cleared of their awful blankness. One morning he woke up and could speak. He said, "morning." But there was a limit to his speech. He couldn't remember anything about himself, not even his name. He seemed to feel guilty about that, as if he were betraying someone.

Houston carved a stick into a hopping frog and gave it to the boy. From then on, men called the nameless boy Tad for tadpole. It gave people a way to identify him, but did nothing to satisfy his longing. "Maybe I'm just dead," he told one of the other survivors who passed it along to Houston.

One afternoon Houston returned to his tent to hear another boy teaching Tad an old colonial arithmetic riddle. "If twenty dogs for thirty groats go forty weeks to grass, how many hounds for sixty crowns may winter in that place?"

It was the double rule of three; Houston had taught it to schoolchildren himself. He rounded the corner and there was a lank young soldier sitting beside Tad with numbers scrawled in the dirt between their feet. One hand was wrapped with rags, and the tips of his fingers were swollen.

"Howdy do, gentlemen," Houston said. "Mind if I sit with you?"

"He's the general," Tad told the new boy.

"I know that," the boy said matter-of-factly. He had a self-possession beyond his years.

"Then you're one up on me," Houston said in a friendly manner.

"Terrell Mott," the boy briskly clarified, practically indifferent to his own name. He didn't give his rank. What else would a teenager be but a private?

Houston took a seat against the log. He stretched his legs, scratched at the lice on his hairy neck. "You two soldiers know each other, do you?"

Tad nodded a hungry yes, but that was just his desire for a friend. Private Mott admitted, "Nope, first time."

"How'd you crush that hand?"

"My horse. It fell on me."

"It doesn't look right to me," Houston said.

"She's crooked all right."

"Maybe you ought to show it to a doctor."

"I did." The boy shrugged. "They said too late. She's set funny. That's that."

Houston liked this boy. There were parts of himself in Private Mott's stoicism. Not much differently, Houston had belittled his own gaping wound in front of General Jackson and then had gone on to fight and take more wounds. It made Houston wonder how many times history might repeat the same story and with what layering of similar details.

"Which outfit has you?" he asked.

"Colonel Neill's cannon. Except there ain't no cannon."

"Not yet," Houston conceded.

"Not ever," Mott bluntly responded. "Some fool had us drown the ones we had. I don't expect we'll see more growing on trees."

Houston didn't point out that it was he who had ordered the artillery dismantled and sunk in the river back in Gonzales for the sake of speeding their retreat. Now he wished they'd hung on to at least one of the tubes.

"Well it's good to see the artillery fraternizing with . . ." Houston hesitated, not knowing what to call Fannin's survivors, "with the rest of us."

"I had some free time. I came over here."

"I wasn't aware we had a math scholar in the army." Houston pointed at the equations drawn in the dirt.

Private Mott ducked his head, mistaking Houston's tease for a criticism. "We were just talking."

"Terrell was at the Alamo," Tad volunteered.

Houston waited for Private Mott to backtrack on his extravagance. The Alamo was fast developing into a nativity of choice. Men who'd never been within a hundred miles of San Antonio could be heard describing with great authority the limestone walls and Colonel Crockett's gigantic arms, and they had invented a host of reasons to justify their last-minute absence at the battle.

But the private didn't retract his claim, which left Houston the choice of treating the boy as a liar or accepting his word. He decided to take Mott at face value. Maybe in fact the Alamo had something to do with his injured hand. If it did, Private Mott didn't elaborate on it except to say, "I got sent out and the others died. And my whole point is, it made me an orphan of a certain kind."

Houston poked a stick at the dirt and maintained his show of unoccupied leisure. But inside he felt jolted. This man-child with his peach fuzz and pimples and gangly arms, this muddy wisp of a private, had arrived at some sort of wisdom. Houston paid attention even while appearing, carefully, to only half-listen.

"Orphans," he prompted.

"Maybe you lose your family, lose your home. Maybe you lose your name, even," Mott expanded. "But in a way, I figure you're better off with none of that, you know."

"How's that," Houston asked, a trifle more earnestly than he'd meant to reveal.

Mott answered with sureness. "A baby doesn't remember where it came from, out of the sky, up from a vegetable patch, what not. But every day now, I wake up and I know right where I came from."

"That's it," Tad said. As if the clouds had opened up and he'd just caught sight of a distant city, the boy closed his eyes and held it inside.

Right then something took seed in Houston's heart. As surely as these boys had lost their pasts, Houston now began to feel himself found. These children had witnessed the apocalypse, but turned it around and made it into a beginning. Having risen up from the dead, they had no time for feeling sorry for themselves, not with so much else to do, a whole future to elect. Houston had listened to and generated enough revolutionary cant to lift a French balloon. He had signed with flourish a declaration of independence and corralled an army of long rifles for a clash. But none of that counted against what he'd just witnessed. Because it was these two boys who had just cast the first real vote for Texas, and it lay scratched in the dirt, a riddle.

CHAPTER SEVEN

HOUSTON LED HIS ARMY up and out from the ravine into the scarlet dawn. Except for Deaf Smith and a few of the scouts, they had yet to sight a single enemy soldier. But Santa Anna's army loomed gigantically, like a bad season, like famine or the plague, all-consuming. Ever since Fannin's survivors had surfaced upon the prairie, bobbing among the grasses like shipwreck victims, Houston had watched his soldiers sober. He didn't regret that one bit.

To Houston's relief his soldiers had finally begun to lose confidence in their abilities with a long rifle and a butcher knife. They quit talking about themselves as legends waiting to happen and no longer spoke of Santa Anna as a bug to be stepped on. The hard truth was sinking in. They might be the children of the first Adam, but they weren't ten feet tall and the enemy was not some treed squirrel open to the shot.

Old Man Groce had sold Houston a splendid horse on credit, and at last he felt mounted like a general ought to be. Both knees were peeking through rips in his tobacco-green pants and the frock coat was falling to pieces on his back, but he didn't mind now, not seated atop this mild-white masterpiece. Saracen was the stallion's name, and he was thirty-four hands high with vast bellows for lungs and muscles that bunched and rippled under the saddle.

Houston stayed out in front of his army. Saracen's frisky spirits made a convenient excuse. In truth Houston was trying

116

to keep ahead of his own doubts. At some point they needed to branch north or branch south. If the goal was Nacogdoches and a feint to pull General Gaines's 6th Regiment across the Sabine River, they had to go north. If Houston meant to turn and fight, he had to go south. Either way risked Texas. By going north they would likely trigger a war between Mexico and the United States, a war that might very well ally Britain and France with Mexico and possibly stunt American expansion on the continent. And by going south they would isolate themselves and face almost certain decimation.

To this point, Houston's cryptic pleas to Gaines produced small results. Beyond allowing the more zealous soldiers—fully uniformed and bearing new Type III U.S. muskets—to "desert" from his army and join Houston's bunch, the old fox was playing the same nervewracking waiting game Houston was. The irony didn't escape Houston: Even as he battled desertion, he was now in the position of welcoming deserters. They were better than nothing, though not much.

When the first of Gaines's deserters had showed up at the Brazos ravine, Houston had imagined the presence of regulars would put some snap in his rabble. With their sky-blue coatees and trousers and eelskin forage caps and squared knapsacks and wooden canteens, the regulars had made an impressive contrast to Houston's tribal bunch slathered with ravine mud. In fact for a matter of two or three days, the regulars had followed orders and kept their area neat and they'd made model soldiers.

But the tug of chaos had proved too much. Gaines's men were almost indistinguishable from his own now. They had bartered off bits and pieces of their uniforms and kits and the result was a hybrid of buckskin and regulation blues and bare feet. It came as no surprise to see their obedience erode and their crisp élan melt to mud. They seemed doomed, all of them, imprisoned with their worst instincts in a cage of their own making.

Unable to decide on the north or south route, Houston kept the army pushed in between, due east, putting off the choice and maddening his officers who saw no strategy, no method, only a slow and shameful drift. What they didn't see was how, when he walked among the soldiers at night and saw them sleeping like dead men on the coming battlefield, Houston agonized over how to keep them safe long enough to make them dangerous.

Five days after leaving the ravine they entered snow, or so it seemed. For hundreds of yards at a stretch, white feathers carpeted the path. "Taking the Sabine chute," it was called, heading for the river dividing Mexico from the United States. These were the remains of mattresses emptied to lighten the refugees' load, here a batch of goose feathers, thirty yards later a splash of stiff pins plucked from chicken breasts and backs, a poor family's bed. They passed furniture tossed into the brush, a set of sky-blue British china lovingly stacked upon a rock, and a dead mule.

A mile later they came upon a dying cow trapped to the neck in a sink of mud. For no reason Houston could see, good or bad, Three-Legged Willie climbed down off his horse and unfurled a bullwhip. Chastising the poor lowing beast with jokes that no one understood, he proceeded to lash it across the face until both eyes ruptured, and even that didn't complete his odd sport. Dumbfounded, Houston was about to draw his pistol, but Deaf Smith shot the animal first with his rifle, then rode on.

Around noon Houston and his soldiers caught up with the refugees. There were several hundred desperate women and children and slaves jammed at a swollen stream. It was raining again. As Houston approached on his stallion, the women set to shouting and wailing for deliverance. He pulled his vest shut—all the buttons had fallen off by now—and steered Saracen into the thick of them.

"Sam Houston," a woman cried out.

The crowd parted for him. Except for a few grandpas with stained white billy-goat beards, the only men in the group were black slaves who drove the wagons and herded the livestock and carried children, white and black, on their shoulders. Some carried hunting rifles and were obviously filling in for their absent masters. The refugees looked little different from the soldiers—emaciated and ragged with wet coughs and pinkeye and shaking with malaria.

"Thank Jesus, we are saved," shouted a skinny woman with her wet dress plastered to her collarbones and pelvis.

In an attempt at rising to the occasion, Houston swept his three-cornered hat in a long-armed presidential arc that embraced them all, but against the misery spread on every side the gesture seemed to him pinched and empty. The smell of sweat evinced how these women and children had fought the wilderness every bit as hard as his soldiers had. What distinguished them from his army was the smell of menstrual blood. It was a raw, fertile, bonding smell and Houston leaned into it like a prisoner catching sight of a butterfly. He hadn't realized how much he missed the presence of women.

"O my strength, haste thee to help me," another woman called up to Houston. "Deliver my soul from the sword, my darling from the power of the dog. Save me from the lion's mouth."

The voices surged. Save for the woman who kept on with her Psalms, Houston heard little of their clamor very distinctly. The women were instruments and their tragedy was music, pure and simple. Their song lifted over the water's loud rush. Mosely Baker arrived and behind him, on a horse sprayed with vomit, John Wharton came in hunched with flu.

"They shall come," the Psalms woman feverishly praised. "They shall declare his righteousness unto a people that shall be born."

Out of the corner of one eye, Houston saw the two colonels shaking their heads in disbelief. It did indeed sound as if the woman was praying directly to him.

"Mosely?" a female voice reached up from the pandemonium. "Mosely, my God, you've come." The sea of hooded faces and white eyes shifted. A spark flashed red in the dark crush of humanity. Part of Houston's heart flew out to the girl, and he wished it were him she was calling. Until then he hadn't known how much he remembered of her: her name, her green eyes, her ferocious pledge to love.

Molly had found her soldier, or him her, or them each other. But whichever way it was, Mosely wasn't prepared. The colonel jerked at the sound of his name. Under the sunburn and whiskers his face blanched. Houston frowned, disappointed by the young man's repulsion. Pretending not to hear, Mosely hauled his horse's neck around and pushed his way back through the crowd, away from her.

Houston rode deeper into the thick crowd, here and there intercepted by faces from another lifetime, half-forgotten images of people who'd once lived in places like Gonzales and San

Felipe and Victoria and Montezuma and Egypt and squatter settlements scattered anywhere like corn seeds thrown carelessly between tree trunks. In a way, though, all of them were strangers to his eye, even the ones he knew, because their defeat and vulnerability looked so alien. They reminded him of the Cherokee people as, year by year, Old Hickory cast them west and further west, out from their gardens, their hopes.

"Why are you massed here?" he asked a hollowed-out woman with buckteeth. She was standing stock-still beside a wagon full of shivering children. "Why is no one crossing?"

She walked over to him, obedient to some idea. Without a word she handed up a bundle wrapped in rags. Houston thought she was presenting him with a gift of food, a ham, say, or a rabbit.

"Madam," he started to thank her. Then he flipped open the rags. Inside the bundle he discovered an infant, cold and blue and with dead eyes staring at him. Houston grunted. He fumbled and nearly dropped the tiny corpse, and came close to cursing the woman, too. But her eyes were almost as dead as the child's.

"Colonel Wharton," Houston shouted back down the line. After a minute Wharton shoved his way through the crowd.

"Take a detail," Houston instructed him. "Bury this poor babe. And see to any other burying that needs to get done." Thinking quickly, he added, "And fire a salute to the dead."

"What in hell . . ."

"These people, they are heroes." Houston spoke loudly so the refugees could hear him. "Heroes." He lost nothing except a little gunpowder to try and raise the refugees' desolate mood. They needed something. They were so spiritless it would be a wonder if they reached the morning, much less their ancestral soil. Louisiana had never seemed so far away.

As his soldiers started to arrive, Houston felt shock running through his army. From infancy these people had believed themselves to be the sons and daughters of giants. But the truth of it was, underneath their sinew and buckskins and gingham and raw knuckles and broken nails, they were just scratching for a place in the wilderness. They called themselves Christians, but even with their Jesus talk, they were really just pagans worshiping the sun, following it west, ever west. And now, like rats in a flood, they were swimming east, out from the rising currents of Mexican sovereignty. It went contrary to everything they had ever known about themselves.

Houston nudged his stallion on to the stream. The refugees would not cross because of the water. There was a bridge, but it lay submerged beneath a foot of rapid water. The bleached-out wood of the passageway was visible through the water, a ghost of a thing. Understandably none of the horses or cattle would cross on it.

"We already lost one to it," a woman with a soggy hat told him. She was sitting under a wagon, the first in line to cross if a crossing ever happened. "I had our nigger swim the stock across. He walked the bridge. But he fell and the gators shagged him, and my cattle, too. Everything except my pony. That was yesterday."

Houston saw the pony waiting patiently for them on the opposite shore, a lonely sight. "No one wants to try no more," the wagon woman said. Houston didn't blame them. The way it sank off into the gloom and far bayou, the bridge looked like a sure walk into the underworld.

So for a day and a night they had sat here piled against the river, waiting for the Mexicans to find them or the waters to wash them out to sea or to get raised up by the rapture, Houston couldn't say what. But clearly they weren't going to move unless they were led across the water.

"Now you'll see, the general will watch over us," a mother told her little girl.

Houston forced himself to be stone deaf to them all. "Keep those soldiers moving," he bellowed back at his officers. And to the populace he shouted, "Let those soldiers come. Clear a way."

This stream needed to be crossed, and quickly. Littered with women and children, the place guaranteed a bloodbath if the Mexican army happened to show up. The civilians would get caught in crossfire, the river would turn red. He had to lead them to safety.

"Your *reata* there," Houston said, pointing at a coil of braided rope in the back of her wagon, "it will make a good hand line, once I fix it on the other side." He stretched out of the saddle and hefted it, a long rope made of good heifer skin.

"Don't you lose that," the wagon woman said. "I've already lost enough things to this goddamn river."

"I'll do my best," Houston said, and fitted the coil over
one shoulder. Then he turned Saracen toward the underwater
bridge and gave him the spur. Through the great white neck
and quivering flanks, he could feel the animal resisting him.
Houston bullied the horse, digging the spur in hard and at the
same time reining him tight.

But the horse balked. For the first time since obtaining the
monster, Houston regretted its size and power and even its
beautiful white color. Atop this Alexandrian stallion, he towered over everyone else in the army. While such a height would
hold his triumphs that much closer to the sky and sunlight, it
would also make his failures that much more conspicuous. *Goddamn my conceits,* he confessed to himself. *Goddamn this animal.*

Saracen trembled between his legs. Houston wanted to lose
his temper and flail the creature with his scabbard. He wanted
to force it to grandly prance across the bridge. What a vision
that would be, General Houston walking up the water. But the
horse didn't share his fascination with magnificent illusions. It
refused the bridge.

Houston got down off the horse. Wharton and Sherman
and some of the other officers guffawed to one another. It had
happened, Houston's fall from grace, and without a tumble,
but a meek dismount. He turned his back to them.

Softly, with nonsense words a man would only murmur to
a horse or a dog, Houston gentled Saracen. Finally, when the
stallion wouldn't stop its quivering, Houston dropped the reins,
just let them go. He reached into his pocket and found a lead
ball. Unseen, he slipped it into his mouth and bit down, the way
Old Hickory had once told him. The *duelo* had been like this:
everything to lose, everything to gain. Houston took the step.
Holding high his saddlebag with the books and his pair of
pistols, he entered the water.

The officers quit their laughter. The people watched him
in their hundreds. He could feel every eye upon him. Oddly,
for the leader of a retreat, retreat was out of the question. He
could not go anywhere but forward.

Step by step Houston sloshed through the shin-high rapids.
The bridge was solid enough, but it was slippery. The water cut
white around his legs. It tugged at him, disputing his right
to pass. A dark green ripple slid against his boot, serpentine,

poisoning his mind with fear. The serpent turned to water. It was nothing.

But Houston had made the mistake. He had looked down. Immediately the water was there, mesmerizing and alluring. He could see the bridge beneath the opaque surface. He could feel it under his boots. But looking at it only made him dizzy. Suddenly he couldn't be certain the bridge was really there.

Houston bit down on the musket ball and forced himself to raise his eyes up. The best thing, the only thing, was to keep fixed on the opposite bank. That helped. It came naturally to him to pay attention to what was out of reach. After the half-way point, the crossing turned easier. The river turned to shallows.

Remarkably Saracen followed right behind him. Houston didn't know the stallion was there until he reached the far shore and turned around. He thought that a fine lesson in independence: Give a people their freedom and they would come along on their own. But then Saracen shouldered him aside and promptly mounted the shaggy pony, which was a mare and in season. Houston liked that even more. Maybe love turned their destinies after all.

He tied a rock to one end of the rope and cast it back across and got a hand line started. After that, the army and the refugees came over the bridge. The crossing took all day long, exhausting the already weakened civilians. For their sake, Houston made camp a half mile from the river. He issued instructions for the refugees to stay with the army for the night.

Even before nightfall it was obvious the combined people meant to throw a feast and frolic. Houston didn't try to stop them, he just posted a rear guard to guard the bridge against Mexicans, and found a spot to pitch his tent removed from the hurly-burly.

The rain quit. The moon rose. The clouds dispersed and a muggy spring heat wrapped the camp. Mosquitoes swarmed up from the swampy earth, and crickets began sawing away in the forest. Gently at first, as if tiptoeing, another sound began to drown out the bug song. It was the sound of dancing and drinking and fighting and loving.

At about ten o'clock Tom Rusk came around the hill and put his head inside the tent. Houston had a little candle going and was reading. "You ought to come to dinner," Rusk said. "There's a lady's requesting your presence. A lady of honor."

"What lady?" Houston wasn't exactly tired, but he wasn't in any mood for fighting with his colonels tonight. The more he kept himself cloistered and remote, the lighter his burden.

"Just come to supper, Sam," Rusk said. "She wants to meet the general of the army. It can't hurt."

Houston groused about the hour, but that was pretense, the sort of thing old men do when they haven't been remembered properly. In fact he'd been lying here curious all evening. It sounded like a whole town's New Year celebration on the other side of the hill. And the prospect of meeting a woman who wanted to meet him made a visit down irresistible. He combed his hair with some precision and knocked the dust off his seat and descended into camp.

Houston's barbarians had outdone themselves. It was an unearthly sight, the banquet they had prepared in the forest clearing. When Houston rounded the hill he was almost cowed by their primal concoction.

A huge bonfire had been built, for lack of space, in the center of a shallow pond, rendering the water like blood and lighting the entire region. Flames lapped at the clear night sky.

Houston made his way through the bedlam of five hundred hungry soldiers and at least as many women and children and slaves. Men were wrestling and fighting in the mud while those with common sense were courting more directly for an evening's company. A few fiddles and the army's drum and a mouth harp had come together to whack away at the same songs over and over. Couples were dancing and singing, skunked on liquid corn. Dogs barked and fought and stole food. Children raced everywhere.

One popular attraction turned out to be an old black conjure man. Houston craned his neck to see over the heads of the crowd and there in the center was a white-haired slave. He'd cut a zodiac into the dirt with a string and a stick and was collecting money for predictions. A lot of soldiers seemed eager to part with their pieces of eight and whatever else the conjure man was willing to accept for payment. It wasn't hard to figure out what prediction they wanted. Just as he was leaving, Houston saw J. S. Neill in the line, and the colonel looked apprehensive. Houston didn't stick around to see if Neill's Alamo luck had run out or not.

Houston came across Deaf Smith hunting through the crowd, his thin lips tight, eyes darting. He was looking for his family, obviously, and not finding them. When he saw Houston, the scout shook his head and smiled, though it wasn't really a smile. "I miss my Guadalupe and the youths," he said. Houston smelled the liquor on his breath.

"Perhaps they've already crossed the Sabine," Houston said.

"I pray God the east is not too strange for her. She's just a Bexar girl, you know."

"She'll get kindness from strangers, Mr. Smith."

"I know my people, though," Smith despaired.

"Trust in their goodness," Houston said.

"You're a wonder, General. I don't know how you do it."

"Trust?"

"I mean, to be parted from your wife, sir."

"I'm a widower." It was a tired lie. Eliza was not dead, she wasn't even divorced from him, not formally. The scout examined Houston's eyes, and it was plain the old gossip about Houston's marriage was fire talk here, too. "What I mean to say is," Houston clarified, "my wife, she's dead to me."

Smith wanted to sympathize with him about it. Houston had seen the look a thousand times over the past few years and it made him weary. He had been laid waste all right, but less by the loss of Eliza than the loss of love itself. Ever since he'd been in search of the outcast in himself and finding some way to bring his wandering to a close. Until this revolution, Texas had seemed an ideal place for the quest. It was teeming with lonely hearts like him, but it was full of hope, too, instances of men who had settled their yearning. Bowie had done it with his Mexican wife, a Tejana version of Eliza: landed, young, connected. Travis had found it with his outlandish whoring, and Austin with his quiet cabin mate, a man slightly younger. Everything was possible in Texas.

"But, General, how do you stand the loneliness?" Smith almost pleaded. These questions, forever disguising condolences or confessions or accusations, could sometimes drive Houston to a rage or into black melancholy. Tonight it didn't

seem to matter so much. He had a lady to meet and the sky was
clear and sweet as a brook.

"Can you keep a secret, Mr. Smith?"

The scout nodded, expectant.

Houston rested one hand on his shoulder. "Then so can
I," he said, and headed back into the riotous din.

The banquet's centerpiece was a table dominated by an
entire black bear, complete with hide, meat, and claws. Locked
between its fangs hung the red, white, and green flag of the
Mexican Republic. A drunken woman dug her hand elbow-
deep into a slit in the back of the giant carcass and wrenched
free a rib that looked well short from cooked.

Besides holding up the black bear, the table displayed a
forest of critters—raccoons, squirrels, two turkeys—plus the
hindquarters and backbone of a roasted ox. Though their flour
supply was limited, Houston saw that Colonel Forbes had dis-
bursed plenty enough for biscuits.

Not much further, ringed by torches, sat the officers' table.
Someone had knocked the sides off a wagon and positioned
kegs and boxes around for chairs. Refugees had donated a set of
china plates and crystal goblets and Irish linen napkins, though
there wasn't a single fork or spoon in the spread. One of Sherman's men, Houston guessed, had stabbed the Buckeye Rangers' standard into the dirt beside the table. The silk flag rustled
gently, exposing and then enfolding the image of a half-naked
woman waving a sword.

Houston joined his majors and colonels and their guests.
Looking around he found hints of the vanity each indulged
when not at war. Sherman's uniform was hard to improve on,
but he'd managed, adding gold and silver epaulets brought
from home to each broad shoulder. Three-Legged Willie had
shaved, badly, and his nicked jowls still bled. He was wearing
his skin cap with its six coon tails dancing merrily against his
shoulders. Forbes and Wharton had their buttons buttoned.
Even Ned Burleson—the most unself-conscious man Houston
had ever met—had made an effort to reform his appearance:
From the shins down he had scraped the mud off his buckskins.

Here and there, like ladies of a royal court, various refugee
women perched on the makeshift chairs. Like the officers they
had taken pains to fancy themselves up. Houston smelled laven-
der water. In lieu of lace or bonnets, two giggling sisters were

sporting blue napkins on their heads. Several had powdered their cheeks with flour to obscure the sunburn, and their gingham and calico appeared damp still from a hasty laundering. Houston tried to select which of these famished-looking women had requested his presence.

His eye ranged down to the end of the table where Molly sat beside Mosely Baker. With her red hair washed fresh in the river and braided back, the young widow had obviously aimed at radiance tonight. But her eyes were raw and swollen and her hands cupped emptiness, limp in her lap. Plainly she'd been crying for hours, and probably not over her dead husband.

It was strange to Houston that he should remember her so clearly from that Gonzales street. Maybe it was a matter of contrasts that pronounced her. Eliza had had the translucence of a cholera victim, all white-gold hair and porcelain delicacy. Houston had watched how men were drawn to her fragility, for it was a perfect foil for their chivalry. Suitors had been drawn to her for much more than that, of course. Through her father, the belle had promised pedigree and wealth and political connections. Indeed, her wedding to Houston had resembled a presidential inauguration with every captain of industry and banker and kingmaker in Tennessee present. And this Molly? Except for her beauty and youth, she was Eliza's opposite in every way. She was just a pauper girl who offered no plantation, no political machinery, no dowry, nothing but the present moment from the toes up. Maybe that was her appeal. She was as graceless and unadorned as Texas itself.

"General," Rusk's voice broke in on his thoughts. The secretary of war was escorting a young man his own height. He was sturdier through the chest than Rusk and he had city clothes rather than buckskins. But they could have been brothers, the two of them looking equally chaste, equally joyful. "I want you to meet a dear bosom friend of mine, Junius Patrick. *Doctor* Patrick, by golly. We shared a childhood together. Now he's come two thousand miles and found us, somehow, in the middle of nowhere."

In the three years he'd known Rusk, Houston hadn't seen him grin half so wide. Maybe this visitant would be the cure for Rusk's moods. Houston pumped Patrick's hand gratefully. "A doctor of medicine?" he offhandedly inquired.

"I am, sir. Transylvania College, the class of 'thirty-three."

"You're a blessing, then."

The doctor made some reply, but Houston missed it. Because at that instant the torchlight flickered and Houston thought his eyes were playing a trick on him. Over Dr. Patrick's shoulder, nestled at mid-table, was Private Lamar. And it was clear from his dress that he was here as a guest, not as help to serve liquor or fetch meat. The little man had somehow infiltrated Houston's elite and was merrily chatting away with Wylie Martin on one side and John Wharton on the other. Wearing his frock coat with a burgundy cravat and a steep white collar, Lamar had done himself the favor of removing his green spectacles. Worse by far, the man had combed his hair forward upon each of his temples in the popular style of Lord Byron, the martyred poet and revolutionary. That happened to be one of Houston's favorite effects, one he reserved for special occasions like tonight. But it was too late to comb his own hair back. *Well then,* he resigned himself, *we'll give them two Caesars tonight.*

"Sam," Rusk murmured discreetly, "here she comes now."

"Ah, yes," Houston said, as if it had slipped his mind. He looked where Rusk was pointing uphill. There was no mistaking which woman he meant.

She was tall, taller than most of the soldiers she passed. Her black hair, caught loosely with a leather whang, created a frame for her extraordinary white neck. Beneath the calico dress, her proportions were long and full, and there was muscle on the inside of her womanliness. There would be thick calluses on her palms, Houston predicted. She was barefoot with a gold band around one ankle. There were copper rings on her fingers and wrists and loops in her ears. She looked wild and uncaptured and Houston was glad now that he'd come to dinner.

He thought he was the only one anticipating her, then noticed that Lamar was fixed upon the woman also. To his dismay the private was actually standing up as if to be introduced. It was absurd, if only because she was a good six inches taller than Lamar. At least the lady made no mistake about which of them was the general. She paused by Molly—a quick touch of two fingers onto the heartbroken girl's shoulder, a whisper in her ear—then circled around to Houston's side of the table.

"Allow me," Rusk took over, "General Houston, here is Mrs. Pamela Mann."

That name sounded familiar, but Houston couldn't place it immediately. He stepped away from the table to perform his bow. An old French fencing master, somehow overlooked by that country's revolutionary guillotine, had once taught Houston the courtly gesture. It involved several stages and ended with a flourish. An inebriated Daniel Webster had once told Houston that he looked like a peacock in rut every time he met a woman. But, figuring the world was no worse for it, Houston went ahead with his bow.

"Madam," he extemporized, "our wilderness has been a dark and cold place. From tonight forward you light our way."

"We'll see who will light which way, General Houston," Mrs. Mann replied. "One thing, though. I doubt we're done with the dark cold yet." Her voice was plain, yet the plainness had power. Up close, her hair was tangled and greasy and she was baked brown from the sun and blue from weeks of woodsmoke. Here was one woman who hadn't spent the day preparing herself for the meal. Houston liked that. She trusted in her presence.

"Where's that husband of yours?" Three-Legged Willie called from downtable. He was very drunk. The coonskin tails flapped against his neck.

"Gone to Luziane," Mrs. Mann said without bitterness. "He's in Natchitoches by now."

"I swear he has an instinct," Willie said. "He's the best I know at keeping one step ahead of whatever it is."

Now it came to Houston. Mrs. Mann was said to be the real genius behind their so-called Owl Creek money. The counterfeited bank notes were nearly worthless in the United States even when they weren't counterfeit, and had ended up following the Manns to Texas. Of late, so many people in the American settlements had gotten stuck with the paper that Owl Creek money had come to be used like regular cash just to maintain its value. Houston appreciated the fact that Mrs. Mann's imagination had become the coin of the realm.

"Let us eat," Wylie Martin barked at them. "I'm hungry."

"But who will bless our meal?" Mrs. Mann asked the officers. The fire glittered in her eyes.

Houston cleared his throat and searched for an appropriate verse. But Lamar, the interloper, was faster. "I would consider it an honor," he said to Mrs. Mann.

"Colonel?" she smiled, clearly uncertain who Lamar was. Houston saw his opening and took it.

"Mrs. Mann, my manners," Houston chided himself. "Let me present to you, fresh from the States, Private Lamar." He didn't bother stressing the rank, and Lamar's wince, when it flashed, was a tiny thing. But Houston had grazed him, definitely.

"I confess, madam, I am green from the States, bright green," Lamar recovered. "Until my baptism in battle, I can only aspire to a reputation as meteoric as the general's."

"It's a good thing we're all democrats then, equal before our food anyhow," Mrs. Mann diplomatically observed. "So why don't you go ahead with your prayer, sir."

Lamar tucked his head down to recall, finally settling on a snatch from Ezekiel. "Ye shall eat the flesh of the mighty," he intoned, "and drink the blood of the princes of the earth, of rams, of lambs, and of goats and bullocks. And ye shall eat fat till ye be full, and drink blood till ye be drunken, and drink sacrifice which I have sacrificed for you. Thus ye shall be filled at my tables with horses and chariots, with mighty men, and with all men of war. So saith the Lord God."

"Amen," Wharton pronounced. "Amen to such a feast. Now eat."

They set to their banquet with fingers and butcher knives, tearing at the meat with their teeth and nails. The ladies were as voracious as the men. Mrs. Mann pitched in, and Houston noticed her preference for the venison and buffalo over the ox. To her very core her tastes seemed to run away from what was domesticated. The animal grease smeared her cheeks and she grew more and more lovely.

There was no war talk for an hour. The conversation wove about, light and airy. The officers openly courted the refugee women. Their flattery was impressive. It was also stolen. Houston recognized at least a dozen lines lifted directly from Scott, that serpent. Sherman and Forbes and Three-Legged Willie seemed most adept with it, offering up bits and pieces about beautiful damsels, the dignity of arms, and the Great Heart. They used "Southron" for Southern, "aristocratical" for aristocratic. Forbes likened their gathering to "Texian chieftains," as if the Anglo-Saxons in Texas went back centuries instead of a scant few years.

Not everyone flirted. Old Wylie Martin was preoccupied with gastric difficulties and finally, to his neighbors' relief, excused himself to go hang his arms over a tree branch and let the wind leak out of him. Rusk and his friend Dr. Patrick were inseparable, engrossed in catching up with all that connected them. Children were constantly barging in, making demands on their mothers and older sisters. And Mosely, who should have been enjoying the rendezvous more than anyone, seemed singularly bent on extending his strange punishment of poor Molly. Gone was his buckishness. The colonel sat there taciturn and humorless. He didn't talk, didn't look around, didn't eat. Molly sat and suffered, too, the unhappiest creature on earth.

Mrs. Mann saw Houston frowning.

"Put down your troubles, General," she said. "It's much too fine a night to waste on worry."

"No worries, Mrs. Mann. It's just my young blade there." He pointed his chin at the starcrossed couple. "I'm beginning to dislike his manners."

She knew who he meant without looking down the table. "He could be taking his news more agreeably."

"What news is that?"

"Don't you know?" Mrs. Mann said. "It's all through the refugees."

Houston shook his head.

"The girl's with child. She found out three days ago."

Houston absorbed the implications with a lagging nod. It came together for him. Molly wasn't going to be so easily freed of her past. Her dead husband had freighted her with more than bad memories. And Mosely wanted nothing to do with it.

Mrs. Mann read Houston's thoughts. "You do understand," she inquired.

Houston paused. "It sounds like I don't?"

"She has your colonel's baby in her womb. He cuckolded a ghost, General, and he got a child." What was Mosely's horror began to come into focus. Then Mrs. Mann laughed, at Houston perhaps, or at Mosely or at life.

The army and the refugees swarmed all around the officers' table, shouting and chewing and running about in their tattered clothes and ragged beards. They were overjoyed to have each other for the night. The moon was binding them, one way or another. Couples moved off into the trees. Inevitably men fell to fighting. Their wrestling turned to fists, the fists to gouging and knives. They bled into the mud as if the bleeding were a sacrament. Their noise soared to thunder.

At the officers' table the conversations revolved around land transactions, the latest price of cotton, and the state of various currencies. Dr. Patrick told them about the release of a group of New York volunteers which had, on its way to Texas, stopped off in Jamaica to plunder British plantations and been captured. He said there had been a new outbreak of cholera in Baltimore. He described Jackson's latest confrontation with the bank. This brought the talk around to politics and the future of Texas.

Houston listened to his officers recite their old litany of woes about Mexican tyranny and taxation and the foreignness of Mexican law. Houston didn't point out that, once "liberated," the Republic of Texas would lay far more taxation and law on their shoulders than Mexico ever had, and these same men would be crying foul upon their own government. And what then, another revolution?

"Gentlemen." It was Sherman, steep with the corn. Beside him one of the sisters with the blue napkins on their heads had acquired the colonel's hat. "We have a poet among us and he has a toast. Give it, brother." He thrust a hand at Lamar, prompting him to stand up. Houston drummed his fingers. The private was certainly getting in his licks of oratory tonight.

"Revenge," Lamar dramatically intoned. "Revenge is all my soul! no meaner care, interest, or thought, has room to harbor there; Destruction be my feast, and mortal wounds, And scenes of blood, and agonizing sounds."

Houston recognized the passage with a start. It was from his cherished *Iliad*. Before he could expose the theft, though, Lamar admitted his borrowing. "It's not my poem, of course," he said. "But we can make it ours if we want. It can guide us if we have the will." He could have been talking about the weather, it was said so mildly.

Houston took a deep breath. So, they meant to twist the lion's tail, to raise up their discontent once again, but this time with the women present to witness it. There was another difference. Tonight the colonels had chosen a private to lead their assault. Old Hickory would have shot the man dead for it, and then shot a second man just to make sure his barrel was clean.

"We must have no more of your runaway, Houston," Wharton started off. "It is time for revenge, goddamn it. Time for destruction."

"We must stand here," Sherman threw in.

"Split the army," Wharton demanded, "half goes north, half south, then catch the enemy. . . ."

"No, no," Three-Legged Willie howled.

Houston saw Rusk and Dr. Patrick exchange a startled glance. They were new to the mutiny talk. So was Mrs. Mann, but it shocked her less. In fact the army's fractures seemed to excite her. Her eyes flashed. She was like pure fire, feeding upon their passion, not their words. Houston pressed his hands against the table and shoved to his feet.

"I look around," he rumbled, "and I wonder to myself . . . at this very moment, while we sit here and our enemy sits out yonder . . . I wonder, Houston, right now, right at this very minute, what do you think Mr. Santa Anna is looking at in his own camp? A table full of good right officers? Men who are ever patient and never tiring in their patriotism and zeal for the cause of defense? Men who bear every incident of the soldier without complaint? Men who are the cream of his army? Men who desire the good?"

He swept the table with a wolfish grin. His officers had fallen silent. All around them the camp was in a state of bedlam. People were howling and gobbling to the starry night sky, imitating hounds or turkeys or spring bears or whatever their favorite animals were. A pack of brawling men collapsed a corner of the bonfire, plunging much of their light into the black pond water. What light was left came from the few torches which hadn't been drafted for use as cudgels. Even those seemed close to blinking into darkness, extinguished by the sheer bulk of their noise.

But at the table the officers' silence shaped a bubble and Houston was its center. He raced to invent his own meaning. He placed his hands flat on the table, bracketing the bones of his meal.

"I wonder to myself, Houston, if Mr. Santa Anna looked around his supper table right now and considered his officers, would he see a round table of buckskinned knights? Would he see in their eyes the spark of God?" Houston dropped his voice a pitch.

"I ask that," he said. "And then I say to myself no, of course not." He grinned at them with a ferocity that was also utter helplessness. They were off balance. So was he. It was a precarious moment.

"No," he mocked them, "of course not. And do you know how I know?" He traveled from eye to eye, from one man's glare to the next man's scowl.

"Because I know that old Santa Anna must be surrounded by wicked men who plot against him every minute. He probably can't sleep at night because he fears his own officers. When I try to imagine him, I see a man who's blown along by whispers. He has to listen to the whispers and go where they say go, otherwise he'll get stabbed in the back and replaced by the next brute. And whenever I think about the coup d'état waiting in Santa Anna's ranks, I say to myself, God, Houston, how lucky you are to have such true and righteous colonels." He lifted his glass. It was, by chance, empty. "Here's to loyalty, gentlemen. Here's to you."

They sat there, stilled by the admonition. Houston's insolence—the rawness of it—stunned them. Not only that, he had spanked them in front of ladies. No one spoke. Teeth gritted, Burleson was beet red with the memory of his own mutinous troops last fall. Lamar looked wonderfully flatfooted.

At last Sherman came to life. "Outrageous," he protested. "To make us into those rascals in Mexico."

"But you forget," Houston reminded him. "You *are* in Mexico."

"And so we are all little Napoleons, is that it?"

"Oh, not so large as little, sir," Houston retorted, and he looked straight at Private Lamar.

"Goddamn it," Sherman bellowed, like a man who'd stubbed his toe.

Houston twisted and carefully spit tobacco juice into the mud beside his chair.

"What of you, General?" Lamar piped up. "We find ourselves painted with dark strokes. What portrait do you paint for yourself? A George Washington for our Texas maybe? Or, maybe just a King Andy." He delivered an academic smile.

"Me?" Houston said softly. He looked around, then fastened upon Mrs. Mann. She had caught her lower lip with strong white teeth. There was his same abandon in her eyes. "Why," he drawled, "I'm just an old moke."

They looked affronted, not knowing what he was talking about. The men who'd been in Texas long enough to understand some Spanish were either too drunk or too slow to see his meaning. The newcomers thought he was playing a trick.

"If you can't speak English, don't speak, Houston," Sherman snapped.

Now Tom Rusk got in on it. He was properly solemn. "Old mokes," he explained, "they are desperate, vicious beasts. Exiles. That's what the Mexicans call old mustang stallions that get driven from their fold by a youngster. And ever after, the mokes wander wild, searching for another herd to dominate. Every now and then you'll see one off there on the prairie, all alone. But every now and then they find a herd, and break it to their rule."

Against the roar of brawling men and the silence of these conspirators, Mrs. Mann's laughter rang like bell music.

CHAPTER EIGHT

HOUSTON MIGHT HAVE GONE LOOKING FOR HER, but the night was too abundant out there. Human musk hung in the air and a million fireflies bobbed in constellations of their own making. It kept him in his tent, propped on one elbow, watching the fiery silhouettes writhe and blend upon his canvas wall, remembering his Plato about shadows and reality. Sleep was an impossibility. Finally he got up to do some work.

With a twist of tobacco to one side of his ink bottle, a strip of scorched beef to the other, Houston sat crosslegged in the dirt and composed another of his anonymous pleas to General Gaines to cross from Louisiana and invade Mexico. This one revolved around fictitious Indian attacks on refugees. Other reports had plagiarized from his army's worst fantasies: Mexican rape, the burning alive of Bowie, the enslavement of white prisoners. His wax taper smoked furiously. Houston wrote with his left hand to disguise his handwriting, but he knew Gaines would see right through it. The theme was too familiar: *Please, Lord, come save us from ourselves.*

When she entered there was no announcement, no request. The tent flap jerked open, his little flame guttered and almost flushed out. The inky smoke stung his eyes. "Sam Houston," she said and planted her bare feet, wide and splayed, beside his letter.

Mrs. Mann had mud to her knees and her blue calico dress was soaked with sweat and raindrops knocked off trees and bushes along the way. Houston smelled human milk.

136

He saw the stains on her bodice and wondered where her baby was.

"You move so quiet," he told her.

She was looking all around the spartan tent, not that there was much to see, just his satchels and a new saddle blanket and a round stone he'd brought in to make a pillow.

"I don't have anything to drink," Houston apologized.

"A bit of that twist will do," she said. Houston handed the tobacco up, and she returned it a few inches shorter. Her eyes were shining. He wondered how this would go next, if it would start with a kiss or just be a straight-out rutting. It had been years since he'd used the Cherokee prayer for winning a woman: *Oh Black Spider, may you hold her soul in your web.* He longed for a kiss, for a soul in his web. But practically speaking, he wasn't about to pass up a chance for some raw congress for the sake of a mere romantic longing.

After a minute Mrs. Mann said, "You have my oxen."

Houston wasn't sure he'd heard right. "Madam?"

"One of your captains came and took my oxen. For your cannon."

So that was it. Disappointment dropped on him like a weight. They had obtained two brand new brass cannon—a donation from the city of Cincinnati—yesterday morning. Colonel Neill had sent his captain around to requisition oxen to haul the artillery. And Mrs. Mann was here to complain.

"I just about shot him to shreds," she went on. "He said the army of Texas was confiscating. I told him to go to hell. I'm not about to lose my oxen to a goddamn war."

"But we have them now?" Houston sighed.

She spit toward the corner of the tent and nodded. "I made it a loan. I told him, you all can use my team provided you're going to Luziane. Go to war, though, I take 'em back. He said, go tell it on Sam Houston. So what is it?"

Houston's eye wandered up her contours. There was all of womanhood in the span between his pristine belle and this bonny amazon. "Mrs. Mann," he said, "every war has its secrets."

"I'm no spy."

"But with all due respect."

"I don't think you know," she said. "That's what the people say. You don't know your own mind." She eyeballed him.

He let it lie. Mosquitoes whined in the heat. A woman

groaned somewhere close by. A man whispered encouragement.

Heart sinking, or sunk, Houston took his own measure. He tried picturing what Mrs. Mann saw at that moment, a balding man sweating on the dirt with some papers of state and a candle. A pretender. He made a motion to get up and see her out, but he felt too drained. He'd once commissioned a painter to render him as a Roman emperor standing among ruins. That was how he felt just now, like a man in ruin.

But then Mrs. Mann came down from her great height above him. She squatted on her heels and rested her forearms on her knees. "You know," she told him, "Jean Lafitte had me for supper once."

Houston blinked at the exotic suddenness of it. He couldn't think of anything to reply except, "Lafitte's dead."

"Oh he was alive, sir." She grinned. "I can testify to that." It appeared as a big saucy parting of chapped lips. Her teeth were crooked and so was the smile, but Mrs. Mann was enchanting him.

"It was out on Galveston Island," she said. "I was a young thing. And he was the laird of a kingdom. It was only one night. One supper. He was a grand man and a grand talker, too. He went on and on about how someday Texas would belong to him and he would be its emperor."

"Lafitte?" Houston snorted. It had never occurred to him the French privateer might have had designs on anything more than his island keep. On second thought it made perfect sense that a pirate would fasten on Texas.

"Oh yes. And he had things there from all over the world. Wine and brandy and Spanish lace," she remembered. "And hard sweets from London and cups from China. In the morning, Mr. Lafitte told me, Look through the booty and pick something, anything, and it's yours. So I did."

"A generous man," Houston said. Some of his spirit was returning to him. Unless he was mistaken, she was weaving a web of her own.

She nodded. "Mighty. He also gave me a child." She seemed to enjoy Houston's surprise. "That was my first. She's mostly grown now."

A smile dawned on Houston's face. He was delighted, utterly taken. What this army—indeed, this whole countryside—

needed was more women, both like and unlike Mrs. Mann. Without women they would end up like Stephen Austin and so many other bachelor colonists in this region, wizened and shrunken like old grasshoppers, shacked up with similar men struck blind by their vision of land and more land, infinite land. But love for the land was not love, it was religion. More than once on this journey Houston had heard his soldiers feeling for one another, eyes closed, shaping themselves into Greek warriors for lack of a woman. They were—all of them—in search of her. And here she was with a crooked smile on her face and a fertile womb.

"You are a rare spirit, ma'am," Houston said.

"It's a rare night," she said.

It struck him that with all her talk about a love child from her bygone pirate chief, perhaps she'd come simply to get a siring. It wouldn't be the first time Houston had been approached by women hunting for seed they judged noble just because it had "governor" or "congressman" attached to it. Not that he objected. Since he didn't believe in God—not the bearded biblical character, anyhow—he didn't have hellfire to fret over. That left only one other danger, the risk of believing in his own greatness just because someone else did.

With one liquid motion—businesslike, as if skinning a colorful animal, a pheasant, say—Mrs. Mann slipped her blue dress up and over her head. The sight of so much nakedness so suddenly left Houston hoarse. "Oh God," he whispered, and felt singularly unsteady for a great general. Still chewing, she smiled her crooked smile and let him look all he wanted.

Finally she said, "I didn't figure you to be such a shy man."

Houston took his turn and shucked his shirt, and she wet her lips seeing his big chest. Then, in the midst of fumbling with his pants, he knocked the candle over and plunged them into darkness. It was intentional. Beyond a point he was shy. Showing the battle and surgery scars crossing his arms and shoulder was one thing. But he'd learned the hard way to conceal the wound. It embarrassed him still that he and Eliza had never consummated their marriage, though at least he'd had the honor of returning her to her father as whole as she'd come to him.

Mrs. Mann reached between his legs and took him in both hands. It was a matter of a minute before she came across the arrow hole leaking into the thicket of loin hair. Her fingers recoiled. That always happened, and things often stopped right here. But then she went on exploring.

"Does this hurt you?" she whispered, touching the wound lightly.

"Sometimes, yes," Houston said.

"Then we need to be careful." The way she kissed him next, he wished for the candlelight. He wanted to see her eyes and hair and lips. But their urgency flooded them. All they could do was hold on to each other for all it was worth.

Afterward she sat with Houston's enormous head and shoulders cradled in her lap, stroking his hair. Off in the distance one of the refugees was singing all alone in the night. It was a woman's song, beautiful and keen, carried from the old country. She sang it in the Gaelic, the song of Scottish exile.

"Thug thu uam gach ni bh'agam, Ann an cogadh a'd aobhar, Cha chrodh is cha chairdean. . . ." On and on she sang to them, like a ghost, like a bird. From his mother and grandmother, Houston knew the meaning, if not, exactly, the words.

"You took from me everything I had, in the war on your behalf/ I am not mourning cattle and sheep, but my partner/ Since I am left alone with nothing but my shroud!"

They are burying us already, Houston thought, drifting near sleep. *Could we be ready at last?* He wasn't the only one listening to the shroud song.

"Folks say you'll take the army right when we go left tomorrow," Mrs. Mann said. "They say you'll go wait for Santy Any in the bayous."

Houston didn't answer. Sunrise wasn't far off, and with it the daily strife. But her breasts were soft and warm against his neck and he felt at peace in her arms, ready to sleep for a century.

"Folks say you'll fight a great battle."

"I'm much obliged to all those folks," Houston murmured.

"Even if they're right," she said, "I think they're wrong. I think you ought not go wait for Santy Any. You ought not fight."

That pricked Houston a little more awake. He had an army ready to kill him for not leading them into a fight to the death, and here was this woman ready to love him if he would quit

Texas altogether. How could that be? What did they want of him? "What ought I do, then?"

"Maybe Texas don't want us," she suggested. "Maybe this ain't home."

"Maybe not yet," Houston qualified it.

"Maybe not ever. I mean, what if. What if we just called it quits and said, Home's where we left it at, over on the other side."

"No more frontier?" said Houston. No sooner did he say it, than the thought made him a little sick, as if someone were locking a door with him on the inside.

"What if we decided to just take care of our children and tend our crops and say Texas never belonged to us anyhow, we didn't lose a goddamn thing by quitting this territory?"

"But you can do all those things, Mrs. Mann. You can cross the river with your children and go to where it's safe. You can make a new home over there and plant new crops. You can say that everything that happened on this side was just a dream."

"But what about you?"

"What about me?" He felt cold. There were temptations all around him. Who was he to listen to? He was their prisoner, confined to their expectations—hers, as well as theirs—a captive of their longing. He didn't dare try to escape them. Without them, without their passion, he would be marooned. The solitude didn't concern him. He was adept at making his way alone. But the emptiness would shatter him.

"Maybe we need you," she said. "Maybe we need you so we can get to Luziane. Maybe we need you there so we can stay there."

"You have your husband for that," Houston reminded her.

"That's not the same."

The most remarkable thing happened then. A tear dropped upon Houston's throat and slipped south across his rib cage. She was crying.

Now he understood, or thought he did. Mrs. Mann wanted to return to the States with everything she'd come with. That included the kingdom she'd built in her head, and that in turn included the king. For her to leave Houston and his army wandering in search of empire—her empire, the same as theirs—would make Texas into a haunting. It would make leaving into

getting left, and she had been left enough. It was something
plaintive like that, Houston guessed.

"I'm sorry," he said.

They must have slept then because Houston came awake
suddenly at the scream. It wasn't yet dawn, but the tent wall was
lit gray. Houston had ended up with Mrs. Mann still naked in
his arms. He felt the rough-woven saddle blanket underneath
them.

It was a real scream, not something out of his dreams, nor
like the alarm that had fooled Colonel Forbes. The edges of the
scream resonated in the air, stitching the other sounds of early
morning: a dove, a horse cropping grass nearby, someone pissing against a tree. Houston tried to disentangle himself quietly,
but she woke up.

"Sam," she sadly breathed. The rapture was already fading.
She had a husband, alive, worthless, cowering in Louisiana, but
a husband all the same. She was no Molly. Houston was no
Mosely. They were too seasoned for that kind of passion and
misery to last more than a few hours. For better or worse each
had a life to return to.

"You didn't hear it?" Houston asked her.

Mrs. Mann frowned.

"Stay here," Houston said, in part to ensure her safety, but
mostly to have someone overseeing his possessions. Things had
a way of walking off in this camp. He got into his pants and
boots and shirt and emerged only half put together. Huddled
to one side of his tent door, Houston's self-appointed guardian,
Tad, smiled his "morning." Then the boy glimpsed the nude
woman inside and went silent. Houston dropped the tent door
shut.

"What happened out here?" he said to the boy.

The boy went on staring at the tent door, blinking wide-
eyed the way lepers did. An expression of disapproval ate across
his face. Houston didn't prompt him again. Other people had
begun to rise up and filter through the camp, between the trees,
all in a certain direction.

"This way," Houston said to the shocked child.

By the time he got to the stream, over a hundred people
had collected. It was almost like a baptism, with the sun throwing peach along the horizon and the water so pure. They stood

in a broad oval surrounding a stout girl who was sobbing and a confused man who was scarcely awake, sitting on his rump, shaking at his hangover. Molly appeared from the crowd and wrapped her long arms around the girl and gathered the sobs against her sisterly shoulder. Mosely appeared. Molly spoke to him, though it was with all the love scrubbed off her face. That was gone, and from Mosely, too. Their beautiful faces had been replaced by two cold stones.

"Fetch a rope," Mosely called out with grim authority. "Get a horse." That was lynch talk. Houston had heard it used a dozen times in his lifetime. When the man on his rump tried to stand, Mosely pushed him down with one foot. Now Houston saw it was the man called Popcorn. At the colonel's direction three men jumped in and pinned him to the ground.

It took no genius to add up the parts. The girl had found him sleeping. Popcorn's raping had caught up with him. Ordinarily that would have been the end of it. Houston would have faded back into his tent and given the incident a half hour to get over with. But this was his army, his people. And justice had to come from the top down or else it wasn't justice.

"What's going on here, Colonel Baker?"

Mosely whipped a glance at him. "By God," he said. "The man defiled a woman. We're going to stretch his bastard neck." He said it like a man eating chalk.

"Let's bring that fellow around to my tent," Houston quietly reasoned. "We'll do things right, Mosely."

Something in Mosely ignited. His eyes sparked. He had hatred in his blood, and to Houston's shock it was hatred for him. "Oh, we'll do things right, General," Mosely shouted.

People cheered. They crowded around. A bareback pony was brought up and a rope snaked up and over a tree limb. Houston saw Ned Burleson's face in the crowd and he was enjoying the predicament. Sherman arrived, and over on the left two more colonels showed up. It was a full audience.

"Stand down," Houston hissed at Mosely, still hoping the defiance was an accident. They could go to his tent and sort this out. Houston could jump up a court martial and within the hour Popcorn could be tried, sentenced, and swinging, and there could be a proper signature to the whole affair. Everybody would get what they wanted.

Houston gripped Mosely's arm, the kind of thing an older man could rightly do. "We'll do this in its proper order," he advised. He may as well have grabbed a wildcat.

Instantly, as if fighting off an attack, Mosely twisted away. When his hand came up there was a foot-long butcher knife in it. It surprised both of them. Mosely swallowed. He held the knife higher between them, like a man contemplating a barter.

"I know the goddamn order of things," he rasped. He was belligerent, but anguished, too. Suddenly Houston remembered Mosely's indecision and helplessness before the mob in Gonzales. He realized that it must have shamed his colonel almost to death, and that his indecision then wasn't going to be repeated now.

"Gig him," someone called to Mosely, deliberately unclear as to which they wanted to see stuck, Houston or Popcorn. One thing was certain, though. The knife was out. Mosely was going to have to use it. That was the imperative and Houston knew it. There might be no such thing as predestination, but the kind of code that came with a drawn knife was the next closest thing. He stared at Mosely through the bright blade.

"Mosely!" The voice crashed against their impasse. Still holding the stout girl, Molly stood facing them ten feet away, but with her eyes closed. Houston had once seen a granny shaman find her trance state that way in a dark Georgia forest. She was going to witch them. Molly ran her tongue across her lips like an archer whetting the feather. But when she opened her eyes and stared at her haunted lover, Molly said nothing. She didn't have to. Mosely remembered himself.

"First things first," Mosely said, and then he used the knife. He bent. With one stroke he sliced open Popcorn's pants.

"Don't you do me." Popcorn thrashed around. "I'll hex your babies and your babies' babies."

Mosely barked his annoyance. His baby was already cursed.

"Mosely," Houston said. He was frightened and sad at the same time. Molly had saved him, but he felt lost. He was losing Mosely. Mosely was losing himself.

The colonel dropped to one knee between the wide open, pinned-down legs. It took no longer than a good grip and a quick pull with the knife.

"Ah Jesus," Popcorn prayed with a shriek. "You did it."

Mosely dropped the palmful of flesh into the dirt and wiped his hand on his leg. Now that it was done, he seemed sick.

One of the soldiers poked the mess with a bare toe. "Ouch," he said, "nuts and pizzle, the works." Men and women were shouting jokes and taunts at Popcorn.

Now Three-Legged Willie appeared, his strange perpetual hilarity illuminated by the dawn. "Up," he said to the prisoner, "let's see you dance." But of course that wasn't going to happen alone. The three soldiers who'd held him down now boosted Popcorn onto the pony. Back in Houston's hometown in Tennessee, the hangman's fee was $2.50. This bunch was more than ready to do it for free. Mosely dropped the rough hangman's loop over the prisoner's head and cinched it tight. Over at the tree trunk, a helpful refugee woman pulled the rope tight and threw a couple half-hitches to tie it off.

The soldiers had to hold their prisoner on the pony so he wouldn't hang himself before it was time. The terrible wound between Popcorn's legs quickly painted the mount red and he kept sliding right and left, magnifying his agony. Houston wished for his pistols, one to shoot Popcorn, the other to shoot . . . someone. The faces in the crowd were hideous. Houston's hands opened and closed on empty air. He stood there horrified by his own inaction.

Three-Legged Willie let go of the pony's reins. The pony sauntered forward, no need for a gallop, and the rope came taut. Popcorn slid backward slowly across the wet horseflesh.

Many in the crowd had seen hangings. The children who were new to it wormed their way to the front or climbed into neighboring trees to watch. They were fascinated but nervous, too, not knowing what to expect or what was expected of them.

The hanging took longer than most because the tree limb bent and the rope was elastic with rain. Consequently Popcorn's bare toes could just touch the earth and his dying brain seemed to register hope. He pushed against the ground and the rope pulled him up then let him down and then he pushed again. Like that he yo-yoed up and down for several minutes, neither alive nor dead, just bounding between escape and surrender with his face going black and his eyes bulging.

"That's the way Colonel Bowie got the Mexicans to talk,

you know," Burleson said. "I watched him at it. Tie 'em up, then drop 'em down, then tie 'em up, drop 'em. Every one of 'em, they talked. Well, whispered."

"He's like a snap of popcorn himself," Willie said. The prisoner's hands and feet kept flexing and springing open. Every time he twitched and jumped the wound sprayed more blood. No one moved from the deep circle of witnesses.

"Goddamn it," Houston swore to himself. It was Horseshoe Bend all over again. Jackson had told his soldiers to count the Creeks by cutting their noses off, and that had led to every manner of cutting: ears, scalps, fingers, scrotums, heads. There had been tales of cannibalism. Lying in the dirt practically dead himself, Houston had seen their gory harvest. He'd never dared to ask the Old Chieftain directly about how he could have let the savagery pass. Of all the brutal things Jackson had done to gain and keep power, it was the one thing Houston despised him for. And now he had his own army. He was the same age as Jackson had been at the Bend. He had an empire to capture, a map to redraw, a people to rule. He was Jackson's protégé. And yet from the start he had vowed things would be different.

"If this is your notion of swift justice, Houston," Wharton spoke facetiously, "Lord help me from you."

"He is the most natural born dancer I've ever seen," Willie quipped, then sang a little ditty. "Hornpipes, strathspeys, jibs and reels/Put life and mettle in our heels." He jigged about on his crutch.

Popcorn's antics went on. His longevity drew admiring remarks. Someone introduced the possibility of freeing Popcorn now that he'd learned his lesson and reinducting him into the army, because "that man don't quit."

Abruptly Deaf Smith was among them. Moving swiftly, like a bird of prey, he got behind the hoicking gasping prisoner and wrapped his arms around the man's waist. The next time Popcorn's feet touched ground, the scout kicked the legs free. Then he leaned back and set his own weight against the rope.

The branch or the rope or both creaked loudly. The weight of both men against the noose was too much. Something had to give and it did. Houston heard the spinal bones pop loose and just as quickly Popcorn grew a ten-inch neck. His legs quit jacking. His hands and feet quit balling and opening. Smith let go. He stepped away with a set jaw, his grim duty done.

"For mercy sake," he said to them and walked off, disgusted. The crowd started to melt away. A few soldiers tarried to discuss dying. Some of the children took sticks and poked some more motion out of Popcorn's dead weight. The long shadow swung back and forth.

"What do you think, Houston?" It was Burleson. "Are they hungry enough when they start to eat their own?"

CHAPTER NINE

WHERE THE ROAD FORKED, there was a tree. Houston found some soldiers standing there gaping up at a dead buzzard stuck belly-out on a sharp twig. A roll of paper fluttered on a bit of string tied to one yellow leg. It was a Mexican custom—the dead bird, the posted message.

Two days ago Houston had sent Juan Seguín north to find General Gaines and his U.S. Army regulars. Now he untied the string to read Seguín's report. The square of paper was blank. Gaines hadn't crossed the border. Houston was on his own.

One fork led toward the Gulf. The other led north to Nacogdoches. Either way the Mexicans were going to chase and fight them. Through force of will he'd kept them out of harm's way for almost forty days and nights. Caution dictated they should aim for Nacogdoches, because even if Gaines didn't invade Mexico and come to the rescue, at least Houston's army could escape into Louisiana. But the army seemed bent on no escape. They seemed to enjoy trapping themselves in citadels and cul-de-sacs and baiting their enemy into attack. Recklessness seemed to be an Anglo-Saxon flaw.

Houston saw his prairie boy Tad hunkered down in the shade resting. Since discovering the general with a woman, he had made himself scarce. Houston had begun to hope the child had attached to the refugee column and made his escape from Texas.

"Which way?" he asked the child.

The boy stared suspiciously.

"I could flip a coin," Houston said. "Or you could say."

Tad shrugged. *Is this the final innocence?* Houston wondered. *To choose not to choose?*

As it went he didn't pick which way the army would turn. The general just sat beneath the buzzard on the tree and watched his troops make their own decision. Naturally they chose the path to apocalypse. They poured south along the trail toward Harrisburg and Lynchburg and the bayou country.

A soldier saluted with more enthusiasm than Houston had seen through the entire march. "I knew you had the Go Ahead, by gad, General."

The word passed down the line: They were heading south. Houston could hear them cheering far back in the trees. As they slogged past, their step quickened, their eyes glittered.

It was a strange feeling to see how his inertia gave them energy. At his weakest, they seemed their strongest. At his most indecisive, they were like steel. He felt transparent. It was a moment not without joy. He had become their vessel. He trusted them to guide him down the right path. Whichever path they chose, it would be right.

"Hurrah for Old Sam," they cheered.

The way children anticipate Christmas morning, Houston's soldiers could hardly wait for their battle. He had never seen men so seriously happy about the advent of bloodshed. These men were. He looked for the smallest hint of dread in them. They had none. They wanted the fight more than anything in the world. Houston concentrated on their glee and sudden kindness to one another and on the yellow sunlight that seemed to release more wildflowers by the minute.

Houston could see their seriousness by the way they'd begun harvesting cobwebs. Every place that might harbor a spider, men could be seen on their hands and knees like boys scrambling for parade candy, hunting up webs. When one got found, they would carefully detach the threads from the anchor points and pinch the web into a ball and store it for later use. There was no better staunch for a bullet hole or bayonet hole than spider silk.

There were other signs, other preparations for battle. One enterprising man turned a good profit hawking little vials of honey with gold filings from Spanish and Mexican pesos. He promoted the concoction as "instantaneous energy" and recommended his buyers imbibe it just before battle. Houston rode past another man preaching a diet of lead shavings as a form of bulletproofing, and saw several others devising little fetishes from feathers and rawhide string and pieces of animal bones. He heard a scholarly debate over seating their musket balls in six-hundred-thread linen—the same as Daniel Boone once used—versus patching with pieces cut from an ordinary shirt-tail.

With the heat of day some stripped to sleeveless leather jackets or went bareback and Houston observed that his men and some of the boys, too, seemed to be sprouting more fur by the day, growing thick mats of it on their cheeks and foreheads and the backs of their hands and shoulders. Some painted their arms and faces black, Creek-style. Men could be seen hardening their thumbnails in the campfires, tempering them like steel to gouge out the enemy's eyes.

The doctors made their own preparations. Even from a distance Dr. Labadie and Dr. Patrick were readily identifiable, for they'd taken to pouncing on every abandoned rag for bandages, tucking the loose ends into their belts and wallets and vests until they resembled tattered clowns. As they walked along the learned men debated cures and techniques and examined local plants for possible use as medicines. Houston rode alongside the two surgeons for a stretch.

"Ah, here, a second opinion," Dr. Labadie said. "Maybe you can tell us your preference, the calomel physician or the steam physician?"

Houston knew both types from his long search for a true healer. "Well, I've been calomized and steamed pretty profoundly," Houston said.

"You sound dissatisfied." Dr. Patrick laughed.

"I'll be most satisfied if you can save even one of these boys without the guesswork that has been practiced upon me."

"Guesswork is all we have sometimes," Dr. Labadie retorted.

"Unfortunately," Houston wryly agreed.

The army worked along the upper bank of Buffalo Bayou until a passage could be cobbled together. They changed over to the other shore with a leaky flatboat and rafts made of logs and house doors that still had the hinges on them, and continued on.

At one final boggy creek they found a stout new bridge of white and blond timbers built by the slaves of four brothers named Vince. After so much wading and ferrying Houston felt cheered by the dry crossing.

On the far side of the Vinces' bridge the army resumed its march. They found themselves upon a virtual island, long and wide and surrounded on all sides by waterways and a lake and swampland. The island was not quite flat, having a gentle spine running from left to right. The grass stood high and emerald green and the field sparkled with brilliant wildflowers. It was a fine day to be lazy. You would never have known they were hunting for war.

Houston had a sense that he and his army could have gone on and on under those languid sunbeams. He conjured up an image of Stephen Austin's painstakingly drawn map of Texas with its blank spaces and medieval notations "mustangs here" and its incomplete borders, and he tried to imagine where they might be and how far they might go. Forever, it seemed. Ounce by ounce they would lose weight and flesh, and finally disintegrate into puffs of wind that never reached an end. The Mexican wind could chase the American wind into infinity.

At the island's upper tip, where the road dipped into a dense pack of trees, they came face to face with the San Jacinto River. The road ran straight into the water.

The river was swollen thick with chocolate brown runoff. The waters placidly funneled toward the sea. They had reached Lynch's Ferry and somewhere among the thick humid shadows on the opposite shore lay the little town of Lynchburg. While Houston sat on his horse facing the river, his officers gathered around.

"Does anyone know where we are?" Rusk asked.

"Does it matter?" John Wharton said. Obviously he didn't know this place either.

"What now?" Colonel Sherman demanded. His shaggy red hair hung shoulder length and his nose had been sunburned so many times it looked like the pox.

"Let's circle round on the plain," Burleson said, "a big circle round and round until they bite our tail or we bite theirs."

"Head west," Mosely Baker declared.

Houston wasn't really listening. He was staring at the rolling water, remembering the raft he'd once escaped with. A squatter had sold it to him and he'd floated down the Mississippi, burying Eliza, forgetting the governorship. For days on end he'd simply drifted with the current, sipping whiskey, chewing tobacco, fishing. With such a raft he could slip away and leave the army to its infernal hunger and bickering and go search for a less difficult kingdom.

"No, we must cross the river," Wylie Martin advised. "We must draw the Mexicans on. Sooner or later, they'll catch us. And then we'll destroy them."

"But gentlemen," a voice spoke behind them, "we're already caught." Over one shoulder Houston spotted Private Lamar. The little warrior must have been dipping into his investors' purse of money, for he'd gotten himself a horse, a huge bay mare with white socks. He looked quite tranquil on top of his saddle.

"Mexicans?" Sherman asked. "There's Mexicans?"

"Right behind us." Lamar pointed back through the trees to the bright green savannah from which they'd come. The officers wheeled their horses. Side by side the colonels held their horses to the edge of the treeline, squinting into the sunlight. Houston shouldered his white stallion in among them.

Out beyond their fortress of shadows, the afternoon had been usurped by insects. Bees cleaved the heat waves. Cicadas buzzed. Beetles quietly rendered the horse and cow dung. Nothing else stirred out there. Paradise lay stunned silly by the yellow sun.

"I don't see a goddamn thing out there," Mosely said.

"They're there," Lamar said. He didn't bother to join the line of horsemen. He'd already seen what they were about to see.

Thirty seconds passed. Perhaps a half mile off a set of Mexican dragoons materialized like August mirages. They halted on top of the long green ridge—a ripple, really—that swelled in the center of the savannah. Their blue uniforms were scarcely larger than summer buds on a gentian. Even at this distance Houston could tell when one of the soldiers took out a telescope and glassed them.

"We've got 'em." Sherman slapped his fist against his palm.

"Who got who?" Rusk wondered. "It looks to me like we're the ones butt up against a river and nowhere to run."

"We've got 'em," Sherman repeated. "Now there will be a reckoning."

After a few more minutes the Mexican dragoons melted backward into the green field, leaving Houston and his army with emptiness to stare at.

"Look there," Rusk said to Sherman. "You scared them off."

"Now what?" Wylie Martin said.

Houston studied the terrain for military advantage, then gave up. The bayou's bosky foliage and the plain's flatness made this place as good as any other.

"Shall I prepare headquarters?" Colonel Forbes asked. Even his ginger whiskers looked excited.

Houston shrugged and pointed at the ground where they stood. He said, "Here will do."

Forbes gave a crisp salute. "I'll see to it immediately, General." He hopped down off his horse. Then he just stood there, at a serious loss. He had no flag, no staff of subordinates, not even a tent with which to establish the spot as anything but a patch of grass.

Houston touched his spur to Saracen's rib and started off along the edge of the shadows. It was up to him now. He had to find some shape in this shapeless swamp. There were no lines in the dirt to connect this impending battlefield, no maps to consult, no natural features that offered a logical defense, no physical reason to turn upon this point and take on the enemy here and now. There wasn't even a sense of geographic drama—a mountain, say, or a deep gorge. All he had was the soft hiss of the river and these flickering shadows among the live oak and Spanish moss. The river and the quiet messiness of the foliage reminded him of Horseshoe Bend.

Houston regarded the sky. Nothing much was written up there this afternoon, just the Gulf clouds bunching in the heat and the sun standing there and some blackbirds going through their mating jinks. Not an eagle in sight. Maybe tomorrow, he thought.

He rode among the trees and came across soldiers gaping out at the meadows, waiting for the horizon to fill with their enemy. "Easy, boys," he said, just to make his presence known. He saw Dr. Labadie sitting under a tree, priming his old musket. "You may prepare your hospital over there, Doctor," Houston said to him.

"Hospital?" the doctor snorted. Their tents had all gone

with the refugees, and so had one of their physicians, a pug-nosed fellow who'd decided he was in love with a farm girl. Their medicine had just about run out, too.

Houston rode on. All told the perimeter stretched a full mile along the crescent of trees. He got all the way to the end of his line of soldiers before the Mexicans reappeared.

To begin with the sound of their coming was muffled by the grassy rise and Houston blamed the cicadas for the strange hum. Then the notes got closer and took on the brassiness of trumpets. The music clashed sharply with the smear of humidity and the tangled swamp brush littering the view.

"I'll be," Houston said. "They're playing us a song."

"Yes," said Burleson, who had joined him. He was skittish.

"Have you heard it before?"

"Oh, yes," Burleson answered. "And, I'll wager it's the same tune Travis and Bowie and the boys danced to."

"A song of the people then."

"You could say so." Burleson smiled sweetly. "Them black hearts call it The Gueeo. That's their music for cutting throats. Can't you hear it? No quarter."

At that an old man with wide bony shoulders and a clay jug on a string perked up. "What you say?" he screeched.

His name was Jimmie Curtis and one of his daughters had lost a husband at the Alamo. Houston know Old Jimmie because he was the oldest man in the army and very probably its meanest drunk. It was said he'd despised his son-in-law before the Alamo fell. Ever since the fall, though, he'd decided there was more profit in loving the son and hating the Mexicans. They'd been listening to him for many long weeks now.

"They mean to kill us all," Burleson said. "Won't be no prisoners."

"Them?" Old Jimmie clenched his fists. "Them kill me? They kilt my Wash Cottle, goddamn 'em. I'll kill them bastards. I'll cut their goddamn throats, I will."

About then a cannon gave a muffled boom. They heard the unmistakable snake hiss of incoming grapeshot. Those who knew what it meant ducked or sprawled in the grass. The rest stood gawking.

The snake hiss turned to rattling as the scattered shot cut through branches and twigs overhead. Metal pattered against tree trunks. Leaves and old dried-out winter pecans came raining down on the soldiers, and those still standing hunched their shoulders up around their ears or ran around.

"Goddamn," Old Jimmie bellowed. "I'll kill them Meskins. I'll kill 'em."

"You, boy," Houston called out to a wiry child. "Get up that tree and say what you see."

The boy scampered barefoot into the upper forks.

"Soldiers and hosses and cannon," he shouted down. His voice was just breaking into manhood.

"How many soldiers?" Houston asked.

"More'n I can count."

Houston didn't despair. Things weren't always what they first appeared.

"How high can you count?" he thought to ask.

"Oh, twenty," the tree boy said.

"Well, how about their cannon?"

"How about it?"

"Is there just one?"

"One," said the boy.

"Where at?"

"Yonder." The boy pointed at an isolated grove of trees two hundred yards away. It stood off to one side of the flatness like an island. With that much for a target, soldiers started shooting randomly at the distant thicket. Their muskets popped ridiculously in the afternoon heat.

"Colonel Neill," Houston yelled at large.

A head popped up from the grass out by where the Twin Sisters, their two brass cannon, had been marooned. The head was followed by the whole lank brown form of J. S. Neill, who warily climbed to his feet. Houston calmly steered his horse out into the meadow.

"You heard that cannon, Colonel?"

"It's a goddamn twelve-pounder," Neill complained. "They can reach from there to kingdom come with a goddamn twelve-pounder."

"You see that thicket?" Houston asked.

Neill nodded.

"Can you place some grape out there?"

"You wouldn't let us practice. These cannon ain't been fired."

"Do your best, Colonel."

Just then a bumblebee or a hornet—something—slapped against Houston's left rein midway between his hand and Saracen's neck. Looking closer, Houston found a neat half-moon bitten out of the leather.

"By gum," Neill choked. His face pinched up. "The goddamn Meskins got snipers shooting at us."

Houston was out of practice at being shot at. But he wasn't about to show his alarm, especially not to Neill. The poor man was more convinced than ever that the Alamo was going to catch up with him.

"Never mind," Houston said. "Let's just rake that thicket there."

Under Houston's watchful eye they dumped in measures of powder, then plucked pieces of chopped iron scrap from an open barrel and slid them down the throats of the guns. They tamped the charges tight. Meanwhile a man with a face full of smallpox scars was striking a small fire in a nest of wet grass. Neill gave the word. Not quite together, but almost, two men took burning twigs and set them to the touch holes. There were two explosions and the Twin Sisters bucked on their makeshift carriages.

"Boy," Houston yelled up at the high branches of the oak tree. His sentinel was perched higher near the top like a treed wildcat. "Say what you see." Everyone went quiet to hear what devastation the Twin Sisters had wreaked upon their enemy.

The boy's report came back through the muggy air. "Don't see nothing," he said.

"Maybe them Meskins gone to siesta," one of the cannoneers cracked.

"I believe we kilt 'em all," his partner decided and patted the thick brass tube affectionately.

The rest of the afternoon went quietly enough except for the occasional boom of cannonfire. Every ten or fifteen minutes the artillery exchanged shots. The Mexicans consistently overshot the Twin Sisters, looping their loads into the trees. Mexican grape balls raked the upper branches, showering men with leaves and sometimes dropping upon them like hard hot berries.

Around five o'clock they took their first casualty, Colonel Neill. Out of some seven hundred soldiers, the Fates touched him alone. The shot sizzled among them, followed by the bleat

of a hit man. By the time Houston reached him, Neill was
stretched out on one side in a cradle of green grass. He had
blood on his hands and a bite stick in his teeth. The veins stood
thick on his neck while he tried hard not to scream. Dr. Patrick
had come out from the woods and was kneeling over him. Men
were standing in a somber curve.

"How bad off is he?" Houston asked, preparing for the
worst. It looked critical, all that blood and the soldiers' gloom.
Houston was awed. Poor Neill's premonitions had come true.

"He'll live," Dr. Patrick pronounced. He stood up and
cleaned his hands on a bunch of grass.

"But he's maimed."

"I can pretty much guarantee he'll walk again." The doctor
had the severity of a gravedigger. "My concern, frankly, is that
the colonel might sit funny for the short term."

Houston digested that. "You're not saying . . ."

Dr. Patrick played it just right. "Yes, sir. I'm afraid they've
shot Colonel Neill in the meat of his arse, sir."

The bite stick snapped in Neill's teeth and he yelled in pain
or humiliation or their combination. The soldiers' faces lit up.

"First blood," one cried out, "the dirty Meskins drew first
blood." They all started laughing.

Houston maintained a straight face. Glory could be a cruel
belle. "I suggest you remove your patient to the hospital," he
instructed Dr. Patrick. The comic relief was almost worth the
loss of Neill, but now he was without an artillery commander.
He looked around.

"You there," Houston said to one of the youngsters by the
cannon. Tad was among them but wouldn't meet Houston's
eye. "What's your name?"

"Ben McCulloch," answered a boy with a blond caterpillar
for a moustache.

"What's your experience with artillery?"

"All told?"

"Roughly."

The boy held up two fingers.

"Two what, son?"

"Two shots, General."

Houston looked at the others. "How about you all?"

A teenager with a goiter and a broken nose held up one
finger. His pinkeyed neighbor shrugged, and their third party

just stared with his mouth open. Houston returned his attention
to the first boy.

"How's your eye, Mr. McCulloch?"

"I was born in Rutherford County, Tennessee, General,"
the lad proudly answered.

"Crockett country." Houston had given up resenting the
congressman's deification.

"McCulloch country, too," the boy said.

"Well," said Houston. "Let's go ahead and make you the
gunny for this piece here."

"By God," the boy whispered.

"Now what I want is, every two times they fire at us, you
fire back one time. That way we save on powder but let them
know we've still got some teeth to our bite. Can you do that?"

"I reckon so, by God."

"All right then."

The two armies traded a few more blasts. Then a sentinel
in the tree—a new monkey, one who could count—announced
that the enemy was pulling back. He called down that the Mexicans had brought up a small mule train and seemed to be
stripping their forward artillery position of balls and powder.
For the moment the Mexican cannon appeared to have been
left without a guard.

Colonel Sherman came cantering out from the right flank
trailed by a small phalanx of younger horsemen, his lieutenants
and admirers. Among them rode Private Lamar with his half
smile and green spectacles.

"General Houston, sir," Sherman addressed him. "My cavalry wishes to go capture that Mexican cannon. That cannon is
naked out there. Until they return with their mules, it is ours
for the taking." Not far in the background Sherman's cavalry
was all ears and radiant determination.

Houston lowered a piece of jerky from his teeth, then re-
tired it to his jacket pocket for later work. "That cannon is
nothing but bait," he said. "They mean to draw us out and cut
us up."

"But you can't mean to wait for an attack, sir." It was not a
question.

Houston wiped his mouth, exasperated. "Colonel, besides
turning this army over to you, what can I do for you?"

Sherman sucked at his teeth for a minute. Clearly he had

promised his cavalry some action. "What about a reconnaissance patrol?" he asked. "We could at least go out and take the lay of the land."

Houston could see the horsemen eager and waiting, and allowed that a little bending wouldn't hurt.

"A reconnaissance," Houston said. "No more. If the enemy appears, I want you to return to camp immediately. Don't bother with their cannon. Do not engage the enemy. We can't afford to lose our cavalry."

Sherman and his horsemen mounted up and hurrahed each other, then streamed out onto the savannah. The golden sun was sinking onto the magnolias, casting sweet long light. With the right imagination, the dragoons looked like knights issuing into a fairytale battle. As they dashed forward the rest of the army cheered.

Almost immediately Sherman disobeyed. He made no pretense at reconnoitering the field, instead aiming straight for the thicket that sheltered the Mexican cannon. Houston cursed. There was nothing to do about it except watch and wait from the trees and hope that Santa Anna hadn't rigged a trap. It was too much to hope for.

No sooner did Sherman and his valiant cavalry crest the slight hill than they came to a halt and wheeled around and came galloping back down. Not fifty yards behind came the Mexican cavalry.

"Goddamn it all," Houston swore. This was exactly what he had dreaded, a battle in the open and with night only a few hours away. There were more Mexican cavalrymen than American, and they were better horsemen and mounted on faster horses. The span between the two cavalries eroded rapidly. The best that could happen now would be for Sherman and his men to swallow their pride and dash back into the safety of the treeline.

For a minute it looked like they might even exercise some wisdom. Sherman's cavalry sprinted directly for the sanctuary of the forest and the Mexicans slowed to stay out of range. But with an audience of hundreds, Sherman's men weren't about to admit defeat so easily. As soon as the Mexicans disengaged and started back across the savannah, Sherman rallied his men with an upraised sword and they spurred off after the enemy. Houston lowered his head in disbelief.

It went on like that for another half hour. The Mexican and American cavalries chased one another back and forth like puppies. Their warfare seemed tiny and irrelevant. For a while no one bothered to fire a weapon. They just took turns pursuing one another.

The Mexicans were armed with tall lances which further cemented the bizarre medieval tone. The advantage of the lances became clear when a half dozen of Sherman's men finally did fire their rifles. In order to reload, they pulled over to one side and several dismounted. It was what the Mexican lancers had been waiting for. They rode pell-mell for the dismounted Americans and would have skewered them, too. But Sherman and his other troops saw the predicament and circled back to protect their comrades.

Houston groaned. It was plain what was about to happen. The Mexicans had divided them into easy prey. A wing of Mexican cavalry detached to the left to engage Sherman's main body, while the remainder pressed hard to ride down the dismounted riflemen.

"Houston," Mosely Baker yelled out, "we've got to go get those boys." All through camp men were priming their flashpans and tamping charges down their barrels, ready to charge out on foot and engage the enemy. But if Santa Anna had prepared this much of a trap, he would surely have the rest of it ready to spring, too.

"No man leaves the wood," Houston thundered to them. "We will not be drawn out."

"But they need us!"

"We need them. We need them to quit the goddamn field," Houston said.

"But they'll be slaughtered out there."

"No one leaves the wood," Houston repeated. Sherman's game of tag had turned deadly. Once again men were going to have to pay the consequences for a foolish and insubordinate leader. First Travis at the Alamo and then Fannin at Goliad and now Sherman with his doomed cavalry; they were being erased from Texas. The Mexicans were simply obliging their suicidal farce.

Now the lancers speared one of the American riders. He fell out of his saddle, still alive but helpless in the grass. Nearby the Mexicans were encircling another of the riflemen. The man's horse had run off and they were on the verge of piercing him from three sides. From Houston's distance the Mexicans looked like sheepdogs cutting lambs out from the herd, one by one.

But then a champion appeared.

Out of nowhere Private Lamar came barreling across the plain on his huge bay stallion. The green grass parted. Lamar cast his horse straight upon a mounted Mexican dragoon. The bay's giant chest rammed the smaller horse and the Mexican flew from the saddle and his horse bowled over sideways, legs kicking.

Lamar didn't hesitate. He spurred his bay and headed into the pack of lancers surrounding the isolated rifleman. Again he used his stallion as a battering ram and for good measure fired his pistol toward the three lancers. One of the Mexicans pitched backward.

Before the Mexican cavalry could recover, Lamar curved back and plucked the rifleman up and onto the rump of his horse. Meanwhile the wounded American had gotten to his feet and crawled back into his saddle. Lamar caught that horse's reins with a low athletic dip to the side.

Leading one horse, riding the other, Lamar returned to the treeline. By the time he got to safety the whole army was cheering his name, and Sherman and his tired dragoons had decided to call it a day and come back to camp.

That night the happy camp celebrated Private Lamar's stirring heroics around their campfires. The wounded rider died, stabbed through the hip and bladder like one of Homer's terrible casualties. Houston couldn't find anyone who knew his name.

CHAPTER TEN

FOR WEEKS ON END Houston had slept three hours a night, no more, sometimes less, opening his eyes to constellations that were only slightly changed from when he'd closed them. Providing sleep came to him at all, he usually woke at two or three every morning and immediately got up, never waiting to see if sleep might find him again. Sometimes he spelled the dawn watch. It was he who beat reveille on the camp drum every morning.

But this morning Houston slept. He dreamed. It was an old dream. He heard a woman's voice, possibly his mother's, or his sister's. Maybe Rusk was right, maybe the belles talked to you from the other side. As always when she called for him, it was dark and starless, a geography of loss and yet hope. *Samuel,* the voice called. *Samuel.* She called his name—the name of God—and it seemed to echo from far away. By the time it reached him, though, the name's greatness had leached out. Its syllables dropped limp at his feet like a dead sparrow.

In his dream he gave chase. Whoever she was, she fled from his heart, from his capturing arms. His feet became hooves and he galloped. His hands became talons. He took wing and hunted her. If it was his pitiless Eliza, it seemed possible he could reconcile with her and have all his ruin and humiliation forgiven. If it was his mother, he could return from exile. If it was the Cherokee girl Tiana, or the lonely queen Mrs. Mann, he could put his wandering to an end. Whoever she was, he could finally go home. But first he had to catch her.

162

As always, she escaped. Houston was left alone. He groaned and burrowed deeper, hoping she would call once more.

"General." His name again, another of its manifestations. "General."

This time Houston came awake. He opened his eyes. And sunlight—brilliant, midday sunlight—blinded him. He had slept into the day!

Deaf Smith was kneeling beside him, dressed in a braided leather jacket that was too short for him. The old scout's sombrero hung against his back on a string, and the sun was lighting his orange hair so that he looked like some archangel with flames licking up around his kindly face. He was a fearsome sight and yet a welcome one.

"Mr. Smith," Houston whispered.

Behind Smith soldiers stood gawking in a distant clump. They'd grown used to being woken by their general. Their expressions at seeing him laid out flat in the dirt in the morning light ranged from curiosity to shock and fear.

"A hot time is preparing for us," the scout quietly reported. The worry sounded in his high voice.

Houston closed his eyes. He felt immensely heavy, as if pinned down. He tried moving his arms, but they seemed far away. Every finger felt tied to the earth. After a moment the sun warmed his blood and some of the weight slid away. He had slept! Houston couldn't get over that. He'd been waking in darkness for so long he'd started to feel like some nocturnal creature banished from the human race. But he was among his people once again.

He blinked at the brilliant blue sky and suddenly what had been missing all these weeks was no longer missing. Houston lifted his head from the pillowing coil of rope. Drafting on vapors high above the bayou, it was his eagle, returned.

"The sun of Austerlitz has risen again," he murmured. It was a morning like Napoleon himself might have wished for. At long last the eagle was with them.

"What's that he say?" a soldier sniffed.

"Hell," someone grumbled. "Who knows." The soldiers dispersed, no longer interested.

Houston rolled onto one shoulder, in toward his wound, and pushed himself to a sitting position. He folded his legs

Indian-style and lay his sheathed sword across his lap, dazed by so much sleep.

"Are you suffering, General?" Smith asked with concern.

Houston shook his head no. There was no suffering to this. His daze felt close to ecstasy. The world seemed remote and peaceful, similar to the garden at Jackson's Hermitage with its fruit orchards and long beds of roses and bougainvillea. But he didn't try explaining that.

"The enemy is increasing," Smith confided. "Santa Anna is getting reinforcements. I counted five hundred. But nobody knows except you now."

Houston struggled to match the scout's concern. "Who knows besides us?" he asked.

"I kept it to myself," Smith said.

But at that moment a horseman from Sherman's cavalry came thundering into Houston's camp. "The Meskins," he yelled. "Look, there's a thousand more Meskins marching in." The man pointed and sure enough, what appeared to be an endless line of dots was moving from right to left across the savannah's far skyline. It looked like a string of tiny ants.

Colonel Burleson heard the alarm and came stamping over, his long rifle in one hand. He was livid. "Goddamn it, Houston," he shouted. "Didn't we tell you, yesterday was the day. We could have fought part of them. Now look, we have to lick their whole goddamn army."

From the other direction Sherman and Mosely Baker and others came riding up. "If we don't attack on the instant, all is lost," Sherman declared. Houston noticed a little silver star Sherman had pinned to his collar, a general's star. He must have brought all the trappings of majesty with him from Kentucky. Now wasn't the time to confront the self-promotion, however.

"Give the go-ahead, let our men fall upon that line of reinforcements," Wharton demanded. "We can destroy them."

"We're outnumbered," Houston said. "It would be a disaster to attack now." Even as he spoke the line evaporated. The savannah was once more empty. Santa Anna's reinforcements had safely made it into the Mexicans' main camp.

"It will be a disaster if we don't attack," Wharton pressed. "You told the soldiers today is the day. Well I say this hour is the hour. We must attack."

"Did I say today is the day?" Houston asked. He honestly couldn't remember.

Wylie Martin shook his weapons in frustration. "You've made us fight you every inch of the way. Today I quit the fight with you. I take my fight to the Mexican."

"If we wait they will come to us," Houston said, knowing the officers would never agree.

"We will go to them," Wharton said.

"Boys," Wharton preached loudly. "There is no other word today but fight. Fight! Now is the time."

"Fight," Burleson seconded. His scorn was a clear warning. The colonels had decided upon mutiny if Houston restrained them one minute longer.

Houston grunted at them, weary of their brittle black cawing. He slipped part of his sword from its scabbard and ran his finger across the rust. "Then fight," he said. "Fight and be damned. But it will be on my word."

"When will that word be?" Baker demanded.

Houston looked up at the sun. His eagle had flown on.

"At one o'clock draw your men into a line."

Their agitation vanished. "Well, then," Wharton said, and rode off to ready his bunch.

"Maybe you'll prove a white man after all," Sherman dared to sneer. Burleson stalked off, the rest of them spurred their mounts away. Houston was alone again with his scout. Deaf Smith waited with his squint-eyed patience.

Houston turned to him. "I have a task for you," he said. "Go wreck the bridge."

"General?"

"Burn it. Or cut it down with axes. But we can't afford to have more Mexicans crossing over."

Smith considered the proposition. "They can still cross lower, down to New Washington, then come up."

"That would take some time," Houston said.

Smith spoke his real hesitation. "If we cut that bridge, there will be no escape," he pointed out. "Maybe some of us would get across the river. The rest would die on these banks."

"Yes," Houston said.

Smith started to ask a question, then comprehended he'd just heard his answer. Houston was indeed sealing them in with the enemy. By destroying the bridge Houston was eliminating further retreat. If the battle went poorly, they would die with their decision.

"You told me a long time ago, it's a sin to kill your command."

"But you heard them. They'll have it no other way."

"I don't like it," Smith said.

Houston didn't either. Part of him thrilled to the act of faith, though. There was a tale that Bowie had once shut himself into a dark house with another knife fighter. Only one man had emerged. This savannah bordered by hyacinths and slow water and yellow sunshine was that dark house. Here was their Alamo.

"I'm not asking you to lie," Houston said. "You can tell the men. Just wait until after the bridge is down."

"I will," Smith said.

One o'clock came and went without the army getting assembled. Sherman's cavalry was all mounted up and ready on the far right flank, and some of the infantry companies showed the beginnings of linear organization. But the remainder of the army was too excited to toe a line.

Everywhere soldiers bustled around for flints or balls or powder horns or good luck pieces, or just to go check on pieces of meat left roasting at their mess fires. No sooner would one decide he was ready than his neighbor would remember something he'd forgotten to do. Houston had never seen so many fidgety men nor so many needing to piss so many times. He finally had to tell them to quit going back in the trees and just piss where they stood.

At around three Houston started an inspection ride down the line. They had been on the trail for weeks—some of them, months—and during that time the army's numbers had vacillated wildly. Opportunists and glory hunters had swelled their ranks as high as a thousand when things were going well. Today Houston estimated there were seven hundred men standing along the front of the treeline. Another sixty or so were mounted to the far right edge where they could sting the Mexican flank. By arranging the men two-deep and spacing them out, Houston got the line stretched hundreds of yards wide. They were going to be attacking a fixed position of unknown strength and he wanted to keep his ranks thin enough so Mexican gunfire wouldn't gouge them too badly.

Houston rode slowly, measuring their chances man by man. He was not encouraged. Some of the men were walking skeletons, ravaged by the army's diseases and by the near famine they'd been surviving. Many had jaundiced skin and golden-yellow eyes and were barely fit to hold a rifle, much less load and carry one. Trembling with fever, a few stubborn souls looked like they were held upright by nothing more than the breeze and a few stems of grass. Here and there he noticed boys who had started the campaign as children and were now sporting little moustaches and creeping sideburns. And some of the grownups who'd begun this as vital men in their prime had turned into graybeards and gaunt scarecrows. Along with losing sleep and weight, they'd lost teeth, hair, and major portions of their clothing. No one among them looked whole.

The long march had changed them. Their physical decline concerned Houston less than how they had altered from what they once were. Two months ago these had been farmers and clerks and physicians and lawyers and laborers and walking poor. They had been fathers and husbands and sons and brothers. But just as the retreat and hardship had melted their muscles down to bone and sinew, so the unrepentant wanting—for land, for money, and finally just for food and a fire and a dry patch of sod to sleep on—had rendered them into something other than what they'd been. Houston could feel it in himself, a hardening that felt powerful and yet regrettable at the same time. He wondered what it could mean and knew he was about to find out.

Their eyes followed him as he rode along. Houston nodded to some, greeted others with a few words about their gun or knife or just said their name. *How many of you will I bury?* he sadly wondered. *Or will you bury me?*

He paused by the artillery. Young Ben McCulloch had pretty obviously picked his cannon gang from among his friends, little different from the schoolboys Houston had tutored in Tennessee. He ran a professional eye across the crew.

"Are you prepared, sir?" Houston asked the cannon master.

"She's loaded up, General." McCulloch pointed at Tad, who held a smoking torch. "Here's my fire. You say when and she goes."

"Good man. Tell me, does she shoot straight?"

"With them chopped horseshoes, she shoots straight plus some. I'd not want to be on the taking end of it."

"Nor me, Sergeant."

It took the youth a moment to digest that. "Sergeant?" he asked.

"I guess so," Houston said. "At this rate, you'll make general any day." The boys in McCulloch's crew were awestruck by what was going on, the promotion, the easy bantering between their peer and the general. "Why it could happen to every one of you gentlemen," he said to the other boys and got a blush out of the whole crew.

"I declare," one of them whispered.

"Carry on, men," Houston said. He gave them a little salute and rode on.

The army was getting highstrung and fractious. Up and down the line men were firing their rifles into the grass and the air. "Stop that shooting," Houston commanded.

"We're just clearing out the old powder," a soldier said.

"I don't care. I don't want one more trigger pulled until I say." But as he traversed the line, the soldiers continued their shooting. Farther on Houston reached Company D just as Mosely Baker was finishing up with a speech of some kind. He turned to greet the general. "I was telling the boys how to take prisoners," he said. "But I'm done. You can throw in, too, if you please. I believe they'd like that."

The soldiers had the bright eyes of starvation. Houston rustled through his old oratory, stirring together the kind of stew ministers dished up for saving souls—a pinch of pepper, a splash of vinegar, some gamey meat.

"Boys," he spoke, "we cannot hope that the bosom of our beautiful prairies will soon be visited by the balmy breezes of peace. . . ." But it was the wrong speech, Houston could tell. He cut himself short. The soldiers' faces had gone blank and resentful. There was a time for high language, and a time for brute, horse-gutting slang, and he had misjudged.

"The boys were just electing a color for our company flag," Mosely informed him. Clearly he was pleased to see Houston at a loss.

"Not white, I trust," Houston joked.

"Well let's just see," Mosely said and he reached inside his jacket. The men's eyes were glittering. Their jaws were set. Duelists had this look on the morning of settlement, a fixity that sharpened certain details and ignored everything else.

"Right here," the colonel said and drew out a square red rag. "It does seem to be that red got voted up."

Houston glared at the grinning colonel. His heart darkened. Company D had made a pact. They meant to kill their prisoners, a devil's work. He bent in the saddle and got closer to Baker's ear.

"No quarter?" Houston snarled. "That's a commander's decision, goddamn it. Don't you dare mount that rag on a staff, do you hear me."

The grin never left Baker's face. Turning to his company, he announced, "The general wants to give us our war cry."

"Hurrah, the general," someone yelled out.

"Give it to us," a soldier called. "We will smite them bastards. God give us strength."

"Aye," said Mosely. "Give us our word, Houston."

Houston straightened in the saddle. Their fighting spirit was stoked hot. He could throw water on it or he could hope for the best and trust in their humanity. They might look and sound like savages at this moment, but once the troops obtained victory, he felt confident they would show mercy. And if they lost to the Mexicans, the issue of taking prisoners was going to be meaningless anyway. At that point, mercy would be something Company D and the rest of Houston's army were on their knees praying for.

Saracen shifted from leg to leg. He swung his great head away from the flies. Houston looked into the faces of Company D and tried to read what was really in their minds. He searched for the right thing to tell them, something about not forgetting the men they were. When he spoke, though, it was only to stammer.

"Remember," he started. "Remember . . ."

Baker usurped the sentiment. "Remember the Alamo," he declared to his company. "Remember Goliad. Remember what the bastards done to us, and goddamn do it back to them. Remember, boys."

"Remember the Alamo!" a soldier shouted.

CHAPTER ELEVEN

IT BEGAN.

A thousand yards wide, the line of men let loose of the woods' edge to drift across the green savannah like thistledown blown by a child. There was no crouching or slinking or bellying forward for these brazen men. They moved upright across the open field as if they were invisible. They could have been the Redcoats walking into Old Hickory's guns at New Orleans, except they had no order to their ranks and talked aloud whenever a thought came to mind, whistling tunes to calm their nerves, brandishing curses and, more softly, prayers. Luckily the meadow dampened their language.

Deciding the two-deep formation was not for them, the men behind quickly skipped up into the front rank and the line fanned wider still. Where soldiers encountered puddles or hurried their pace or helped to push the Twin Sisters or paused to fix a shoe or tighten a belt or pick a burr from between two toes, the line bent and wavered. As they walked men and boys fiddled with their flints and hammers. Miraculously no one tripped and pulled his trigger. The dominant sound was of sick men coughing and wheezing for breath and of the grass whipping slickly against their pantlegs. Their military inexperience wrote itself all across the plain in a large messy scrawl. War had no poetry in their big hands, no elegance.

Houston rode well ahead of them, thirty yards in front, nudging his white stallion back and forth along the line, trying simply to keep them at the same pace. A mile separated them from the Mexican camp but it could have been all of Texas between them and any other human being, enemy or otherwise. The plain was empty. It was peopleless. Even the meadowlarks had quit singing.

Up ahead the savannah swelled so imperceptibly that the only way to actually tell there was an incline was the increasing heaviness of their two cannon. The artillery crews and various wagoneers had tied rawhide ropes to the gun carriages for pulling, but soon soldiers were having to push, too. There was a definite angle to the plain and it was tilted against them.

No one could say for sure what might lie on the far side of that rise. Houston couldn't imagine how a Mexican encampment ought to sound or smell. Even ahead of his troops, cleared of their stink and noise, he couldn't sense a thing. He was puzzled, too, that the enemy had no patrols out. It was conceivable that Santa Anna had crossed over the river or pulled back to another position overnight. What if they reached the crest of the hill and found no one left to fight?

The army went on shoving through the sunbeams and lush green like there was no end to the afternoon. Their immodest Liberty fluttered in the breeze. Her bare right teat rolled in and out of the folds. Someone had attached a belle's white glove to the very top of the staff and every now and then it filled with air and seemed to be pointing east toward Louisiana. The piece of red cloth that Company D had fixed to a stick disappeared. Apparently no one wanted to be troubled carrying it anymore. Houston told himself that the soldiers had put its grisly message out of mind.

Ten minutes went by. It seemed like an hour. The men broke a sweat. It gleamed like hog grease on their faces. Big white clouds scudded against the south horizon, a ghost armada docking upon the Gulf.

Without warning a horseman suddenly came dashing from the forest to their right. Dozens of soldiers threw their rifles up to their shoulders just in case the stranger needed knocking out of his saddle, but it turned out to be Deaf Smith. The old scout sped along the serpentine line. His Spanish pony's remarkable long tail streamed out behind. As he rode Smith gave his news to anyone who wanted to hear it.

"The Vinces' bridge is burnt," his voice squeaked at them. "I burnt it out. The bridge is gone."

Houston watched for their reaction.

There was a faltering. All along the line men missed a step as the scout went sliding past on horseback with his terrible message: Retreat was impossible. Smith's few words staggered their momentum. Like a field of grass caressed by a breeze, the line bent. For a moment it seemed the whole army was ready to stop and reconsider its extreme course. But then Wharton commanded the musicians to start their flute and drums.

It took the three musicians a minute to coordinate their rhythm. What finally appeared—more mud than song—was not a martial step but a popular tune about lovemaking. The momentary confusion melted off men's faces. The soldiers resumed their deadly march. Those who knew the words sang to themselves. Those who didn't hummed and grunted along.

Will you come to the bower I have shaded for you?
Our bed shall be roses all spangled with dew.
There under the bower on roses you'll lie
With a blush on your cheek but a smile in your eye.

The sight of soldiers—especially these anarchists and land thieves—marching into battle with romance on their lips charmed Houston. It made him believe more than ever in them. Only yesterday the Mexicans had played death threats to them. In return they were throwing a love song back to the Mexicans.

With no forewarning they topped the grassy rise. Houston was first. It was such a subtle prominence he didn't know this was the top until he was actually on it. To a man the whole army came to a halt on every side of him. The drum beaters quit and the flute's trill died with a whistle.

"I'll be goddamned," said a soldier.

The Mexican camp lay before them, no more than two hundred yards away. Spreading from their left across to the savannah's center, it looked a mile wide with white tents and beautiful red and green and turquoise blankets and serapes propped on sticks for shade and men and horses milling among the trees lining the bayou. Little brushstrokes of smoke rose from fires that had been banked for the afternoon. Except for some cannon near the midpoint and the long tangled breastwork made of single-axle Mexican wagons and chopped brush and tree branches and saddles, it looked like a traders' caravan.

Houston pulled out a telescope and searched in vain for sentinels or roving patrols. What few soldiers he saw were gossiping or lounging about, and not one was looking in their direction. A man appeared from a small lake in the rear, riding one horse bareback and leading another two dozen from their watering. In the whole camp Houston counted only five horses that were even saddled up.

The Mexicans were asleep!

"Can it be?" Houston asked Deaf Smith.

Smith kept silent. He wasn't the sort to enjoy surprise, making him the sort who didn't like to show it. But the scout was surprised. Houston could see it in his lips which moved like an old man's trying to read a primer to himself.

Down the line Mosely Baker summed it up. "We caught 'em in their goddamn siesta."

Houston went on studying the camp, trying to unravel its details. He sniffed at the air. Folded within the woodsmoke, the scent of corn and chiles came to him, a lunch of tortillas. He could see where the reinforcements who'd arrived that morning were fast asleep in a meadow to their left. No doubt they'd been marched through the night. Their stands of muskets were clumsy and many had fallen to pieces.

Houston slowly comprehended the opportunity. The Bible and the *Iliad* thundered with such moments, when events cracked open under the weight of their own predestiny. It seemed incredible to him, but the gods had wrapped Houston's army in clouds and transported them here to fall upon these Mexicans in their magical sleep. There was no other way to explain it. This was meant to be.

With a hiss that ended up ringing, Houston drew his long sword from its scabbard. "Now," he cried out to his army. "Fire upon them. Now's the moment. Fire away!"

What followed was supernatural. Not a shot banged out. Not a man pulled his trigger. There was silence.

Houston looked around at the army, stunned, thinking they must not have heard him, for they surely hadn't come these hundreds of miles just to have a look at the Mexican army and turn around.

"Fire," he bellowed again. The advantage was theirs, but only for the instant. They had the high ground. They had surprise. They were prepared and the enemy was not. But all of that could change in the space of a heartbeat.

"Goddamn you. Fire away!" Houston yelled at them. It was as if he were a ghost.

Instead they moved down the rise, slashing through the grasses with their whip-whip of long legs. Right and left men and boys looked to their pans to double-check their powder, some blowing out the old powder and splashing in new and closing up the pans. The sound of seven hundred rifles cocking clattered like locusts. Then they stabbed down the rise in cold silence, each man making for the point closest to him.

The long line wrapped around the camp. Like wolves they started loping faster, some even with a big-footed sideways gait. And still no one fired. The Twin Sisters screeched on their ungreased axles, rolling downhill now, moving hotter and hotter. From here on there was no stopping.

Houston dug his spur into Saracen's side, thinking that if he could just get far enough ahead of the tide, it might look like he was in command of it. With the wind in his eyes and beard, it felt like an abyss had opened up and he was plunging over the precipice.

The first fifty yards vanished in a blink. Saracen strained to outstrip the pell-mell warriors. The stallion's muscles sprang and gave and seemed ready to sprout into vast wings. Flanked with equal halves of his army, Houston felt like his horse was already flying. He bent toward the pommel, and held his sword out.

Saracen reached harder. White foam lashed Houston's face. The earth shook beneath the stallion's great hooves. Houston tried braking his horse just to reassure himself of his control. But the giant animal ignored the rein. If anything, the horse deepened his stride.

The army closed on the camp in a din of pounding hearts and chattering teeth and footsteps falling like fists on a drum. The breastworks, so solid at a distance, became an intricate weaving of wood and leather that wasn't solid at all. Suddenly, up close, there were a thousand holes in that puny wall. The holes gaped as actual gateways.

On the far side of the breastwork the few Mexican soldiers

on their feet began to notice the havoc descending upon them. Houston saw them look up from their card games or pieces of beef and tortillas or their afternoon conversations. Like men peering up at a cloud that's just blocked the sun, their faces took on a gentle inquisitiveness. Even when they saw Houston with his enormous wings spread on either side the soldiers didn't startle, not initially. Houston watched one man in particular, a slender young man standing near the cannon with a book in his hands, and he was touched by the reaction. The young Mexican wasn't alarmed. He seemed fascinated and actually marked his place before closing the book.

When the gunfire came it crackled in a long ragged popcorn volley on Houston's left side. He shot a glance down the line. The far flank—infantrymen in the 2nd Regiment—had nearly tagged the nearest corner of the breastwork, down where the Mexican reinforcements had gone to sleep. They would be waking now.

The Twin Sisters boomed. Chopped scrap and horseshoes flashed wide of Houston on either side, sizzling through the fat summery air. It pattered against the breastwork and Houston saw three Mexicans promptly vanish, caught at head level by the metal hail.

Now the rest of the army added their musket and rifle fire to the breaching. Their muzzleloaders banged and popped and roared. Some snapped on damp powder or bad flints. Any general in the world would have preferred his army to walk in order and fire all at once, in effect creating a huge, moving shotgun. But that was out of the question with these men. Houston was grateful just to have them pulling their triggers at random.

The air whined and zipped. Houston realized he was too far in front of the line because most of the lead was coming from his own men. He hauled on the reins again and almost sliced his thumb off. But the charging stallion had lost its mind to the sheer motion and refused to be harnessed in.

Houston cast a glance back at his army and saw, to his horror, that the horse had taken him directly in front of one of the Twin Sisters. The barrel's mouth had no lines or angles supporting it. It was just a black hole surrounded by concentric circles and on top a flaming torch descending to touch it off. *So this is how it ends,* Houston thought, *in a mess of iron.* There was no time to duck nor even feel sorry for himself. It was going to be over that fast. But in the next instant he saw a head jut up from behind the carriage wheel and the torch lifted away from the touch hole. It was Ben McCulloch. The boy snatched off his slouch hat and waved it madly at his general.

Each of the Twin Sisters boomed a second time. Brushed by invisible fingers, the grass quivered in waves that expanded outward from the smoking muzzles. Again Houston heard the mangling loads beat a devil's tattoo against the breastworks and the cart walls trembled and a saddle slipped from the construct.

A Mexican soldier poked his handsome head above the breastwork, for all the world a ground squirrel stretching above his hole. It was the wrong moment to get a view of the *norteamericanos*. That quickly Houston saw the long Indian hair lift backward and the beautiful face jellied with gore. Immediately it was gone. With a single blink Houston would have missed the awful sight altogether. But he had seen it. And now his fear became terror.

Inside the breastworks hundreds upon hundreds of soldiers were rising up from the grass and running about in disarray. They jostled one another and yelled and pointed to the north, the dread north. The soldiers rushed about, grabbing muskets from stacks and tripping toward the wall of carts and branches under their officers' screamed directions. Houston saw a small forest of gun barrels lower onto him. Once more he tasted the certainty of his own annihilation. On a command the Mexicans fired. Their volley was even less disciplined than the Americans' had been. It erupted with a loose sporadic cadence. The balls sang in a thick curtain that passed fully ten feet overhead. Houston breathed his relief. It was true what they said then, that the Mexican army was taught not to aim.

The Mexican volley did have one effect, though, and that was to turn Saracen away from the enemy line. Houston had grown up hearing stories about men whose fiery steeds had carried them right into the enemy camp, delivering them to torture or ridicule. At the first puff of shot powder Saracen veered away from the breastworks.

Without slowing his magnificent pace the stallion now went galloping in a bead for the western sun, equidistant between the Mexican and American lines. His long legs pumped at the earth. The beast seemed ready to run all the way off the battlefield and over the bayous and across the prairies into deeper Texas. For just an instant Houston imagined galloping all the way to the Pacific Ocean. *I'll go,* he thought to himself, and he leaned closer to the white neck.

But their fantastic course abruptly closed off. Up ahead one of the Mexican cannon belched a load of grape. Not missing a stride, Saracen looped around and reversed his direction, this time bolting for the east. It looked to Houston as if he was doomed to be carried hither and thither at his horse's fancy.

"Hurrah, Old Sam," someone shouted loud. They thought Houston was rallying them.

Back and forth Houston raced in the crossfire. Both sets of foes had found their trigger fingers now and Houston found himself bracketed by walls of gunfire on either side.

Wide streamers of dirty white gunsmoke began to fill the emerald plain. The smoke blotted out the light, then parted to rake them with sunbeams all over again. But the darkness was fast overwhelming the light as the smoke clotted in greasy clouds overhead. Less than two minutes had passed since the Americans had started down the rise, enough time for a soldier to shoot and stop and reload three or four times. Whenever they felt like it Houston's soldiers came to a stop in the grass and yanked out their long ramrods and eyeballed measures of powder from their horns into the throats of their gunbarrels or poured it premeasured from paper cartridges. A number had squirreled extra balls in their cheeks and would spit one into their fingers and seat it on the patching. A quick jab of the rod, a splash of powder in the pan, and they were off again.

It all happened willy-nilly. They ran wherever they wanted, fired at whatever interested them. As his horse careened back and forth Houston scanned his army and saw nothing but lone men acting out their own individual conceits of combat. Nowhere did he see more than three men working in unison. For the most part they performed like a nest of mice chasing after sunflower seeds.

Saracen continued his terrified dash between the gunfire and Houston simply hung on, every now and then lifting his sword overhead for the sake of appearances. Over where the 2nd Regiment was making contact with the breastworks, the dozing Mexican soldiers had woken to a nightmare and panicked en masse. Houston saw the Mexicans' entire left flank

crumbling in rout. The reinforcements—hundreds of them—
were crowding backward into the main camp like sheep. Not
one in ten had a weapon in his hands. Adding to the chaos the
Mexicans' bareback horses had broken loose within the camp
and were stampeding in a wide crescent, trampling tents and
fires and anything else in their way. The long string of tethered
hobbled mules was inspired to a wild frenzy of hopping and
kicking. The confusion was contagious. Other portions of the
Mexican army were beginning to run, too.

But long sections of the breastworks were still abundantly
manned. There was still fire in the Mexican belly. Houston
could feel their heat on the side of his face. Some of Santa
Anna's soldiers had seen more combat in revolutionary Mexico
than most Americans ever dreamed about. Providing their army
didn't melt away in complete panic, these veterans were perfectly capable of turning back this free-for-all offensive, and
Houston knew it. The Mexican resistance—which Houston
measured in the quantity of firepower—seemed particularly
potent surrounding each of the cannon emplacements. As Saracen carried him irresistibly to the east, Houston spotted Tom
Rusk galloping across the meadow with his buckskins flapping,
trailed by Dr. Patrick. The doctor suddenly doubled over in
the saddle, clutching at his stomach. His beaver hat toppled,
followed by its gutshot owner, and Rusk reined short. "We've
breached the flank," Rusk yelled at Houston. "We're inside their
line."

Then Rusk leapt to the ground and knelt over his fallen
comrade. The young man's tall hat had landed upright on the
ground and stood beside him like a faithful dog while he
writhed every which way, tangling his legs in the grass. The
young man cried out, "nothing, nothing, nothing." It was suc-
cinct as Houston went galloping by, unable to stop.

All along the breastwork the army was closing with the
Mexicans. Those who had any wind left were howling and
screeching and yelling Remember the Alamo, Remember Goliad. The ones who knew better didn't say Goliad, but the proper
name La Bahía, which they pronounced Laberdy. *Remember*,
they shouted. The notion that memory could justify and even
vindicate them was like acid liquor.

The battle coalesced on every side of Houston. It flooded
every sense. Wherever he turned he was in the thick of it. The

scream of men and horses and gunfire orbited him. Gunsmoke thickened into an ugly yellow fog. It buoyed him like a myth. He began to lose his fear. Suddenly it was so easy to believe he was untouchable, because no dreamer ever died in his own dream. And outside the borders of his ferocious imagining there was only Texas and Texas was desire. She had killed off a thousand men, but for him her arms were wide open. The truth of it surged through his heart. She had selected him. He was the chosen one.

For the first time in his entire life Houston felt certainty. He had been in revolution since childhood, mounting one ambivalence after another against the world. It could end now because it could begin. He was freed. Against that even the possibility of death lost its value. He was freed of it all.

Houston quit sawing at the reins. There was no use trying to slow whatever was going to happen. Instead he leaned into it and gave it speed. With both legs he clutched hard at his stallion. He dug his single right spur into the ribs and cried, "gee haw," and slapped at his flank with the flat of the sword.

Saracen jumped to clear a keg. It was an ecstatic leap and Houston filled it with his sense of utter liberation. The horse kicked loose of the earth and thrust high with his giant head and Houston thought, Man and beast, they were joined together now. They had become his eagle.

In fact it was the stallion's way of dying.

They began to descend. Saracen's leap had not taken them very high at all, but it seemed to Houston like an infinite descent. Time slowed. He heard the air whistling out through holes in his stallion's great lungs and the blood frothed up like sea spray. It riddled his calves and thighs with red foam.

My God, I've killed us. He had punctured his horse with the spurring, Houston was sure of it. But then, more rationally, it came to him that they were bullet holes. With the realization came two, then three more bullets. The balls struck like an ax bit seating deep into soft wood—big, solid, chunk-cutting sounds. The horse quivered.

And still they fell. Texas loomed beneath them. The land took on a transparency. Houston saw the underworld through it. They were going to be swallowed. His rapture turned to dread.

Saracen landed gently. His legs crumpled under him but

somehow the animal kept upright, tumbling neither to the right
nor left. Houston found himself deposited onto his feet. It was
stupefying, to be one moment slinging sunward upon a huge
winged horse and the next to find himself reduced to standing
stock-still upon the earth. His flesh weighed gross and heavy on
his bones and he felt captured all over again.

Saracen died the way a mountain dies, his bulk occupying
the meadow like some immovable geological fact. With their
furious ride across the battlefield forever a thing of the past,
the animal's body cooled by slow degrees. Houston stood there
and watched. The stallion didn't scream or roll or kick at the
sky. Hot blood pumped out through the holes perforating his
smooth white rib cage. The vast head sank. All Houston could
think to say was "We came a long way to get here." He murmured it. Then the horse was dead.

The battle returned to his senses in bits and pieces. The
double bang of muskets sparking the pan and igniting their
load roared in a wide sheet of sound, mostly from the American
side now. Men scampered about yelling blank excited syllables
at one another.

Houston looked around him, dizzy and a little sick to his
stomach. The world seemed larger than when he'd been
mounted. The view from the saddle had been an expeditious
one filled with swooping urgency and a million quick images.
On foot, though, it seemed the horizon arced all around like
the lip of a vast bowl. His feet felt bound by the soggy ground.
Time moved sluggishly down here. And as his soldiers came
advancing through the high grass they looked to him like gam-
boling, famished predators moving upon a sick calf. The deft
elegance of the raptor was gone, replaced by whatever it was
going to take for them to quit being hungry.

The wave of Americans stormed past him like the cold
north gusting. Houston called out to them, relieved to be in
their midst. But no one stopped. No one showed the slightest
recognition of him. They surged around him and went on,
leaving their general flatfooted and with his jaw agape, stranded
there beside the shattered hulk of his horse. Three men in
ragged city clothes galloped past on farm horses caterwauling
at the top of their lungs. One jumped over the dead stallion,
clipping Houston's saddle with a hoof. Houston had to leap out
of the way or be churned under. Old Man Curtis loped by with

a hatchet in one hand and in the other a musket with smoke pouring from the muzzle. "You kilt my Wash Cottle," he screeched madly. "Remember Wash Cottle."

The Mexican breastworks were useless against the tide of wild men. The more nimble among them vaulted over the collection of sticks and saddles and boxes. Most just shoved and scrabbled their way through as if the piled-up wall were a drift of powder snow. Houston took a few steps one way, then returned in a daze to his horse.

Glancing down, Houston saw the rust-stained dress sword hanging loosely from his right hand. He hefted it back into his grip and twisted around in a circle, wondering what to do next. Saracen's death had robbed his momentum. There seemed to be nowhere for him to go and nothing for him to do. Alone he stood there frozen and immobile while the rest of the solar system slung around and around him.

"General," he heard, and there was Colonel Rusk on horseback, leading up a second mount by the reins. The colonel had blood to his elbows and the horse he offered to Houston had gore smeared over its neck and shoulders and all across the saddle.

"Are we carrying the day?" Houston asked. Rusk seemed not to hear him. Houston pulled himself up into the bloody saddle, seating himself with a wet plop.

"Hell yes," Houston grunted, feeling considerably better with a horse situated under him and with this elevated vantage of the land. At eye level with Rusk now, Houston saw tears streaking the colonel's grimy cheeks. Dr. Patrick must have died. How many other casualties might be lying in the grass, Houston couldn't guess.

Rusk didn't wait for another word. Vengeance showed like lockjaw on his square face. He kicked his horse and bolted off, leaving Houston to investigate the battle's progress. He'd lost all sense of the army's direction and timing. With the sun buried in the thick sulfurous blanket of gunsmoke Houston couldn't remember how long the battle might have been raging, nor even which way their camp lay. He wandered about, chewing at the gummy smoke.

The breastworks had been shattered. Hundreds of holes had been shouldered and kicked and rammed through the loose construction and Houston's army was deep inside the camp now. Soldiers—both Mexican and American—were running everywhere. The stampeding horses and mules had chopped dozens of Santa Anna's small slender infantrymen to bones and rags. Officers' tents had been plowed underfoot and scattered campfires had spread into the wet grass, where they smoldered with thick white smoke. The livestock was running in giant revolutions and the humanity swirled in crazy paths. The maelstrom defied all prediction. Houston couldn't determine who was winning and who was losing. He wasn't certain how victory should have looked.

To the far left, down where the 2nd Regiment had overrun the sleeping reinforcements, men in buckskins and homespun were circulating through the grass, every now and then bending over to worry at things on the ground. They seemed casual in their motion.

But near the center, where the Mexican cannon had been placed, the battle was still a pitched contest. Under the calm direction of a tall Mexican officer, artillerymen and other soldiers were trying to hold off the enemy long enough to jam another load of grapeshot down the tube and fire. The officer's uniform jacket was open and his long silver hair hung like a lion's mane. His men scrambled to obey, but they were losing against time. Perhaps a hundred Americans had surrounded them and suddenly they were pouring gunfire into the position. The Mexicans pitched and blew backward and sideways, raining blood and bits of flesh on one another. They fell against the caisson wheels and hugged and slapped at the cannon barrel, screaming and praying.

Somehow the silver-haired Mexican officer was left standing alone among the ruin. Neither running nor flinching, he simply folded his arms, and waited for the American riflemen to finish frantically reloading. Something like a smile crossed his face. Houston needled his horse to a sprint, making straight for the officer. Here was a rare man worth preserving. Empty-handed, he could look into a gunbarrel and smile and wait.

"Hold your fire," Houston yelled at his men. He reached the outer ring of shooters in time to knock one rifle off its mark with his sword. The rest cut loose at will. The balls knocked the officer ten feet and nearly cut his head off.

Instantly the Americans swarmed over the artillery with butcher knives in hand. Even shot to pieces some of the Mexicans were still moving, but not for long. The Americans fell upon the bodies, two and three and four to a man, and their knives and gun butts slugged down and up and down. Elsewhere short brown men and boys in pieces of blue and white and red cotton uniforms were scampering about, some toward the lake behind camp, some toward the timber and bayou, some even toward the American camp. Most had tall gaunt pursuers who ran after them screaming and shouting.

A Mexican boy suddenly materialized from the grass and dashed straight against the right shoulder of Houston's horse. He was slight and his impact barely raised a twitch. A deerfly would have gotten more attention from the horse. The boy bounced backward, then scrambled to his feet and stood in place. There was not a hair on his smooth walnut face and he looked barely twelve years old.

"That one's mine," a big man cried out. Houston remembered this fellow. He was a farmer from Georgia who had cried one night talking about his sweet wife and red soil. "I seen him, he's mine." He slashed through the grass with his old musket at hip level and pointed at the child's head.

"Leave that child alone," Houston ordered.

The farmer glowered at Houston, then recognized his general. An ugly joy crossed his face. He didn't object, just let his rifle muzzle drift up from the ground so that it was trained on Houston. It was a lazy accidental kind of motion, but there was no mistaking the knuckles squeezing white around the stock. The man waited curiously to see what Houston was going to do about it.

"Get that goddamn gun off of me," Houston said.

The farmer looked down at his gun and feigned surprise at its direction, as if the thing had a mind of its own. Then he swung it back toward the Mexican boy and coldly pulled the trigger. The ball passed through one thigh bone and shattered the second thigh, too.

"*Madre de Dios*," the boy shrieked. He fell in a pile of limbs into the grass.

"Goddamn you," Houston said to the farmer.

"Remember the Alamo," the farmer crowed hoarsely.

The little boy reached his arm up from the grass. "Me no Alamo," he pleaded.

The farmer yanked a huge scoop of a knife from a beaded

sheath and bent over the boy. Houston raised his sword to strike the man down, but when he swung it was with the flat of the blade. The big farmer didn't flinch. Houston tried to bring himself to run the man through, but couldn't. He turned away from the gutting and rode slowly across the plain.

The battle was no longer a battle. It was a hunt. Everywhere Houston turned his soldiers were tracking and seizing prey. They pounced on the slightest movement of grass, scything it away with their gun butts or with knives and swords. They uncovered Mexicans crawling away or lying wounded or on their knees praying for salvation or just for their souls. The few who had muskets in their hands immediately tossed them down and threw their arms out in surrender. Most had no weapon at all.

Houston led his horse through the carnage between curtains of noise that was even thicker than the gunsmoke. It was a hideous passage through sights and sounds he'd figured were closed off to him forever. Horseshoe Bend had been mean and ugly. But at least there the Creeks had fought to the end. They had been a foe. Here the Mexicans were no longer even fighting. They were simply dying.

Houston was stunned. It was beyond his comprehension how quickly his army had spun out of control. The men had never truly been in *his* control, there had been symptoms of that all along. But he'd believed they were at least in control of themselves.

"Cease fire," Houston shouted as he rode among them. It was the wrong command. Bullets still hummed through the air, but the crackling of gunfire was moving off to the south and east, over in the direction of the bayou. Here on the savannah and in the camp Houston's men had largely given up on the tedium of reloading. Instead, in their madness, they had turned their guns around to use as clubs. A soldier never clubbed his gun unless he was desperate, for it nearly always broke or bent the weapon. But the only desperation Houston could see here was a race to feed their growing blood frenzy. They moved like hounds baying up a panther or a bear.

Five men in a mélange of tattered city clothes and buckskins discovered a Mexican cradling his dead comrade's body. He was weeping and rocking the gray corpse and it was clear from their identical faces that these two had been brothers. Houston spurred his horse and bore down on the scene. From far away, it seemed to him, his voice reached in among the circling men.

"That's enough now," he said to his soldiers. "We have won. Texas is ours."

"Not yet it's not," one retorted. "We got to break their defiance."

"They've had enough," Houston said.

A fellow with wide fat cheeks and a pistol said, "Whatever you say, General."

"That's what I say," Houston said.

Houston pulled his mustang's head up, unexpectedly proud of himself. They were going to listen to him. It was in his power to stem this killing fever. But no sooner was his back turned than the pistol went off. Houston swung around and the one Mexican was slumping across his brother. His bare feet were still twitching as the soldiers set upon the pair of brothers with knives, working them like a pair of beeves. In shock Houston drifted on, going nowhere in particular. He had become a tourist in his own war.

"Houston," someone yelled at him. It came as an accusation, perhaps, or a warning, or an identifying. He heard the rifle go off and glanced to the right. Down by his foot a bluebonnet toppled off its stem, sliced in two. Houston saw the flower tumble. The bullet snapped a hole in his boot. Inside the leather he felt his ankle explode.

"Ah God," Houston roared. He reached down for the boot. He needed to tear it away and empty out the pain. But the little mustang was screaming and already falling. It was all Houston could do to keep his sword—the damned sword—away from his face and hope the horse wouldn't crush his shot ankle.

The little horse dropped hard, flailing with her hooves to fight death's talons off her belly. She was too late for that. Her belly was already open. It emptied out. Yard after yard of slick viscera dumped loose like eels escaping. When the mustang got a smell of her own insides, she screamed again, and Houston shoved himself loose before she could roll over on him and break his spine or climb to her feet and bolt off in a death gallop, dragging him caught in the stirrups.

He hoicked and pulled himself through the grass, putting distance between him and the mustang's slashing hooves. When he was far enough away Houston jammed his sword into the turf and, with both hands hooked under his knee, pulled the wounded ankle closer for a look. There was a finger-sized hole in the boot right above the Achilles heel and blood was pumping through it. It seemed entirely possible that his foot had been severed in there and might come loose with the boot. He decided to leave the boot on.

His vision went black for a moment and he slid backward into the grass. Then he noticed the butterflies. There was a flood of them just above the grasses. Agitated by the war or just by the advent of sunset, hundreds, thousands, of orange and black and red and bright blue butterflies were beating at the sunlight, hovering at thigh level all across the plain. They could have been a million flowers set free to fly about, it was that pretty. Houston took a breath. The air was sweeter down here, even with the stink of fresh horse gut. If he closed his eyes, the smell of spring grass almost returned him to the days when a child named Samuel had crawled among the cornstalks and rye. He opened his eyes and there, high overhead, hung a canopy of smoke and killing and manhood—legends, remote and epic.

A lithe childlike figure came running through the grass and Houston thought it was a rescuer, but the boy was simply running past.

"Wait," he called, then, more hopefully, "Tad?"

Since that wasn't the boy's name anyway, he didn't slow down. Houston lunged and caught him by one tattered pantleg. Now that the fight had gone hand to hand the Twin Sisters were of no more use and their crews had abandoned them to get into the thick of the fight. The child had a knife in one hand.

"I need a horse," Houston said to him. "Go catch me a horse, son." It wouldn't do for him to be afoot, nor to be chasing about trying to wrangle a mount. In the middle of storm and strife a commander was supposed to be commanding. *At the battle of San Jacinto men fought and died and Houston caught himself a pony.* Maybe Crockett could have turned such a thing to advantage, but farce wasn't Houston's strong suit.

The boy tore away from Houston's grip and growled, crouching in the grass. Houston took his hand back, unnerved. A grim incandescent gleam lit the boy's face and there was not a hint of recollection in his bloodshot eyes. Only an hour ago— no, less than that—Houston had teased this boy and his crew into blushing. It might as well have happened in another century, on another continent. The way fever victims sometimes did the child had boiled over. The world had become a stranger to him. At any rate the general was a stranger. The boy raised his knife, a thin clasp blade. Houston saw blood on the metal and dripping from the boy's knuckles.

"Oh, child," he murmured sadly. Whether it was seeing Houston's white skin or hearing words spoken in English, the boy decided against killing him. He lowered the knife and rushed on wordlessly. Houston felt heartbroken.

Now the pain began. Like a mean dog that lets go just to get a better grip, the pain slipped a little, then tightened with a vengeance. It bit harder, then bit some more. Houston put his head back. He wanted to howl but didn't dare. *I am their general.* The reality wouldn't let him go.

Men sprinted by in the high grass. He heard their laughter. Children playing tag on a summer eve. Houston almost called to them but didn't, not sure if they were friend or foe.

"Found him," a man sang out happily. The whip-whip of more legs through grass joined the finder.

"Four inches?" one of the men offered to his partners. "Anybody wager?"

"Five," someone said.

"Five then. But hold that little pilgrim tight. This will take some scientifical doing."

A man's voice turned into a woman's. The shrill cry rose higher. What was remarkable about it was how long and unbroken it went on. Houston stared dumbly at his bloody palms. Tears welled up and fouled his vision. He blinked them away and saw a tiny butterfly fixed on the toe of his boot, resting.

The woman's scream ran out of air. It became a man's voice again, Mexican. *"Perdónelos,"* it said. *Forgive me?* Houston wondered. Then he realized the man was forgiving his captors for whatever it was they were doing.

"One more inch," the gambler urged.

"Goddamn it," someone complained.

"He's took the dark leap," another voice observed. "Wasn't but four inches."

"You lose, George. I told you. Wrong rib."

George grumbled. "He was too skinny, by God." They turned the Mexican's body loose and it flopped heavily on the ground. Houston's father used to bring home meat that way, near dusk, dumping it off the rump of his horse. It would drop to earth with a finality that said the spirit was gone, the animal would never move again. Houston closed his mouth. The butterfly was gone.

"There's another," someone yelled and off they went, slashing through the grass. They left Houston alone. He didn't dare call out to them. He remembered Robinson Crusoe choosing solitude over the company of pirates and cannibals.

The mustang's eyes were wide open. After a while the big rib cage quit and the viscera quit pumping. It was none too soon for Houston who found himself getting irritated that life would hang on so long and for no good reason except the pure suffering.

"Goddamn it," he groaned at his leg. But at least he'd found a safe refuge. With cannibals and cavalrymen streaming back and forth across the battlefield he had this cup of grass to call his own. They could have their battle. If not for the demon gnashing on his leg bone, Houston might have gone to sleep.

"General?"

Houston started. Behind him, practically overhead, a rider was sitting with his back to the sun. Houston squinted in the smoke and flashing sunlight. Blood and gore glistened on his slick leather suit.

"Mr. Smith?" Houston said.

"I thought sure we lost you," Deaf Smith said. A tinge of grief still painted his voice. Smith's bay snorted then stretched his columned neck down and took a mouthful of grass from beside Houston's head.

"Here I am," Houston said.

Smith dismounted. He wrapped the reins around his fist, taking no chances on getting stranded in this ocean of grass. "Is that the whole of it?" he asked, pointing at Houston's ankle wound. The way he said it diminished the wound. It didn't lessen the pain, but the pain took on an odd poverty. Suddenly Houston knew he was going to have to rise up and reenter the dangerous sky and try to lead these rebellious souls to some sort of salvation.

"I've finished resting," Houston said. He took Smith's hand on one side and the bay's stirrup on the other and hoisted himself to standing. The effort almost cost his consciousness, but he managed to stay upright until the fainting passed. He pulled his rusty sword out of the wet ground and surveyed the battlefield. Where two thousand men had been joined in a semblance of battle there were now fewer than two hundred in view. Houston looked all around. It was as if the savannah had swallowed up both armies.

The hiss of bullets had largely stopped. Houston could hear wounded horses screaming and thrashing in the grass. Others just stood in place, tired from so much running around. Most grazed peacefully, though a few hung their heads and bled through the nostrils. Houston's questioning look prompted Smith. "They've gone to the bayou," he said with disgust, "back in there by the lake."

Houston didn't know what to make of that. He heard a clattering of gunfire from behind the trees Smith pointed at. Here on the plain, though, some of the quiet was beginning to return. Maybe the killing hadn't been so bad after all.

And yet Houston realized he was wrong. They hadn't won Texas. They hadn't gained a peace at all. They might have won this day, but only over a fraction of the Mexican army. After today's fight his soldiers would be tired and disorganized and their weapons would be broken from clubbing. They had just made themselves eminently vulnerable. They were in greater peril than ever before. At this very moment a hundred armed Mexican soldiers under a single good leader could sweep them from the field.

"Are you sure the Vinces' bridge is down?" Houston asked.

"Burnt out," Smith said.

"But you're sure," Houston reiterated. He scanned the western reaches for any new Mexican battalions. There was nothing to see. But he was losing blood, and he'd struck his head when the mustang fell, and the smoke was thick. A fresh new army could have been three hundred yards away and invisible to him.

"I must speak to the men," Houston said. "I've got to warn them, get them organized." His head ached. He wanted water.

"They won't hear you," Smith said. "Maybe later. When they come back to us."

"Come back?" But Houston knew what the old scout meant. The bloodlust had to cool. Suddenly Houston slumped. The string went out of his good leg and he barely managed to catch himself against the bay's saddle. He was panting and lowered his head. His boot was filling with blood faster than the bullethole could drain it. Blood seeped over the top.

"Take my horse, General," Smith said. "Go back to camp. You've got nothing more to do out here. When it's over and done with they'll stray home."

Smith was right. The battle was finished. It had been finished almost before it began. The rest was sheer homicide. It couldn't even be called vengeance, what was going on. Almost none of these men had known their so-called brothers at the Alamo and Goliad. They weren't killing out of any genuine spirit of revenge. Remembering was just an excuse. They were killing because no one could command them not to. And that meant Smith was mistaken. Houston had things to do out here.

"If you'll oblige me with just a little push, Mr. Smith." He couldn't stand on his right foot long enough to get his left in the stirrup. With Smith's help Houston crawled and humped his way into the saddle. Smith handed up the dress sword, which had acquired a sideways crook in the metal.

Houston set off through the veils of smoke, aiming for the lake. Along the way he discovered where many of the Mexican soldiers had disappeared to. In a sense the earth *had* swallowed them up. Singly and in bunches they lay twisted and heaped and stretched out in the grasses. Passing through the shattered breastworks, Houston found men so shot up that their flesh hung in tatters. He looked for the Mexican general who had stood by his cannon so nobly. He was able to find the man only by his mane of white hair, what was left of it. Over in a pile of boxes what was left of a human body had been stripped and mutilated. Someone had lifted the richest part of the scalp.

Deeper in the camp Houston could tell where his men had lost patience with reloading. The corpses were hacked with butcher knives or their skulls and faces were caved in. Houston told himself this was war. He insisted upon it. But it didn't work. This was an outright massacre. Forever more it would be the face behind their mask.

Houston searched for the body of a white man, any white man. He found none.

At his approach dozens of his soldiers lifted up from their looting and knife work. They didn't look to see who the rider was, only to judge if he could be killed. They emerged from collapsed tents like vultures drawing their heads out from a buffalo carcass. Several were cutting away dead men's noses and ears, no different from what Old Hickory had ordered at Horseshoe Bend. As if questing for some deepest forbiddance, some of the corpses had been opened up and their livers and hearts stolen. Houston weighed how much this might be his own fault. Could it be that he had failed them, that they were innocent and didn't know better? Perhaps he should have instructed them about the temptation.

I will cut down the man who makes a meal of this, Houston tried to declare. But his voice wouldn't come out. He could scarcely breathe. He rode on. What looked like a windfall of sticks and twigs littered the ground. They were British muskets—Mexican issue—that had been thrown to the ground by fleeing soldiers. The discarded weapons cracked and snapped underhoof, so much kindling.

The trail of bodies led on and on, through the timber, out to the lake. That was where Houston found the rest of his army. The Mexicans had fled to the water's edge with an eye to crossing the bayou and escaping into the far thickets or following the San Jacinto downriver to the ocean. Maybe some had made it. From the looks of things, probably none had.

The problem, once again, was illusion. What appeared to be a narrow span of shallow water was actually deep and rimmed with swamp mud. No better mantrap could have been devised. Here was proof that God didn't belong to the Papists, not the God of mercy anyway. The killing Houston had witnessed on the savannah didn't begin to compare with the horror at this false crossing.

Like sheep bunching at a gate, the Mexicans had bottlenecked against the water and their enemy had come right behind. Utterly desperate the Mexicans were leaping and crawling and wrestling over one another in an effort to get away. The muddy beach had sucked many to a standstill, where they'd been bludgeoned and stabbed and shot. Between the blood and the bayou slime that plastered them, the Mexicans looked less like humans than amphibious creatures hatching out by the hundreds. Their slick limbs tangled and writhed. They had no faces, just muddy masks with holes for eyes and mouths.

Houston had never heard such howling and screaming in

his lifetime, and that included hearing Red Sticks burned alive at the Bend. Hell wasn't just a place of fire after all. It was a place of water also, and Satan's gang wasn't demons but the very men Houston had embraced as children.

The Americans lined the banks. The killing was festive and hilarious and neighborly, exactly like a turkey shoot. A good number of them had thrown away their own guns and taken up the British muskets left behind by the Mexicans. They picked out targets and bet on them and congratulated one another on what fine shots they were. One man killed another sharp-shooter's target. The two men goddamned each other, but in a friendly way. No matter how many they shot down, there were still many more Mexicans to kill.

Houston watched from the trees, his mouth slack, his heart dead. He was shattered. This was wrong. This was evil. Was this Texas?

Over and over Mexicans in the rear of the press turned around and tried to surrender. They were clubbed down or cut open. Only a few still carried their muskets, and those were wet and useless.

The muddy flats teemed with Mexicans dragging them-selves toward the water. Bodies with their heads and limbs shot away stood at grotesque attention, jutting upright among the reeds. The mud was paved with many more bodies, which helped the Mexicans following to reach the water. There they simply died in greater numbers.

The water housed its own terrors. Much deeper than it looked, the narrow channel had drowned or slowed countless men who now floated on the surface or sank. It was awful to see hands reach up from the depths and catch at struggling soldiers and drag them under, too. The heads of dead and living men bobbed up and down in the water and these provided the shooters with a greater challenge. The blasted remains stuck above the water like bony chalices. In the center of the channel men and horses had piled so thick in the water they formed a bridge. It too was deceptive. The limbs twitched and moved and snared men trying to climb across, and then they too were shot and added to the bridging.

Houston knew his men would keep shooting until they ran out of powder or the sun set or there was no one left to shoot.

Someone had to put a stop to it. But how? Would these animals even understand human language anymore? He told himself to heel Smith's horse forward, to trumpet his wrath upon his own soldiers. But his spirit felt snapped. He shrugged in despair, then shrugged again. *My children.* More minutes passed. Houston sat paralyzed in the shadows.

When Tom Rusk came onto the scene his hat was gone. His hair was slicked back and he was in a frenzy. Houston was sure he'd come to avenge Dr. Patrick's death. But Rusk's grief had changed, it had somehow reified.

"No more," he shouted hoarsely. "Cease your fire."

He caught a man's musket barrel with his sword and the gun went off, making a little geyser in the water. He hooked another man's barrel and rode his horse into a pack of marksmen, knocking one flat in the mud.

"These soldiers have surrendered," he yelled. "They are prisoners."

Three soldiers took aim at Rusk. "Go on now, Colonel," one of them warned.

Rusk shook his sword at the would-be assassins. A rangy man with a sandy bush for a beard lowered his rifle and grabbed at Rusk's reins. "Let loose," Rusk said, "let loose or I'll kill you."

"Ha," said the man and he yanked the reins left, turning the horse sharply. He pulled a knife. For a bad moment Houston thought he was going to reach under and slit the mare's throat or else hamstring the colonel. Rusk thought so, too, Houston could tell by his frantic twisting in the saddle.

Houston broke from the trees. "You," he shouted at the soldier. That was all he could think to say.

"Sam," Rusk yelled, "we must stop them." He tried to kick his assailant away. But the soldier let loose of Rusk's reins and stepped back and swung his knife in a wild arc. He slashed the horse across the rump, a deep long slice. Rusk reached out to strike the assailant with his sword, but the mare's eyes turned backward at the pain and she tore away, her reins snapping loose.

"Sam," Rusk cried as he got carried off into the distance.

Rusk's lonesome cry cut at Houston's despair. "Cease fire," Houston called. "Do you hear me? They are my prisoners."

"No such thing," said a man with a beard pink with brains.

He had appalling lost eyes. But Houston refused to look away from them. He made himself search the man's face until he found, under the smoky filth, a spray of boyish freckles across the man's squashed, broken-down nose. It was there, the innocence, and Houston spoke to it.

"The fight is gone out of them. The fight's gone out of all of them."

"Says who," the freckled man retorted.

"I say so. And I'm your general."

"So you are," the man said. "Then I'm sorry for you, General."

Houston flinched. The rest of the men were peering at him through dark sockets, their teeth white in blood-soaked beards. They looked almost incapable of speech.

"You give us a good slay," the freckled soldier said. "It's a shame you can't see it through."

His neighbor spoke up. "These are hard times. You go back to camp, sir. We will finish things for you." Houston recalled the man was a store clerk in Sherman's militia.

"Aye, sir, you get gone," someone else said.

Another in the bunch raised his rifle and snugged it tight against the skull of a Mexican on his knees.

"You can't," Houston said. The backbone had fallen out of his voice, though. He was simply playing out his part in this thing, the same as he'd played it through the whole campaign, the same as these men were playing out their parts. Homer was right. Men were puppets in the hands of gods.

"Can't?" said the soldier.

The rifle went off. The Mexican's face flapped open like a Chinese box. Houston didn't look away. He told himself he had no right to look away. Some of the pieces patted softly against Houston's cheek.

"Let me deliver you," Houston murmured. But they had returned to their killing and he sat there, invisible. Houston had thought he was done with retreating. He'd told himself this battle would mark the end of his running away. From here on, he would face down the dictator that was his own memory.

But he had lost.

Without another word of protest Houston gently guided Smith's big bay away from the slaughtering and turned his back on his men of faith, his buckskinned crusaders, his heroes. Shoulders hunched against the gunsmoke, he returned to the American camp a mile away. There he lay down against a tree to watch the sun flare above the western magnolias and night come on.

CHAPTER TWELVE

LEG-WEARY AND POWDER-BURNED, with knuckles scraped and fingernails broken and bearing the nicks and slices and bruises of their frenzy, the men straggled back to camp under a three-quarter moon. Houston lay against a live oak and watched them straggle in, his skull propped against the gnarly bark. His ankle throbbed. He didn't move.

Some limped from twisted knees or sprained ankles. Some arrived emptyhanded, too tired or forgetful to carry the weight of a gun. More than a few showed up naked above the waist, their shirts having gotten clawed away. Their eyes were bright red from the acid gunsmoke. To a man they looked dazed and hollowed out.

Those with the strength left threw chunks of timber on the banked fires and blew the embers to flaring. The camp lit up. Men wandered through the trees trying to remember where they'd stashed their possibles that morning. In the space of an afternoon, their whole world had changed. They had left their past forever. The men didn't hurrah or yell their triumph. Seeing the army as it pieced together in the firelight, any stranger would have guessed these soldiers had just lost their battle.

One man circulated through camp with words of cheer. Houston could hear his voice. "Boys," he declared to packs of men, "this was the day. Our children and grandchildren will hail this as the greatest day of the nation. They will say the hand of God reached down and struck our dark-skinned enemy.

196

They will say that we have brought light to the heathen. Today is the day we have won all Texas." Then he moved on through the trees to find a different group and say it all over again. Houston saw him passing a fire. It was Colonel Forbes.

Incredibly there were prisoners. A Mexican officer had gathered enough of his troops together on a spit of bayou to make a formal surrender. Despite the hours-long slaughter, or possibly because of it, a small contingent under Tom Rusk had accepted the surrender. Quickly, at double time, Rusk had herded the prisoners back to the American camp without being spotted by his own army. Now the prisoners stood in a makeshift corral of tree limbs and bonfires. They were guarded over by a handful of soldiers draped with pistols and shotguns on ropes and holding beeswax tapers in their hands. Between the heat of the bonfires and the soldiers' hands the candles melted fast, dripping wax over the men's fists.

Judging by the guards' menacing glares at the huddled prisoners, none seemed to realize they were guarding the captives from their captors as much as against their escape. But the killing fever had petered out. Houston's men were too exhausted to make a run on the corral. Just as Deaf Smith had predicted, the wild soldiers had returned to their humanity. For tonight, at least, the prisoners were safe.

The men were too fatigued to eat what little there was: some bits of cow, some ears of raw corn. But thirst raged among them, and even those ready to collapse in the dirt managed the extra distance to the river behind camp where they drank and drank and drank. Just as thirsty, the prisoners cried out for water. In their bracelet of bonfires they looked like damned souls begging for relief. Except for an occasional American who took pity and tossed them a gourd of water, their pleas went unanswered. The guards grew angry with the noise and demanded quiet. But the wounded were out of their heads and kept on screaming for water and for their mothers and for Maria.

"Water those men, goddamn it," someone finally demanded. Houston recognized Burleson's voice. When no one responded, Burleson got to his feet. "Some of you, help me."

After a while a figure rose up from the ground and collected gourds and with Burleson began shuttling back and forth from the river to the prisoners. Their path took them close to where Houston lay. The firelight revealed Burleson's helper, the thin child with a goiter, one of Ben McCulloch's cannon monkeys. Houston wanted to ask what had happened to Tad, but didn't. He wasn't sure he cared anymore. Burleson quit after two or three trips. The boy with the goiter didn't. He labored mechanically for what seemed like hours, his bare feet slapping the dirt. Water spilled from the gourd holes, soaking his clothes. Little by little it washed some of the blood from his pants.

"Can you spare some of that?" Houston begged on one of the boy's passages.

Gradually the battle smoke cleared away on the night breeze. It was a relief to smell fresh air, but with the smoke gone the mosquitoes pounced on them, adding to their misery. A nest of ants had found his leg. The pain overrode the tickle of their creeping, but he could see them coating his pants and boot. Ordinarily the thought of insects crawling in and out of the hole in his ankle would have bothered him. From long ago he remembered the maggots, white and alive, in the meaty gouge of his groin wound.

The stars came out and Houston stared up at them with his mouth open. There was a design up there but he just couldn't seem to find it, not upon the tides of his delirium. He faded back and forth from one battle to the other, from one wound to another. It was strangely conceivable to him that he might still be that young soldier and that he was lying near death at Horseshoe Bend and everything since was just a dream. He reached deep inside, demanding some proof of which Houston he really was, the boy or the general. High overhead, deep in the carved moon, Old Hickory's skull smiled down on him. "I'm your bastard now," Houston murmured.

All over again he saw his mother's gaunt face, practically scarred by the tears she had wept thinking him killed under Jackson. He raced down wilderness traces, through ramshackle settlements, up rivers dotted with squatters turned yellow with disease, across a land of ambitions, into the halls of Congress. He kissed Eliza, held the long, heavy hank of golden hair in one palm, saw her turn away from him. His effigy burned in the streets. His exile turned to water, the Mississippi, a raft, and there was Bowie again, whispering *Texas, Texas.*

"Texas," Houston hissed at the stars.

Many hours passed and on every side Houston listened to wounded men babbling in English and Spanish. At some point he felt his head lifted off the knotty root and water slid between his lips and down his dry throat. He choked weakly and opened his eyes. Rusk was kneeling over him, gourd in hand. His face was nearly black from gunsmoke, and for an instant Houston was reminded of the Cherokee's Negro clown who had once parodied him.

"Am I dying, Tom?" Houston whispered.

Rusk had run out of tears to weep. "Here," he said. "This is for the pain." He held out a small green bottle with a bit of rag for a cork.

"I found this in Junius's kit," he said. "Laudanum. It's more opium than alcohol, I think."

Houston sipped at the liquid, then took some more. "How far is the dawn?" he asked.

Rusk averted his eyes.

"She'll be a beauty," Houston confided.

"Rest, sir."

"But the dawn . . ."

"Soon," Rusk told him. Then he was gone.

I have no one to pray to, Houston realized. *There is only memory.* Covered with insects, he let his eyes close and joined with the voices of his past.

"General."

Houston woke. The sun was coming. Along the eastern horizon the stars were disintegrating in a peach blush. It was going to be a hot day. Strangely the bonfires were still blazing away. Any other morning they would have died down by now. Even exhausted the men had kept the fires stoked large. Houston thought that odd.

"It's me, Labadie." The surgeon turned slightly and the firelight and dawn showed he was painted with blood from his side whiskers and bald spot to his brogans. Houston remembered the wounded. The doctor would have been attending the casualties all night long.

"This boot must come off," Dr. Labadie said.

"Don't go ruin it with a knife," Houston said.

"General, the boot's ruined, and I must see your leg."

"It's the leg I mean. No cutting." The pain he could stand, and the pathos, too. Certainly there were enough one-legged warriors in the world to keep him company. What Houston could not abide, even drugged and half delirious, was the thought of more mutilation. He'd lost one wife, in part over the wound in his groin. If ever another came along he needed all the wholeness he could summon, and that included two legs.

"Now, you know, General," Dr. Labadie tsk'd. "I can't say yet."

"I can," Houston pointedly informed him.

Dr. Labadie pulled a butcher knife from a back sheath and held it up. "I can wrestle your boot, sir. Or you can let me use this."

Houston took a deep breath. It was going to begin now. Once the boot was open the doctors would have him. The suffering could go on for many years. Houston had forgotten the pain, it had grown so constant. But when Dr. Labadie slid his knife inside the boot and began sawing apart the leather, Houston jerked up onto his elbows and tried to back away from it all.

Colonel Forbes joined them. "It was a great victory," he brayed hoarsely. Houston smelled the liquor on him. It took a moment for Colonel Forbes to see what Dr. Labadie was doing. "General," he said, "you're shot."

"How many wounded do we have?" Houston thought to ask.

"Wounded? I don't know." Colonel Forbes spoke up. "Our latest count shows we lost four of our men. Dead."

"Four?" Houston marveled. Could it be? He must have seen a thousand bodies on the field yesterday. And they had lost only four?

"I'm doing my best," Dr. Labadie said to Houston.

"Of course," Houston assured him, very close to vomiting from the pain.

"Courage, sir," Colonel Forbes said. He staggered.

Finally the doctor laid aside his knife and pried open the boot. It wasn't so bad to look at. There was no gruesome twist to the ankle. The foot was not hanging by a few tendons the way Houston had feared. The bullet had entered on the side and torn the skin open. What showed was mostly gristle and bits of white bone. Houston had seen far worse.

Dr. Labadie took the leg in his hands and held the ankle

higher to the light. A month of rain had rotted the bottom of his pantleg. Soaked in blood, the raggedy edge looked eaten by something alive and mean. "This will hurt," Dr. Labadie said.

Houston tried to imagine his leg was a hundred miles away, that it was someone else's. Dr. Labadie gripped the ankle and hoicked it this way and that. He was firm and vigorous in his inspection. Houston roared. He jerked his leg away. He had thought their long march and all the nights spent sleeping in the dirt and mud would have hardened him to pain. His softness mocked him, though. He emptied his stomach onto the dirt.

"Help me," Dr. Labadie told Colonel Forbes. "I need to poke for scraps of metal. It's a mess in there."

The colonel had grown pale. "Courage," he muttered. He didn't move to help.

"For God's sake," the doctor said. Drawn by Houston's shout, other men had gathered to watch. Houston felt awfully far down in the middle of their circle, like a lamed rabbit surrounded by giants. "You," the doctor said to one, "come over here."

Through the nausea and haze of pain, Houston recognized his young cannoneer, Ben McCulloch. "It's me, sir," the boy said to Houston.

Houston summoned his dignity. "I may buck, Sergeant," he said. "You hold tight."

"I will," the boy said, and hugged the leg a little closer.

The knife went in. Houston gasped at it. He tried not to let the men see his pain. He told himself they didn't deserve his agony. After ten minutes he would almost have preferred amputation to Dr. Labadie's meticulous probing. The doctor made physician noises. His knife—McCulloch's scalping knife —scratched against the exposed bone and worked between the gristle. Spotting a piece of shrapnel the doctor picked at it, worrying it up through the hole.

Dawn broke with Dr. Labadie still at work. Houston was drenched in sweat. He watched a shiny black beetle creep through the weeds, a long meandering journey that finally brought it into the light of day.

"Copper," Dr. Labadie pronounced, holding up a bit of shrapnel. "A new development over lead. It goes to poison after a while."

"Inhuman," Colonel Forbes said.

Dr. Labadie quit digging. "I'm tired," he said. "This will take surgery, I'm afraid."

They had him now, Houston thought. One surgery would lead to another. They would whittle and pare at him and when they were finished he would have scars on top of scars and another wound that wouldn't heal.

While Dr. Labadie bound the ankle in rags, Houston asked about the prisoners.

"I'm pleased to inform you, General, six hundred enemy are in our hands," Colonel Forbes reported. "I'm even more pleased to say that by subtracting that number from the Mexican muster list, we seem to have killed nearly six hundred fifty. That figure will climb as their wounded die off."

"Hurrah," Dr. Labadie woodenly stated.

"Not since the invention of gunpowder has modern warfare witnessed such a miracle," Colonel Forbes insisted. "It's a sign from God. We were destined to this."

Houston licked his lips. Destiny? He would have spit, but all the sweating had dried him hollow. "Which group is Santa Anna with?" he asked.

"Sir?"

"Is he a prisoner or is he dead?"

"The devil escaped. Deaf Smith has taken a patrol out tracking."

Houston weakened. He lay back against the tree root.

"Colonel Forbes," he continued, "you will detail a party to take stock of the enemy camp. Get a full inventory of the spoils. Round up their livestock. Collect their weaponry. Bring their goods and supplies to this camp."

"Yes sir."

"One other thing," Houston said. "I want no plundering."

Colonel Forbes looked shocked. "These men are patriots," he protested.

"Goddamn your patriotism," Houston whispered. Overhead the leaves were blending to solid green. He fought the weakness. There was too much that needed doing for him to go slipping away like this. But he lost consciousness anyway. His old dreams flooded through. She appeared. She fled. The seduction and escape went on and on.

Houston woke to a name being roared through camp. The name trailed off across the bayou like old thunder and he was too late to hear anything more than that it wasn't his name. Beyond that nothing was certain. He was disoriented, unsure if this was even an awakening.

It was dark and the bonfires were roaring and snapping and the ants and mosquitoes were everywhere. Out of the corner of one eye Houston saw his lower leg bound in bloody bandages. His seat was wet and he smelled urine, his own. There were more fires than last night and they were bigger, downright huge, and beside them lay quarters of cow or longhorned heads ready to be cooked. Here and there Houston saw canvas tents that had been brought from the Mexican camp and erected among the trees. Dozens of skinny mules and ponies stood hobbled in the shadows.

A good number of Houston's soldiers were wearing pieces of Mexican uniforms with red cuffs and shoulder boards, many with gaping holes and slashes in the blue cotton. Many were draped with beautiful serapes or carrying the more exotic weapons they'd picked up, long, polished lances and straight-bladed sabers. One gentleman had on a helmet with a Grecian crest of horsehair and white trim and a giant hole blown through its rear.

A day had passed, then, obviously a very profitable day. But for all the raucous costume-ball of new acquisitions, the men had a strangeness in their eyes. They didn't look joyous, not even the ones who were drunk, and there were plenty of them. Ordinarily they would have been joking and bragging and bartering at a time like this. But something had happened, Houston could sense it.

"General." It was Moses Bryan, his doe eyes large and bloodshot. He lifted Houston's big head to the gourd and gave him a long drink.

"A little more," Houston rasped. Rivulets poured down his whiskers, streamed across his neck. He held on to Bryan's arm and emptied the gourd onto his head. It was brackish and warm in his mouth but cool on his face and that meant he was feverish. Houston made an effort to get his elbows under him. He gained a few inches, then the strength went out of him and he dropped flat onto his back again.

"You're weak. You've been out of your head, talking all day."

He lay still and let the blood return to his brain. The dizziness passed. "Did Smith find Santa Anna?" Houston asked.

"A group of Mexican dragoons got all the way to the Vinces' bridge. Santa Anna was with them, but he slipped away. They're still looking." Bryan paused, then went on.

"They've been killing everyone they find along the path. Smith thinks you're dying. He said the Mexicans have killed you. Last evening they cornered a Mexican officer who said he was Santa Anna. Smith cut his head off with a saber. But it wasn't Santa Anna. They're still looking."

Houston had meant to lead them through the labyrinth into bounty and sunshine and goodness. Yet here they were, mired deep among the swamps, dressed in dead men's clothes and painted with blood. "Tell Mr. Smith I'm not dying. And tell him stop the killing."

Like a starved man smelling food, Bryan leaned in toward the words. Hope mingled with the disbelief on his face. "Stop the killing?" he repeated.

"Tell him I want the runaways kept alive. No more killing."

"I'll tell him. He'll listen to you."

"I want—I need—Santa Anna alive."

The Mexican *caudillo* deserved to be confined like a wild animal and displayed the way the Romans used to with their foreign captives. But something more than that appealed to Houston. If they could take alive this monster who had ordered the execution of five hundred unarmed prisoners at Goliad, and if they could sustain him and perhaps even find his humanity, it would be at least a step toward proving their superiority. Houston's men needed some act to distinguish their butchery from Santa Anna's. At least Houston needed it.

Houston turned his eyes back to the men. "What's wrong with the army?" he asked.

Bryan looked over at the fires. "It was a bad day today." His domed forehead wrinkled.

"What happened?"

"We went back through the field." Bryan swallowed. "You told us to go and we went."

"Yes."

"Well the animals came through last night. And the sun was hot today." Bryan was grimacing. "I've never seen such things."

So that was it, Houston realized. They were haunted. They had walked among the ghosts and bones. He knew what they must have seen. The wounds would have opened wider beneath the fangs and beaks of predators, and the sun would have split them wider still. There was no worse sight than human flesh reduced to carrion.

"You ordered no plundering," Bryan went on, his voice almost too soft to hear.

"And they plundered." Houston wasn't surprised, not a bit.

"And more," Bryan said. He halted again. "Some of the men . . ." Bryan's voice faded away.

Houston didn't spare him. "Tell me," he insisted.

"Some went through the dead," Bryan spoke. "With knives."

"I know," he said.

Bryan looked sick. Houston pitied him. *You want it back, don't you? But it's gone.* If only they could retrieve what was lost so easily, by simply blaming its loss on an accident. Or on madness.

"It was only some of the men," Bryan added. "The rest were sickened. They would have nothing to do with it."

Houston snorted. Their humanity had arrived a day too late.

"And there was something else," Bryan said. "There is a woman."

"You found a woman?"

"I don't know who saw her first. She's a Mexican woman. A camp follower, probably. I've seen her. A beautiful woman. Very beautiful."

"She's dead?"

"Killed."

Houston made a guess. "And my heroes mutilated her as well."

"Oh, no, General. No one would defile such beauty."

He talked as if she were an angel fallen to earth. "I don't understand, Mr. Bryan. More than six hundred men were cut down yesterday. This is just one whore."

"You don't understand?" Bryan pleaded.

Houston regained his patience. "Your chivalry is admirable," he said. "But with so many bullets flying yesterday, an accident to a lady was inevitable."

"But that's just it, sir. It was no accident. The men are quite upset. She was stabbed with a saber."

Then a saber, Houston almost snapped. But there *was* a difference. Between random bullets and a handheld sword there could be all the difference in the world. "Nonetheless," he said, "in the heat of battle, with all the smoke, it could have been one of her own. . . ."

"No sir," Bryan said. "It was deliberate. There were witnesses. And they have identified the killer as an American officer."

Even foggy with pain and lost blood, Houston saw the implications. His soldiers were killers, but they were southerners first. And a woman, especially a beautiful woman, was supposed to enjoy the protection of their arms, especially a southern officer's arms. Under ordinary circumstances this might have been a serious charge. But Houston found it hard to believe that, on the day after a massacre, anyone besides an overwrought nephew of Austin's would really care. He was wrong.

"What officer?" Houston asked.

Bryan was about to answer, then held up a finger and said, "Listen."

"What is it?" Houston asked.

"They're doing it again," Bryan said. "All evening . . ."

Now Houston heard it.

From far away an American voice was floating through the trees. "Who killed the woman?" it cried out.

What happened next stunned Houston.

Hundreds of voices lifted up from around the different fires. It was like some ancient Greek chorus chanting to the dark night wind, and Houston suddenly recognized that this was the same name he'd woken to. All in unison they roared it to the stars.

"Colonel Forbes."

Houston lay there speechless. He was incapable of making sense of the moment. If Old Hickory himself had commanded them to shout all at once, they wouldn't have done it. And yet they had just answered the crime with one voice. They were subordinate after all. The force of their obedience—the unrequited mystery of it—frightened Houston the way it evidently frightened the men. Something had been unleashed among them.

CHAPTER THIRTEEN

IN THE MORNING, at Houston's order, the army returned to comb the fields for whatever remained of the Mexican arms and war machinery. Grumbling, the soldiers fanned out and set off. By daylight their dread was manageable, but the bodies had begun to decompose. Even at this distance Houston could smell the death.

With the men off to scour the fields, the camp quieted. Houston forced down a little scorched beef and some coffee. After a while he felt strong enough to have a passing soldier prop him a little higher against his tree root.

Like hogs sensing the autumn slaughter, the prisoners had been agitated all night. But they visibly relaxed once the bulk of their executioners departed. They quit milling around in the pen and got on with the task of daily subsistence. Mexican officers detailed some of their men to scoop the human dung off to one corner. Soldiers started fires to cook the bull that had been driven into their enclosure. Under heavy guard five tiny Mayans began an endless round of hauling water from the river to the pen. Houston could see a row of bare feet, their wounded who had died. Some of the Mexicans joined in little songs of prayer that sounded almost serene. Houston closed his eyes and listened.

Before long Houston's colonels began to drift over. "They say you're dying," Three-Legged Willie said to him. He had a sword cut across his pegleg.

Houston was in pain and the fever and blood loss had

wracked him. All he could do was lie there as the officers surrounded his carcass. "It's not true," he said.

"Sure looks true," Willie said.

Burleson wandered over, his homespun jacket split open along every seam. Wylie Martin looked like he'd just won an election, all teeth. And Sherman had added another silver star to his collar, although for the sake of modesty he'd pinned it to his opposite collar and kept himself a one-star general. Forbes entered on horseback and dismounted with a flourish, showing off a magnificent sword. It was obviously plunder. Crowned with an eagle head, the hilt had gold wrapped around carved ivory with silver inlay. The eagle had eyes made of rubies. The scabbard alone was more handsome than any weapon Houston had ever seen.

"Yesterday it belonged to General Antonio López de Santa Anna," Forbes announced. "Today it belongs to me. And for you, General Houston," he opened his hand, "the snuff box of Santa Anna." On his palm lay a pure gold box.

Houston was too dismayed to speak. The audacious colonel had helped himself to the best of the plunder, and, worse, done so in front of the entire army. It was a terrible example, one bound to cause resentment. No wonder the men were making a sacrifice of his reputation.

"Sit down, colonels," Houston said. "Tell me what's going on out in the world."

Burleson led off. Captain Seguín's *vaqueros* were reporting that major elements of the Mexican army were still advancing from the west. They numbered in the thousands and were led by an able corps of generals.

"You worry over nothing," Old Wylie chastised Burleson. Apparently they'd been arguing among themselves.

"We have to prepare," Burleson insisted. "They'll come for us now."

"Didn't we just take on twice our numbers and thrash them down?" Sherman said. "Let them come. If they want death and destruction, we have plenty to spare for them."

They bickered for an hour, by which time clusters of soldiers were returning to camp from the battlefield. They cut through the grasses with their arms and hands full of clothing so stiff with blood it looked starched and with weapons and other trinkets. Behind them the sky was thick with carrion birds wheeling. The soldiers had dread and nausea written on their faces. Clearly the fields had grown more horrifying.

Surrounded by his child troops, the cannoneer Ben McCulloch came in wearing a hat woven out of grass and palmetto leaves. He carried the same shattered expression as the rest.

"Hail that soldier," Houston said to Burleson.

"Boy," Burleson shouted. "Come over here."

McCulloch approached warily.

"Sergeant," Houston addressed him. "Report on what you found out there today."

"Out there?" The boy had been among ghosts, Houston could hear it in his voice. His Adam's apple squeezed up and down. "Sir, the hands . . ."

The hands are reaching up from the field. Houston could see it still.

"The eyes are gone, sir. The birds come. And not a one has his eyes left." McCulloch was in shock. The child was no longer a child.

Colonel Sherman leaned back, lighthearted. "I hear the buzzards will eat the horses, but won't touch the greasers for all the spice in them."

"Oh no, that ain't so," McCulloch said. "The animals been eating on everything out there. Why there's arms and legs scattered from here to yonder."

"Do tell."

"Yes, sir."

"And the woman?" Houston interrupted. Colonel Sherman ate his grin. The other officers glared at Houston with the contempt of victims. As for Forbes, he froze.

Until that instant, Houston had considered the charge against Forbes just a malicious invention. He was an ass and the men had been rankling him for weeks. Now he was dipping into the plunder while the rest of the army was forbidden to. Even if Forbes actually had sabered her, Houston would have excused the act as an accident.

But Forbes was guilty. He had killed the woman, and not by accident. Houston was taken off guard. He didn't know why he knew exactly, not after all the deception and death that had passed to now. But Forbes was guilty. He stared straight ahead.

"I went up to her," McCulloch answered. "She's just lying there on her back. Yesterday I'd've said hush, she's sleeping.

And she was so pretty. But today . . ." He screwed up his mouth and whispered the rest. "They took her eyes, too, sir."

Suddenly Forbes erupted. "I demand a court of inquiry," he yelled out. "By God, I am innocent."

Sherman reached over and patted the colonel's leg. "Of course you are, man. There's no need for a court."

"By God." Forbes shivered. "I demand to clear my name. I demand an immediate court of my peers. I demand . . ."

He would have gone on demanding, too. But something was going on among the prisoners. It began as a murmur and rapidly built into a leaf storm of words, and it reached over to Houston and his colonels.

Forbes quit his shouting and they all looked across at the corral of captives, then out to where they were pointing. It was midday and the sunlight was yellow and jumpy on the green grass. Deaf Smith was wading through the emerald glister on horseback with a bedgraggled imp of a Mexican mounted right behind him on the rump. The scout had taken a prisoner.

At first Houston thought the prisoners were celebrating the sight of one more living comrade or perhaps cheering his two days on the wing. For his own part Houston was relieved to see Smith with a prisoner in tow, for it meant the old scout had quit the killing as Houston had ordered.

"What's that they're saying?" Burleson said.

Now Houston paid attention to the clamor.

"*El Presidente*," the Mexican prisoners were crying out. "Santa Anna."

"Can it be?" said Houston.

It was so.

They brought Santa Anna before Houston, who lay against the oak tree. A huge crowd of Americans developed, some carrying rope for a hanging, some guns and knives. In their bloody battle-torn uniforms, they looked like a graveyard in rebellion. It was not an auspicious start for the emperor of Mexico.

Dressed like a circus monkey in a slave's cotton pants, a moldy leather cap, a discarded round jacket—once blue, now a patchwork of rainbow colors—and a linen blouse with diamond studs, Santa Anna stood there with one hand upon his heart. When they'd rousted him from his hiding place in the bayou that morning he'd been wearing a pair of red silk morocco slippers on each foot, and carrying a box of chocolates and a gourd of water wrapped in a white sheet, looking more ready for bed than escape.

It was impossible to say which was having the worse effect on the prisoner, the thick ring of men clamoring for his immediate death, or their laughter at his scavenged costume. His fingers trembled like a very old tailor's, rebelling in principle against his overall stillness. Otherwise the captive managed to contain his agitation. He had black eyes and a long neck that tapered aristocratically.

The men swarmed together in the manner of peeking at a human deformity or some exotic animal. In a way Santa Anna was both, part Napoleon and part Don Quixote, a creature of the New World that could only have flourished in a place like Mexico City. Or, Houston reminded himself, in Washington, D.C. Here was a figure of such charisma that, with words alone, he could carry an army of seven thousand men and women and children a million miles from their jungles and huts and cities into this hostile North called Texas. Here was a butterfly who'd presumed to change the world with the brilliance of his colors.

How powerful he must be, Houston thought. *He has so much to teach me.* Houston's rabble was of a different mind, of course. They took one look at Santa Anna's wonderful strangeness and his magical authority and howled for his extermination.

"Hang him."

"Shoot the son of a bitch."

Old Jimmy Curtis was present. "I'll nail him to a tree and skin him piece by piece. Give the bastard to me for what he done to Wash Cottle."

With every shout Houston's gunshot throbbed a little harder, reminding him that his own chances of surviving the birth of an American Texas probably weren't much better than Santa Anna's. He wanted to bellow for silence. But he was enough of a spectacle already, filth encrusted and lying in the dirt, a general with no uniform who had pissed his own pants. He did what he could to put a little more elevation in his prostration and wished there had been time to have one of the beautiful Mexican blankets spread underneath him. There was no excuse to let down his own theater, not even with a mortal wound.

"One of you men bring a crate for my guest to sit on. And

you," he pointed at a bald fellow with bad teeth, "go fetch some coffee and meat over here."

"For him?"

The cluster of men grew larger, reminding Houston of magpies that multiply around a bright object. A wooden ammunition box got hauled over.

With the timing of a natural-born diplomat, Moses Bryan forced his way through the crowd and took his place beside Houston. Houston fastened his gaze upon the slender prisoner and closed out the yammering crowd. "General," he began, "would you have a seat, sir."

Bryan bowed slightly and introduced himself to Santa Anna, then softly translated Houston's invitation to sit on the crate. Santa Anna dipped his chin with courtly acceptance. First, though, he asked Bryan to formally present him to Houston as one ruler to another, name first, followed by his credentials, a long list.

"Also," Bryan went on translating, "he wishes to put himself at the disposition of the brave General Houston. He asks to be treated as a general should be treated when a prisoner of war."

"You can tell the general his treatment won't be one bit worse than what our men enjoyed as his prisoners," Houston replied. It would have been a lie to promise anything more, and the Mexican seemed satisfied with Houston's candor.

Santa Anna seated himself with a tired whispered "ay." He was visibly relieved to descend beneath the canopy of death threats and hostility. He kept his back straight and his expression firm, but Houston didn't miss how under his sunburn and the mud on his face he was pale and weary. He sat still with flies buzzing around his head. Houston had wondered what this notorious ruler would look like. Would he have decadent eyes or hands crisscrossed with battle scars? Would he have the clenched jaw of an Andrew Jackson? What Houston saw was an ordinary man who had reached high, only to fall. But he had managed to land on his feet, that was important. Yes, there was much to learn here.

"Does the general have any immediate needs?" Houston asked Bryan. The young man had crouched upon his heels between the two generals. He relayed the question, then the answer.

"He says it would be a courtesy of state if you would allow him one of his own aides."

It brought to mind the world of diplomacy Texas would now have to engage in. Lead balls and butcher knives could gain them only so much. "Fair enough," Houston said. "Who among them survived?"

"Let's see," Bryan considered, "there's Juan Almonte."

"Almonte's in the bunch?" Houston hadn't known. "I'll be." He'd met Almonte several years earlier when a group of Mexican scientists and officers passed through Texas on a fact-finding expedition. Almonte had charmed the Anglos with his perfect English, his fine humor, his understanding of American and European ways. He was the bastard son of a priest, Morelos, who was a great revolutionary hero in Mexico. Not long before the firing squad got him, Morelos had sent his child to the United States for safety and education.

"Yes," said Houston. "Bring Almonte over."

While they waited for Almonte to be brought, Santa Anna swallowed a piece of Houston's opium and took a sip of water. It would take ten minutes or so for the medicine to melt into his veins, but already his anxiety seemed to be loosening. He looked at Houston with an expression—a blink, a tiny dimpling—that bordered on fraternity. Houston had noticed the bonding effect of opiates before, but this was different. Encircled by a lynch mob with ropes and guns and drawn knives glinting in the sun, this was more like two men being trapped in a tiny cabin by a terrible hurricane. In a sense that's what it was, the storm of history.

Santa Anna spoke. Bryan leaned down toward Houston's head. "The general asks, how many thousands of soldiers did you use to defeat him?"

Houston was tempted to inflate the actual figure. But Almonte and some of the other Mexican officers would surely have estimated his troop strength by now, and anyway the truth was more satisfying. "Less than eight hundred," Houston said.

When Bryan told him, Santa Anna's face congested. His black eyes flared, as if Houston had just insulted his intelligence. Then he decided it was a joke after all, and smiled. Finally, with another glance around, he realized it must be the truth and something like beatific resignation surfaced. Houston watched the emotions slide across his face. He'd known only one other man whose countenance could leap from the lion to the lamb so naturally, and that was Old Hickory.

"He begs your indulgence, sir. Would you kindly share with him the status of his army?"

There was no reason to hide the numbers. Houston said what he knew, that the Mexicans had lost as many or more men as were now in captivity. Santa Anna looked proud, even redeemed. The figures suggested a great sustained defense by his men.

"And the president asks, how many casualties did we sustain in storming their position?"

"What are we up to now, Mr. Bryan?" Houston said. "Nine dead?"

"I don't know, General."

Houston set his jaw. "Ten. Tell him, ten."

Santa Anna was a professional soldier in a country wracked with revolution. He had probably been in more battles than all of Houston's army put together. He was experienced enough to recognize a massacre. Again his small, square face washed with feelings. He flushed with anger. *Yes,* thought Houston. *Rage at us. Make us ashamed.* But that wasn't it.

"The general hopes that you reserve no contempt toward the Mexican people for this disgrace. His reinforcements were raw recruits. They were still learning courage."

Houston recoiled. Hundreds of men had been killed in the *caudillo*'s name, and all he could think to do was accuse the dead of cowardice? Suddenly Houston suspected Santa Anna might harbor the darkness they accused him of.

"The general notices your leg wound," Bryan said to Houston. "It looks very serious to him. But he has no doubt you will recover. He said great men are prone to injury. The leaders of nations get brought down by scratches and bee stings, not war injuries like this."

Houston was disappointed. He'd expected something more intelligent than flattery from Santa Anna. There was another burst of Spanish, and Bryan's eyes widened. He translated. "The general adds that, at this moment, he would give his fortune for a wound like yours. He would gladly sacrifice his right leg to the peace and prosperity of Mexico. For such a wound, he would give all Texas."

Houston was quiet. "He said that?" he whispered.

Bryan was astounded, too. "All Texas," he repeated.

But before they could explore that opening any further,

Almonte appeared. Pushed and pulled through the mob, he arrived with a very sour look on his face. Houston couldn't say if the sourness had more to do with being manhandled or with seeing his cowardly president. It struck Houston that the Mexican army might very well have been more freighted with intrigues and plotting than his own. Certainly, Almonte's greeting to his supreme commander was less than enthusiastic. He bowed in his destroyed uniform. In turn Santa Anna indicated a space—on the ground—where he wished Almonte to sit.

"General Houston," Almonte said, then sat. He was a squat copper-colored man with black eyes and a pleasing smile. He wore what was left of his uniform with splendid indifference, like an actor who has finished yet another performance.

"Señor Almonte," Houston greeted him. "Excuse me, but I don't know your rank."

"Oh, that." Almonte dismissed it with a snap of his fingers.

"I'm sorry to see you in such circumstances," Houston said. "You've come a long way to reach such hard times."

He recalled encountering Almonte on a wooded trail in eastern Texas. They had kept their conversation safely away from matters of Texas, instead discussing a recent novel, *Frankenstein*. Houston had found it decadent and a waste of time. Almonte had called it political, a novel for the New World.

"General Houston," Almonte said. "With all due respect, it was my intention to express those same sentiments to you."

The Mexican referred to Houston's overall situation. This tattered prisoner didn't think himself defeated at all. To the contrary, Almonte was actually offering his condolences in advance for what he saw as Houston's inevitable defeat by the rest of the Mexican army. It wasn't an insult, simply a prediction, and one offered straight to his face in the heart of the American camp. Houston laughed, delighting in the man's courage. The bald soldier bringing more coffee glanced up, startled by the laughter, and spilled half the cup on his hand. Almonte smiled wider. They understood one another.

"Well here we are," Houston said. "In a revolution. In a new day. A new Texas."

"Revolution," Almonte repeated slowly. "Let me give you a warning, General. We were born in revolution, too, just like you Americans. Maybe you know this, maybe you don't, but it seems that everywhere we Mexicans turn anymore there are no more landmarks, no more dreams. There is just the land, just the people. I had always thought that revolution would be like the sun rising. But for Mexico revolution has brought darkness."

"I blame false prophets for much of your anguish," Houston said. He looked at Santa Anna to see if the leader of Mexico was following any of this exchange. Santa Anna was looking at his fingernails.

"We believed in a man," Almonte shrugged. "We followed him to Texas. He told us he was the lord of men. He told us to do things and we did them. We believed in him even when he was wrong, because we did not trust ourselves to know what was right."

"There are burdens to empire," Houston said.

"Perhaps," Almonte said. "But my general is a bloody man. For every one of you Americans who has died, this man has killed a hundred of his own people over the years. After the rebellion in Zacatecas last year, blood ran in the gutters. Almost two thousand of my people . . ." Almonte flipped his hand over and shook his head sadly.

"You're a curious fellow," Three-Legged Willie leered at Almonte. "It sounds like you just asked us to do your dirty work for you. We could take care of a whole lot of your problems with one bullet."

Again Almonte shrugged. He neither confirmed nor denied it.

"But how's this for an idea," Willie said. "How about we kill you instead and send this boy home and let him run your country into the ground." Willie laid one affectionate hand on Santa Anna's shoulder. Santa Anna glanced up and smiled robustly. "If he's as bad a president as he is a general, we could own Mexico City inside of ten years."

"You could do that," Almonte said.

"You can't do that," one of the soldiers in the crowd shouted out. "You can't let Santy Any free. Not after what he done at the Alamo."

"Remember the Alamo," someone brayed.

Santa Anna needed no translation to understand. His eyes showed that he knew what was brewing and it frightened him. But suddenly he caught sight of his own sword on Forbes's hip and his face changed. His fear turned to catlike curiosity. He leaned toward Almonte and spoke into his ear. Houston watched. Almonte whispered back to his commander, pointing at Forbes.

Forbes saw their attention. Resting one palm on the sword hilt, he lifted his whiskery chin and fixed the two prisoners with an indignant glare. Santa Anna asked another question, his finger aimed at the red-haired American, and Almonte nodded, then dipped closer and went on whispering. The American colonel had a reputation among the Mexicans, too, it seemed. Forbes licked his lips nervously, finally looking off in another direction.

When Almonte spoke it was loud enough for others to hear. "The general compliments the great army of the north," he said. "He compliments you for burning all of Texas to the ground. He said you must desire this golden land very much. Above all, he compliments your leaders. He says that only great leaders would have had the nerve to sacrifice two hundred men at the Alamo and another six hundred at Goliad. He says Travis and Fannin were truly military geniuses. He said that, before, he thought such men were common thieves. But now he knows better. He said you are great *caudillos*—military dictators— maybe greater than himself."

Almonte finished with a deep lungful of the fetid air and smiled with remarkable white teeth. He seemed highly pleased with his commander, or with himself. It amounted to a death wish.

In that instant Houston came close to loving his enemy.

The Mexican's insult was breathtaking. For all to hear, this thin doomed man in red slippers had just charged Houston and his colonels with presiding over every horror that had taken place in Texas. And there was no way to deny it short of admitting they had failed as rulers. Few in the mob understood that Santa Anna had just laid his curse upon them. Indeed Houston heard several mouthing to themselves snatches of the translation, enchanted by their enemy's praise of them. But Houston's colonels heard it for what it was.

"We stand accused of being miniature conquistadors with dreams of Mexican gold stuck in our skulls?" Willie was laughing at his comrades, goading them on. It was clear what outcome he wanted. "But gentlemen, if we are *caudillos* in whiteface, then it makes our grand war of Texan independence nothing more than an act of petty conquest. In fact, Colonel Sherman, it makes you and your patriots into mercenary hirelings. That doesn't have such a pretty sound."

"Kill him," Sherman said.

"I'll skin him," Jimmie Curtis shouted from the crowd.

Almonte watched the proceedings with grim amusement. A look of alarm was spreading across Santa Anna's face, and Houston suddenly wondered if perhaps Almonte had put his own twist on the translation.

"But what does he mean by this?" Colonel Wharton demanded. He was genuinely bewildered. "Doesn't he realize we hold the power of life and death over his head?"

Houston didn't answer the obvious, that they intended to kill Santa Anna anyway.

Now Private Lamar stepped forward. He faced the crowd and held up his hands for quiet.

"Lamar," Houston growled. But Lamar turned his back to the general.

"We have snapped the back of the heathen," Lamar spoke to the crowd. He was a little hesitant, not quite used to leading a coup. But he bulled on. "We have defeated tyranny and brought liberty and acquired a country for our own. Now, as free men, we must define ourselves."

The men listened, mostly because they knew he was going to give them what they wanted. Houston's colonels were nodding their heads.

Lamar pointed at the ground beneath his feet. "We cast a shadow," he said. "We walk in the glory of the light. But we cast a darkness, every one of us. And it is up to every man to say what part of us is the light and what part the darkness. And that's what we must do today. Determine what is right from what is wrong. Determine what is just. Because justice is honor."

"I'll yank his heart out," Jimmie Curtis howled from the crowd.

"Give us honor," someone yelled. "That's what we want. Give us the bastard."

Somebody fired a musket into the sky, then more men did, too. Lamar looked uneasy. He blinked and looked over at the officers. Even lying down, Houston felt rocked by the crowd's hatred and savagery. *I give them to you,* Houston thought to Lamar.

"That's it, then," Burleson said.

Now Mosely Baker and some of the men lifted Santa Anna by the elbows. They herded him up against Houston's oak tree. The mob thickened, recommending its various methods—rope, gun, or blade. Colonel Forbes drew the sword with the jeweled eagle hilt from its sheath and it looked as if Santa Anna were going to die on his own steel.

The Mexican's moment of bravado had elapsed. His shoulders folded in like a flower in wilt and he bleated for Almonte. But Almonte had stepped back and was looking away. To Houston's disgust, so was Lamar. Having triggered the killing, they were suddenly too polite for it.

The rabble closed tighter. Their ranks thickened. The stink of dead men's clothing mixed with the sweat and horse and dung smell. Their bloodlust had no bottom to it and Houston hated them for it. Once they finished with Santa Anna, Houston knew they would work their way into his officers, then all the rest of the prisoners. The killing would go on for days.

Houston reared up onto his elbows. The pain nearly drove him back against the tree root. But he'd resided among these barbarians as long as he could stand it. Now, even if it killed him, he had to get away. He was almost wild to be separate from them. If he died twenty feet away, at least it would be twenty feet traveled against their tide.

The mob crowded around and past him, jockeying for a view of the treeside execution. Houston battled their legs and feet and hips. He shoved at them like they were dumb cattle. He slugged at the meat on them, but they scarcely noticed.

Somehow he hoicked himself around onto his knees, then managed to get his good foot planted. Pulling against the thick tree root, he rose up.

A soldier bumped him. He rocked off balance and touched down upon his wounded ankle. Bones grated. The shock started to crumple him, but with an ungainly hop he kept himself upright. He roared at them. It wasn't a word or a thought, just a noise to clean his mind.

Men and boys fell back from him, alarmed by the sight of this giant shaggy beast. He was feverish, swollen with insect bites. Even hunched with pain and faintness, he was taller than the crowd. He cranked his head to the left and a long string of drool whipped across his beard and cheek.

The mob stilled. A space cleared around Houston and he teetered in its center. They stared at him, frightened by his madness. Over their heads he could see Santa Anna pinned against the tree by a dozen hands, but still alive, unharmed. The sword gleamed in Forbes's fist.

Houston twisted to the other side. The camp had frozen. His shirt hung open and he saw the skin of his belly pale against his square brown hand. His hair rattled like a mane, heavy with grease and blood. Houston straightened his back and pushed the hair from his eyes. For a moment it seemed to him that he towered over the entire world. From such a height it seemed he could see down into their very souls. He could see himself in them.

At last, with his heartbeat sluicing rivers through his veins and the sunlight ricocheting from his eyes, Houston met their dumb gawks and perplexity. There was only one thing to do really.

He winked at them. For some reason it worked. They backed away, as if he'd breathed flames. Finally a word came to mind. It seemed like a word men usually shouted. But when he spoke, it came out as a tiny question.

"Honor?" he said.

Then the blood squeezed from his head. His wings melted. He began to fall. But even as he crashed to earth and a hundred hands reached out to catch him, Houston saw Santa Anna stand away from the tree. For the moment he was spared. For the moment Houston had won.

CHAPTER FOURTEEN

HOUSTON OPENED HIS EYES to find the night lit white. The camp was an inferno. Whole trees had been chopped down and toppled into their bonfires. Flames licked so high the stars died. The heat was astounding. A greasy sheen of sweat coated Houston's naked chest and belly and he felt roasted whole. White ash covered the bandages on his leg, the same ash that layered the mules and saddles and leaves. The leaves had shriveled. Men walked around panting.

The army was afraid of their field of ghosts. Houston knew it instinctively. But if they meant to blot out the night, it was going to take whole forests, whole towns, even all of Texas in flame. Because just above their cup of fire and sparks and exploding wood, the darkness hung like a vast animal, waiting.

"General?" Tad had returned. He was squatting by Houston's head. A dusting of ash powdered his thick black curls like fine snow. Two or three live cinders twinkled on top of his hair. The boy looked old and hoary, but also, with the bits of fire on his head, he looked strangely celestial.

"Why?" Houston rasped. *Why have you returned to me?*

"I brung you water," Tad answered. He held out a gourd. Behind the boy, other soldiers—mostly Fannin's survivors, but with some new faces thrown in—hunkered or lay catnapping in the dirt, ready to protect him or do his bidding or simply watch him sleep. He wondered what had occasioned this royal guard, then hoped they weren't just his burial detail.

Houston accepted the heavy gourd in both hands and

tipped the hole over his mouth, dousing his thirst. He let the trickle soak his hair and swept it across his hot chest where it steamed in streaks. He murmured thanks.

Bryan appeared from among Houston's guardians. His round forehead glowed in the firelight. "The men have been praying for you," he said.

Houston didn't believe that for a minute. "I see the leg is still on," he grunted.

The intense light skewed the camp's lines and shadows, casting a fabulous scene. Their beards and long hair flickered like liquid silver and every eye gleamed white as ivory. The weaponry had a golden solidness to it and the men seemed taller somehow. Soldiers moved through the hot vapors like slow statuary. Miraculously the air stood clean of mosquitoes.

"Who kilt the Mexican woman?" a distant voice called out. The men were still at their penny game of penance and blame. Houston waited for the chorus. But the hue and cry had evolved. They had added some variations.

"Who stole the sword?" another faraway voice asked.

"Who hid in the grass?" a third hollered.

And closer: "Who took them scalps? Who took them ears?"

"Who plundered the dead?"

As before a chorus of shouts pronounced Colonel Forbes's name.

Houston went cold. He stared at the darkness poised over their light. They were confessing their sins, the entire army. They didn't know that they were confessing, of course. Colonel Forbes made a fine scapegoat and they were primitive enough to still believe a blood sacrifice was the same as exoneration. But it was a confession. They had sensed evil among themselves. And they were crying out for pardon.

Houston listened to their echoes. Someone took up the cascading interrogation, then another voice. They breathed in the stink of their butchery and breathed out syllables of guilt. Clearly they were haunted. But who was it they were crying to? Who did they think could forgive them?

A molten figure approached through the heat vapors. His silver face became flesh. His armor became blue homespun. It was Burleson. "You're alive," he said to Houston, neither pleased nor disappointed. He was just registering the fact for himself.

"What time is it?" Houston asked. It was a strange thing to ask in the middle of nowhere. It didn't matter and Burleson didn't answer.

"Nearly midnight, sir," Bryan said. He closed his watch and tucked it back in a pocket.

"You hear 'em?" Burleson growled. The voices were like sniper fire, randomly snapping in the distance. Who had been the coward, who the butcher, who the thief? Always with the same answer.

"Colonel Forbes demands to clear his name," Burleson said. "He wants a court of inquiry. Tomorrow."

"And who will sit on this court?" Houston asked. "His friends."

"Friends?" Burleson snorted.

Houston shrugged. "Peers, then."

"Officers," Burleson stated.

"It would be a whitewash. You know it. They would make jokes, then declare him innocent."

"Will you endorse the court?" Burleson insisted.

"Is he guilty?"

Burleson drew a breath and sucked at his teeth. He waved at the voices. "They talk about everything, on and on. We have to put an end to it."

"An end?" Houston asked. He felt burned down to his essence. Things seemed very clear to him. "Let's say your court pronounced Forbes innocent, then who would the army have to blame?"

Burleson didn't think about it. It didn't interest him. "No one," he said. "It would end."

"And that would be good for Texas?"

"We have a country to build. Yes or no. Will you grant Forbes his court?"

"I don't know," Houston said. More troublesome than an innocent verdict would be a guilty one. What then? Would Forbes's punishment return them to innocence? Or would it simply cheat them all of their guilt?

A gun went off on the fringe of light, then several more: nervous sentinels, or perhaps just drunks. Out near the shadows one of the sharpshooters yelled, "Goddamn ye."

A second man shouted, "Quit your fire. It's Old Deef acoming."

Houston rested his head back. His scout was still going out to see the world, still returning to camp to tell them about it. Maybe Smith could find a way for them.

Burleson continued standing there, his shadow razor sharp across Houston's body. "We have learned the government is returning upon the *Yellowstone*," he said. "They'll come here first, to see the victory." That would suit the colonels, Houston knew. The way domestic cats showed off their dead prey, the colonels would display their battlefield.

"So the government finally quit their running, too?"

Burleson wasn't amused. "They're coming," he repeated, "and if we don't have our affairs in order, by God, they'll order 'em for us." He lowered his voice. "We're the goddamn army, Houston. It's time for us to clean the blood off ourselves. Give Forbes his court before Burnet's jackals come and give it for him. It's our affair, not theirs."

Burleson was at least partly right. Once President Burnet and the rest of his pack showed up, the troubles would only mount. One answer would be for Houston to declare martial law immediately and supersede the chaos that was approaching. A warrior king seemed to work for Mexico, why not for Texas? It seemed a moot point, though, if Houston was just going to die.

"I don't see the difference," Houston said. "We hold the court or Burnet does. Either way the colonel will have his good name restored. And these men will be silenced."

Burleson chewed on a tag of his beard. "What is it you want, Houston?"

Houston looked at the camp. It seemed crowded with more soldiers than he could remember. He wondered if new companies of men might have arrived from the States. But as he looked around all the faces were familiar and marked with their passage and battle. They were the same army, the same numbers. The difference was that they had herded together into the light, even though the light—the heat—was too much and was going to drive them back into the darkness. Waving flags and baying their ferocity, these men had come to seize an empire. Yet now they were scarcely able to occupy the night.

"Not this," he answered Burleson.

"Goddamn you," Burleson despaired. "You might as well die."

"No sir," the boy piped up from beside Houston. His alarmed voice sent a rustling motion through the other soldiers watching over the general. Someone murmured. They were all watching now.

Burleson frowned and dropped his voice. "What is it about you, Houston? You say nothing. You lead nowhere. And yet they believe in you." He was genuinely baffled.

Deaf Smith appeared, leading his horse by the reins. His leather sombrero was thrown back and his orange hair jutted like flames. He didn't blink at the heat of their bonfires. He seemed not even to notice it.

"Where have you been?" Burleson demanded.

Smith squinted at him. "Seguín's *vaqueros* won't come into camp. So I went out to them."

"They won't come in?" Houston asked.

"They're hard men, General. But they want to keep their souls."

Houston didn't want to know what that meant. He didn't ask. "What do Seguín's spies tell you?"

"All three elements of the Mexican army have come together at the Brazos. There are thirty-five hundred soldiers two days from us. And Urrea is with them."

"Urrea?" Burleson grunted. "Are you sure?"

"These *vaqueros*," Smith said, "they know where to hide. They catch the Mexican soldiers bringing messages or trying to run back to their villages. And they know how to get information."

"Then we've lost," Burleson said. "Urrea, with so many men . . . we wouldn't last an hour."

Houston marveled at the man's abrupt gloom. Burleson's faith was an inch deep. But that was logical, given that their ownership of Texas was barely three days old. It put to mind that these men needed more than just land and sunlight. They needed belief.

Burleson tried to recover himself, piecing together a plan. "We need to warn the *Yellowstone*," he said. "And in the morning we need to get away from here. We need to ferry our men across the San Jacinto. And the armament. And the spoils."

Burleson stopped. "The prisoners," he remembered. He cut a glance at Houston and Houston knew his thought. If they meant to retreat—to run for their lives, this time—they couldn't reasonably bring the prisoners along. Nor could they turn them loose. The last time Burleson had paroled Mexican prisoners—back in December in San Antonio—he'd made them swear never to fight in Texas again and they had broken their promise. This batch of prisoners would, too, and men like Burleson would see no sense in fighting the same soldier twice.

"What about the prisoners?" Houston muttered.

Burleson snarled. "This is war," he said.

Smith was looking off into the night. He wouldn't be part of any mass execution, not a second one. Houston knew the scout would simply vanish before the dawn. *Why not?* Houston thought. *I'll go with him, into the north.* He remembered that book Almonte had enjoyed: Frankenstein's creature had fled north, too. He wondered what a land of ice might look like.

An idea came to Houston. "Where is Santa Anna?" he asked.

Burleson's eyes hooded over. Had they killed the general after all? Houston started to curse, but that meant filling his lungs with the stench and he stopped. "What have you done?" he said.

"He's over there," Burleson answered. "Off a ways so no drunk will accidentally shoot him."

"I want to talk with him."

"You already talked with him."

Houston didn't argue about it. He waited.

"Goddamn it," Burleson swore. "He's nothing but mischief. But I'll bring him to you."

Houston shook his head no. "I'll go to him."

"With that leg?" Burleson sneered. When Houston didn't balk, he said, "Then go."

"Boy," Houston said to the child hunkered beside him, "will you help me stand?"

He reached up and placed a hand on Tad's shoulder. The bones in the boy's shoulder were delicate and pronounced. Houston felt them through the Mexican uniform. The child was emaciated. They all were. Even the living were turning to skeletons. Houston had acquired an empire of bones.

With his two huge scarred hands, Burleson could have lifted Houston off the ground and carried him anywhere. But Houston didn't ask and Burleson didn't offer. Houston struggled upward, biting against the pain. The boy's hands slipped and clawed at Houston's greasy flesh. Bryan stepped in, but Houston was an enormous man and his help wasn't enough. Finally Deaf Smith dropped his reins and shouldered the other side of Houston and got him upright.

Houston held on to the old scout and the boy, helpless without their support. He was gasping and the heat and strain were sweating him hard. He couldn't see how he was going to make it across camp and into the shadows Burleson had pointed at, not this way, not even dragged between Smith and the child. "The horse," he requested, ready to faint.

They worked Houston up into the saddle on Smith's horse, the mustang mare with white feet. It was the second time Smith had loaned him his horse. Houston found the left stirrup and let his right leg dangle free.

"Do you want me to come along?" Bryan asked.

Houston nodded yes. "Colonel," he said to Burleson. "Don't you do a goddamn thing unless I say."

Burleson spit.

"And you," he said to Deaf Smith. "Go eat."

The scout said, "I will." He turned away and the leather in his braided Mexican jacket creaked.

Hooking the reins, Bryan led the horse on foot. The boy trailed beside Houston's bad leg. The three of them moved through camp. The heat was even worse up here off the ground. Flushed and squeamish, Houston bent forward, quivering, both hands clenching the horn. He came close to asking them to lay him out in the dirt again. But as they moved into the shadows the air cooled and he felt better.

Through the trees Houston saw a bubble of firelight. A brace of armed men was sitting beside some torches jammed between tangled roots. They looked at ease, like a hunting party lounging with tall tales and full bellies. Closer up their faces had the same famished lines as the rest, though. None stood up as Houston's bunch approached, but he did notice three guns pointing in their direction. When the soldiers saw who he was, they took away their trigger fingers and let the cocks down to half-cock.

"Howdy do, General," one said.

"I'm looking for Santa Anna," Houston said.

Behind them the shadows moved. Something glinted in the

torchlight. Houston peered at the darkness. Someone was in there. Then he saw the man. The men. There were two of them, chained to the tree like hounds.

Bryan led the horse to the very edge of darkness and there Houston found Santa Anna with his hands roped together and a length of chain running around the tree. On the other end of the chain was Almonte. Apparently Houston's officers had decided to reward the disloyal aide by attaching him to his *presidente*.

"Colonel Almonte?" Houston called to the shadows.

"Ah, General." For all its urbanity, the voice sounded so American. "I feared you were dead." Almonte didn't seem particularly relieved that Houston wasn't.

"Not yet," Houston said.

"I feared we were dead, too."

Houston was blunt. He offered no optimism. "Not yet," he repeated. Then he added, "Have my soldiers fed you supper?"

Almonte was stoic about it. "A little water would suffice," he said.

Houston handed down Smith's water gourd, and Tad high-stepped through the mangrove roots to give it to Almonte.

The soldiers went back to their gossip and their jug. Their torchlight flickered, making the shadows slippery and liquid. Houston eased himself from the saddle and Bryan and the boy helped him lie back among the slick roots.

He rested for a minute. From this place you could hear the river sifting by on its way to the ocean, and Houston imagined that if they slept tonight, the two Mexicans would dream of sailing down the waters to friendlier shores. A quarter mile away the center of camp gleamed brilliantly, another world.

"For saving his life, the president is profoundly grateful to you." Almonte spoke from the darkness. Clearly the Mexican colonel was not. He shifted and his chains rattled. "But why? Why not let this evil man die?"

Houston peered into the gloom, trying to locate his only hope. Santa Anna's eyes glittered. They were like unhealed wounds in the darkness, moist and pained. When he saw the flash of white teeth—a smile, a grimace—Houston looked away.

"Texas," Houston answered.

"Of course." Almonte's tone was bitter. He knew why Houston had come. And the depth of Almonte's bitterness told Houston that by coming here he might actually profit. Almonte was a genuine patriot. Santa Anna was not.

Almonte tried one more time. "General Houston, I appeal to your honor." That word again. "We are prisoners. And the president is under sore duress. He is at an extreme disadvantage in any negotiations. And any agreements made at this time would be null and void."

It was impossible not to admire Almonte's resistance. Even chained in a swamp with killers for guards, he was trying to protect his nation from its own president. But Houston was just as intent on exploiting the moment. He considered having Almonte unchained and taken back to the corral of prisoners. Then again, there might be uses for Almonte, maybe for his knowledge of international law.

"Nevertheless," Houston said to Almonte.

"I see," Almonte said. He was gracious.

"If you prefer, I can have you removed to another tree," Houston offered.

"Oh, I am quite used to this tree," Almonte said.

Bryan nestled himself among the root system in order to be close to the conversation. The boy was content to squat at Houston's feet and wait.

Houston didn't waste time. "I want President Santa Anna to order his generals to surrender the Mexican army," he said. "Further I want him to formally acknowledge the separation of Texas from Mexico and to recognize Texan independence."

Bryan politely waited to see if Almonte would translate. Almonte heaved a sigh, then got on with it. Bryan monitored the interpretation and nodded his approval to Houston.

"His Excellency states that he will do nothing to disgrace himself or his nation," Almonte replied. "Many Mexican soldiers have died here and at the Alamo and elsewhere in his name."

"I wouldn't like to see our two countries go to war," Houston said. "Not in anyone's name." He watched carefully and it happened. Santa Anna literally blinked. He said something to Almonte, who apparently disputed his commanding general. Santa Anna responded with an angry torrent of Spanish.

"If the United States Army has crossed the Sabine River, it will mean war between our two countries," Almonte stated.

"That would be a terrible thing," Houston said. "But perhaps it doesn't need to come to that."

"A surrender by the Mexican army is out of the question," Almonte warned.

Houston had figured as much. Such a surrender would imply the defeat of all Mexico. Even for a man like Santa Anna that was too much. "Surely there's a way to avoid a confrontation," Houston said.

"General Gaines must withdraw immediately," Almonte answered.

"He would never agree to that," Houston bluffed, "not unless the Mexican army were to withdraw also. Call it an armistice. Sometimes it's better to stop the bloodshed and let the passions cool."

Almonte was silent for a long minute. Houston made his face a mask of patience. Everything depended on what came next. If Almonte balked, if Santa Anna refused—if they doubted Houston's desperate little fiction—then the rest of the Mexican army would advance and destroy this so-called Republic of Texas. The two Mexicans talked.

"What would constitute a negotiated withdrawal?" Almonte's voice was full of caution.

Houston had put little thought into the proposal, much less its details. "We would instruct General Gaines to pull back into the United States," he invented. "You would instruct your troops to withdraw from Texas."

Bryan was looking on with disbelief. Only minutes ago, it had seemed they were doomed. Now, through a cheap trick and by playing to one man's cowardice, Houston was cobbling together a nation.

"And the prisoners?" Almonte asked. He meant the Mexican prisoners in Houston's hands. Houston addressed the American prisoners in Mexican hands.

"Any prisoners of war in Mexican custody—any still alive—you will liberate immediately. Once your army evacuates Texas, we will parole all prisoners of war in our keeping, including yourself and General Santa Anna."

Almonte soberly relayed this. Santa Anna considered Houston's concoction of terms. When he spoke, it was with an authority Houston hadn't heard him use since being captured. Almonte demurred. Once again Santa Anna tongue-lashed him, but Almonte shook his head no and wouldn't convey the message.

Santa Anna's face took on a prayerful joy. He began speaking rapidly and melodiously, at sudden and complete ease. Once more Houston marveled at him. The man was metamorphic, one moment a worm wriggling for his life, the next a butterfly born to be an emperor. Almonte tsk'd as if hearing something unclean.

"What's he say?" Houston asked.

Almonte cocked his jaw, deciding there was some grim satisfaction to be had. "His Excellency was just remembering the first time he came to Texas. It was a quarter century ago. He was a young and ambitious lieutenant. He wanted to climb life's staircase four steps at a time. He came with the army under a brutal general named Arredondo. They came to rid Texas of your *tumultuario*, your dregs from the Mississippi, who were trying to steal our land even then. But on that occasion the North Americans were not so lucky. It was a swift battle. Afterward, when the North Americans were dead, Arredondo hung their bodies in the trees of Medina like fruit, and the people of San Antonio came out and chopped off the arms and legs and called the North Americans dogs. For many, many years, there was no more trouble in Texas."

Houston stayed hushed. Santa Anna could have been describing Houston in his own youth at Horseshoe Bend. "A curious memory," he commented.

"You remind him of Arredondo," Almonte said.

"He's mistaken."

"Perhaps. Never mind."

For a long minute Houston felt unclean, too. The fact of the matter was he had more in common with this ruthless dictator than with any other man in Texas, indeed in all of North America, unless one counted Old Hickory. They were one and the same, generals with bloody hands and wild appetites and a habit of operating on the periphery of human behavior, upon the blank spaces of half-drawn maps. They believed in their own destiny and imagination was their only law.

And, really, what was Texas but an act of imagination? Houston tried to articulate what that name conjured up for him. In the name of their revolution he had galloped back and forth across this thing called Texas. He'd fed upon its animals and crops, breathed its air, swallowed its dust and rain, woven between its lightning and northers, and slept and bled on it. Texas was in him. It was in his gut, in his blood, in his lungs. Most of all it was in his head, or his heart, wherever the seeds of imagination got stored.

Santa Anna was still prattling on. Almonte had quit listening. He looked off toward the bayou, then back to Houston. "We have lost Texas," Almonte sighed. "And you have won it. I see that now."

Houston wished he felt the same certainty. Even if the Mexican army never attacked again, there were the Comanches and land speculators and mercenaries and an empty treasury. No infant had come into the world less prepared than this new nation of Texas.

"We're Americans," Houston said, as if that explained everything. Even as he spoke, though, it sounded foolish to him.

"And we are Mexicans," Almonte shrugged. "The difference is that we have grown tired of illusions. But you North Americans, somehow you manage to go on believing in your flags and independence and martyrdom. You believe in your own propaganda. I can see already how your people will declare that this battle was a great miracle. And that, General Houston, is your victory. You have won over history. You have defeated reality itself. Texas is yours."

Houston regretted having to spoil the Mexican's grand gesture, but a prosaic answer was the brick he needed. Everything else could be built upon that. "Will you order the withdrawal?" Houston asked.

Almonte glanced at his chimerical president, adrift in his private memories, and sighed. "Yes," he said.

It was done.

Texas.

Houston gaped up at the constellations. This place was his now. It was a special moment, a triumphant moment. He felt the serpentine roots against his back. He willed them to bind him to this land, now and forever.

Instead the roots pushed at him. They stood hard and held him at a distance. He could as well have been in Timbuktu or meandering in the upper Rockies. Even now the land was like an ocean to him. He might as well have been a mariner for all the belonging he felt. All through his life it had been this way.

No sooner would he arrive than he was gone again. And he wasn't alone. Already he'd heard some of these men talking about going after Santa Fe and even California and a place called Nicaragua. In their minds they had already gone ahead. For himself, he wanted it to be different this time. But he didn't know how.

Suddenly Houston couldn't stand to be here any longer. After so much reckless momentum, the river sounded too slow and the Mexican general's voice seemed infinitely long, a memory without end. It was almost as if Santa Anna's imprisonment were his own, as if they were now chained together by their agreement and were bound together for the rest of time. No, he couldn't stay here one instant longer. He had to escape from this dungeon of shadows.

"I'll leave you now," he said. "Mr. Bryan will get ink and pen and paper so that the general may draft his order of withdrawal. I'll have it carried to your army posthaste at the crack of dawn."

Almonte had retreated to silence.

Houston struggled against the slick roots. But now that he wanted to leave, they clutched at him. His hand slipped and he ended up deeper in the woody limbs. His leg hurt all the way into his spine and lungs. He grated his teeth and tried again.

Bryan came over and fumbled with Houston's armpit. In the darkness it was hard to make out how badly the general was knotted in among the roots. "Go fetch a light," Bryan told Tad. Then the chains rattled and Houston felt another set of hands at his elbow. It was Santa Anna. "Ah, *mi hermano*," the monster whispered with concern. My brother.

I am lost, Houston thought. Then the torchlight was bathing them and Houston was lifted to his feet. Bryan brought the horse close. Houston mounted, his leg bundled like a leper's claw. He looked down at the boy holding the pine knot.

"Stay here with Mr. Bryan," Houston said to the boy.

"I'll go with you," Tad said.

"No. Someone has to watch over our two prisoners. You're sober, they're not." Houston pointed his chin at the guards. "I need a man I can trust here. This is the future of Texas you're guarding."

The boy looked dubious, but he didn't talk back. Houston leaned in the saddle. He took the torch. It crackled and the horse shook the sparks off her neck. "And while you're at it," Houston said to the boy, "water and feed General Santa Anna and Colonel Almonte. Take what you need from those guards. Tell them I said so."

"I will," the boy said.

Houston nudged the animal with his left heel, just enough to get her in motion. Ever so slowly she started for the main camp, winding between the trees. He could feel the weariness in her plod. Smith must have ridden her far that day. The woods darkened. Houston twisted around to see Santa Anna one last time, but the little cup of light had been swallowed up.

A branch reached out and scratched against Houston's cheek. He ducked it. A moment later the horse brushed against a tree, tangling his good leg. Houston kicked it away.

Somehow the woods were growing denser and darker. He looked for camp to orient himself. It was more distant than it ought to have been and yet its brilliance blinded him. The men must have dragged half the forest into their fires.

Ye are the light of the world, Houston could practically hear Old Hickory reading the night prayer. *A city that is set on a hill cannot be hid.* But what was this city they were building? What had they gained, and at what loss? And could he ever hope to live in it? It seemed fitting their great triumph should be blazing away, not on a hill, but in the deepest swamps.

Houston looked away and the darkness was inviting. He'd been surrounded by men and their violent intrigues for too long. Solitude and peace were almost forgotten things. The night air tugged at him. It was cool and liberating and quiet. *I could ride away and never be missed.* It was a romantic notion. But Houston was known to obey such things. Since childhood he had always taken sanctuary in darkness and Indian tribes and finally liquor and the sweet opium. For all their bold talk his Anglo-Saxons didn't like to venture much beyond the penumbra, and that was a blessing because it took just one step beyond the light and he could be alone.

The horse scraped against another bristle of twigs, this time snaring Houston's torch. He pulled and orange sparks showered to the ground. The flame waned. The darkness swelled, a little bit dangerous, a little bit seductive. The thought came to him, Why return to their crucible of guilt? He listened and heard the distant howl of wolves. They called to him.

Houston dumped his torch into the damp grass. The light vanished. It was that simple. He was alone.

He turned the horse away from camp, away from the river, away from man. A Gulf breeze was blowing ever so gently, bringing the smell of rot with it. But Houston found it perfectly natural that destiny or desire or whatever this was would call to him in the wind. Houston pawed at the invisible branches and twigs reaching out to scratch and claw him. There was no way to protect his ankle, though. Once, then twice, it scraped against the trees. Smith's horse was reluctant at first, both tired and hungry. But Houston was insistent.

Abruptly they broke from the woods and the savannah opened magically beneath the full moon. It was beautiful out here. The grass was a plain of silver filleted with shadows. It seemed to stretch forever. Houston heeled the horse with his left boot. He rode south. The breeze was drawing him onto the battlefield, of course, but that was all right. There would be peace among the dead. They would leave him alone out here, at least until dawn, and maybe by then he would have decided some things. The further he rode, the righter it felt.

Animals abounded, a surprise since Houston had figured the field would be largely still and lifeless. It was alive with night creatures skittering through the grass. Wolves yipped and barked. Houston could even hear the snapping of their teeth as they fought over meat. Here and there owls jumped up from their feast and blotted the moon with their wings.

As he mounted the ridgeline overlooking the Mexican camp, the stink blasted him in a wave of corruption. Dead, his enemy were putting up a better defense than they had in life. Houston wished for the torch. His elation at being free of the army was quickly eroding into childlike fear. Maybe he'd gone far enough.

Suddenly it seemed unwise to go any deeper into this open field of corpses. Ghosts aside—and it was impossible not to believe in them on a night like this—his dream spirit was at large out here. Whether she was a ghost herself, or a muse, or just his own memory in ricochet, Houston sensed danger. Over his shoulder the northern horizon glowed with the American fires. He started to rein around. But once more his name seemed to respire in the breeze.

Samuel. It was the wolves, of course, or the wings of night birds. The breeze rushed in again, and with it the possibility of discovery. The grasses bent and shifted under its breath. It wicked the fever heat from his forehead. The moonlight washed him. He felt drawn on. There was no resisting this.

As he rode on, the horse's hooves snapped a wet twig, then another. The gleaming white sticks lay among the grasses and Houston tried to think how willow switches—what else could be so white?—could have been blown so far inland. He was still a hundred yards from the Mexican breastworks. Then he saw an uneaten foot at the tip of one stick and realized these were human bones. The animals had scattered the remains everywhere. It was a ghastly sight. Houston found it hard to believe a human being could be rendered to sticks and rags and shadow so quickly.

He urged the mare forward. Under the moonlight the shattered breastworks looked like the long broken backbone of a whale. Houston guided his horse through the wreckage and entered camp. The only tents remaining were so shot up and burned that no one wanted their cloth, even for scraps. A big gray wolf loped past with a rib cage in its jaws. The horse shied sideways. Houston wished for his brace of pistols, then tried to remember if those had been stolen, too. At any rate, all he had was his whittling knife.

Smith's mare stayed spooky, her ears perked. She lifted her legs high and fancy, ready to bolt. Houston could feel her loathing in her neck muscles. They meandered through what was left of the camp, traversing bald patches of earth where the grass had lit on fire, circling piles of broken boxes and kegs and ruptured tents. The dead lay everywhere. Their hands clawed at the moonlight. Their empty sockets stared up at Houston. The breeze played with his hair, cooled his sweaty trembling.

Houston didn't know what to look for, which direction to take, how to navigate this geography of ghosts. He just rode on and on, slowly turning here and there, accepting the horrible sights as part of his patrimony. Between him and Santa Anna, Texas had gained a dark underworld to go with its golden sunshine.

It occurred to him that he might search for the body of the Mexican woman. Every other man in his army had visited her. Now was his turn to be her pilgrim. He would see what she had to say to him. Houston set to tracking her.

It was an impossible hunt, one without landmarks. She had been sabered among the grasses, that's all he knew. Any pathway of footprints that led to her body would be overlaid with a hundred other pathways. The field was crisscrossed with purposes. Besides that the animals had probably dispersed her parts across the acres and miles.

Reason told him he could never hope to find her. But if reason were his rule, he'd never have come to Texas in the first place. He searched on. Leaning right, then left in the saddle, Houston rambled through the savannah. He kept out of the trees. Even if she was in there, he couldn't have seen her without a torch. Moonlight was his only hope.

After a time Houston suspected he might be tracking himself in the grasses. Certainly the dead served as no landmark. Stripped of clothing and flesh, they were anonymous, all the same. However varied they had been in life, in death they only repeated themselves.

Houston's leg burned with pain. He felt lightheaded and thirsty. It seemed like months since he had eaten more than bits off a corncob and he was famished. And it was hard to imagine how one more pile of bones could speak to him any more clearly than all the rest. But he kept on.

He made another pass through the camp, then curled outward behind the camp, taking the Mexicans' line of retreat toward the bayou lake. There were far more bodies along this corridor, far more scavengers. Wolves and coyotes and birds scarcely lifted from their feeding as he rode by. He stayed away from the water's edge. The trees and brush were thick with shadows, and he could hear the alligators bellowing and stirring the water. The woman wouldn't have been killed so close to the water anyway, otherwise the soldiers would have mentioned the lake as a landmark. Also the reptiles would have dragged her off the first day. Houston doubled back, working laterally.

In that way he found her. It could only have been her. They had put her under a little mound of earth and rocks with a cross of tied wood. There was no name on the cross, and Houston couldn't be sure this solitary grave contained her. But one of his men had taken the lady's glove from the staff of their liberty flag and bound it to the cross with twine. The white fingers hung delicately. Men had laid flowers here.

Houston sat in the saddle, shocked.

His barbarians had buried her the way they would a wife or a sister or a daughter. The grass lay tramped flat by hundreds of pairs of feet. This was no ordinary grave.

On a whim he lifted his bad leg over the horn and turned belly down to slide from the saddle. The instant he touched earth, Houston realized this was a mistake. He was weak as a baby, and climbing back into the saddle was going to cost him a lot of pain. He was down now, though, and decided to get his look.

Bits of metal glittered on the grave. Houston bent close and saw they were lockets and a few coins, both American dollars and Mexican pesos and cut-up quarters of each. Slips of folded paper stuck out from splits in the wood. Ever so gingerly Houston knelt on the soft turf and reached for the cross. He plucked one of the pieces of paper loose and unfolded it. Inside was a poem. It was impossible to make out the words by moonlight, but the form was clear, and so was the intent. The soldiers were singing to her.

Who were these men? In the form of Colonel Forbes, they had killed her and it made no sense that one more death should touch them so. But at least they were touched. Houston let go of the poem and it fluttered off in the breeze.

He listened for her voice. He put his hand on the earthen hump. Behind him the mare reached for some grass and started chewing. *I've crossed the world to find you,* Houston thought. *I've conquered it. I'm here. Now speak.* But she said nothing.

Off to the side something stirred in the grass. It was large, judging by the noise. Houston glanced up in time to see a sizable furrow seal together again in the grass. It could only be a wolf.

His first concern was the mare. Without her, he was lost. He was unarmed and no one knew where he was. He could die among the dead. The animals would eat him to bone and he would disappear. He would be forgotten.

The horse had pricked her ears up and she was following the sound. Slowly so that she wouldn't startle, Houston stood on one leg and reached for the dangling reins. He almost got them, too. But the grasses whipped open. Houston caught a glimpse of some lank white animal. At the same instant, the mare reared and screamed. Her hooves missed Houston's head by an inch and he stepped back, twisting his bad ankle. He fell to the ground, screaming. Then she was off, kicking right and left at the ghosts. She matched his scream, and the last he saw of her was a silhouette along the luminous north horizon.

After a few minutes Houston pulled himself over to the grave where he lay exhausted. Even in pain he was embarrassed by his situation. He couldn't walk, and crawling was out of the question. Pulling himself through the remains would be more than he could stomach, and the wolves would get him before he got a hundred yards.

"Goddamn it," Houston swore at himself. He'd survived battles and a duel and outlasted a coup by his own officers and outsmarted an emperor. He'd faced bullets and malice and towering storms. He was the commanding general of a republic, for God's sake. And now, because of a sentimental urge, he faced getting eaten by a wilderness of his own making.

Houston set his back against the grave mound. He fished out his clasp knife and got the blade locked open, and tried holding it one way for sticking and jabbing, then the other way, underhanded, for ripping. Knife fighting had never been an interest of his. Unable to decide which was the superior position for impaling a wolf, he stuck the knife into the dirt beside his hip and cast around for other possible weapons. The only things close at hand were rocks from the mound, and he piled a few within easy reach. That was it. *Houston's last stand,* he snorted, *my own private Alamo.* It wasn't going to be much of a fight.

For a long while he just waited. Clouds drifted in from the Gulf, menacing his moonlight with temporary feints. His ankle was hurting worse now and his leg felt hot to the touch right through the homespun pants. The limb was infected and he half wished the wolves would take just those couple feet of spoiled meat for their meal, say from the thigh down.

When the wolf didn't reappear, Houston began to relax. With his back against the grave, he listened to every motion and whisper in the air, alive to the sounds. But the night had become as still and quiet as the dead woman under his back. Cloud shadows streamed over him, only to pass. He located a few of his favorite constellations in the gaps. He shivered. He sweated. He tried to remember snatches of the *Iliad* to stay awake. Finally, deciding the mare had kicked the animal senseless or scared it off, he let the fever have him. That was when it chose to attack.

A gust of wind parted the savannah. The moon covered over. The cloud passed. With a howl the creature leapt at him.

Houston was surprised less by the attack than by the fact that this was no wolf. "God," he shouted. The instant he saw what it was, Houston wished to the deepest part of his soul that it had been a wolf.

It was a man, naked and bearded and fouled with mud and excrement. He was lean, nearly skeletal, and obviously mad. His ribs bulged in the moonlight. In one hand he clutched a human arm bone, partly eaten.

Houston had no time to grab either his knife or a rock. He could only cover his head to fend off the awful club. A cloud sank them in blackness. The assault evaporated. By the time Houston lowered his arm, the lunatic was gone, into the opposite band of grasses.

It was a ghoul. Houston had heard of such things, but never actually seen one. Poor wrecks who had lost their minds to battle, they lurked on the field, feeding on whatever they could find until disease or starvation or a farmer's bullet took them. They could haunt a region for years, spoiling crops with their bad luck, bringing drought or earthquakes or locusts. Sometimes they even outlasted the memory of the battle and became forest legends no one could explain without invoking the devil.

The savannah would provide a banquet for a cannibal like this one. Houston shuddered. He was certain the creature was a Mexican soldier who'd escaped the slaughter and didn't have the sense to reach his own lines. That made Houston's situation even more precarious, an enemy gone mad. He palmed the largest stone in his pile and prepared for any further assault. It wasn't clear the man meant him any harm, but if he did, Houston was easy pickings.

The scavenger came a second time, sprinting from a different direction. He darted out in a moon shadow. Houston threw his stone and by chance caught the man on one leg, tumbling him and drawing another inhuman cry. The clouds parted. The moon illuminated Houston's predator just long enough to show fresh scratches on his body, either from animal claws or tree limbs. The most terrible aspects were his blue eyes and red beard. This was no enemy soldier. It was one of Houston's own men. Houston thought he recognized the wild man as a land surveyor from the Red River country who'd joined up in March. He started to call a name—any name—but the man recovered his footing and limped off into the grasses again, still bearing his bone club.

Five minutes passed. The mad soldier attacked again. This time Houston missed with his first stone, then tried again with no luck. Suddenly the rocks seemed to weigh a hundred pounds. He wanted to sleep, not fight. Even sitting with his back against the grave, he could barely keep upright.

The naked man darted close and struck Houston on the shoulder and side of the head—what felt like a big meaty palm slapping him—then raced on. Houston saw that a hand was still attached to the bone. He panted for breath; his nausea mixed with terror and spoiled his delirium.

The lunatic was growing bolder, circling the grave mound. Houston grabbed for his knife and held it up so the moonlight glinted on it. If the animal recognized the knife as a weapon, he didn't show it.

"What do you want?" Houston demanded. There was no answer. He had reached the very edge of the world. Language meant nothing out here. It was only a matter of an hour, maybe minutes, before he was going to pass out and get brained with that hideous club and picked apart for meat. It was unthinkable. But he wasn't going to last until dawn.

And then the earth parted—or the grasses did—and a figure with flame and sparks for wings came descending upon them. Mounted on a horse with thunder for hooves, the fiery angel became Deaf Smith with a torch in each hand. He drove at the madman, stabbing with one torch and throwing the other at Houston's feet.

Smith wasted no words on a creature so obviously beyond reason. He just swung the torch in searing arcs that bent the lunatic close to the ground. "By God," the scout shouted, "by God." His disgust was like a living thing.

At last, with a whimper, the madman threw the arm bone at Houston and scampered into the grasses. The field sealed shut behind him like a pool of water and only the grass stirred.

Smith's horse reared—the same mare with white stockings that had bolted and left Houston stranded. She must have returned to camp. How Smith had known to come out here,

Houston couldn't say. The scout pulled out a big pistol. He pulled the cock on it and started to give chase. But Houston stopped him.

"Wait," he said.

"I'll be back," Smith promised. "First I have to hunt that thing down and shoot him."

"No sir," Houston said.

"That one's lost to us forever," Smith insisted. "He won't ever come back."

Houston's dread and disgust were receding, even though the arm bone lay across his legs. There were human teeth marks on it. "You're probably right," he said.

"Then let me shoot him down. The man needs to be gotten rid of. You don't leave a rabid dog to wander and bite someone else."

When Houston didn't answer him, Smith added, "He would have killed you." He stood in his stirrups to try and keep the creature in view.

"I don't think so," Houston said. And suddenly he believed that. He cast away the gory limb, then wiped his hand clean on the grass. His composure was returning. Now that Smith was here and he was safe, Houston's supernatural combat seemed foolish and exaggerated.

"It's just a poor critter," Houston said.

"No," Smith said. "That was a man." But he was calming down, too. He took a deep breath, then half-cocked his pistol and dismounted and brought over a gourd of water. He meant to hold it for Houston whose hands were shaking, but his own shook, too.

"He has suffered his share," Houston said.

"But we can't have him running loose."

"He was protecting her," Houston explained. Until that instant Houston hadn't even considered the possibility. The words just came out.

"Dear Lord," Smith whispered.

It was a simple thought, but Houston knew that was where the greatest truth hid sometimes. Then it came to him. The clouds scudded away and the whole field came clear.

"Maybe they know what's wrong, after all," Houston said. "Maybe they just don't know what's right."

Chapter Fifteen

"Samuel?"

He stirred at her calling.

There was a babel of excited voices out there, a rushing about that shook the earth. The air stank of rotting flesh still, but it was nearing that point where life takes over and taxes the dead and makes them yield the future. He could smell the edge of fertility. Flowers would bloom and break down the remains. Cattle would eat the bones for their salt. Crops would grow. Childlike, her voice was inviting him to resurrect himself and join the green riot of spring.

Part of Houston wanted to stay in the darkness and sleep on. Even in here the terrible wound hurt him, and it would become much worse if he emerged. In here he could close himself to the pain forever. But to sleep would be to end the dreaming, and there was too much of that left to do.

The choice was his. He chose. Houston clawed his way from the dark belly, out into the light. He opened his eyes and she was waiting, high overhead and wearing the golden sun for a bonnet. He blinked at the radiant image. Her hair hung in long braids and she had been crying. She had been grieving over him.

"Mama," the girl said. "He's awake, look."

"Hush, Rose," a woman said. "General Houston has fever and he's dying. Give him peace."

"But he smiled at me."

"Come away now. You've seen him. Let the other people have a look, too."

The girl disappeared, pulled away by her mother. Houston jerked at the full brightness of the sun. Other faces, other shadows replaced the child.

"Is that him?"

"He is the hero of San Jacinto."

Houston let his head loll to one side. The *Yellowstone*—her name was painted in black on the hull—sat upon the silky red waters, her twin smokestacks billowing white clouds upriver upon the northerly breeze. Parts of her deck and the engine room were walled with stacks of cotton bales, five hundred pounds each, against Mexican bullets and cannonballs.

The ship had come then, and with it people. It was impossible to say how long the *Yellowstone* had been here or how long he'd been unconscious or what exactly was going on. Houston studied the crowd for clues.

His barbarians were mixing with clean new folk. The soldiers were easy to distinguish by their rags and animal skins and the gunsmoke bluing their flesh and the filth and gore caking their long hair and beards. They looked so thin and frail among the well-fed newcomers. Houston saw Ben McCulloch and his gang of cannoneers in the shade of a tree, gawking at a ring of strangers that was gawking at them. The warriors were children once again, accepting bits of food and candies from the crowd, blushing at praise, wearing garlands of bluebonnets and paintbrush. Could it be there was a return to innocence?

In another part of camp, soldiers were hawking battle trophies to the tourists. Houston saw a shattered Brown Betsy held aloft, then a boiled human skull. Elsewhere he saw people carrying scalps like colorful ribbons at a county fair, and a gentleman strolled by wearing a necklace of blackening Mexican ears.

Houston felt someone's fingers plucking at his clothing. He looked down and a friendly enough character was sawing through the cuff of Houston's left pantleg with a shiny butcher knife. He gave a big smile that showed more gum than teeth and said, "Pleased to meet you, General."

Houston figured the man was a freshly landed surgeon. But once he got the pants cuff cut free, the man put it in his pocket and walked off. Now Houston saw that he was missing swatches of homespun all over his clothing. The souvenir hunters had been busy while he slept. At this rate the emperor truly

would have no clothes. After a minute another fellow decided
to take a piece of Houston's ankle bandage. Houston aimed a
kick at the man's face with his good leg. But to his chagrin he
barely had the strength to raise his knee a few inches and the
foot stayed put. The feeble motion didn't deter Houston's tor-
mentor one bit.

"Someday people will say it was you fathered a mighty
nation," the man cheerfully explained while he cut away at the
crusty rags. "There will be cities and ships and trains called Sam
Houston, maybe even mountains and oceans. Why, if I ever
have sons I mean to name every one of them after you. And
their children and grandchildren will have this relic to remember the father of Texas."

"Get off." Houston tried bellowing. What surfaced was a
high-pitched creak. He had seized tight inside and his tongue
clapped like dry meat. The carrion birds had taken human
shape and he was helpless to stop their cannibalizing.

"Clear away," someone demanded. "Goddamn it, give the
general some blue sky." Tom Rusk shoved his way through the
spectators, and he was trailed by Dr. Labadie and another man.
When he spotted the fellow snipping away Houston's bandage,
Rusk sent him backward with the flat of his brogan. "Back off
of him, you jackal. Get on." When the crowd still didn't disperse,
Rusk drew his sword.

"I'm from Tennessee and we're free men," a tall man in
bright yellow buckskins shouted back at him. "Don't you order
us."

"We'll go where we goddamn please," another declared.
"Texas is a free country, or ain't you heard."

The possibility of a ruckus drew more spectators. *The mob,*
Houston wearied, *always the mob.* If they weren't burning him
in effigy they were worshiping his very rags and bones. Houston
felt sick enough to puke, but his stomach was empty. The crowd
grew larger.

"We're Texians," a fat man with red cheeks shouted at
Rusk. "Maybe *you* ought clear away."

The tourists and curiosity seekers jostled closer.

"Texas belongs to us now," the Tennesseean in buckskins
declared. "Before he come here to fight to the death for American democracy Old Davy told me, Be sure you are right, then
Go Ahead. Now here I am. And I ain't budging."

From out of nowhere one of Fannin's survivors—a stick of a man—appeared in front of the hardy Tennesseean. He didn't speak a word nor give the fellow a chance to even smell him, which might have backed anyone off. Instead he made a quick little motion. There was a glint of steel, then a scream, and the yellow buckskins acquired their first blood. The Tennesseean clapped both hands to his split earlobe and dropped his long rifle and his neighbors backed away from the drops of blood.

"Look it there," a man said, "jingle-bobbed, by God."

"Maybe he'll hear better now," Rusk said. "Maybe you all will."

Since that seemed to be the end of the controversy, the crowd lost interest almost immediately. The spectators trickled away, going off to bedevil the Mexican prisoners in the corral or to buy trinkets or dicker over military land bounties that Houston's soldiers were eagerly pawning off. Houston closed his eyes for a moment and listened to the bustle of commerce. Off in the distance he could hear an auctioneer offering Mexican mules for sale.

Dr. Labadie gave Houston some water. "You must have given your kingdom in hell," he said, "otherwise you couldn't have come back to us. You've been under, sir, deep under two days and two nights."

Rusk led the stranger forward by the elbow. The man was gray and emaciated, a thousand years old. "This here is Dr. Kenner," Rusk said. "He lost a boy at Goliad and the Mexicans shanghaied him to tend their army. Somehow he made it through the battle. I wanted him to take a second look at that ankle there."

"I'm sorry about your son," Houston said.

"I met you once," the gray man said. His voice was dull. His ordeals had cost him a chunk of spirit and Houston wondered whether his senses were addled. He didn't want a crazy man fiddling with his ankle, but when the two physicians squirreled down to peek inside the ankle wound Dr. Kenner was the gentlest.

Rusk sheathed his sword with a hiss and a crack and sat on an ammunition box beside Houston's head.

"Where's the president at?" Houston rasped. He was asking about Santa Anna. Rusk took him to mean the president of the Republic of Texas.

"Burnet came in on the *Yellowstone* just about an hour ago," Rusk said. "But I don't think you want to see him, not at present. That old boy doesn't like to get his thunder stolen and you stole it. He's using some strong language just now. He thinks you ought to be court-martialed."

Houston smiled at that, even at the price of splitting his lips. "What charge?"

"Victory." Rusk shrugged. "He's trying to convince the citizenry you could have won at Gonzales the same as you won here. He says if you hadn't run away, you could have spared the Republic all the excitement."

"I'll be," Houston said.

"Nobody has much taste for his nonsense," Rusk added.

Dr. Labadie pulled something out of the hole. "For Christ's sake," Houston gasped.

"He's very near to lockjaw," Dr. Kenner said to Dr. Labadie, probing carefully. "The line of infection is creeping. See there?"

Whatever the two physicians were doing to the ankle, it felt like wickedness itself. Houston didn't look.

"And the Mexican army?" Houston asked with teeth gritted.

"Santa Anna wrote the order," Rusk said. "Deaf Smith delivered it. The Mexicans have begun to withdraw. One of Seguín's men reports that Santa Anna's troops have demolished the outer walls of the Alamo and sunk their cannon in the San Antonio. Looks like we're the new landlords."

"Tell me Santa Anna's condition," Houston said. "I trust he's been unchained from that tree."

Rusk and Dr. Labadie exchanged a look.

"The man is suffering severe melancholy," Dr. Labadie wiped his hands on his pants. "Every time I try to bleed him he refuses. He only wants his opium. I've warned his guards to watch out for suicide attempts."

Houston frowned. "I don't understand. He should be pleased. On my promise, he's going home."

"He's partway there anyhow," Rusk confirmed. "He's aboard the *Yellowstone*. But not for long, not if Burnet gets his way. It seems a brand new company of volunteers has showed up from the States—fancy uniforms, a flag, the works. They're mad as can be at missing the fight. To make up for it they want to hang Santa Anna."

"What an odd people," Houston whispered.

"Burnet has fastened onto the popular sentiment," Rusk said. "He thinks an execution would help promote the health of the nation. He wants Santa Anna returned to shore for a court martial. But there's some boy who won't budge from the *presidente*'s doorway. He's mean as a cat. Says it has to be you to tell him quit before he'll quit."

Tad was still doing his penance then. "Good for him," Houston murmured. "Did you tell Burnet I gave my word?"

"Moses Bryan has testified to that effect repeatedly." Rusk ran his fingers through his thick greasy hair. "But Mr. President claims you exceeded your authority. According to him you had no right to negotiate on behalf of the Republic."

"There wouldn't be a goddamn republic if I hadn't traded." Houston wanted to be angry, but there was no time. He had to try and think around the problem before he passed out again. It seemed the future of Texas, at least the future as it involved him, was going to jerk forward in these spasms of consciousness.

"When does the *Yellowstone* depart?" Houston asked. The sooner the steamboat left, the less chance Burnet would have to destroy Houston's pact with Santa Anna.

Dr. Labadie looked up at Rusk. "It departs when you do, Sam," Rusk said. Dr. Labadie lowered his head again.

"Leave Texas?" Houston protested. There was too much to do, an army to dismantle, a government to build, visions to articulate.

"You can't stay, General." Dr. Kenner was firm.

Dr. Labadie amplified the thought. "Without the most advanced medical care you'll be dead inside the week," he said. "I've informed Captain Ross you need immediate evacuation to New Orleans."

Houston dreaded facing the surgeons in New Orleans. But he didn't contradict Dr. Labadie's directive. After so much misery and darkness and violence, he'd never thought to see civilization again.

"The problem is," Rusk took over, dipping into his dry Georgia stoicism, "you can't stay, but you can't exactly go either." He spit. "Burnet caught wind of the plan to get you on to New Orleans and right away he declared the *Yellowstone* a government vessel for the conduct of state affairs only. Since your wound doesn't qualify as a state affair, he's not going to allow you passage."

It amounted to a death sentence, a mean act even for
Burnet.

"New Orleans, Sam. Newspapers."

Houston nodded. History began with words, and he was
about to have the first one. Newspapers meant votes, and the
revolutionary convention had set September for the Republic's
maiden election. In short the temporary president feared his
temporary general. He was strangely cheered. Burnet's action
was an overt form of assassination, and Houston doubted the
citizenry would much approve of killing off a great war hero
like himself. Whether he let Houston go or stay, it seemed
Burnet was going to lose some votes today. "Too bad we have
to wait until September," Houston said.

"You're not dead yet," Rusk observed. "Captain Ross is
refusing to cast off until you're brought aboard."

"So we're in checkmate, Burnet and me."

"There's a way through this of course."

"Do tell."

"A swap. You for Santa Anna. We take him off and put
you on. That way Burnet saves face. And you save your life."

Houston dropped his head back on his bundled-up coat
and closed his eyes. The flies danced on his face. The stench of
death closed over his mouth. The air was thick and oppressive.
He felt staked to the dirt.

More than anything he wanted to be away from here. One
word and he could be carried aboard the *Yellowstone* and borne
away. The sea breeze would clean him. The waves would lift
him toward his home, away from Texas so that he could be
healed and return to Texas.

But the same word that would save him would betray him,
too. He had promised the Mexican general his life in exchange
for Texas. And Santa Anna had kept his end of the bargain.

"Make the swap, Sam. If it was his to do, Santa Anna would
give you away in a heartbeat." There was anguish in Rusk's
voice, rare for him. Houston hadn't realized how much the
colonel needed a leader.

"I was just thinking of another piece of business," Houston
said. "I was wondering, whatever happened with Colonel
Forbes?"

The detour annoyed Rusk. "Pay attention, Sam. We're talking about your life here."

"Tell me," Houston said, "do the men still shout his name?"

"Every night, louder and louder."

"And what about his court of inquiry? Has he whitewashed his crime yet?"

"Not yet. There's been no court. He's still waiting your approval. He can freeze in hell for all I care."

Houston took a breath and released it slowly, making a decision. He hardened his heart. He went ahead.

"Tell him to go ahead and collect his friends," Houston said. "He can have his court. He may retrieve his reputation from the shit pile."

Rusk's brow wrinkled up.

"Is there a problem with that, Tom?"

"You acknowledge that what Forbes did was a crime."

"He's guilty as the devil," Houston affirmed. "In cold blood he sabered a defenseless woman."

Dr. Kenner had paused with his ministration. He was listening intently, as if he'd known the woman on a personal basis. Maybe in his terrible journey she had woven a kindness for him.

"And yet you'll authorize a whitewash?" Rusk said.

Houston nodded.

"You're contradicting yourself."

"I guess I am."

"Then tell me one thing. If you were to sit on Forbes's court, how would you judge him?"

Houston smiled. "Innocent," he said.

A stormy look invaded Dr. Kenner's face and Houston suddenly wished his foot was beyond the physician's reach.

"But you just said he's guilty," Dr. Labadie interrupted. "We all know he's guilty. What about the truth?"

"We left a lot of things at the border, gentlemen."

Dr. Labadie didn't like hearing that. "What about atonement?" Clearly he was one of those who'd been howling Forbes's name to the moon and also, clearly, one who'd done his share of the killing.

"I'm afraid atonement is a luxury."

"A luxury!"

"For civilized men," Houston said.

"But something terrible happened here," Dr. Labadie insisted.

"Listen to me," Houston said. Even speaking so softly was

wearing him out. "We are creating a nation out of air and dreams. For a while it will be as delicate as a butterfly. We must protect it from the memory of itself, from the mud and filth and night. We have been the barbarians at the wall of an empire called Spain. But from this day forward they must be the barbarians at the wall of an empire called Texas. So, the woman, the dead, the atrocities, all of it . . . forget, just forget."

Dr. Labadie was offended, that or bewildered. "And this is how you would baptize Texas? By telling the people just forget?"

"You gave us a battle cry, Sam," Rusk reminded him. "You told us to remember."

Houston labored to stay conscious. They needed him. It was time to quit burning down the night.

Houston raised his arm and jerked at the jacket under his head. But the blackness swirled up and he had to let his arm go limp.

"Doctor Kenner," he whispered, "in the pocket, please."

Dr. Kenner lifted Houston's head and pulled the jacket free. He found Houston's whittling knife.

"No, the other pocket," Houston said.

The doctor dipped into the pocket and removed a half-eaten ear of corn. "This?"

Houston took the corn. "Give my men these seeds. Tell them go get some land. Tell them go plant some corn."

Dr. Kenner understood. He gripped the ear of corn.

Rusk leaned forward. "Is that all you've got to say, Sam?"

"No," Houston whispered. *Save me so I can save you.* "Get me on that boat."

They carried him aboard the *Yellowstone* as if it were a Viking funeral ship. Men and boys and what few women had traveled in lined the way. There was winter in their eyes. Soldiers who had swallowed their enemies' blood just days ago wept. Some cheered him, calling huzzahs for Old Sam, but even they looked dour and bleak. All in all it was better than an election because their grief and forlorn faces gave Houston his mandate. If he died, they would remember him. If he returned, they would follow him.

Burnet was nowhere to be seen, nor were most of Houston's

colonels, for they had closeted themselves in a tent for Forbes's court of inquiry. He looked for Mrs. Mann—her or Molly—in the line of faces, but that was a useless search. If they ever met again, she would be changed and so would he. Everything was going to be different from now on.

The procession came to a halt at the gangplank. "First we got to off-load Santy Any," one of the stretcher bearers said to Houston. After a few minutes the Mexican general was marched off. Terrified at being returned to captivity, he had eaten the remainder of Dr. Labadie's opium supply. He stumbled and would have fallen over the railing. But Tad was there. He caught the *caudillo*'s arm and helped him navigate the walkway.

Scattered voices called death threats at the tyrant. Overall the crowd observed his pathetic descent in silence. Leaning heavily upon the boy's shoulder, Santa Anna passed Houston's makeshift stretcher. It would have been his right to shout at his betrayer, to condemn Houston with a pointed finger. Houston almost wanted him to. Instead Santa Anna delivered a presidential salute, a loose thing that transcended its military roots. Houston summoned his strength and returned it.

Then Santa Anna was gone, back to his chains and tree and drunken guards. Houston rose up above the earth. The stretcher tilted and he saw the river surging against the wooden hull, the ship rocking gently, tugged seaward. The twin smoke-stacks with their crenellated black borders towered overhead pouring white smoke into the sky.

"Welcome aboard," a Yankee scarecrow greeted him. "I'm Captain Ross. It would please me very much if you'd accept my cabin for your own."

"Much obliged," Houston rasped. "But the open deck will do." The air was fresher up here and he wanted to be outside where he could see the sky shift colors and the birds fly and the battlefield recede between banks of green. He wanted to know the moment this river opened onto the ocean.

Captain Ross led the way, directing that the stretcher be laid on the forward deck. He opened a pocketwatch, scanned the bustling shoreline, and announced that they would be casting off in ten minutes. A whistle blew to call in the tourists for their return excursion.

This section of the *Yellowstone*'s deck had been cleared of the protecting cotton bales. Houston had a view of his distant battlefield. It was a flat place, empty to the eye. Except for the buzzards and ravens billowing over the savannah, nothing suggested that so much as a life had been lost here nor a nation gained.

The *Yellowstone*'s crew busied itself taking on the last cords of wood cut for her by the army. No matter how much wood the soldiers were giving to the steamboat, Houston knew they would have saved plenty for themselves. He wondered how bright their campfires would blaze tonight. By dusk he would be far away from them. They would have to hold off their siege of ghosts without him.

Several of the tourists strolled onto the deck, casting reverent glances at their bedridden celebrity. One of the men carried a bright white skull, boiled clean. His friends took turns poking their fingertips into the bullethole through its forehead.

A cry filtered up from the bayou reaches. "Samuel? Where's he at? I want that Samuel Houston."

The voice was female and for a minute Houston hoped this woman might be the Hellenic bride of his imaginings, the call he had come to Texas for. He yearned for her to be beautiful and luminous and loving.

From his stretcher, Houston heard the sound of bare feet slapping on the deck, and then an old woman in muddy gingham planted herself in his sunshine. She had nose hair and dewlaps and red hair gone to white and could have been one of Macbeth's witches.

"You're Samuel Houston?" She sounded disappointed.

"I am," Houston confessed.

"I'm Peggy McCormick," she said. When that didn't provoke the right response, she added, "Peggy's Lake. That's mine." When that, too, failed to register, she said, "The lake you filled with Mexicans."

"Ah yes, Mrs. McCormick."

"Don't you Missus me," she snapped. "I come to say take them dead Mexicans off my league."

"I cannot," Houston replied.

"You can, goddamn you. They haunt me all the day and all the night I live. My cows will chew the bones and spoil their milk. Now take them Mexicans off."

Behind the white-haired fury the tourists were grinning broadly.

"But, Madam." Houston rummaged through his bag of oratory. "Your land will be famed in history. Here was born, in the throes of revolution and amid the strife of contending legions, the infant of Texas independence. Here the scourge of mankind, Santa Anna, met his fate."

Peggy was unpersuaded. "To the devil with your glorious history," she barked. "Take off your stinking Mexicans."

"Madam," Houston consoled her. "I can't take them back."

On shore excited men were loading and firing off their newly acquired muskets. Chains rattled. The vessel was preparing to debark. A crew mate came up to lead Peggy McCormick down the gangplank. "We're casting off," he said.

"I ain't leaving," Peggy declared.

"Come on, old woman."

"Not until I get my satisfaction."

"Try to understand," Houston reasoned with her. "You have all the time in the world now." Her eyes hooded over. She suspected a trick. But it was the truth, all Houston had left to offer. He turned his face away and when he looked again, Peggy was gone.

The ship cast loose. The sun rotated in a sweeping arc through the sky. They were leaving Texas. The cheering on shore grew fainter. Captain Ross gave the soldiers a blast of his whistle. The gentlemen with the skull were animated. They leaned against the rail, pointing at whatever there was to see out there.

Houston lay his head back, suddenly exhausted. His great quest was coming to an end. At last he could sleep.

But then a shadow swept across and lit on him. Like a huge raven pouncing on carrion it stayed fixed on his body and it was cold. Houston bent his head back and saw one of the smokestacks blocking the sun. It was chilly in the shadow, too much like night.

"Boys," he called. The gentlemen at the rail heard him and came over.

"Would you move me out of this shade," he said.

They lifted his stretcher carefully, straining as if he'd taken on the weight of granite. Stepping over a pile of rope, they placed him more strategically. "General?"

The sun was warm against his face. He shut out the earth and the sky and took a deep breath of the light. "Thank you," he murmured. "Here will do."

The footsteps moved off. "The general is sleeping," one gentleman whispered. Finally Houston knew he was by himself. That was when he opened his eyes and it was there, that single bead in the sky, his lone star waiting.